MAN OF THE HOUSE
by
Matthew Shaw
ISBN: 978-1-9996623-4-9

Published by

PUBLISHING
i2i Publishing.Manchester.
www.i2ipublishing.co.uk

Prologue

David Denby remembers the start of the war very well. It had been big news for a while, all the build-up, and he had an insatiable interest in anything related to it.

It fascinated him: whether he was listening to the radio, to the news bulletin, during light, summer evenings; or reading newspaper reports first thing, before leaving the house for school. It didn't matter how far-removed the world of war and grey-haired political leaders might appear to be from that of a thirteen-year-old in rural Yorkshire, David wanted to know everything. He would find out about, say, the rising tension in the Sudetenland, practically study it, so far as he could, and once he was done, he would turn on to something else, another place, another figure, with the same enthusiasm.

So, David remembers the start of the war well because he had been reading up on it, learning about it, for months. He could tell you intricate military or diplomatic details the average adult wouldn't know.

But David remembers for another reason too…

He remembers because on the day the war began, his father died.

PART ONE

Family History

To do with the Entrance Test

"Turn over your papers and put down your pencils." The voice of the bushy-moustached schoolmaster rumbles from the front of the hall, ricocheting from one wall to the next, via the ceiling, and into David's ears. He drops his pencil, instantly, flipping his test paper over too. Glancing either side of him, David catches the eyes of a few of the other boys – some look relieved, some more worried than before the exam began. He ruffles his fair-brown hair with his right hand, his nerves only just starting to lift like an autumn morning fog. He looks around, properly, taking in the vastness of the hall, its imposing beauty, as the sun drips in through tall, slim windows, lighting up the room in sections.

The schoolmaster collects in the papers. David sits four tables from the front and on the second of five columns. He looks again at his exam script, at the date printed on the cover, 15TH MAY 1937, and as it's taken from his desk, he slumps back in his seat. Nothing left that he can change, no part he can have any effect upon, he gently squeezes each finger in turn, massaging them after the strain of two hours non-stop writing.

"Now…"

The boys all look up.

"Stand quietly."

They stand.

"Put your chairs under your desks." The schoolmaster watches them as they do it. "And you may go."

In silence (who'd dare break it?), they leave the hall.

David only knows one of the others taking the exam. They go to the same infant school in the village. Once he makes it out of the main hall – flanked strikingly with huge portraits and grand, carved panelling – he finds him.

"Robert?" David taps him, from behind, on the shoulder.

"Oh. Hello, David." He turns to him with a grimace. "That was really difficult. Don't you think?"

"Oh, yes – much harder than I expected," replies David – though, really, the opposite thought is running through his head: he didn't think it was all that bad.

They make their way down a short corridor and out into the entrance hall, which is as dramatic as the room they have just spent their last few hours inside. When he had arrived, thinking ahead to the test, David struggled to focus on anything else. The same was true in the exam hall itself. Before the test papers were given out, he couldn't bring himself to look up, to acknowledge anything of the room other than the table and the chair he occupied. Now, as he moves along in a steady, schoolboy current, he finally sees. Overawed, he does not speak, just looks, lets his eyes flit from one thing to another. He notices the domed ceiling. The chattering voices around him are amplified by it, and the stone floor makes a slightly out-of-time marching sound as they all head towards the doors in their nicely-polished, saved-for-best shoes.

Meanwhile, in the yard outside, there are clusters of waiting parents: mothers mainly, expecting the best. They stand, looking assured, convinced that their child will emerge through the dark-wood, church-like doors, return a smile, and announce, confidently, how well they think they did, how no question left them stuck for an answer.

All of them, that is, but for one.

One mother waits, instead, with an agonizing fear right inside her, bubbling away. She had never wanted him to take this exam. "It'll put too much pressure on the little lad," she had told her husband, after once watching him sweat over his schoolwork. She only agreed because it was entirely his idea, something he really wanted to do – more than anything else, he'd said. But, knowing that, reasoning it in her head, over and over, like she has done these last few days, hasn't eased this parent's mind.

So, Esther Denby waits for her son, alongside the other mothers with their certain kind of pride. She waits, nervously, to see what is set across his face: the one thing that can tell her how he's done, how he feels, really. And when she sees him coming, looking for her with one of his glowing, toothy grins, she smiles too – for the first time that afternoon.

David leaves Robert's side, both of them spotting their parents and moving, wordlessly, in opposite directions.

"Who was that, love?" Esther asks.

"Just Robert Fitzgerald." Like she should know him better than anyone.

"Oh, right. How do you know him?"

"He goes to school. He's in the other class, but... I didn't realise he'd be here today, not until..." He trails off, distracted by the hugs and conversations filling the schoolyard.

"Well, that's nice, isn't it? It'd be good having someone you already know going here as well."

Walking out through the school gates, they head towards the main road.

David's smile has gone now. Thinking about what he will say, how he will summarise the whole morning, he wonders whether he did as well as he first thought; doubts start to fester and ferment inside him.

"So...?" Esther finally begins the line of questioning she is most interested in. "How did it all go, then?"

"Well..." He hesitates. *How did it go?* He was so nervous – he remembers that. The palpable worry. He remembers dreaming up all the snags he might come up against. "I don't know," he says.

"Well, what did your friend think?"

"He found it really hard."

"And – did you?"

Again, he hesitates. It *was* difficult; but he knew that it would be. He had to work hard to answer everything in the precise detail he desperately wanted to. But he does remember, also, thinking, right at the end, that it could have gone a whole lot worse.

"What did *you* think?" his mother asks him again.

"It was hard. I was really rushing to write everything down."

"Right..." She gestures with her left hand, encouraging him to go on.

"But..."

She nods; smiles.

"It wasn't as bad as I expected." David, at last, answers directly, more confidently.

And Esther looks relieved to hear those words. "Well, that's good, isn't it?" Her smile – it's refusing to leave her lips now. "I'm very proud of you, you know that?"

David looks at his feet. He's never sure how to take those sorts of comments – any time he's praised it feels like he's put on some clothing that's too small or made from unbearably itchy material. It's uncomfortable.

"How about we get off a stop early and get some fish and chips for tea – to celebrate? We'll get some for your sister, too."

"And Dad?" He couldn't wait to tell him how it had all gone.

"Yes. Can't forget *him*, can we? Though they might be a bit cold by the time he gets home."

"He won't mind."

"No. I'm sure he won't. Come on."

David nods, unseen weights lifting from his face, from his mind, his sunny grin emerging, effortlessly now – a mirror for his mother.

At the bus stop, a mother and son are already waiting. David recognises him from the exam. He has a pile of blonde hair that, every ten seconds or so, he pushes out of his eye-line. It's immediately familiar, tied to that exam hall. They sat across from each other and, when the schoolmaster called time, he was the first boy he'd glanced at. He looked as though he'd found the whole thing a bit tricky. His mother smiles, quickly, briefly, at them, while he keeps his eyes stuck to the grassy ground.

"Hello," Esther says, cheerily. As it leaves her lips, in that way, for a second, she looks surprised by how it sounded; she folds her face back into something less jovial, more neutral.

The other mother simply nods, quickly and briefly again.

Esther looks down at the boy.

"He's not saying much today," his mother quips, sharply, her short, tight lips refusing to form anything but a slight, straight scowl.

David turns to look down the road, hoping to see a bus already on its way towards them. Instead, he spots another pair, another mother and son, coming along the path. They're in conversation. Or, more accurately, the mother is – the child nods, repeatedly, with a frustrated scrunch of his cheeks. She's telling him something he doesn't want to hear, something he already knows, guesses David.

"David?"

He turns to his mother.

"Are you all right?" she asks, almost whispers.

He nods, a few times, a little like that other boy, but without the cross, crumpled face. "I'm fine." Because it's been a period, building up to this day, of uncertainty and pressure that he's tried his best to keep hidden – from everyone. After all, he'd insisted on taking the exam. It had been his decision. And, now…? Now that he'd done it…?

"Sure?"

"Definitely," he smiles, slipping his hand into hers and looking back down the road, squinting into the distance for the first sign of their bus.

***

The early-summer sun picks through the murky clouds. David walks home from school, moving like an animal in pursuit of the right scent: this, then that, grabbing his attention. He tightrope-walks along a wall, before jumping off, finding a loose stick, and using that to search in the bushes or long patches of grass. He listens in case he is close to some sort of bird or, perhaps, a frog or a grasshopper. (They had just studied frogs and toads in school that afternoon, so they're on his mind, the possibility of seeing one.)

At a brisker pace, he would be home in around ten minutes, but on these still, warm evenings, David enjoys taking his time. He likes the endlessness of where he is, of all that surrounds him. When he stands, stretched tall on the wall, he can see laid out, at either side of the road, box after box after box-shaped field – and each one, save for what grows inside them, looks exactly the same, dimensionally identical. There's an enduring, comforting notion to that, he thinks – as though this will always be.

Small cottages, the odd farmhouse too, begin to interrupt the flow of fields around him. Greenfield Cottage, the first he walks by, is set back from a low, un-pruned hedge. The stonework mimics the privet and, also, the garden – chaotic, decaying, given over to the passage of time. David's never met the people who live there, wouldn't even know what they looked like, but it is occupied. He knows this much. Because each morning he sees two milk bottles have been delivered, left on the doorstep, and then every evening, on the return journey, he checks to see that they're gone.

David continues scuffling along, passing several more cottages, before reaching a rusting gate. The gate which means he's home. David pushes it open, giving it a little lift too, so as not to get it caught on the stone step, then wanders down the dried-mud path. Before opening the front door, he can hear his mother saying something, most likely to one of his younger sisters, something that sounds a little like…

Not home yet.

And…

We'll have to wait.

He opens the door, as softly as he can.

"Oh. There you are." His mother turns to him as he jumps over the threshold, bursting through in a half-hearted bid to surprise them. She straightens up too – having been bent down talking to Josie. "I thought maybe you were coming home via Beverley, the time you've taken."

"Sorry. We learnt about frogs today. And sir said that if we looked hard enough we might see one on our way home."

Josie, once hearing the word 'frog', starts to jump up and down, legs fixed together. "*Raaak, raaak.*"

"Right. Any luck?"

"No," laughs David, dumping his school bag on the simple, oak table and joining in with his sister's amphibian imitation game. "Until now!" he declares, grabbing hold of her. "Caught you!"

"Careful," says Esther, when Josie typically yelps and pulls away.

"Sorry."

David removes his coat. Hangs it up by the door. Josie goes off and sits on one of the wooden chairs by the fireplace. The burning wood and two oil lamps, set down in opposite corners, light the room dimly but sufficiently. The bare, wood boards are covered by a dark, blood-red rug, worn by years of trodden-in dust, dirt, and left-to-stain spills. The dining table – which the five of them just about fit round – fills the middle of the room, the chairs currently distributed haphazardly around the place, a couple by the fire (the one that Josie sits on and one other), one next to the window, and the remaining two where they should be. David sits on one of them; begins pulling out his schoolbooks.

"Do you have much homework tonight?"

"A little bit. We have to write a story that has an animal as the main character. Maybe I'll write about Josie the frog," he says, glancing across the room. Now she's peering into the cradle their baby sister, Lily, is sleeping in, quiet and settled.

"Well, before you get started, there's one thing I've got to show you. It's just in here. Wait there." Esther disappears into the kitchen – a thin, sliver of a room set at the back of the cottage. She returns with a letter.

Josie leaves Lily's crib to stand beside her mother. "Can I give it to him, Mum?"

"I suppose so."

And his mother passes the letter to Josie. She then gives it to David, mouth wide open – perhaps because she's carrying on her frog-act after all and hoping a few flies will foolishly buzz inside.

The letter is addressed to MASTER DAVID DENBY – his first personally sent mail, that is besides birthday cards from grandparents and aunts.

"Can you see where it's come from?"

David rotates the envelope: notices something, on the back, in the top-right corner; a return address. "It's my entrance exam results," he says, with a gasp.

"I know."

He gently bites his bottom lip, considering what he holds in his hands for a few moments, the weight this piece of paper carries. But this hesitation does not last long – seconds only. The worries David imagined on the day of the test have completely faded over the weeks since. Now he just wants to know. He rips into it. Looks it over carefully.

"I passed, Mum. It says I passed."

"Oh. I knew it."

(How? Did she peek?)

"May I see?" Esther asks, taking the letter from David's outstretched hand.

She reads the whole thing, twice, her eyes darting side to side. And as she scans the lines, a certain kind of pride bubbles and simmers inside her, threatening overflow.

"Well done, love. Me – and your Dad – we knew you'd do it."

David stares at her, beaming proudly. Josie starts up her frog impression again, spurred on by the raised voices and smiling faces. But David looks on; he doesn't join in. He suddenly feels much older. The excitement, the satisfaction and pleasure from achieving what he'd wanted to, fills his head along with all that this could mean in the years ahead. He breathes quickly and shallowly, loudly too, exhilarated, as though he's just returned from a mile-long sprint.

One Day

Over the hum of voices in the school hall, a man checks his wrist and steps forward. David recognises him as the teacher who oversaw their entrance test – the headmaster, Mr. Greening. For a moment, he stands still, his head scanning the room at a deliberate, slow pace, as if he is trying to catch each boy's eye in turn. Then he speaks. "Quiet, please."

Silence settles.

"Thank you. Those of you not in the upper-third should know better than to speak in the assembly hall. I hope we don't have the same problem tomorrow morning."

David watches those around him. Every young head is focused on the front, on the man standing there, speaking to them.

Prayers are read. One of the upper-sixth-formers leads them at the lectern, with what David assumes to be just the right amount of volume and reverence. And, then, a hymn is sung: the tune carried by the senior boys' choir. David, and his friends around him, try their best to join in.

"Now…" Mr Greening speaks again, sending the boys who read and led the singing back to their places. "I'd like to welcome all our brand new upper-thirds. Perhaps the rest of us could give them a round of applause, to help them feel welcomed? After three, then. One… two… three…"

A thunderstorm of handclaps erupts. The noise loosens some of them up. One, nearer the front and to David's right, with a short flash of red for hair, appears to be attached to some strings, the operator of which is having enormous fun, shaking their puppet aggressively by the arms. Others, meanwhile, break into excited smirks; a few tilt their bodies round to look behind them at the older boys.

"Excellent." The schoolmaster starts to break the flow of applause. Again, it takes just a few seconds for his folded-arm stance to have the required effect, returning the room hush once more. "It's a new school year," he continues. "I trust you have all returned ready to work as hard as you possibly can. After all, we expect nothing less here – as I'm sure you've heard me say many, many times. I want to hear some good reports from all the teachers at the end of the day; I will be asking – particularly about you, here, at the front." His eyes scan the rows of nervous first years. "Now. Let's not delay the learning any longer. Leave the hall, please, in absolute silence." Then the schoolmaster stands back against the old, wooden-board stage, his speech for the morning seemingly finished.

The senior boys start lining out. Single file. Silent, as instructed.

After briefly peering round, David re-directs his gaze to the front. The stage looks like it hasn't been used for a while, un-maintained. The arch above it could do with another coat of paint, or two. He noticed it, too, after the entrance exam. It stood out in comparison to the finery displayed elsewhere.

"Upper-thirds – turn and face me." Mr. Slogee breaks across David's thoughts.

Mr. Slogee is the head of the first year (and also teaches chemistry) and met David and his new classmates in the playground that morning. The breeze messed up what remains of his black hair and he appeared to have an obsession with removing his glasses and giving them a swift, thorough wipe on his teacher's gown. He lined the boys up at about quarter-to-nine and led them into the main hall. Apart from introducing himself, he said nothing else and just pointed to the floor where he wanted them to stand. One by one, they each followed the other. And when a new row needed to start, Mr. Slogee beckoned them over with a few expressive flicks of one long, bony finger.

"Now…"

The older pupils continue to leave the hall.

"I hope you have all brought your lesson timetables with you." He eyes them inquisitively. "Is that right? Did everyone receive them in the post over the summer?"

There are no dissenting answers, no confusion (*what's he talking about?*) as far as David can see from his quick scan of the bodies around him.

"Good." Mr. Slogee points to the main doors. "This way, then. Follow me."

The classroom is cramped. There are three long, varnished-wood benches with room for twelve pupils perched on stools along each. They sit shoulder to shoulder, David in the middle row. He looks up from the physics work he's re-reading to see the time. The clock, a sort of miniature grandfather fixed to the front wall, has almost reached four – his first day minutes from being over.

Below the clock on the wall, David observes Mr. Marston sat at his desk. He remembers how short he appeared when he stood beside the chalkboard, raggedly writing that lesson's work. The teacher lifts his head from the papers he's been intently working at to check on the rest of the room. David tries discreet side-glances. Next to him, some boy called Simons is hunched over his book, scribbling answers whilst also scratching his head with his free hand – stimulating his thinking muscles, perhaps. And Robert – a few heads to David's left – is hard at work too, tongue flexed in concentration.

"If anyone has any of this left to finish, I want it done for homework and handed in at the start of our next class. However, if you finish now or in the next few minutes..." Mr. Marston carefully instructs, glancing up and behind him to the clock, as if to make sure he definitely had the correct time, "Then come and put it here on my desk." He indicates which part of the desk he wishes the work to be placed on.

David continues checking his answers. Once he's sure it all looks right, he stands and pushes his stool noisily out of the way. Heads rise from books and several boys fill the following silence with forced coughs. David places his exercise book on the teacher's desk.

"Thank you..." Mr. Marston starts – then falters to a stop.

"Denby," David offers.

"Denby," he smiles. "I will remember names eventually." He lays the work down to one side, hoping more will come and form a pile.

David walks back to his seat, head down, suddenly feeling embarrassed.

"Anyone else?" He leans back and waits for responses.

Further footsteps stutter into hearing. Someone else has finished.

"Ah, excellent. Thank you..." Mr. Marston takes the boy's work; reads his name. "Thompson. Good work."

David watches as Thompson strides back, his brown, curly hair bouncing in step. He wears a pleased grin as he settles back on his stool.

Mr. Marston gets to his feet, the time just approaching four. "Right, the rest of you – I want that finished for homework. Understood?"

Those brave enough, mutter a reply, "Yes, sir," while the others nod slowly, shyly, in response. The best he's going to get from them.

"Very well." The bell intervenes. "Class dismissed."

One Weekend

David kicks a stone ahead of him. It bobbles along, across and over the drops and bumps in the road. The midday sun burns into the back of his neck; he scratches where heat and skin meet. Leaves bristle as the delicate wind drifts through the countryside. He can barely feel it brush past him, but David knows it's there, all around him, by the movement in the trees and the gentle waves of the long, raggedy grass beside the lane. Off to his right, David spots the straight, precise progress of a steam train. It chugs and it grunts, splitting the fields apart. And now, having seen it, David imagines the people on board, peering out the window into the far distance. Who knows? If he can see them, perhaps they can see him: a dot of a boy on a country lane.

He arrives at Robert's house. Robert lives in a run of five cottages, each with well-groomed front gardens.

"Good afternoon, young Denby," Robert's father welcomes him – at first just a voice, until David sees him crouched down, examining the plants with a trowel. "And how are you on this fine Saturday?"

"Well, thank you."

Mr. Fitzgerald stands up. "Excellent news." Stretches his back muscles with a twist and a sigh. "I'll get Robert for you, shall I?"

"Yes, please."

"Robert!"

Right on cue, he comes piling through the open door. A black-and-white Border collie follows, tail-wagging, tongue-panting. "Hello, David," he says, immediately turning to his father. "Can Antsie come with us? Please?"

Flashing his eyes to the brilliant blue sky, Robert's father exhales a long blast of air and slips his lips into a straight, uncertain expression.

"Please?" Robert's almost on his knees.

"Well, I suppose."

"Yesss."

"Just don't go too far."

"We won't." Robert looks almost as excited as the dog. "Come on, then, David." And he bounds off: as though, at all costs, he must keep up with Antsie, who's pelted up the lane, nose first.

The sunlight seems to have grown stronger. David's hands feel sticky, his hair wet with sweat. He watches Antsie, her every move fascinating him. She arrives at a tree hanging over the road. Lifts a leg. Little wobble. Then steadies herself. Does her stuff and moves on. Disappearing behind the long grass.

Then in the bare, harvested fields David suddenly notices a pheasant shyly pecking at the ground: radiant, red feathers.

"Look, Robert." David points.

"Oh, well spotted."

It's searching for seeds and bugs. They watch for a little while, a few still moments, before Robert turns away and carries on down the lane. David waits, however, and Antsie pads to his side, wanting to be stroked, to take his attention from the bird she hasn't even noticed (and if she had, what would she do then? Who would she be most interested in?).

"Come on, Antsie." David starts catching up to Robert, his attention successfully deflected from bird to dog and back to his friend.

Another train clatters past. They try to glimpse it, struggling to orientate themselves, unable to pinpoint where the railway lines lie amongst this stretch of farmer's fields and country lanes. The sound of the train's progression (away from the station or into the station – they can't say which) lingers, dancing in David's eardrums.

"Rag *b-ohhh-ne!*" A shrill voice cuts across the fading mechanical waltz.

Robert glances back behind them. "Here, girl," he says, to the dog. "Off the road."

"Rag *b-ohhh-ne!*" the voice repeats itself.

The boys shift on to the roadside, out of the way. Antsie does the same – either out of obedience or an attempt to mimic her human companions.

A horse-drawn, rickety wood-cart trundles round a tight bend in the lane. Antsie turns and barks at it.

"Quiet!" Robert snaps back, through tense, clenched teeth: as though he is now the mimic.

The cart moves slowly, cautiously, piled mountains-high with pieces of household furniture – dining chairs stacked on an upturned table (part of a set, presumably); a couple of cabinets that remind David of the one they have at home which stores their best crockery and fancy glasses (family heirlooms, apparently, from his mother's side); a battered cooker; old, rusting buckets; and an oak wardrobe, turned on its side. It all contributes to the weight and the strain on the patchy-grey horse tasked with moving it down the far-from-smooth lane.

Up ahead, there are a few houses. No doubt, going that way, they'll try for more things (*that poor horse*), then go back to their rag-and-bone yard, wherever that is (close by, David hopes... *that poor horse, that poor horse...* runs, gallops, unhindered, through his head).

Finally, the heap of junk comes level with Antsie and the boys, as they trudge slowly through the overgrown grass.

"Afternoon," grunts the rough-haired driver, tight-hold of the reins. Horse and man bounce past. The hardworking animal cannot keep to a straight track, the road a mess of potholes and bumps. The man lowers his head. David suddenly spots a boy sitting beside him. Their sun-strained gazes cross. He's a little replica of the rag-and-bone man – quite clearly his son, the next-in-line to the family trade. Antsie keeps barking. Robert tries holding on to her. The father smiles; reveals a depleting set of yellowing teeth.

Despite all its pulling, the horse quickly takes the man and his cargo beyond the boys and closer to the houses ahead.

"Rag *b-ohhh-ne!*" He calls on, announcing their approach, giving time for more, no-longer-needed stuff to be brought out.

Once they're clear, David and Robert return to walking on the road – though it is bumpy, it's far less so than the clumpy, grass verge. Antsie continues barking her doggy lungs out, standing, now, in the middle of the lane as if assigned to guard it.

"Quiet now," Robert tries again.

But it's not until the horse and cart are out of sight and earshot that she finally abandons her offensive.

"Good girl," sighs Robert, adding, with a grin that looks both pleased and relieved: "She's very obedient, isn't she?"

Just as they themselves arrive at the houses, they move off the lane and cross into the square fields. The sky above them has completely dissolved itself of clouds and they head towards the shade of a copse. Through the middle, dividing the little wood in two, runs a stream that – if you were to follow it all the way – cuts across the centre of the village. With his shoes off, his trousers rolled up, David stands in the water. The level is as low as he's ever seen it down here – a result of the very hot summer, possibly – and with a twig, he prods at the submerged stones: inquisitive mind in overdrive; sifting through for something from the nature books he knows so well; something he's not seen before. Robert sits on some exposed tree roots, wriggling and squirming to get comfortable. And Antsie lies at his feet, tired, content – a little wet also, up to her legs, after playing herself sleepy in the beck.

"What do you reckon, then?" Robert pipes up.

But David's concentration is fixed, instead, on lifting a rather large, pinned-down stone. His tongue licks his bottom lip – such is his focus.

"David?"

"Sorry?" He gives up; looks away from the water and at his friend, hearing the rock drop and settle back into the mud. "What did you say?"

"School – what do you reckon?"

"I like it," he replies, simply.

"Mmm."

"Why? Don't you?"

"Oh, no, I do – I just wondered what *you* thought."

The sunlight breaks through the trees behind Robert. David is, momentarily, blinded. Raises a shielding hand to his forehead.

"I mean, I didn't know what to expect, you know…"

Robert nods; reaches down to stroke Antsie. David returns to his nature-hunting; stick searching and probing the stream for signs of life. Though it's hard to conceive of anything existing in this very shallow, muddy water. It hardly covers David's feet.

"And I'm glad I found out you were going there too," adds Robert.

"Same here."

"I know we didn't really know each other that well before, but…"

"We do now," David finishes.

"Exactly."

David hops out and perches next to his friend. He looks at his now-brown feet. Begins brushing off lumps of muck and shards of stone.

"And I like William too," Robert continues.

David nods, just as Antsie starts cleaning his feet too, her tongue working between his toes.

"But what about Thompson?"

"What about him?" The dog's warm tongue really tickling now, David pulls his feet away.

"He's like your shadow," grins Robert.

"Or I'm his."

"Maybe."

Charlie Thompson is the boy from the physics lesson they had on the first day; the only other one to complete the work in class time. In the first few weeks of term, that pattern has continued itself: he and David have always been first to finish every lesson, and always in about the same time too. (Who came first? The Denby or the Thompson?)

"I don't know," sighs Robert. "I think he thinks he's better than us – better than you."

"Well, maybe he is."

"What? Just because you're on a scholarship and he isn't?"

David shrugs his shoulders. But the very same thought *has* crossed his mind too.

***

One particular moment occurs to him. Again, it was their first week; they'd just had a really tough mathematics lesson.

"Someone might get to thinking you're copying off me, Denby."

"Sorry?" David turned to find Thompson catching up with him. "What did you say?"

"People might think something's going on – you and me, finishing at the same time."

David said nothing at first.

Thompson raised his eyebrows. "Don't you think?" he reiterated, push-push-pushing for a response.

"What? That, because I'm one of the scholarship boys, I must need someone to help me get the work done?"

"You said it. Not me."

"But it's what you meant, isn't it?"

Thompson shrugged his shoulders. Smirked a smile. "You tell me, Denby. You're meant to be the clever one round here."

When have I said…?

"Just saying." And Thompson bounded off down the corridor. "See you in chemistry."

***

"Anyway…" Robert stands; yawns. "We should start walking back."

Antsie rises too. Presses down on her front legs, tensing, giving her hind end a satisfying stretch, ready to go.

"What time is it?" David asks, now also on his feet.

"Not sure. Late enough."

The clammy heat still sticks to David's skin. "My tummy's starting to rumble," he says.

"Mine too. Did you not hear it a few seconds ago?"

"Is that what it was? I thought it was the rag-and-bone man again."

The boys and the dog, wander out of the copse. Crossing, this time, through a sheep-grazing field, they make it back on to the lane and, more directly than before, quicker too. They each head for home.

On the Bus and in the Schoolyard

Half-past seven. The chill, sharp breeze disturbs David's newly-trimmed hair, blowing it in all directions. He places his hands in his coat pockets. Drums a beat, with his feet, on the ground. Anything to counteract the cold. Mounds of dry, split leaves, which have all lost their green and summery colours, pulse and lift as the wind crashes through them. Some collide with David's feet, gathering together into new, smaller piles, while others are taken past him at a greater height, one coming to rest, suddenly, on his right shoulder. He pushes it off. Catches it in an open palm. Runs a finger along the veins, tracing them like a river on a map.

The harsh, rolling notes of an engine fade into hearing. David steps on to the rough-stone road, burying his feet in a deep trench of crisp leaves, and arches his neck so that he can see as far along the lane as possible. It takes a few moments for it to appear, for sight and sound to combine, but soon David sees it coming around the corner and on, to where he waits: one lone guard stood to attention at a country lane bus stop. It's become some kind of habit: the patient silence as the bus pulls into position, the open doorway at the back carefully lining up with where David stands, ready for a swift, effortless boarding – a re-run of that which passed the day before and will, undoubtedly, take place tomorrow too, under near-identical circumstances.

David hops on. The conductor greets him with a delighted smile.

"Good morning, young man."

"Hello."

He hands David a ticket, then tugs – once, plainly – on a short stretch of string hanging directly to his left. The bronze-coloured bell – covered maze-like in scratches – chimes, telling the driver to continue along the lane.

David is one of just six boys on board, as many as there ever is at this stage of the journey. And they're all older than him. He fights the bumpy motion to the front, sitting, as usual, behind the driver's cab. He shuffles his bum into the hard-cushioned seat. Then, as comfortable as those seats allow him to be, David shifts his gaze to the dim, wind-swept view outside that, only seconds ago, he was a part of. He squints through the speckles of grit and dust pasted on either side of the window. With one out-breath, he clouds a circle on the glass. Pokes at it with an index finger. Then wipes it off with one swift stroke.

David has memorised the route, knows clearly the order in which people get on board. He knows that Robert, for example, will join him in three stops time.

They pass the same-as-every-morning fields: the vibrant, vast squares of rapeseed; the house-shaped hay bales, standing solitary, at intervals, as though keeping watch. They reach the grazing, black-and-white Friesian cows – forty or so of them (David remembers counting once, or struggling to, in the short time he had as they drove past) – and, when the bus goes by their field, David knows the next thing he'll see is Robert, waiting near two other lads in matching uniform.

Robert stands behind the taller boys. This happens every school morning. He doesn't look at them, appears not to acknowledge their existence in any way. But David knows what his friend is thinking. He knows that these others will, without a word or gesture, be first in line to jump on board – some important, unspoken rule dictates it. So, Robert keeps his eyes stuck to the ground, hard at work, studying something intensely, his messy, golden hair whipped about by the wind: never left to settle in one place or shape for very long before another rush undoes the work of the last one. And as the bus moves to a slow halt, Robert does what he has never been told to; he lets the older pupils on first – a re-run of a re-run that will likely be done again the next day.

"Did you manage to finish the history homework?" Robert asks, as soon as his backside hits the bus seat, intimidation all gone. He doesn't even look at David: just sighs, pushes out a breath of air that lifts wisps from his long, blonde fringe. He rests his school bag on his knees and begins to peer inside, thumbing books and papers.

"Yes," David answers, simply.

"You did? All of it?" Robert continues to search his bag, rooting through its contents, now, with increased vigour and pace. "Huh. Course you did. Oh, come on – where is it?"

David laughs, silently, within. *Give him time. He'll find it.* This feels like another re-run.

"Got it," Robert finally says, relieved. "Thought I'd lost it for a second, there."

For the first time since Robert got on the bus, they make eye contact. He smiles – almost apologetically. And with that expression, one David has seen before, it's as if he's saying he understands how, really, he is being rather annoying; *but if I don't ask for help,* David imagines his friend's inner monologue, his mind's reasoning, *how else will I learn?* David, though, actually quite likes this dynamic. It isn't an every-morning-without-fail event. But it does have a certain level of regularity: provided their homework quota stays roughly even, David can expect this same scenario to play out several times a week. See, Robert always turns to David: both out of convenience (they share a bus journey; are best friends) and because a pattern has sprung up (namely, this pattern: David will know the answer – he just will, as far as Robert's concerned, no matter what it's about). And David doesn't mind how often this happens – that, perhaps, you could say, it happens *too* much. He doesn't even care that answers, which took him time and dedicated concentration, are given over to someone else as if they're co-architects, deserving of equal recognition. No, because this way David has something to offer: a mind that has rapidly, in the few weeks they've spent at Grammar School, earned him a reputation (with both teachers and classmates) he is keen to keep and eager to build on. It's a symptom of something David is becoming increasingly proud of, something he likes to be known for – no matter what people like Thompson say (and actually, he is the only one who says it).

Robert flattens his bag into a makeshift desk. He lays his homework papers on it, smoothing out the creases with his right hand.

"Which bits were you stuck on?" David leans in to read Robert's scribbled-on sheet.

"Well, I did do most of it. So…" He fingers rings round the completed parts. "What happened when, where, how it started – I could do all that. It's just the last bit, here, where you have to…"

"I see." David spots the unanswered gap.

"I just don't understand." Robert turns from the page and looks at David. His eyes widen. *Help me out here*, he seems to be saying.

David lifts his satchel from the juddering bus floor, opens it, and finds his own copy of the history work. "Here…" he says, passing his answer sheet over. "That's what *I* put. I think it makes sense."

"Thanks." Robert's relieved smile clear and audible through just that one word. "I'm sure you've got it right." He looks over David's precise, neat answer; a product of a few evening's back. "Right, I see – I hadn't noticed that." He shoots another, quicker smile at his friend – as if to say: *but, of course,* you *would* – then reaches inside his bag, locates a pencil, and starts to write.

David leans back in his seat.

But Robert's concentration lasts barely a minute. He looks up from the paper balanced on his bag. Sighs: then says; "History really gets on my nerves, you know? It's just dull. Even this Great Fire of London stuff – it sounds good, but, you know, hardly anyone got killed. And Parfick's drone of a voice doesn't help, either."

David laughs again – this time letting it spill out a little, so that his friend might notice. Though he agrees with none of it. Especially the bit about Mr. Parfick.

"Anyway…" Robert returns to his work. "You don't mind me using this as inspiration, do you?"

"No, go on. Glad I can help."

"Again," Robert adds, knowingly.

"Again."

He continues scribbling his answer, checking, every few lines, that he's not straying too far from the script provided. And while he does so, David turns to the window. The sun is, very slowly, making a way through the heavy cloud cover. Still, the wind appears to be as lively as it has been all morning: severely bowing the bulky, oak arms that belong to the clutch of trees they now drive past. David spies a gull fighting its way to who-knows-where; observes it battling against the forceful currents, persisting, only to find a few wing-beats forward are easily negated by a strong gust effortlessly pushing it several more backwards.

"Done," sighs Robert, returning David's work back to him; placing it on his knees as they bounce in time with the heartbeat of the bus. "Thanks. Appreciate it."

David puts his papers away, trying hard not to curl or bend the edges, easing them in with a flat palm.

"I wonder what we'll be going on to next."

"I thought Mr. Parfick said something about the English Civil War," David replies, vaguely – though he knows exactly what their history master said. "But I could be wrong."

"Sounds about right."

"You should enjoy that a bit more – plenty of people died then."

The noise on board builds. David glances behind. The bus is almost full; each row of seats now occupied by at least one other person. Rather than talk above the racket, David looks outside again, at what they pass by. Brick and stone forming more of the landscape; the open farmland and watercolour villages shifting into their opposite – the crammed confines of the city. It still looks like a pre-dawn scene, very little sunlight breaking through the thick, defensive clouds that, along with the wind, marks this day. A Thursday. Another school day for David, Robert, and the other boys, all dressed in their red and black, sitting on their blue and white bus. Thursday. Another day at work for those just arriving at the factories and warehouses, shops and courtyards, that line the main road: Zernys Dyers; Reckitt & Colman's; Boots, the chemist; the blacksmith yard; Boyes; William Jackson, baker, grocer and butcher.

Then amongst the dirty smoke and concrete, David spots something else. Every morning, he looks for it, watches as it disappears behind them.

It is there to mark something out.

A signpost.

Pointing to ST. ANDREW's DOCK.

Which is the place David's father goes to work.

Each day, he leaves the house before David – and returns a good while after him too. He sets off, washed and fresh, and comes back covered in dirt and grease all across his rough-skinned face and arms, his hands often scarred, his whole body and his clothes, too, smelling (like everyone who works on the docks) of rancid fish guts. David's father is a strong man – though you wouldn't know it, looking at him. He lacks the broad shoulders that normally benefit those who are required (for this is his job) to move wide, weighty boxes stuffed full of ocean produce. But none of that appears to matter, according to his mother. "There's not many that are more respected down at that dockyard than your father is," she told him once. And he knows this, himself. David can't recall a time when, being out with his father, they haven't come across someone he knows from the docks. "Who's that, Dad?" David will ask. "Oh, I just work with him, son," comes the predictable reply.

And the docks sound fascinating – like the world of nature and history, full of noise and movement, vibrancy and life. And David's father seems to know about everything that happens there, is well fed on whatever story happens to be going around, whether it's the one about Harry Best and what he got up to the other weekend or the one about Dave Camfield and his ridiculous, disgusting home-brewed remedies. And, likewise, David is nourished on these things too (the stories, not the possibly poisonous potions). His father loves to recite the conversations he's heard or been a part of during each day – does so with intense energy and animation – and David is a captive, hungry audience. Then, besides that, he's let in on bigger, perhaps more truthful accounts; ones that tell of trawlers heading out to sea for months on end, returning with far less than they had intended and hoped for. Or not returning at all. David is told how the ocean is a beast like no other, that if you underestimate it once, come to what may, at first, appear to be the most reasonable conclusion about what is possible, what that vast, mucky-green animal (in the muddied North Sea's case) is or isn't capable of, it will come back at you in a way you hadn't imagined, in a way that changes you forever. "And I know, son. Believe me." With this short, haunted statement, these watery anecdotes will typically conclude. And David knows the words are true because he knows that, before he became a general dockworker, his father used to be a trawler-man.

"Nearly there," groans Robert.

"What?"

"Just saying – we're nearly there."

"Oh."

David turns again to the window; begins to see what is, actually, there. Rather than the dockyard or some wind-battered trawler in Arctic waters, he sees far calmer sights. The smart yellow and white-brick houses, their flourishing gardens, followed by the very fancy appearance of the National Picture Theatre; one sure signal they're at the end of their journey to school.

He lifts his bag from the floor, up on to his knees. Checks it over. Another one of his habits – every morning he does it, to be sure – despite the fact that one of his school-night routines, also, is to carefully re-pack his things. All of which means, by the time the bus is about to drop them off the following day, David already knows, really, that everything will be there. It's just the final look-through of several more before it. Unless some slight split let rip and made a hole in his bag during the journey – and the country lanes *are* very bumpy. But that's yet to happen. (And will it ever? Really?) And anyway, even if something had dropped out between here and home, he can hardly go back and find it now.

"Look, David..." Robert points, across the gangway, to the footpath. "There's William."

David strains to see past the bodies and heads that restrict his view of the street. William Field – who they befriended after just a couple of days – lives in this part of the city and is walking the last few paces of his own, shorter school journey. His bag hangs down from his neck, across his chest, and he kicks it along, as though the pull that then runs through the strap is the lone momentum tugging him forwards.

David and Robert stand – just as others do – battling against the declining, slowing motion of the bus. They haul their own book-filled satchels over their heads, David's thudding heavily on to his left shoulder.

"All right – off you get, then," the conductor calls out, once the bus finally nods to a stop.

Robert waits while the gangway fills up, a steady stream of different heights and stages of maturity. Seeing this, David realises how he and Robert are also a part of some far more consequential journey. Not just the one to school. Or the one heading off the bus. (But, a journey to – where exactly? To a life of work and parenthood, a repetition of the life David knows his parents have made for themselves, following in the tradition others, their own parents, set before them?) Back on the school bus, it's hard to see where others are on that route. But the physical difference is obvious: some boys' heads even nudge the ceiling; they loom, tower, above David and Robert. So – in that sense – it's only natural. They wait until last, until the final seat has been vacated. Another custom silently observed, a different sort of tradition, a re-run and a foreshadow at one and the same time – they've done it before and they'll do it again.

"William!" Robert shouts above the schoolboy chatter.

He's up ahead, walking towards the main gates. Maybe he didn't realise which bus was emptying and who might be on it.

Or maybe he didn't see it at all – the bag-kicking game taking up the whole of his attention, letting nothing else in. Whatever he did or didn't see, he certainly missed Robert's enthusiastic wave through the breath-flecked window; a triumphant greeting that (on this evidence) found its way to nobody.

Robert hollers again, his call rising over the messy melee of voices. Some lads glance back, wondering who's shouting so loud – *what's got into him?* Thankfully – because David isn't sure he could stand Robert calling after him a third time; his ears still ring from the previous attempts – William's one of them. He begins his retreat, dodging the crowd of school pupils like it's the rugby field.

"Morning, you two."

"Hello."

"Hello, William." Robert punctuates his words with a thump to his arm.

William yanks it to his chest. "Ouch!" he yelps. Faint giggle. "You got me there."

"Just being friendly."

"Well, you didn't have to be that friendly." William's face scrunches up – though, David suspects, that expression makes far too much of it. William and Robert have an odd sort of friendship, unlike the one that exists between David and Robert or David and William, for that matter. It's a rough, one-upmanship sort of thing, which David struggles to fully take part in. It's a game, essentially – but nothing close to the one they play each day in the twenty minutes before the school bell rings and lessons begin. That game is one all three play.

"Sorry, William – don't realise my own strength sometimes. Maybe a bit of running around will sort it out."

"You think?"

"It could work," he shrugs. "And, if not, I could always hit you again in the same place. The impact might push the pain out… or something."

"Is that right?" William plays along.

"Absolutely. That's solid science, you know – isn't it, David?"

He may not say much during these exchanges, but once the conversation turns factual or, indeed, scientific, then David is called upon to join in. In everything academic, he's seen as the de-facto authority, the one to whom all questions are put and expected to be answered, accurately, and without need for further reference. Still, that is a bit of a stretch – even for David's brains – but he's fortunate to have never been asked anything beyond his intellect. So far, that is. And, besides, this enquiry is less serious. They often are when Robert's asking them. If he's questioning David without a schoolbook in hand or outside a classroom, it can be safely assumed that a genuine answer isn't really necessary. So, knowing this, David continues the game.

"That's right," he says. "I remember hearing it in a biology lesson one time."

"Told you so," Robert quips, in William's direction.

They pass through a tightly-packed playground. Huddles of friends; the occasional ball game played among silver birch trees dotted about, helpfully, in rough, football-goal shapes. Opening out at the north-facing side of the Grammar School – a larger, squarer yard. The boys head that way. It's emptier, less full of the babble and shouts of the previous area; filled, instead, with more green, more plant-life – grassy borders packed with shrubs, trees, some of which are huge, over-hanging chestnuts that, at the right time of the year (which happens to be this time of the year, in fact), produce an abundant harvest of conkers. (David has his own conker collection at home, around the one hundred mark, at last count, and most of that number has come from these very trees, gathered and bagged during break times.)

The boys discard their bags, dumping them alongside a few dozen others. Robert and William swing theirs by the straps. They land with a muffled thud. In contrast, David sets his down gently, to one side, hoping it won't get buried, squashed, weighed down, as others are added to the pile.

David much prefers this part of the school grounds. As much as they can, the trees and plants remind him of the countryside.

But, also, he likes it because it is the place in which they play their playtime game.

"Right…" begins William. "I'm off to my hideout." He runs off towards a weeping willow, leafy fingers reaching right to the ground. "Don't look," he calls back.

David and Robert do just that, following orders they don't really need to. (*Why don't they watch him? It's not like he can stop them.*) They turn to each other, serious concentration settling in their faces and through their minds.

The game has begun.

David becomes Corporal Denby; Robert – Sergeant Fitzgerald. They scan the area into which William (who plays the bad guy, General Field) has disappeared – not even the hint of a black blazer in the mix of autumn shades. Cautiously, they move out; then part. Robert thrusts his arms in David's direction, telling him to go to the far corner. This is their usual line of attack: head to opposing ends of the undergrowth (which, like everything else, has a name-change and becomes, The Forest), a kind of pincer movement. So, carefully, quietly, David moves through – he plays his part – knowing full well William's somewhere inside watching everything he's doing.

***

The game has begun. And William is its inventor. That's why he gets to be the bad guy. Each morning, they play the same thing out, adding to its storyline day by day. It came from the bedtime tales his father would tell him. Sadly, those nightly narratives have stopped now. William's father said he was too grown up for that sort of thing, that he no longer needed a story to help him on his way to sleep. "You're growing up. Some things should be shelved and left in childhood." Except, William couldn't leave them there. The stories have stayed with him – and, more than that, he's taken ownership of them. He's carried them on, added to them. For a while, it was a solitary activity, played out at home (with the use of a dozen or so tin soldiers), or just in his head. But as he got to know David and Robert, he found that he was opening up this part of himself and letting them join him in his story-world, just like his father would do for him each night when he was younger.

Back when they first started playing this game – which has never been named or has no particular purpose or ending point (so, a bit like most things) – David wondered where it came from, how William could have dreamed it up. His answer, the one above (that it came from stories his father told him at bedtime), didn't seem sufficient. It led, naturally, to a second question…

"So, how did your father think of it, then?"

"Oh. I don't know. I'll have to ask him," William replied with a decided smile.

And he did.

The next day, the first thing he said to David and Robert was: "I asked my dad – about the stories."

Now, if he's honest, David had forgotten all about this. (He can have moments like that. He doesn't remember everything, as much as Robert and William would never believe him should he tell them so.) Nevertheless, his interest in the story's origins returned immediately. But at first, for a few seconds, William said nothing more; perhaps intending something dramatic or suspenseful. Instead, they continued to walk, in silence, towards the school gates.

David coughed. Birdsong cut across from the roofs above and around them.

"And?" David asked.

"He wouldn't tell me."

"Oh."

"He just looked sort of surprised – couldn't believe I'd remembered."

"Right."

"Then he said it wasn't important and to forget about it."

"That's odd," thought David, out loud – not quite the reveal he'd hoped for. (And a feeling that there was more to it hung around. David remembers it nudging him here and there throughout the rest of that day.)

"Oh, well," Robert joined in. "If we don't know where it came from, we don't know – but at least we can still play it. We can, can't we, William?"

"Course."

So, by the time of this Thursday in October, it feels entirely theirs. It is the thing that fuelled their friendship – it watered the ground and caused it to grow – and now, if they were without this game, and the stories it emerged from, their days at school would have something vital missing.

***

David crouches. Pushes aside a low-hanging branch. From a shedding, nearly leafless bush flies a startled blackbird (a female, because it's actually brown not black). David watches it land on the roof above the doorway they'll soon be walking through to their first class. It looks down at the shouting, playing boys. Then flaps off, dissolving into the dirty grey-blue.

After playtimes packed with battles and fights, William has been pushed back to his hideout. David and Robert think they have him cornered, that there's nowhere he can escape to, that nothing can come of his plans for world domination – which, let's be honest, is what all good bad guys want. (*Good* bad guys – now there's an oxymoron.)

It's deep and dense inside this so-called forest – in the boys' well-formed imaginations and in reality too. David squints to see Robert at the other side, mirroring him. But he can't. The undergrowth is far too cluttered. All David *can* see is one branch followed by another (and another and another), on and on that way, layer upon layer of branches merging with a few still-green bushes and tree trunks of differing widths to create a blur of rough browns and fading greens.

Then one dodge under a protruding tree limb and David can suddenly see William, his red and black uniform undoing every attempt to blend in and keep hidden. He has his back to David – must be keeping an eye on Robert, he thinks – and between them, there's a wide, knotted chestnut. David lines himself up with it. Squats, careful that nothing gives him away; no crackle of leaf or burst of twig. He grips the tree trunk. It should keep him concealed – even if William should turn around, out of curiosity or alarm.

Time appears to expand during this no-man's land between arriving for and starting school. It somehow feels like there is more time, like a minute takes longer to count out – bizarre and impossible though that is.

After a few minutes (or whatever time-scale it feels has passed), William rises. He still has his back to David and, to keep him in view, David stands too, tenderly, precisely, his blazer scraping against the chestnut tree.

Then he peers round it, just as...

"Got you!" declares William, through what sound like clenched teeth.

...just as Robert gets himself caught.

...just as The General grabs hold of him.

David pulls his head back round the tree, his hands gripping it hard, the roughness of the bark scratching his palms. *What now?*

"Do you give up? Do you?" He can hear his comrade being interrogated. It gives him no other choice.

David pads lightly over the fallen leaves, amazed that William or Robert still haven't heard him; he'd have thought the sound coming from his pounding chest alone would've given him away by now. When he gets to within a few paces of them, David points two fingers into a pistol shape and jabs them at William's back. "Let him go." He presses harder. Feels his fingers boring shallow imprints into his friend's skin. William tenses. Straightens. Takes an audible, deep breath. Then gives off a reluctant sigh.

An English Lesson

The school bell rings. Ten-to-nine. Lessons begin. Learning – for David, the greatest game of all…

Pushing his way out of the undergrowth, the low branches poking and scratching at his uniform, David goes to collect his bag. Robert and William follow, untangling themselves: from each other and from the game.

"Good morning, gentlemen," Mr. Slogee greets them as they cross through the double-doors; his face, as ever, stern and grim. "Straight to first lesson, please," he says. "Chop, chop." Then, rising on to the balls of his feet, he hollers over their heads, "Hunter!"

The English master, Mr. Johnson, stands at his desk, watching while the class fills up.

"Sit down, then, boys," he says.

William's place is at the back, along the left-hand side, and David and Robert are in the central column, three tables apart.

David takes out his things, arranging them neatly in a line. He looks across at Simons, catches him planting a flemmy cough into his hands.

Even with the blinds pulled up, the light lingers dim and dull. Mr. Johnson checks his watch. No one dares move. It's two minutes since the lesson should have begun. From out in the corridor, David can hear running footsteps. Mr. Johnson glances at the classroom door (clearly, he's heard it too) just as Michael Francis rushes in, filling the last seat without a word or look.

"Right…" The English master moves out from behind his desk. "You know what I'm going to say, Francis."

The lad nods.

"Another five at the end." (He says it anyway, for arguments sake.) "*Don't* make it any worse."

"Yes, sir," Francis mumbles.

"Good. Let's start."

He picks up a stack of books and starts passing them out, one per pupil. A copy of their current text, JUDE THE OBSCURE by Thomas Hardy, lands on David's desk. He's had this exact one before: recognises the squiggles on the title page, the initials, JCW, scrawled in blunt pencil across the bottom-right corner.

"Now, where were we? Who's going to begin for us?"

Thomas Farnham raises his hand, low and timid. He sits directly in front of David – which makes him next to read.

"From chapter one of the sixth part, please, Farnham."

Thomas' shy voice echoes round the room, hanging quietly in the ceiling.

"Louder, boy."

He raises the volume slightly and David follows the words on the page, before glancing down, turning to the next one, wondering which paragraph he'll be asked to start from.

After Farnham's gone for about a page and a half, Mr. Johnson interrupts. "Denby – your turn."

""They turned in on the left by the church...""

David does his best to make himself heard – he doesn't want Mr. Johnson ordering him to speak up. But it's a challenge in this old, musty schoolroom – just because of the creaks and groans these aging buildings naturally make, not to mention the noises made by other people in the class, and out in the hallway, that then rebound from one wall to the next, or play about over their heads before dropping boomy and confused to straining, schoolboy eardrums.

""...And to criticise some details of masonry in other college fronts about the city."" David reaches the end of a paragraph, a page or so later.

"Thank you. Watson, please," Mr. Johnson butts in again, passing the reading-baton on. A pattern that continues for the whole lesson: each boy covering about a page and a half, in turn, in the order they're seated. David reads three times in all – so does Robert, so does William.

Then, after fifty minutes, the bell in the clock tower chimes. First lesson finished. (Next lesson – Latin. From one language to another.)

"Right, then – homework." Mr. Johnson brings things to a close, bell-tones fluttering in the background. "To begin with, I want a summary of what we've just read…"

(He always wants a summary of what they've just read.)

David picks up his pencil.

"Then I want you to ask yourselves this question – what is it that originally motivates Jude Fawley to pursue a college career and, if he'd been successful, how do you think it would have changed the novel? Two pages on that, please. Hand it in, next lesson."

David jots that down into his classbook.

"Now…" Mr. Johnson stands.

The boys copy – chairs scraping along the floor. David knows what's coming. They all know.

"Francis. Here." He points to a spot in clear view of the whole class, then lifts something from the coat rack. "Put out your… your left hand, this time."

Michael does it.

The English master raises the slim length of wood over his head. It brushes the white, wispy tufts that make up the remainder of his hair. Then, without warning, he drops it down on to the offered hand.

David hears it slap on skin. Watches as it happens two more times. Throughout the spectacle, the room remains silent. No one coughs. No one mutters or gasps. They've seen it plenty of times before.

"Now, tomorrow – do try and arrive on time, Francis. I'll be checking up on you."

The boy nods, his eyes stuck to the ground.

"Class dismissed."

Mr. Johnson moves from desk to desk, collecting in the books, and David does all he can to avoid his eye. He carefully repacks his bag, swings it over his head, and makes for the door. He can see Robert and William waiting for him outside, in the corridor, but...

"Oh. Sorry."

David and Francis bump into each other, by the door. David can't help noticing the red marks on Michael's left hand (more than just one lesson's worth, surely), how shaky it is.

"Sorry," David says again.

"No." Francis follows his gaze; pockets his hand. "Doesn't matter." And rushes out of class.

Ten-past five. David gets off the school bus, back where the day began. A vibrant pinky-red spills across the sky. Darkness begins to flicker and blink in his eyes. He looks around, trying to adjust to the lower level of natural light. The fields, the fading birdsong, remind him of scenes from the novel they read in class: scenes of Jude Fawley in Wessex countryside daydreaming about his life and what it might be like, how much better it would be, if only he could attend university. David has similar ambitions, finds strange comfort from this closeness, their shared dreams for things far above the normal reaches of a son of a dockworker or an orphan sent to live with his great-aunt.

If he stares hard enough, stars are faintly visible; distant dots of fire set against the gradually blackening canvas. The thick clouds of the morning have fallen completely away and, as David keeps looking, new stars appear, burn up, come quickly into focus: several every second, the more he studies the evening sky over and around him.

He's not far from home now and his mind tracks back again to the English lesson, to the homework they were set. He tries to think in deep, perceptive ways about Jude and the characters and places of his story, just like Mr. Johnson would want (no, expect) him to...

But Michael Francis pushes all of this out. Instead, it's his story David finds himself trying to understand and re-write.

It's not like he hasn't seen it before, some lad being punished. And, more often than not, the lad being punished is Michael Francis. And it's not his hand held out, waiting to be whacked, or even it *being* whacked – that isn't what's getting to him. It's what it looked like afterwards, by the door. He tried to hide it, but David definitely saw it, bruised and shaking. He'd always assumed that Francis didn't care, that – for whatever reason – it just didn't get to him. (After all, Francis said it himself, didn't he? "Doesn't matter." Before rushing out of class.)

But that can't be true – can it? No matter how many times – it can't be something you just get used to. David imagines, for a moment, what it must feel like; hopes he never has to experience it… first-hand (so to speak).

As he approaches home, makes out, like stars in the night sky, the faint light from the oil lamps, David realises something else: that – besides apologising for bumping into him and asking him, early on in the first term, if he knew the way to the toilets – he's never really spoken to Michael. He's never really seen *anyone* speak to him. Perhaps he should do something about that.

Stories

Michael Francis lives a few streets away from school in a slim, terraced house. David knows this because William told him. And William knows this because he, too, lives in a slim, terraced house down the neighbouring street. Besides that, there's just one other thing David's been told about Michael Francis. In fact, it's a story everyone in his year group has been told.

It's a week since yet another English class closed with a caning. And each one after has ended the same way – not to mention those of a few other subjects. Being late; having the wrong equipment (or having none at all); unfinished or non-existent homework – Michael's been rapped for all of that this past week.

Lunchtime. After stopping off in the library, David is alone. He jogs down the staircase, two steps at a time, his mind heading for the schoolyard. He expects Robert and William will be in the usual spot. But from the height the stairs give him, David notices Michael sat on one of the wooden-slatted benches, cut into a shallow alcove.

"Hello," he says.

Michael is cramming his lunch into his mouth. ("No one's racing you for it," David's mother would always joke when he ate that way at home.) He looks up. "Hello," he splutters through a mouthful of sandwich.

"Mind if I sit down?"

Michael swallows heavily. Glancing at the spare half of the seat, he shuffles over to one side, making more-than-adequate room.

David sits; takes out his packed lunch. The brown-paper bag rustles as his hand sinks in, reaching for a cheese and pickle sandwich. David peels back the greaseproof sheet, holds it at eye-level, inspecting it for a few seconds, then starts to eat. He smiles after his first bite. "I really like pickles," he says, struggling for something to talk about.

Michael says nothing: barely nods in response. A few more silent moments scuttle past, marked by passing pupils.

"And I mean I really, *really* like them." David tries to tease out the beginnings of a normal, back-and-forth discussion. "If I could eat just one thing for the rest of my life – it'd be pickles."

Silence. Again.

David picks up the grocery bag, peering inside for a thing to give his attention to. What's left? Another sandwich (cheese and pickle, obviously), an apple and a pear. He takes out the second sandwich, unwrapping it.

"Those stink so much," Michael says finally, wrinkling his nose.

"Sorry?"

"The pickles – they smell awful."

"Do you think? That's the best bit to me," says David, grinning and, lifting it closer to his nose, inhaling deeply.

The lunch hour hurries past. David glances at one of the mounted clocks that hang on every corridor wall; there are five minutes before the bell.

Once they started, conversation built and flowed. From disagreeing about the stench and taste of pickles, they went on to talk about what really is the best type of sandwich. (Michael likes cheese too, but with onion or, sometimes, tomato.) Then they moved on to other things – the frustrations that come from having younger sisters; their shared interest in creepy-crawlies and slimy amphibians; the graveyard near school and whether, as many would say, it really is haunted – though it is, you would think, the most likely place spirits would inhabit. All little, insignificant things – but David now feels he knows Michael infinitely more.

"I guess you really want to know about my Dad," Michael mutters, during a momentary lapse in chat.

The rumour, the story going around; David had almost forgotten about that.

"Everybody wants to know about that," he says again.

David shakes his head. "It's nothing to do with me."

Michael sighs. "Well, it's true. But..." Michael speaks louder; turns to face David. "It's not as bad as everyone makes out. I mean, we needed the money. Things are expensive these days – Mum always says that. School's expensive." His shoulders drop. "You see: it's my fault Dad stole all that money."

***

"What's guilt feel like, Mum?"

Esther looked down at her son, puzzled. They were walking home from the bus stop. David had just finished his first day at school and she'd wanted to collect him, hear how it all went. David told her everything – all about his lessons and the new things he'd already learnt; the teachers and the other pupils: who's nice and who's not so; the quirky beauty of the building.

So, when their conversation took this sudden shift, it surprised her. "Sorry? What's put *that* idea in your head?"

David matched his mother's stare. He thought it was obvious. "Because of the story we read in English class. I was just telling you – the one about the two brothers..."

A long time ago, there were two brothers. They led a very comfortable life – an upbringing blessed with luxury. Everything they asked for was given to them; nothing was denied them; and, one day, each knew they would be getting an enormous inheritance from their wealthy father.

Now, the second brother was not as patient as his older sibling. He knew his share would be huge. He knew, also, that there was a vast, ceaseless world of riches and pleasures, beyond the many riches and pleasures he'd grown up with, and he couldn't wait any longer to experience such things.

So, the second son asked for his money. He knew he was going to get it – so why wait? The father, reluctantly, agreed – for it was what his son wanted. But there was one condition tied to his agreement; if the younger son took the money, he would have to leave his father's house, the only house he had ever known, and start again, somewhere else, alone.

The thought of all the money he'd be getting far outweighed the comfort he was used to, so the next day the son left his father and his older brother and the house he had grown up in. He travelled a long distance, eventually reaching a vast city that appeared to stretch out forever.

At first, he had a wonderful time. He stayed in the finest hotel the big city had to offer; he became friends with its most affluent and influential people; ate and drank the most delicious, expensive things.

Then, one day, he discovered there was no money left. It had all gone. And he had bill after bill, and account after account, outstanding, demanding to be settled and nothing to settle them with. The son realised, therefore, that he must get a job and, humiliated, he started by cleaning the rooms of the hotel he had just been staying in.

Quickly, he fell into a pit of despair. How had his life turned out this way – his extravagant, abundant life where everything he could ever want or need was his? It didn't take long – not many fresh bed-sheets were laid – before he decided what had to be done; and though he really, really didn't want to do it, he knew he had to.

So, he left the city with its amazing things (which were now well out of his price range) and began the long journey back to the father, brother and home he had left behind.

Now, while he was still some way off, his father saw him approaching. Ever since his youngest son left, he had been watching and waiting. And on this particular day he spotted a broken, dishevelled man in the distance.

Could it be?

He looked again.

Lifted a hand to his forehead.

Is that…?

His eyes piercing the horizon, he realised that it was.

And so he ran.

And when he reached him, he threw his arms around him.

The son began to apologise for all the things he had done wrong: for leaving and for wasting away his inheritance. I'm sorry, sorry, sorry... I'm so sorry, sorry, sorry... He repeated over and over. How can you possibly forgive me?

But his father raised a hand to his son's lips. There's no need, he began. You have returned. And that is all that matters.

"Mr. Johnson said the younger son felt guilty – but what does that *feel* like?"

David's mother expelled a sigh. "You're putting me on the spot, aren't you, love? Will it be like this every day?"

"No, I just wondered – that's all."

"Right, well – I suppose the person in the story knew he'd done something wrong, that he'd made a mistake."

"But, how?"

"Well, *you* must know when you've done something you shouldn't have."

"I guess."

"You can't stop thinking about it – can you?"

David shook his head.

"Well, that's guilt – that's what it feels like."

An old man wobbled past on his bicycle, bits of road firing off the wheel-spokes and showering David's shoes.

"Have *you* ever felt guilty?"

"Gosh. I'm not sure. I suppose." She scratched her left arm. "But it depends."

"What do you mean?"

"Well..." She rubbed her neck with her left hand. "You should never lie – should you?"

"No," replied David, plain and simple.

"But..." She hesitated, before plunging on: "What if I tell you or your sister a *little* lie to make you feel better or to keep you safe?"

"Have you ever done that?" David jumped straight in.

"That's another subject." She smiled down at him, the question (*wouldn't you like to know?*) flickering in her eyes. "All I'm saying is there are times when… well… you know when you've done something *really* wrong by the way it plays on your mind, don't you? Or if it's hurt somebody else."

"But what if you haven't done anything wrong and you still feel guilty?"

"Sorry. Who are we talking about now?"

"No, it's just a question."

His mother sighed; took a few steps before speaking. "I suppose someone could blame you for something that wasn't your fault. Or you might even start blaming yourself."

David nodded at the stony ground. They continued down the lane, the failing light casting long shadows in front of them.

"So – what are those little lies you were talking about?"

His mother looked down at him, flashing a grin. "Come on," she said; then quickened her pace. "Almost home."

***

The bell goes. David hears it ring-ring-ringing through the open doors several yards to their left. The corridor fills up. David and Michael put their lunch things away.

"You're wrong, you know?" David says, standing, ready to set off for geography.

"What?"

"About your dad. It's not your fault he's in prison."

"Maybe."

"No. Definitely."

A Fresh Piece of Family History

The clock at Paragon station strikes the eleventh hour. What had just filled the square – the engines, the chatter – cuts to nothing. David watches the people around them take off their hats and bow their heads. His father does the same. So, David does the same too, focusing on the paving, the straight-line cracks, like some endless maze.

Silence, but for some crows calling overhead. David resists looking up. Feels his heartbeat throbbing under his school shirt.

The silence continues.

Then the sound of a cannon breaks in: one sharp, ear-popping blast, David's chest leaping. This time he does raise his head; a swell of dark, rain-heavy clouds, not far off. Around him, people start speaking again. Slowly, city centre normality returning. Cars stutter off. A train bellows. Shop doors ring and clatter shut.

David turns to his father, who smiles down at him. "It's good we could both come down here together, eh?" His words very nearly lost in the swamp and symphony of the conversations meshing together around them. David doesn't attempt a reply. Even his thoughts feel drowned out.

"Morning, Bill." Someone shouts through the crowd. A man wearing a mud-green mackintosh walks towards David and his father. "I thought I might see you here."

"Is that right?"

They shake hands.

"And good morning to you, young man." The stranger reaches down and grabs David's hand too.

"Frank – this is my eldest, David."

"Well, it's a pleasure to meet you, David. Your Dad, here's, told us a lot about you."

"Nice to meet you, sir," David replies, as clear and polite as he can make it.

The man smiles, showing off a hole where a front tooth should be. "Here, Bill..." He turns again to David's father.

"Have you…?" He pauses, lowering his voice to a level David can just still hear. "Have you heard any more about The Kingston Rose?"

"No, Frank – not since a few days back."

"Ah, me too."

They both look down at the floor – considering what to say next, perhaps.

"This just reminded me, you know?" sighs Frank, nipping his bottom lip with his teeth. "I know it's not quite the same, but… you know…"

David's father nods understandingly.

"Anyway. Best be off."

The two men repeat the handshake and then, after patting David firmly on the back, Frank disappears into the swarm of people.

"Just someone I work with, son." David's father scratches his unshaven chin. There was no need for him to explain. "Now…" He claps his hands together, rubbing them frantically. "Let's see if we can't get a bit closer, eh?"

As they wade through, David strains on to his tiptoes, trying for a clearer view of the bright-white statue in the middle of the square. Surrounded by drab-stone buildings and grey skies, it seems much too white, almost ghostly. It's a war memorial for a conflict fought nearly forty years ago in South Africa. Lots of men from round here went out there – many of them never coming back. Like trawler men that cast off to the cold, cold seas and end up finding ceaseless rest right there, underwater, many miles from home. The sculpture, shaped into two soldiers (one rescuing the other), was put up to remember those that lost their lives out there in the hills and plains of the former colony. It lists fifty-seven names. Fifty-seven lives. And David's grandfather was one of them, his name written, somewhere, on the plinth the statue rests on.

David reaches out to touch it. Then thinks better of it. (*Is that allowed?*) He glances either side, at the other people crowded round. He watches his father searching the list.

"There he is," he points. "You see the name RUMBLE?"
David looks. Finds it. Nods.
"That's your grandfather – your mother's father."
RUMBLE, D.   PRIVATE,
NORTHUMBERLAND FUSILIERS.
KILLED IN ACTION.

"Northumberland?"
"That's the regiment he served with." His father points again at the base of the statue. "And you see his initial is D? That stands for David. We named *you* after him."

David never knew that – a fresh piece of family history, of his own personal history in fact. "What happened to him?"

"No one's really sure, son. Not precisely. The most we know is he died in battle." He tries a smile.

David looks more generally at the monument, at some of the other names. NEALE. RADCLIFFE. RAMSEY. SEWARDS. Possible relatives of those standing next to him and his father now.

Drizzle starts to slick the pavement, brushing and tickling David's hands and neck.

"Come on, then." His father rests a hand on his shoulder. "Let's get you back to school."

To Do with Thompson

Raindrops drum the roof of the school bus. The kind of thunderous racket David pictures his grandfather being caught up in four decades back. Perhaps it sounded just like this the moment he...

"This better stop soon," says Robert, above the din.

David narrows his eyes, straining to see through the spray and the haze plastered on the bus windows. "I expect it'll be over soon," he says, with a hopeful grasp. (*Please let me be right, please let me be right...*) He pokes his nose against the glass. Winces at the coldness his skin meets.

But when the bus reaches its final stop, nothing has changed. The rain falls just as hard. Harder, if anything. David and Robert rush towards the school gates, dashing up to the first doors they find and stumbling inside. David runs a hand through his dripping hair. Tempted to shake himself dry like a dog after a swim. His clothes, even those a few layers down, are soggy and squelchy and, when pressed in a particular spot, water dribbles up and out of the fabric, similar to fresh water springing from the ground.

Robert's just the same. "Look at this." He holds out his arms, squeezing the baggy material from one sleeve, wringing it out like a cloth. A small puddle gathers round his shoes.

David laughs.

"Just great, eh?"

"Come on," David says, leading the way to the common room.

The empty corridors were a clue – the rain-soaked playground, too. David's never seen it so packed, the fireplace barely visible over the bodies surrounding it. Flickering and dancing, the flames shape shadows on the pale-painted walls. The chatter echoes and booms. In one corner, Michael Francis is hunched over a book. David starts to go over, but Robert grabs his arm.

"What?"

"Are you sure?"

"I told you – it's fine."

"But maybe he wants to be left alone."

"Well, we'll ask him, then."

They walk over.

"Morning, Michael. How are you?"

He takes a moment to look up from what he's reading. Rubs his eyes and replies; "I'm fine, thank you."

"Can we join you?" asks David, pointing at Robert a few strides behind.

"I guess so." Michael straightens up, crossing his legs and laying the book on his lap.

David sits. It feels like landing bottom-first in a pond. Robert joins him down on the carpet. By the look on his face, he's suffered the same sensation.

Glancing at the ceiling, David picks out the fine lines carved into the coving – there's always something you can notice for the first time. The rain hammers at the window they sit beneath, the cold from the blustery wind seeping in. He looks at the faces on the walls: portraits of those from throughout the school's long history – Andrew Marvell, John Clarke, Joseph Milner; all of them writers, as well as former masters, interspersed alongside others involved in financing the school from its earliest days in the 1400s up to more recent patrons.

"So, what're you reading?"

Michael holds up his book. "Latin."

"Irregular verbs?"

Someone almost tramples on David's toes. They hold up a hand for apology.

"Oh, we're being tested, aren't we?" Robert groans. "Can't wait."

"Me too," agrees Michael. "Until it's over."

Robert sniggers.

"Denby!" A voice sounds out from the huddled crowd of wet boys. "Over here, Denby!"

"Who's that?" asks Robert, standing.

"Fitzgerald! Get Denby, will you?"

"Oh, great." Robert sits back down. "It's Thompson."

"Thompson? What does *he* want?"

"No idea."

"Well, where is he?" David gets to his feet. Spots Thompson waving to him.

"You seen him?"

"Yes." David stoops to collect his bag. "I'll go see what he's after."

"Oh, right. Want me to come?" Already halfway up.

"No. I won't be long. You stay here."

"Oh." Robert hands Michael a shy smile, slumping back to the floor.

David finds Thompson by the fire, hands out splayed, red and glowing. He taps him on the shoulder. 'morning."

Thompson turns around. Strange grin. "You look soaked."

"I am."

He steps aside, makes room by the hearth.

"Oh. Thanks. How'd you get such a good spot?" asks David, stretching and flexing his fingers, the heat already starting to tingle them dry.

"You know – just lucky," he shrugs.

David rubs his hands. Then holds them out again. Looks around him at the, mostly, fifth and sixth formers doing the same thing, fiery grins. "Did you want me for something?" he asks.

"Oh…" says Thompson, like he's just remembered. "I was wondering whether you managed that geography homework."

David nods, pulling his hands back to his side.

"And how did you find it?"

"Fine. Why?"

"Oh, no reason." Thompson puts his warmed-up palms together. "No reason," he repeats.

Well, if that's all… David turns to leave.

"Wait. No need to go just yet – you're still not dry," says Thompson.

"I think I'll survive, thanks." David pats his damp blazer. "See you in first period."

"Oh. All right," Thompson stumbles a response.

David starts pushing back through the crowd. The further out he gets, the younger (and shorter), generally, the boys become. He finds Robert and Michael where he left them, pleased to see them speaking to each other, wide smiles and frantic gestures. He drops his bag on the floor by Michael's feet.

"What did he want?" asks Robert, looking up.

"Not sure, really." David settles down again. "It was just about the geography homework."

Michael skims through his Latin book.

"What've you both been talking about?"

"Hennessey the classics master, mainly."

"And we did try to predict what Thompson wanted," adds Robert.

"But we were wrong."

"We didn't get close."

"No," says Michael, with a snort.

David looks to his toes, wiggles them, feels sodden socks sticking to softened skin. Michael puts his book back in his bag.

"I wonder where William is."

"Not sure. No sign of him in that lot?" asks Robert.

David shakes his head. "You know him, though – he'll already be waiting outside physics."

"True," Robert sniffs.

"He won't have thought to meet us in here."

The common room starts to empty. David checks the time. Nudging them both, they stand up just as the bell sets the school day officially in motion.

"Right..." Mr. Finch, the geography teacher, starts another lesson. "Let's begin with the homework you all handed in last time."

David straightens in his seat.

"Witney?" He takes the first book off a thirty-something pile, scanning the room. "There you are." He finds the right page. "Good effort, though *please* work harder on your presentation – as I keep on telling you."

Mr. Finch flings the exercise book across the room. David watches its progress to the back row. Witney's chair yelps as he bends down to gather it from the floor.

"Rogers… Rogers…"

The boy raises his hand.

"Again. Good effort. I think you get the idea."

Throws it out and picks up the next one.

"Now, Harper. *Wrong.* That's all I'll say on that one."

It whizzes past David's left-hand ear and on to the desk behind him.

"Now, Thompson…" Mr. Finch continues. "Big surprise this. I don't think you've understood this, have you?"

Thompson stares silently at the teacher. Mr. Finch passes it to the front row so that it can slowly work its way back to the third.

"Just read what I've written. Ask me at the end if you're still not sure."

David notices some lads with hands over their mouths, hiding smirks and chuckles. That was very nearly his reaction too. But, looking Thompson's way, seeing his fallen face, the way, now, he's grimacing at his work, David regrets the quick glee that boiled up so easily and readily inside him. He catches Robert's eye. He's doing nothing to hide his grin. *Poor Thompson,* he mouths, between both hands, the sarcasm and delight clear in the exaggerated movement of his lips.

Once all the homework's been returned, and the new work's been explained, the class works in quiet. Mr. Finch sits at his desk, marking another form's books – and mentally rehearsing his comments, perhaps. The gold-coloured clip of his fountain pen catches the pale light trickling in and the wind clatters against the flimsy glass.

Every few sentences, David raises his head. Most times out of ten, he notices one of his classmates casting a discreet glance

Thompson's way, pleased that, for once, he's sweating over his work too. David wonders if it were him, and not Thompson, would they react the same way? He'd like to think not. But, then – why wouldn't they?

Leaving the classroom, David and Thompson cross at the door. David tries a nervous smile.

"Well done, Denby," Thompson says through tight-together teeth. "Mr. Finch is obviously an admirer of yours. What was it he said? "Flawless as usual.""

David shrugs his shoulders.

"Enjoy it. I won't slip up like that again. Promise you."

"But what does it matter?"

"It just does." And he pulls away, walking swiftly, purposefully, to their next lesson.

The Radio... And What It Says

Winter, 1938. A fresh covering of frost glitters the ground most mornings and indoors, even close beside the fireplace, the flames crackling and spluttering away, David can make clouds of exhaled air.

His father enters the room, having been out chopping firewood. "Right..." he says, smacking his hands together and going over to the wireless.

David looks at the clock; it's that time already. He, too, rubs his arms roughly as if ruffling the fur on top of a dog's head; sits up straighter in his chair. (He can remember his father bringing the radio home, several months ago. He brought it in, clutching it like at any moment it may leap from his hands, and told David and Josie, along with their mother, to gather round while he set it up. They waited, still and quiet, for the first words to break through. It popped and it hissed, like a fire. Then it spoke.)

Kffffffffff.

He turns the dial. It always starts with a storm of radio buzz.

Kffffffffff.

Pip.

Kffffffff.

"Oh. Nearly there, son." The hazy, audio-fog about to lift.

Kffffffffff.

"...-casting Corporation. The time is six o'clock on Saturday the twelfth of February. This is the evening news bulletin."

"Just in time," David's father sighs into his armchair, closing his eyes and crossing one leg over the other.

David stares at the radio: still finds it hard to believe that this voice, someone's voice – someone's father, probably – could be speaking to them all the way from London, just through this little box.

The bulletin opens with an update on the Spanish Civil War and the number of British-born soldiers (volunteers for the Republican side, fighting as part of a multi-nation group known as the International Brigade) that have lost their lives or been injured in recent clashes.

Then it moves on; the announcer continues: "In Berchtesgaden, on the border between Germany and Austria, Chancellor von Schuschnigg of Austria and Chancellor Hitler of Germany met today. The German Chancellor forced the Austrian Chancellor to allow greater Nazi participation in the Austrian government, with the threat of German invasion should Chancellor von Schuschnigg refuse."

David shifts position, his legs suddenly tingling. This settling down to listen to the news bulletin (except on Sundays – it doesn't broadcast then) has become a sort of tradition, for both David and his father; it's grown to be a fixture of their lives – another habit, another re-run – and, as far as David can recall, that German man's name seems to have been a part of it, too, the whole time.

He whispers it to himself, eases it out slowly. *"Hit-ler…"*

***

And each morning, this tradition continues. David scours the newspaper – once his father is finished with it, of course – searching for that name; a fascinated, greedy student of these far-off events, his appetite never quite satisfied.

And, what does he find?

The story goes on – history lessons for a future set of schoolchildren written every day, for David to read with his breakfast.

Britain steps in. Their aim is to contain the situation, to temper Hitler's ambitions. The British embassy in Berlin suggests the Germans help lead a group of nations to rule Africa – if Hitler gives up plans for border expansion. He flatly refuses and, in March (on the twelfth again – something about that date, perhaps), German soldiers move in and occupy Austria. The invasion is called *Anschluß*, which means 'link-up', as though it was some asked-for change, an accession to the current, public mood. But, maybe it was. Because a month later (though, this time, on the *tenth* of April – pity the pattern couldn't continue), the Austrian people, soon-to-be-Germans, vote in favour of unification (their so-called link-up) by a staggering 99.73%. Apparently, even Hitler was surprised.

***

"You be von Schuschnigg, William. And Michael – you could be…" He looks to the ground for an answer. "Miklas, maybe?"

Michael smiles. "Imaginative, David."

"It's a real person. Honestly."

"Sorry, David – what did you say *my* name was?" asks William.

"Von Schuschnigg."

"Von *Schuschnigg*." William tries it for a fit. "How did you come up with that one?"

"I didn't."

"What, so…? How, then?"

"It's the name of the Austrian Chancellor."

"Oh, right."

A pause.

"And…?"

"And…" David starts again, his answer obviously not as self-explanatory as he thought. "Austria has just been invaded by Germany – right? By Chancellor Hitler – remember?" He *had* tried telling them. "So, *we're* going to be the Germans…" David whacks Robert's arm. "And you and Michael are the Austrians and you've got to stop us invading."

So as the real narrative unfolds, as Europe alters (irreversibly?), David uses the names and events, as he reads and learns about them, to add colour to their game. They become a part of its story.

But.

Hold on.

What's going on is *actually* going on. It isn't just some made-up story. They're not just made-up names. One way or another, there will be an impact – there will be massive, far-reaching consequences. Even from this distance, David can see that clearly, looming, growing. And it stays with him, the reality of it. It plays on his mind, all the questions, confusion, uncertainty…

***

The newspaper rustles. David's father gives it a good, firm shake. "There you go, son," he says, his face emerging from behind the headlines and newsprint.

"Thanks."

David takes it and starts to read. Scans the front page. Lingers at the grainy picture of a uniformed man, saluting straight and upwards.

"Dad?"

"Yes, son?"

David runs his eyes back over the headline accompanying the image.

HITLER DECLARES HE WILL DESTROY CZECHOSLOVAKIA BY MILITARY FORCE

"Why's he doing all this?"

"Who?"

David points at the man.

"Well, I don't know exactly." He scratches his forehead. "I suppose there's just people in this world that feel they have to be in power – no matter what."

David squirms in his seat.

"Look…" his father continues, realising he hadn't given the answer David required. "How about speaking to one of your teachers, eh? They're bound to know more than me."

"Could I?"

"Why not?"

The birds are in full voice: all that can be heard, all that accompanies the swish-swish David makes as he pushes his way through the long grass beside the road. He cannot identify them, individually, by their songs, by sound alone – though he'd like to, would love to have that kind of knowledge and ability. So, David relies, instead, on his eyes and what he can remember of the nature books – along with those on other subjects – he devours at home. In the undergrowth, sparrows jump from one branch to another, jittery and nervous, never remaining in one place for very long. Others, the odd blackbird or robin, appear from out of the honeysuckle hedgerows, springing on to the road ahead – their tiny, five-pronged feet landing where David, also, is about to step.

Time stretches and widens on these walks. And David likes that. It means he can let go of any preoccupation about needing to be somewhere – right now or very soon – and allow himself to be taken over by all that surrounds him. Because everything has significance – the way the wind moves the branches of that tree out in the middle of the hay-stacked field; or how that starling blindly senses a worm beneath the surface, leaps to it, severs in two, and swallows in seconds.

It is some strange between-time, so far as the weather is concerned. But summer *is* close to flowering, spring is nearing an end, and these birds (the sparrows, the starlings) were some of its new-borns, eager and jumpy, everything a new discovery. They're learning every day: how to fill their stomachs and what with; what or whom to avoid; the best place to shelter when the clouds let out their powerful rain. And David watches them, listens to their song-language too, as he makes his way to the bus stop every school morning. And just like them, David is learning too. He is discovering, unearthing, taking things in – whatever new piece of information it might be – with an enthusiasm that is unquenchable, an innate desire to expand his knowledge up to the nth degree, the farthest it will go. Because, to David, nothing is off limits; there is no place of disinterest.

He smiles to himself, at the fields as they look back at him, at the birds as they sing (to him? That's what it feels like sometimes). It all belongs to an unceasing natural order – so does that worm he saw get ripped apart. It belongs to a circle of events that will repeat in time with the seasons and the days of the year – human constructs dictated by the way the natural world has forever done things.

The bus stop is opposite a row of half-a-dozen buildings. Each one of them a business, all family-run, all lit up and open by the time David's there waiting for the school bus, staring across at them and their insides. He leans against a sunken fence-post, folding his arms. Mrs. Habley from the bakery scrapes a chalkboard sign along the stone path. Props it up against the shop wall. In thick, white letters it declares: FRESH BREAD. JUST BAKED. David scrunches his nose, catching a breath of that fresh bread. He sniffs again, this second helping smelling different, and another noise chimes in, clashing with the calm, melodic birdsong; the sound of metal thudding on wood. It turns David's attention to the butcher shop, two doors down. That's what he can smell. He breathes out, deeply, trying to mask it, get rid of it. The warming, bakery scent mixing with what drifts over from the butcher's yard – the stench of iron and slaughter.

David stares at the place. Red and pink pig carcasses hang lifeless in the shop window, their front legs dangling, limp and stubby. The two colours streak like contours on the pages of an atlas; the red marks flesh and the pink shapes out the fat, chewy bits David always eats around. He pictures himself inside, in the room where the hacking and cutting happens, the floor covered with deep-crimson puddles. He thinks of a battlefield, remembers the newspaper stories, the radio bulletins, Austria, Czechoslovakia: themselves now battlefields, invaded nations, blood-covered floors.

It feels like the ghost of war is everywhere right now. His grandfather (after whom he is named) comes to mind, how he never came home... And something David read a few days ago, hinting at wider conflict if things get worse... If Hitler keeps on... If... If... If... And who'll be the ones to stop him? Men from this country, like the ones fighting in Spain? And what sort of age will they be? David wonders. His father is thirty-five. Is that too old? Too young? Or is it just right?

"Sir?" David approaches Mr. Parfick's desk, the school bell that rang to end the lesson still playing in his ears.

The history master turns from wiping away that morning's chalk marks, flicking his long brown hair out of his eye-line with a short shudder of his head. "Yes, Denby?" He taps down the board-rubber on the scratched-wood desk, expelling with it a breath of chalk dust.

"I have a question, sir."

"Oh, yes – and what might that be?"

"Well, sir, it's about what's been happening..." He pauses. "In Germany."

"Ah." Mr. Parfick sits down. "And what is it that you want to know precisely?"

"Nothing in particular, sir – it's just something that I'm interested in, but... I don't quite know what to make of it all." David plays his worries down.

"Well, it's all going on at a relative distance right now, but..." He breaks for a cough. "I suppose that could change very quickly." The history master's eyes catch a streak of sunlight streaming through the blinds, glinting a watery blue. "One wrong move from any of the diplomatic parties and, well..." Mr. Parfick leans back in his creaky chair. (Clearly, he's said his lot – which wasn't very much, as it turned out.)

"Right. Thank you, sir."

Mr. Parfick stands, removing a jagged pile of books collected after class. He places them in their space on the bookshelf, to where they came from beside volumes about the French Revolution (and the royal family it sought to remove) and the great explorers (Raleigh, Columbus and the like) who discovered – and, also, helped colonise – previously unknown parts of the world. (And look what that set in motion. Isn't Hitler merely continuing in their tradition?)

"I'm afraid, Denby, the situation is so… changeable – it's hard to know with any real authority what will come of it all."

"Yes, sir." David wanders back to his desk, begins gathering his things together, while his teacher returns to tidying away the mess of another lesson.

"Denby?"

He looks up from his almost re-packed school bag.

"Don't hesitate to ask me about this again – as and when you need to."

David nods. Slight upward fold creasing his lips: a relieved, shy smile. "Thank you, sir."

"It's quite all right."

David flings his bag over his shoulder and leaves the classroom. *As and when you need to.* Maybe Mr. Parfick will regret making that offer. David still doesn't know what to think. The questions remain. Confusion lingers. And uncertainty casts a very real shadow.

A Fire Called Unstoppable

Midday. The sky is lit up. But not just by the sun. Flames reach like church spires and a vast swelling of smoke obscures the perfect blue.

Robert arrives at David's front door. He's panting and wheezing.

"Have you run all the way?"

Robert nods, waving his hands in the direction he's come from. "White City's on fire," he splutters.

"What?"

"Look."

He points towards the city boundary, towards the pleasure grounds at White City. They've been there almost twenty years and, from this distance, a few miles away, David can, quite clearly, see them ablaze. Just last summer, he'd been there to the ice-skating rink with Josie and his mother. She'd promised them another trip there this year.

"Mum! Come and see."

"Come and see what?"

She joins them in the doorway, discarding a tea towel on the dining table.

David and Robert point together.

"Goodness!" she gasps. "Where's that?"

"White City, Mrs. Denby."

"Oh, my." She puts a hand to her mouth. "What a shame."

They stand watching for a few moments. David can't help noticing less birdsong than normal.

"I remember the fireworks the night it opened. Me and your Dad watched them right here." She points down at the doorstep.

"The fire engine arrived just before I left," says Robert, his breathing even again. "Then I came here." He looks at David.

"Oh – can we go and watch, Mum?"

She peers back into the quiet house. "Well… I don't see why not. Just be back for tea."

"I will."

Robert leads the way. The grass everywhere is dry, the soil cracked and parched. A heatwave hit this summer. Perfect weather for the school holidays. But it no doubt helped the fire spread too. The closer they get, the more the smoke fills the lane and hides the fields. David's eyes well up and sting and he can feel it tickling his throat.

A man with straggly-grey hair approaches. "Not much to see now," he informs them, walking on.

But they carry on anyway.

Then David starts hearing the snaps and thuds of splintering, smouldering wood. He thinks again about the threat of war, about where its battlefields may lie. This place, not all that far from home, has just that appearance today.

They're close to a hundred people, watching the firemen work.

"Not many left," says Robert.

David looks again. "Really?"

"There were a lot more earlier."

"I guess it's dying down," David reasons.

They watch for a little while; work their way to the front of the crowd. Just one more hose flows, jetting over the summerhouse roof. The stadium – nothing left but a charred frame; the ice-skating rink too – swallowed whole by the fire. At the roadside, a lot of the fire fighters stand by the trucks, packing away the equipment, patting each other on the backs with blackened hands. A few others walk through the now-destroyed grounds, turning ashen piles over with their boots – examining what remains underneath, then moving on to the next burnt-out heap.

They decide to leave.

"Well, that was exciting," says Robert, once they can breathe easier and see clearer.

"Mmm. Think I missed the best bit, though," adds David.

"You did, really." Robert smiles (*but I didn't*, flashing in his eyes).

***

David looks in the newspaper the next day. Perhaps unsurprisingly, the events of the fire are given a good chunk of print. Apparently, the sun shining on the stadium windows is how it started – and once it began, once it took hold, well... The report uses the word 'unstoppable'.

Which puts David in mind of something else, of someone else. He turns back to the front page.

A History Lesson

Josie plays by the empty fireplace. She sits cross-legged, dangling a one-armed teddy bear above Lily's head. Lily reaches out for it: lunges, every now and then, when she thinks her big sister is about to let her take it.

"Come now, Josie – don't tease your sister like that."

"Tut." She drops the toy; it flops to Lily's feet and she bundles it to her chest, grin pasted thickly across her face. Patience pays.

David returns to his homework. Runs a finger under the last thing he wrote.

His father sits down next to him. "What's this, then, son?" He leans in, blocking the light. "What's that say?" He tries to read David's writing. *"P-p-poor lee…* What?"

"It's French, Dad."

"Oh. That explains it." He pats David proudly on the head. Messes up his hair. "I'll let you get on."

A new school year. The last fizzled out and, in a similar way, the drama playing out in Europe subsided too. Hitler's declaration back at the end of May – to destroy Czechoslovakia by military force – appeared, at the time, worryingly imminent. David imagined that, in a matter of days, the country would no longer exist, that, by the next evening news bulletin, Germany would have consumed it entirely, like the fire consumed White City. But (…questions, confusion, uncertainty – all present and correct…) in the end, nothing actually came of Hitler's Czech threat.

Over the summer, in the disputed region – a place on the Czech-German border called the Sudetenland – there materialised nothing more than ruptures and in-fighting between those that sympathise with Hitler's plans and those that (obviously) don't.

But as September arrives, as David's school uniform is put on for the first time in a long time and his evenings are once more filled with homework, tensions in that tetchy part of central Europe flare up again.

"It's almost six, son."

David looks up from his French work. His father stands next to the dark-wood cabinet, tinkering with the dial on the wireless. He closes his schoolbooks, piles them at one corner of the table as the bulletin crackles to life.

"The time is six o'clock on Tuesday the sixth of September. This is the evening news bulletin. In Germany, the National Congress of the governing Nazi Party has begun in Nuremberg today..."

David read something in the newspaper about this. They call them the Nuremberg Rallies. They've been held annually for five years now – ever since Hitler became German Chancellor. According to the radio announcer, when Hitler speaks there this year, it's likely he will indicate decisively whether there will be peace or war with Czechoslovakia. David can already guess – with some certainty too – which it will be.

So, the story goes on. Yet again, a country's future dangles in front of him.

And sure enough, by the time October breaks through East Yorkshire, with its reddening trees and cooling winds, all the diplomatic manoeuvres and long-into-the-night negotiations fall away, and Germany begins another invasion.

The news comes out in pieces. And with each piece, David gets a greater sense of events. The German plans seem obvious: we *will* take the Sudetenland. Britain – and others – try to talk them round. But the Germans remain firm behind their demands and, thinking it the only way to prevent more widespread conflict, the British, French and Italian leaders sign an agreement with Hitler allowing Germany to invade and annexe the Sudetenland. (By the way, the Czechs are *not* invited to these negotiations.)

***

"Settle down now, boys…" Mr. Parfick calls the lesson to order.

Desks close. Chairs screech. The wood floor catches the light.

"Good." He comes out from behind his desk: stands central, slight lean to the left. "So, we find Napoleon contemplating a retreat. A retreat like nothing he had encountered before. There may have been troubles for him in Spain and against the armies of the British and the Prussians, but the size of the problem he faced in Russia – in part, because of the size of the country itself – was something altogether different, and something Napoleon had not foreseen." The history master holds his stare in one place, as if addressing someone pinned to the back wall.

The class stays silent. And you might be mistaken for confusing that with keen interest. David *used* to assume that. He'd say to Robert or William afterwards: "That was interesting, didn't you think?" Convinced they too had just been sat there immersed in Parfick's narrative. "No. You're kidding, aren't you?" they'd always reply, eyes red from trying to stay open.

Once Mr. Parfick starts like this, a whole lesson can disappear – and David loves it when this happens. He remembers their first history class. For most of it, Parfick did just this. It was like he was telling them a story. That time it was about Christopher Columbus discovering the Americas, and David listened intently, sat straight, his chin resting on his hands, elbows propped on the desk.

"As much as he didn't want to, Napoleon could see that he wouldn't be able to take Moscow. Nor could he stay there and hope the situation turned to his advantage – the city had emptied itself of provisions and people; all that remained were convicts released from the prisons. So, in October – four months after the invasion began – Napoleon started his Great Retreat. Now…" Mr. Parfick addresses the boys. "Can anyone tell me what other element might have caused problems for Napoleon and his army?"

David glances either side. He can see heads bobbing, half-asleep – the low, morning light casting dreamy minds.

"Anybody?"

David thinks he knows. He raises a hand.

"Denby?" Mr. Parfick smiles.

"Winter, sir."

"And what about winter?"

"Well, sir, Russia is a very cold country – especially in the winter."

"So...?" He's still smiling.

"So, it will have made it far harder to retreat in those conditions."

"Good, Denby. No need to be so reticent about it – that's quite correct. The Russian winter; an unconquerable force. Napoleon and his army began to travel from Moscow in the direction of a place called Kaluga, knowing there they could find food and other supplies. But..." He raises an index finger. "They were met by troops led by Field Marshal Kutuzov and this forced them north, back the way they had come through the bare, scorched lands along the Smolensk road. Then winter really hit. Short on supplies and under regular attack from local villagers and Cossack fighters, the French had to retrace the steps of their original invasion. In December 1812, by the time Napoleon's Grand Army left Russia, around half a million men were lost. Many had died in battle or been taken prisoner at earlier points in the campaign, but many more had simply succumbed to the harsh conditions of their retreat."

Here Mr. Parfick pauses. Picks up a pencil. Twizzles it two or three times from finger to finger. David looks up, watches fragments of dust fall like snow.

"Now, I think we'll leave Napoleon and his men there, for the time being. Instead, I want us to consider something else." He scans the classroom. "So, you'll need to be sat up straight for this. I want you paying complete attention." He claps. "Come now, Latchmore – that means you. Simons – you too. Let's have you concentrating." His voice always suffers slight cracks when it's being authoritative. It matches the thin lines creeping down from the ceiling. "Does anybody read a newspaper?" he asks.

Several arms go up. David flings his into the air.

"Good. And those of you who do, I wonder if you recognise any of the things we've learnt so far about Napoleon." He pauses again. "There's a man – a politician, in fact – with similarities to Monsieur Bonaparte. Have any of you noticed this?"

David leaves his hand in the air.

Parfick gives it a few seconds. "That's quite a few of you. Good." He gestures for hands to be lowered. Breathes out. Then carries on: "It puzzles me that the lessons of history are so often ignored. We should look to the past – not to replicate it – but to avoid the mistakes those have made before us." He leans against his desk, appears to make eye contact directly with David. "This man I'm talking about – and I won't name him. In fact, we could call it an addendum to your homework – if you don't know who I'm referring to, then find out for next time. But this man is doing just what Napoleon did. He's threatening war. He desires the apparently limitless expansion of his nation's borders and, what's more, the spread of his twisted ideology."

Through the window, the sun at last starts showing some colour.

Mr. Parfick coughs. "It wasn't quite my intention to talk about such things today, but I think it's important you know something of the times we're living in. In many ways, I can teach you no greater lesson than that." He sits down. A startled look on his face, he leafs through papers and books strewn over his desk. "Right. There are forty-five minutes left. In your books and using the Heggerty textbooks – Wilson, can you hand those out? – I want you to summarise what we know so far regarding the events of the Napoleonic Wars. I'll have them in at the end, please."

"What was *that* all about?" Robert jogs to David's side, followed closely by William and Michael. They walk down the hallway, hemmed in at all angles. "What do you reckon?"

"I reckon…" He stops. They should know, really. He's tried telling them.

"You reckon what?"

"I reckon you should ask Parfick about it." And David carries on along the corridor.

They reach the playground. Under the horse-chestnut, they start to eat their lunches. Conker shells and golden leaves littering the ground.

"You know?" Robert spits through a half-chewed sandwich. "I think Parfick's right about one thing."

"And what's that?" David asks, after a mouthful.

"He said history teaches you the things that should be avoided. That makes sense. *I* think…" He takes another bite. "History lessons should be avoided." Robert lets out a wide-mouthed laugh, showing off too much of his food.

"Good one," sniggers Michael.

William agrees.

And David just carries on with his lunch, munching mouse-bites out of his apple.

Winter Days

The sun rises from behind the hedgerows, an orange glow flooding the lane. The cold air, colouring his skin, wakes David up – stirs his mind to life. He looks around. Late November: autumn shedding into winter. The icy dew glistens, reflecting the emerging light, and there's a satisfying scrunch under foot. David wears a scratchy, knitted scarf and gloves – recent gifts from an aunt. In spontaneous waves, a chill wind passes through, causing his eyes to water. With one covered finger, David dabs away the wet.

At the roadside, and in the fields, the bare trees resemble skeletons; ghosts of trees that, just weeks ago, were full of colour and movement. Further on, there are a few reduced to stumps – cut down for whatever reason (diseased or just in the way?) And all around him, the song of morning plays. David scans the honeysuckle and long-grass verges for its source. He can hear it. Hear *them*. But, see them…? Nothing. Which makes him think. What if all of this were gone – the fields; the birds; that sycamore; the lane stretched ahead and behind him; even his own house? What if something powerful, something relentless, ripped through? David pictures it: the destruction; everything gone; wiped out; smoking wrecks of rubble; a fresh start on this clear, fresh morning.

Up ahead, the growing brightness behind him, David can trace the faint outline of the moon; a blotchy white stamped on pale-blue.

He yawns. Wipes away another pool collecting in his eyes.

Reaching the shops, awnings hang out, advertising signs stand guard. A hunched man, white hair and flat-cap, leaves the newsagents, hugging a paper to his chest. Over at the bus stop, David rests against the broken fence. A small flock of starlings fly a mid-air dance. He waits there, perhaps for as long as five minutes, watching the birds, having landed on the oak trees, pick at the stripped branches.

The bus arrives when it always does. Mr. Winfield, the greengrocer, puts out the last of his stock (the cauliflowers and cabbages, stacked neatly and invitingly – *what would happen if I pulled one out?*). Then – and it is only then, when the stock is all set up – David hears the drill of the engine, like a far-off wasp, and sees the bus turning the bend several hundred yards away. It's a well-rehearsed play: another re-run, adding to the pile like heaped cabbages and cauliflowers.

The bus rolls to a halt and the conductor calls everyone off. Unlike last year, David and Robert are no longer last into the gangway; a few boys, still looking lost in their uniforms, give way and let them past.

Jumping down on to the pavement, David hears Michael's voice. "Over here!" he shouts, an awkward smile stuttering to life.

"You all right?" asks David.

They pass under the arched gates.

"Oh, yes – thanks." He sounds surprised to be asked. "Are you two?"

"I'd say so," David answers, looking at Robert to check if he's telling the truth. He can speak for himself, but Robert's state of mind is another thing completely. "Shall we find somewhere a bit warmer?"

The common room – as usual on days like this – is full of people. David can't see the fireplace, just parts of its white-painted frame when someone for one moment changes position.

He spots William – talking to some other lower fourth formers – and William spots them. He wanders across, placing a hand on Robert's shoulder and giving it a rough squeeze. Robert squirms. Pulls away. "Aaah-owww!" They exchange smiles, suspicious at first, then wider, friendlier.

"What you talking about?" asks William.

"Nothing, really," admits David. "But I think Michael wants to tell us something – don't you?"

"Yes. I do." He breathes in, about to begin – then thinks better of it. "Wait. How did you know?"

"I could just tell," replies David, simply.

Michael leans in; speaks softer. "We found out that my dad…" He pauses; starts talking even quieter. "That next week, my dad'll be coming home." His smile returns, fires up quickly and sticks there. He looks from one to the other to the next. They say nothing at first. "Well?"

"Well…" starts David, scratching his neck. "That's really good news, Michael."

"Of course," William mutters; then more confidently: "That's brilliant news."

"Yes. Brilliant news," agrees Robert.

***

Next week came and next week went.

And it was as if the previous week had never happened. It was as if that conversation had never happened. As if this… "We'll go fishing along the river. And I can show him how good my schoolwork's getting. Then, we'll probably eat something special for tea and, before bed, he'll read us a story – he *always* used to do that…" As if that had never happened either.

And David just couldn't understand it. From that, to this.

He wanted to say: "How did it go, your first weekend with your dad home?" But he waited. Assumed Michael would come right out with it, before they even had a chance to swap their good-mornings.

Then when he didn't, David waited some more. Surely, he'd tell them at break-time.

No.

At lunchtime, then?

No.

From that, to this. From wide smiles, words tripping over each other, to silence and a look like ice.

***

Another week came and went.

David doesn't understand it.

Walking home from the bus stop, dusk seeping in, the countryside feels like an entirely different place. The ground is damp. A long drizzly downpour just ended, every now and then, David stumbles over potholes filled with rainwater and, with each footstep, hears a muddy squelch. He hums a tune. And the blackness surrounding him makes him up his pace. The wind too, whipping and whistling against David's back, pushes him along. The trees creak in the gusts and – when they do – David breaks from his tune, casts a glance either side, then carries on his made-up song.

He just doesn't understand. Michael still isn't saying anything. What could have happened? He can imagine. He and Robert and William sometimes talk about it, when Michael happens to be elsewhere; their voices hushed, conspiratorial.

"Perhaps he didn't come home after all."

"Maybe he's not like he remembers him."

Streetlights hover in the gloom. David is nearly home. Pavement replacing grass, his steps become surer, more measured, and before he knows it, David is softly shutting his front door.

***

First period; physics with Mr. Marston. The teacher stands at the blackboard, hurriedly scribbling equations and diagrams with a scraggy bit of chalk.

The door opens.

Marston turns from his work. "What time is this, Francis?"

Michael stops still – caught out. "Sorry, sir," he stutters.

"Why are you so late?" Marston casts a glance at the clock.

"Erm. Well…" He screws one foot nervously into the floor; speaks in mumbled monosyllables. "My uniform, sir… well… it weren't quite ready first thing this morning, sir, so we… well…"

"Sit down, Francis. You've held us up quite enough for one lesson."

"Yes, sir. Sorry, sir." He rushes to his seat.

Before long, this is a regular occurrence.

History. "And why have you not done your homework, Francis? Everyone else has." It takes a lot to rile Parfick.

English. "Have I told you to put your things away? Francis!" That cost him three on the right hand.

French. "Come on – it's not a difficult question. How might you reply to this…?" Mr. Trevithick swings his yardstick at the board, before readying it for Michael's palm.

From that, to this. At least the Christmas holidays will give the bruises time to fade.

One Morning

"Oh. Nice to see you, David. He's not quite ready yet, but come on in." Mrs Fitzgerald steps aside.

David wipes his feet, untying his shoes and unfurling his scarf.

"Have you eaten yet?"

"Yes, thank you." (Fried egg and buttery toast, wolfed down before running around here.)

"Well, come on through."

She leads him from the little entrance hall into the kitchen. Robert's sat finishing his breakfast.

"Sit down, love," says Mrs. Fitzgerald.

"All right, David?" grins Robert, his cheeks bulging. "Want some of my toast?"

"No, thanks."

"Suit yourself. More for me." And he crams another slice into his still-full gob.

"You'll choke if you're not careful," says his mum.

He splutters an apology.

"Right. I'll just be outside, sorting this washing out."

"All right."

"You'll let me know when you're going out, won't you?"

"Yes."

"Good." And the boys watch as she squeezes through the back door, her arms full of whites.

"I'll just be another minute," says Robert. "You sure you don't want anything? Or a drink?"

"I'm fine, thanks."

"I thought, first, we might go up to my room for a bit."

David nods. It *was* rather cold outside. His toes and fingers still tingle; his cheeks feel like cold metal.

Robert takes them up to his bedroom. On the wall, along the staircase, there's a row of small portraits mounted in circular picture-frames, stepping-stones up the wallpaper. Somewhere, David can hear a clock ticking. It reminds him of school.

"Where's Antsie?" he asks.

"Outside, I think."

Robert nudges his bedroom door open with a foot. Directly opposite, there are two shelves stuffed with toys. He takes down an old biscuit tin from the bottom shelf. What's inside shunts about. They sit down and Robert tips the contents out: toy-soldiers, a lot of them chipped or missing long strips of paint, revealing their silvery torsos. Robert picks a few up. "Go on," he gestures. And David does it too. They make the men walk, talk, then clatter them into each other, kicking, punching.

"Can I be good, and you be bad?" asks Robert.

"I suppose."

They split the lot in half – which gives them about twenty each. David lines his up, ready for attack. He picks one to be Hitler – the least damaged.

Robert holds one of his men up, looking him over. "Nice to meet you, Prime Minister Chamberlain," he says, with a smile. "Is that right?"

David nods.

Then they begin playing out a war not yet begun.

But it's only a matter of time, surely?

Thinking about the newspaper stories, the radio bulletins, it may appear that nothing much has changed in the last few months; Czechoslovakia's borders, beyond the Sudetenland, have remained untouched.

But David knows it won't stay that way for very long.

When it comes to these games, then, all David can do is imagine the next step. Which might just be a good thing, really. That way it can end how he wants it to. He reacts to Robert's gun sounds – *b-b-b-b-b-b-b* – knocking several men over in one swipe. He voices them with shrieks and yelps; gives them German names he's picked up along the way – Friedrich, Otto, Ludwig. (The sorts of names that, now, David can't imagine belonging to anyone who might, say, read a bedtime story to their child – or even force a smile. Anything like that just seems beyond the nature of someone called Dietrich or Hermann. The names – and, therefore, the men to which they belong – sound so stiff and resolute.)

David's army is quickly defeated: left scattered over the carpeted battleground. Which is probably just as well, the tin-soldier he called Hitler lying, also, amongst the dead.

Robert holds up his two main commanders. "We won!" he tells them, almost as though part of him expects them to shout a reply or plunge a triumphant fist into the air.

Then he jumps to his feet, grabs another tin from the same shelf the soldiers came from, and, sitting back down, shoves the fallen men out of the way – *that's it, see you next time* – lifting the lid.

"Look…" he grins. "These are all the rocks I've collected down at the stream."

David peers inside.

"This one's my favourite."

Robert grabs it – a dark, nearly-blue colour with little white specks. He passes it to David, who moves it from hand to hand. The white bits like tiny ridges, snow-topped hills on the stone's surface. Robert chooses another: swirly shades of grey, reminding David of the marbles his sister got for Christmas. David puts the first rock back, rearranging those on top to see what lies underneath. There's another covered in sweeping swirls, browns and creams this time. He scoops it up. There is a roughness to it. David examines his right palm; a fine layer of white dust coats his skin.

"Oh. I got that one somewhere else," says Robert. "Not from the stream."

David turns it mid-air.

"It came from the seaside."

"Oh."

David's never been to the seaside. But he remembers Robert telling him that each summer holiday that's where he and his parents go, for a week, to Scarborough to stay with his aunt and uncle and cousins.

"I could have brought back lots more," he says. "There are some that are just plain white, like the whitest white you've ever seen, then others that are bumpy and a real dark-grey colour. I even saw an all-black one once, but I couldn't reach it – because it was down in this rock-pool." Robert then started telling David about the crabs and molluscs he and his cousins found in those pools, the way their legs went crazy when you picked them up. "Anyway..." he continues, back on track: "Then Philip, my oldest cousin, he's *sixteen*, grabbed this stone, the black one, and said he was keeping it." Robert sighs. "And I couldn't find another one like it. I looked for ages."

David returns the beach-stone to the tin.

"Want to go out now?" Robert asks, eyes straining in the sudden glow filling the room.

"Good idea." David starts tidying.

"Leave all that. Mum'll do it."

"Really?" David still wants to tidy, but his friend is already out on the landing. He gets to his feet and follows.

Outside, the sudden glow gone, David starts regretting their decision to leave the house. They walk down the centre of the lane. David watches as his breath goes before him, sees it drift and mingle with Robert's.

They arrive at the pond, white fence circling one half. Mallard ducks sit, spread out, on the raised banks. The boys approach them, their cotton fists stuffed with bread scraps Robert's mother didn't mind them taking. They sit on the wrought-iron bench and start feeding the ones closest. David aims for their open beaks.

Very soon, just as the whole group crowds the bench, they're both empty-handed. Robert holds up open palms. "None left. Sorry." Then, changing subject, adds: "I hope Michael's all right."

"Sorry?"

"Michael. I can't help wondering what he'll be like when we go back."

"Oh. Right. Me too."

"Don't you think it's strange – the way he was?"

David nods, then looks down at the ducks pecking at the dewy grass. He points one of them out. "That one there's got a limp."

"What?"

"Look…" Still pointing. "The female just here – she's limping."

"Did you hear what I just said?"

"Sorry. Carry on."

Robert sighs. "No, it's just…"

"Just what?"

"Well… what if Michael isn't there when we get back?"

The ducks' quacks get louder; a man under a black umbrella spreading seeds and crumbs several feet away.

"What if when we go back to school, *he* doesn't?"

"But why wouldn't he?"

"I don't know. I just can't help thinking…"

"Thinking what?"

"Well, you know… His dad's just got out of prison."

"Right." David tries working his foot into the hard ground. Some of the mallards return to the water. "I can't work it out, either," he says. In many ways, he's stopped trying to. "It's like he became a different person."

"Well. More like the old Michael."

David pictures him getting caned; the blank look on his face. "We'll have to try and say something," he decides.

Robert nods. "Like what?"

David shrugs. "Don't know yet."

To Do with Mr. Francis

With the holidays over, David's plan has grown no bigger. All he knows is that something has to be said, that this slide backwards has to be stopped, no matter what the consequences. But *something* is all he has. As yet, it is an idea with no form or shape; a mere suggestion.

"Thought of what you're going to say to Michael?" asks Robert, a few bends into the bus ride.

"Me?"

"I thought you said…"

"No, I said *we* should say something."

"Right." Robert glances across at the empty pair of seats opposite. "Any ideas, then?"

Three stops later, there's not a spare space on board and, annoyingly, one of the newcomers near the back has opened a window. The chill reaches David's scarf-less neck; makes its way down his spine.

Robert turns around. "Who's…?"

David looks too.

Impossible to tell, but if it's someone older than them, they'll say nothing; and if someone their age or younger has done it – again, they'll say (and do) nothing. Just grumble and hold their coats and blazers tighter to their chests.

"You could…" begins Robert, back on to the Michael Francis problem. "No – that won't work."

"What?"

"No, nothing."

Through the window, David watches the fields become busy streets. They pass the road to the docks.

Robert keeps muttering to himself – another idea coming to the boil, maybe. David stares at him – but, a watched pot… and Robert offers nothing. David presses a hand against the pane, the engine's vibrations throbbing in his fingers. Two men pull out a green and white awning: one stretching on his toes, the other, still stretching, but stood on an overturned bottle crate.

He starts to mutter too, staring down at the moving floor… *Think… Think… What can we say?* An apple rolls to his feet. Shouts from behind. David sends it backwards. *Think…*

"Could we…?" David suddenly realises. "Could we not just ask him how his Christmas was?"

"Right…" Robert doesn't sound entirely convinced.

"Because if he talks about the school holidays – and the things he did – he might mention his dad."

"I suppose, but – you know what – I've just realised something." Robert smiles. "We don't actually know for certain that his dad is why he's suddenly changed."

"No…" David gives him a chance, all the time thinking: but we kind of do, really.

"There could be another reason."

"Except…"

Robert looks down at his lap.

"He started acting strangely at exactly the time he said his dad was coming home, so – I can't see how it could be anything else."

"True," says Robert, rubbing his eyes. "You're probably right."

The bus jolts.

"We're here already." David sees the school gates, the busy playground. "I didn't realise we were so close." He remembers the council offices on the junction, then after that…

They stand. David lifts bag over head and on to shoulder. The gangway fills. He's careful not to catch Robert's heel.

They walk through the schoolyard. David looks either side of him. No sign of Michael. If he'd arrived already, they'd assume – because it isn't that cold, and it isn't raining – that he'd be here, somewhere in the yard. And if Michael were here in the yard, surely, he'd be there by the chestnut trees, sitting on the low wall.

But he isn't.

The wall is vacant, waiting for them.

So, they both go over to it. They sit and they wait on the patient bricks.

William arrives. They talk about their Christmas break, about Michael, and then, like when the bus jolted to a stop, the bell rings without any of them anticipating it. David looks uncertainly at both Robert and William – like there must be some sort of mistake.

In class, Mr. Winsome has his back to them. He covers the blackboard in fractions and measurements. The electric lights a weak white.

David sits down, takes out all that he needs for a mathematics lesson – pencil, ruler, book. He lines them up straight and tidy, turning around. Robert's rooting through his bag, two seats behind, and, on the back row, William's sat idly tapping his pencil on one finger.

Mr. Winsome finishes with his chalk, chucking it down on his desk and folding his arms.

The bell goes again. Michael still hasn't arrived. His is the only unfilled place.

"Right, class – let's make a start..." Mr. Winsome explains what's on the board. David tries his best to concentrate. "So, the two becomes six when you carry the..."

The door opens.

David sees Michael.

"Francis. I wondered when you might grace us with your presence."

"Sorry, sir," he says: less a mutter, more an unapologetic scowl.

"Sit down. We'll deal with it at the end." And he continues his explanation.

"Now then, gentlemen – stop there." Mr. Winsome stands. "Francis. Here, please." He points with his cane. "Stand there. That's it." He looks over the rest of the room, a vague smile, then, silently, holds his hand out for Michael to copy. Mr.

Winsome re-positions it slightly to his right. Then he hits it three times.

David winces at every one. But Michael hardly moves, his face set.

"If this happens again..." says Winsome, after the last. "I'll send you straight to Mr. Greening and *he* can deal with you. Understood?"

Michael nods.

"Good. Off you go – all of you. And if you didn't finish today's work – hand it in to me, *completed*..." He looks down at Michael again. "Next lesson."

They catch up with him in the corridor. "It's fine – forget about it," he says, before they have a chance to speak.

David looks at Robert. Not just yet, he thinks.

They go out on to the playground. First period is followed by a fifteen-minute break, which is then followed by two more classes, before lunch. The four of them stand there in a silent circle, each staring at the concrete.

Robert talks first. "So, what do you reckon?" he asks, vaguely. "Are we going to get homework in every lesson?"

"I hope not," William answers quickly.

David grins, then looks for Michael's reaction. Nothing. Head tilted downwards. Hands stuffed in pockets.

Robert tries again. "French could go either way – Trevithick sometimes lets us off."

The upper fourths' football game seems to be turning into a rough rugby scuffle. David comes close to being knocked over.

Michael suddenly looks up. "Will one of you help me with the mathematics work? Because I – you know – I missed the beginning. I didn't really follow what we were meant to do."

David nods. "Now? Or at lunchtime?"

"Wait till lunch," he says. Then he breaks the circle. "Going to toilet."

"Right. See you in French," David calls after him.

"It's a start," says Robert.

"What? *That*?"

He nods.

"I suppose it's been a while since he asked for our help."

"Maybe he won't be that bad, if we just come out with it."

"And what do we say?" David needs convincing.

"One of us…" He means David. "Just needs to ask him what it's like now his dad's home. Simple."

"Does it have to be me? It is *your* idea."

"But…"

"You'd do it much better than me," David says, with a smile; a blatant try at flattery.

Robert looks confused, oddly tempted.

"Well?" David doesn't know if he can hold the expression any longer.

"Let's just see what happens at lunch."

In the schoolyard, whenever something is discarded – a bread-crust or an apple core – two or three gulls swoop down. David enjoys what follows – the fights and mid-air steals, the *gah-gah*ing arguments…

Mine.

No, mine.

No. Mine…

Sometimes, a crow or, even a starling, might try to cut in. There's one just now (a starling) taking on two herring gulls over a piece of greaseproof paper. The gull that arrived second wins; its grip firmer.

William wanders over to the bin. Sparrows and starlings fly away, startled. Crushing his rubbish into a ball, he chucks it in.

"Want to look at that mathematics work now, Michael?"

He almost smiles. "Yes, thanks." Then opens his bag.

David picks at his chin, finds a few crumbs he'd missed earlier, then reaches into his bag. "It's pretty simple, really. It shouldn't take long."

A few minutes – that *is* all it takes. Michael completes all but the last couple of questions. "I'll do the rest tonight, at home," he says.

"And...?" David looks at Robert...

Who takes over: "And, so..." Robert stutters at first. "What's it like now your..."

Is he going to back out?

David nods, mouths the word.

"Now your dad's home?"

Michael had been scratching at the wall, bits of cement under his fingernails, but when Robert finishes the question, he quickly begins stuffing his bag full again: mathematics book, ruler, pencil. "Just remembered," he manages to say, now standing up. And then he's gone, lost amongst a yard of red and black.

***

"So, what was it Winsome said? If this happens again, I'll send you to Mr. Greening? And there he is, waiting outside the schoolmaster's office."

It's the second time this week. His head rests sulkily in his hands, but he sneaks a look at the sound of their footsteps. He smiles, just slightly, then remembers where he is – and why – and plants his head back in his hands.

When they're around the corner, beyond earshot, David says: "He clearly isn't happy..."

"Obviously. But if he doesn't talk to us, how can we help him?" William sounds more frustrated than he probably is.

"Maybe he doesn't trust us enough," suggests Robert.

"Why wouldn't he?"

"It might not be anything we've done, William. But – if he can't trust other people..."

"Like his dad," Robert helps.

"Exactly. So maybe he doesn't know whether he can trust us either."

Afternoon break. The playground. The only time they get to talk to him that day.

"So – what?" asks William. "The Sud-whatever-land has gone now?"

"Germany invaded it – right, David?"

"The Sudetenland – yes – and the next target could be the rest of Czechoslovakia. So, good guys..." He points at himself and Michael. "We'll be Czechoslovakia. And you two are Germany again."

Robert and William exchange nods. Understood.

"So, you want to play?" David asks Michael.

He shrugs. "I guess." Which is about as enthusiastic as he's been for a while.

Under the shadow of the horse-chestnut trees, David and Michael find their starting place. David's wary where he walks. The other side will have planted bombs. And they could be anywhere. He lifts a branch for Michael to duck under, curving it like an archway. Now, they speak less with the formal language this game began with – David is no longer Corporal Denby; Robert's stopped being called Sergeant Fitzgerald; William has given up the name General Field; and when Michael started playing, well... the name-changes had all but been abandoned by then. Instead, they take on the names of actual politicians and military officials – informed, of course, by David and his daily reading of the newspaper. And, in the same way, this place is not called The Forest – that became too restrictive, too prescriptive. Because sometimes it plays the part of a battlefield; other days, it's a fortified city; and today, it's a borderland, a hinterland.

David and Michael hide behind the elder bush. It may not obscure them for long – the branches yet to leaf and flower – but it will give them enough cover to wait and observe. Any moment now, Robert and William are due. Because this is the frontier, the unmarked line separating the two, so if they want to invade, this is where they must begin. David leans back against the wall, patches of which have been taken by ivy and clematis. He dusts off the soil coating his trousers and shoes, like toast crumbs off the tablecloth, and looks across at Michael. It's hard to tell if he's playing along; he's next to him, followed him this far, but…

"All right?" David asks.

He nods, but in that quick, flinching way that suggests he actually isn't.

Suddenly, David feels brave. The game may not change names anymore, but it can still change other things. "Really?" he whispers.

"What do you mean?"

"You seem to have…" David pauses; glances at Michael, his gaze grounded. "You seem to have changed, recently."

"Right."

He isn't arguing. That's something.

"Well…" David ventures further. "You seem to have changed *back*."

"What – into a frog?"

David smiles, but Michael didn't sound like he was joking; looked even less like he was. "No. I didn't mean. I meant… back into the Michael who was always in trouble."

Then Robert and William appear, their arms shaped into rifles. David rests a hand on Michael's shoulder. *Ready*, he mouths, then leaps to his feet, his own hands held like a gun. He fires at them. *B-b-b-b-b-b-b.* They shoot back. *B-b-b-b-b-b-b.* Then Robert and William stop. David lowers his hands too. *Surrender? Victory?* He turns around, sees Michael right where he left him, completely motionless.

"Michael?"

David steps back; moves towards him. But he gets up, steps over a fallen oak branch, and runs off across the schoolyard.

"I shouldn't have said anything. I just thought… I don't know."

Robert's head nods with every bump the bus carries them over. "It was worth a try," he says.

"But – now what? What if he never speaks to us again?"

"It won't be that bad."

But what if it is?"

"We'll think of… something."

That word again. That faceless, empty word.

***

"Hello, Michael." David sees him outside the toilets. He'd ignored David all through morning lessons. But he decides to just plunge right in. "I'm sorry about what I said yesterday."

His hands are folded behind his back, pinned against the wall. Someone comes out of the toilets. A half-screamed laugh when the door is opened. Someone else goes in.

"Do you forgive me?"

Michael shrugs his shoulders, familiar squirming feet, then he makes to go. "I've got a detention," he says.

"Oh, right." David moves to let him past. "Bye, then." He watches Michael slope off down the corridor, turn a corner, then heads out to the playground.

Robert and William ask him where he's been.

He tells them about speaking to Michael.

"Was he all right with you?"

"He was just quiet," says David.

"He's always *just quiet*."

"I know. You feel like you're upsetting him, or annoying him, but he never lets you know because he never says anything."

"Where is he now?"

"He has detention. I think it's with Marston."

"The homework?"

David nods. "And for being late."

***

The next day, Michael isn't at school. Which doesn't surprise David. He missed a few days towards the end of last term and – what with all the canings and detentions – this term is beginning to play out precisely like the last. At least it's one day in which he can't get into trouble.

Then again…

"It'll just be a cold," reasons Robert. "He'll be off for maybe one more day – if that."

"You think?" David isn't so sure. He's started wondering – like Robert in the holidays – whether they will see Michael again at school.

"Trust me."

"Come on, David," William joins in. "Robert's right. He's not going to stay off because of anything we've said. He doesn't care what people say about him."

"No. It's the complete opposite, William." David's sure about this, at least. "He *does* care what people say about him. Except – I thought he was getting better at it. But now…"

"All right. Fair enough. But he must know he can trust us."

"I don't think he does anymore," says David, glumly. "Otherwise, if there is something bothering him…"

"Which there clearly is," adds Robert.

"Right. So why isn't he telling us?"

***

The end of another geography lesson. The low light fills the classroom in square blocks.

"And what's your excuse this time, Francis? Why have you nothing to hand in?"

Michael sits dead-straight in his seat.

"Because if I remember rightly…" Mr. Finch moves out from behind his desk. "I asked everyone to attempt it – no matter how little you manage. One side of paper would have been perfectly acceptable. But nothing?" He slams an unexpected hand on the desk. Watson jumps in his chair. "You didn't even try." He goes to the left side of the blackboard. "I'm very disappointed, Francis. I thought we were getting past this," he says, quieter, picking up the usual punishment. "Stand where you are."

His chair scrapes sharply, no doubt marking a faint, new scuff on the floor, and when Michael puts his hand out – and as it's hit; once, twice, and a third time – David spots the slightest of shakes. He's seen this little flinch take over, understandably, once the ordeal is done, but during... Even when Mr. Marston is ready to go (and, apparently, no one canes worse – even Mr. Greening), David is struck by how still Michael can hold his hand, even as it's hit and the split-second after.

"Right," says Finch, putting it back in its place, propped by the board. "Class dismissed."

David, Robert and William chase after Michael – he rammed his things into his bag and burst out the door, nearly knocking Simons on to the coat-stand – but when they catch up to him, neither one of them knows what to say. Still, Michael doesn't make an excuse or disappear elsewhere, so...

"Wonder what sort of mood Hennessey'll be in?" David just tries acting normal, as though the caning never happened.

"Grumpy, I say," suggests Robert.

David watches Thompson overtake them. He always has to be first in line outside the classroom.

"There'll be something he's not happy about," says William, catching Michael's eye. "What do you reckon?"

They join the back of the queue.

"I don't know," he says – his response to everything.

Mr. Hennessey appears in the doorway. "Lead in, please, Thompson."

David trails into the classroom behind Robert. Stands in his place. He looks across at Michael on the right-hand column, two seats further forward, sees him swaying – ever so slightly, but ever so noticeably – his weight passing back and forth, from one foot and then to the other. A kind of anxious restfulness; the last place he wants to be in class is stood up. Because, usually, that only means one thing.

Hennessey waits until the last lad, Vicars, has reached his seat, then says: "Take out your things, gentlemen, and sit down." He goes over to the windows; puts up the blinds. Then, back at his desk: "Now – I'm coming around with a test paper..."

Someone sighs. Sounds like Whitton.

"*Quiet*. I'm coming around with a test paper," he begins again. "Put your names at the top, please. It *should* take you less than an hour, but we're going to spend the whole lesson on it. I want complete silence..."

He puts one on David's desk. David adds his name, neatly, in the top-right corner.

"There should be nothing in this that you don't understand, nothing that I haven't already taught you – so, no excuses." He hands out the last half-dozen papers and walks back to the front, looking up at the clock, then again at the class. "You may start."

"That wasn't too bad, actually," says William, once they're outside and started on lunch.

"I suppose," agrees Robert. "I always expect the worse from Hennessey. But he must like confusing us. I mean, what was question... whatsit... question four all about?" He looks at David.

"Was that the one with the prepositions?"

"Prepositions?"

"Where you had to cross out every preposition and put in the correct one."

"Oh. Is that what it was on about? No wonder." Robert sighs. "Well I got that one wrong, then."

William sniggers. So, does Michael – the faintest of whimpers, like a smuggled puppy hiding in his satchel has just whiffed their food.

"How did *you* find it?" David asks Michael.

"Me?" He stabs a finger at his chest.

David nods. Who else?

He picks up his cheese sandwich – takes a bite – before answering, simply: "Fine. It was fine."

"Good." David feels oddly relieved, like his whole experience of the test and the lesson rested on how Michael felt about it.

"Oh." Robert nearly spits out half his lunch. "I heard a bit of the bulletin last night, David. But I didn't quite follow what…"

David jumps straight in. It's all the encouragement he needs; the vaguest mention and he'll fill in the blanks. "So, Germany, having taken the Sudetenland ("You remember where that is, don't you?" he asks them. "Basically, it's bits of north, southwest and west Czechoslovakia."), they then did what many thought was their plan all along and invaded the rest of Czechoslovakia. And what people are now talking about, what you'll have half-heard on the wireless, Robert, is that Poland is where they're heading next."

"Right." Robert finishes his sandwich, his shirt covered in breadcrumbs, then dives into his lunch bag for something else.

David picks his up again, nibbles round the edges – that lovely, sweet tang coating his tongue. He could have gone into more detail – like how most of the people in the Sudetenland are ethnically German and actually wanted to be invaded – but he thought that would just complicate things. Even after hearing the news bulletins and talking to his father about them afterwards, and then reading and re-reading the newspaper reports, he can still find the story snarled up and knotted in such a way that it just becomes an impenetrable mess. The difference, though, between David and his friends is that he really quite likes that – the necessity to dig deeper, how it all links together, even if it's in the most confusing, untidy way. He has a notebook at home. Inside it he records what he learns about Hitler and Germany, anything with the vaguest connection, and he'll often look back through them too. Because it's all linked, one way or another; the next story in the paper is, very often, the consequence of something that happened days, weeks or maybe months earlier.

David waits for Robert and William outside the second-floor toilets. Michael stands beside him, his arms folded, one leg lifted, foot resting against the wall.

"Birch'll tell you off. You know what he's like."

Mr. Birch is the caretaker. You rarely see him round and about the school. But at the first opportunity, he'll break cover if he sees some lad ignoring one of his many fussy notices.

"Good point." Michael straightens up. "Actually, there was something I wanted to ask, quickly, before the others come out."

"Right."

"I know I haven't said anything…"

'You've not said much at all, really,' thinks David. 'This is the most I've heard you say all year.'

"But it's my birthday next week."

"Oh. I didn't…"

"And my Mum's been trying to get me to invite one of you round for tea."

"Right."

Michael turns to face David: a strange kind of pleading smile.

"Oh. You mean…?" David points at his chest, feels the hard bone through his skin.

"If you want," he mutters, with a shrug, turning away again.

"No. I mean, yes. Thanks."

"It's just my Mum – she thinks it'd be nice…"

"No. Thanks for inviting me. I'll have to check with *my* mum, but…"

Michael looks more unsettled now than before he started speaking – disappointed, even; like, really, he hoped David would turn him down.

I don't have to… Not if you…

He remembers how Robert looked when he invited them all to his house last year. This is the complete opposite. But, he did say it was his mother's idea, didn't he?

David stows his bag between his feet. He always gets the window seat. Because Robert gets off first.

"It's Michael's birthday next week – Wednesday, I think…"

"Really? I didn't know."

"No, me neither. But his Mum's been telling him to invite one of us round for tea."

"Oh."

"And he asked if *I* wanted to."

"What? And you said yes?"

"Course."

"No, right – it's just… Aren't you a bit – you know – worried?"

David breathes in; gives it a moment's thought. "No. I'm more surprised."

From that, to this.

***

They say goodbye to Robert. A group of lower fifths follow him on board the bus, pulling stupid faces, then laughing shyly as the conductor gives them their tickets. The same sort of thing carries on along the pavement – lads in threes or fours, grinning and guffawing.

"That wasn't too bad – eh, Michael?"

"What?" He looks up.

They'd just been given their marks from the Latin test.

"The test results," says William.

"I suppose." Michael goes back to studying his shoes.

There's a crowd of kids in uniform outside a sweet shop. Most of them peer through the glass, their breath obscuring what's on offer. A few go in. Some more come out, holding their paper bags open for their friends to gaze inside, wide-eyed. Next door, the pharmacy, and after that, the bakery, shoemakers and, at the end of this block, the greengrocers; they just don't have the same attraction for the schoolboys. Those that have coins in their pockets (and, probably not coincidentally, uniform that isn't stretched or threadbare) tend not to spend them on a few oranges or a fresh roll; liquorice and peardrops seem, every time, like the more preferable option.

"If I ask nicely..." William looks back at the sweet shop. "My Mum'll give me two-pence or three-pence, so I can stop there on the way home – won't she, Michael?" As if David would never believe him if it were just one boy's word.

Michael nods.

"And what's your favourite?" asks David, never having been given money to spend as he pleases in a sweet shop – or, any shop, for that matter.

"Sherbet." William smacks his lips together. Michael wrinkles his nose. "And I always get some black liquorice for Michael." William sticks his tongue out. "Can't stand it." Michael opens his mouth, about to say something, then William bats the question back to David; "What do you like?"

"Oh, I don't know, really." His grandma let him try one of her boiled sweets when he was a lot younger. Just the once, though – he spat it straight out, all over the rug. Then, sometimes, at home, he's offered a mint imperial – they're his father's favourite – but that's about it...

"There must be something." William prods harder.

"Mint imperials, I suppose," he says, shrugging – like father, like son.

"Oh, boring."

"That's not a proper sweet," adds Michael.

"Can you buy them in a sweet shop?" reasons David. He's not actually sure – he's never set foot in one, so how would he know what they sell? But he feigns authority with his I-get-top-marks-so-I-must-be-right voice.

"I guess so," William admits. "Anyway. This is Michael's road..."

"Oh. Is it?"

Michael doesn't answer, just looks at a few of the houses, as if to check.

"See you tomorrow," says William.

David and Michael set off down the street. The redbrick houses match each other in appearance. At the right-hand side, there's a front door, then to the left, two windows, one above the other. And after every second house, there are arched openings, little walkways, which follow all the way down – so Michael informs David – to the ten foot.

Three lads – about nine, ten years old – kick a football in the road. "Hello, Michael," says one, his black hair a sweaty mess.

He doesn't reply – David smiles to compensate – just says: "Here we are," turning the handle and opening the door of number twenty-four.

David steps in after him. Smells burning wood. Michael drops his bag by the staircase, gesturing that David can do the same. He hears someone in the kitchen. Plates moving in the sink.

"Home," says Michael, a strange sort of groan, oddly prolonged, continuous and monosyllabic, and David wonders whether anybody further into the house will have been able to hear it.

Michael leads the way into the kitchen. The linoleum creaks.

"Good. You're back," says his mother, turning around. She picks up a tea towel, dries her hands. "And you must be David. Ever so nice to finally meet you."

She's a short lady. David almost feels taller than her.

"Did you have a good day at school, love?"

Michael mumbles something. Shrugs and looks at the square table, squashed in one corner.

"What about you, David? I never get any sense from him these days."

"Yes. It was fine – thank you, Mrs. Francis."

"Oh, good – but call me Ms. Grayling." She smiles. Then pivots round to the stove.

"Oh, I didn't…"

"No, no – don't worry. Now…" she says, stirring the vegetables with a wooden spoon. "Tea's not far off. Fifteen minutes, thereabouts. You two go off upstairs till then and I'll give you a shout when it's ready."

There are two beds in Michael's room.

"Where's your sister?"

"She's staying with my aunt."

"Oh, right." David looks at the shorter bed, the sheets neat and untouched.

"I don't really have anything we can play with," says Michael, going over to the window, lifting the net curtain up and over his head. "I like to just look out here."

David looks around the room first, turns full circle on the spot. In the small gap between the two beds, on the floor, is a rug – the colour faded. Looks as if it might once have been a deep shade of blue. The walls are bare, apart from a clock opposite Michael's unmade bed, next to which there is a set of drawers. David wanders over to the window, kneels down next to Michael, and pulls the curtain over himself. The windowsill is just the right length for both of them to lean on, side by side. David links his fingers and props up his chin.

Michael's bedroom stares out on to the cobblestone backyard. The gate, painted green, swings open. David can see into the alleyway, which looks to run along behind the whole of the street. In the left-hand corner of the yard, there is the tiny outhouse – the door, like the gate, half-open. The same pattern follows in the next road. David can see the backs of the houses, over their walls: the slate roofs of their toilet sheds; the back doors – one or two open, letting the air in: whites on the line; some kid playing with a ball; throwing it up and catching it, throwing it up and catching it, throwing it up and... looks like he dropped it that time.

"Do you play out much?" David asks.

"A little."

"So, do you have friends round here?"

"A few."

David looks back at his friend's room, his vision veiled a yellowy-white. "Why's your sister not here?"

Michael sighs. "Please – you've got to promise not to say anything." He prods at the windowpane. "She's helping us out – my aunt – because…"

Then he ducks out from under the net curtain; goes to sit on his bed. David follows him.

"I was so excited – wasn't I? – when I found out my dad was coming home." Michael tries to raise a smile but gives up after a few seconds. "We knew he'd be – you know – let out some time, but…" He shrugs his shoulders. "I don't know. When he came back, he wasn't like I remembered him."

David wants to ask how old Michael was when his father went away – all the time they've been friends, he's never known that, and only now has the question occurred to him.

"He came home, and he and Mum went into the kitchen. They closed the door and it was really quiet and, when they came out, my mum looked really upset. Then he went upstairs, and I heard him in their bedroom. Mum didn't say anything. She just stood there looking at us. Then he came back downstairs with a suitcase, kissed me and my sister on our heads, and… We haven't seen him since."

"I never… Michael, if I'd…" David blurts out a trail of unfinished sentences. "You must've…"

"But, please – you can't tell anyone about this. Not even Robert or William."

David nods. How can he refuse?

"Anyway…" he sighs. "I don't think I'll be at school much longer."

David looks at his friend's reddened hand. "Is that why…?" He points at the bruises.

"No. It doesn't bother me anymore," he shrugs.

Exactly what David had suspected, but still odd to hear him say it so matter-of-fact.

Michael's mother shouts from the foot of the stairs. He stands up, goes to the door, still speaking. "I mean, I don't want to leave school, but… I don't want to…" He rolls his eyes, looking for the next words. "I don't want to get too upset if I have to…"

"Right, boys," says Michael's mother, when they join her in the kitchen. "Would you set the table, please?"

Michael silently shows David where things are kept. Then they lift the table out from the corner and spread a tablecloth across it. Michael sets the placemats, laying them down over the red rose pattern, and David follows round with the cutlery.

She turns from the stove. Smiles broadly. "Lovely."

Michael nudges David's arm; points to one of the chairs.

"Oh, yes – sit down, love," she says. "Both of you." Starts making up a plateful. Turns back to them. "Birthday boy." Puts it down in Michael's place. Repeats for David.

"Thank you, Mrs. – I mean, Ms. Grayling."

"Don't fret about it." Glancing across, Michael's already three mouthfuls in. 'slow down, love," she says.

David picks up his knife and fork. Looks at what he has – a slice of gammon, some carrots and cabbage, and a few boiled potatoes – and begins to eat.

"Is it all right for you, David?"

He quickly swallows a bit of cabbage. "Yes, thank you."

"Good." She smiles again. "What about you?" she asks, just as Michael's bitten into the last of his gammon.

He nods.

'sorry it's not the best joint." She pokes at it with her fork. "It was all I could afford."

"It's fine," says Michael – the first thing he's said since they came downstairs. 'tastes great, Mum." Lumpy cheeks and quick grin.

When they've finished – when everything's been eaten, cleaned, and put away – David and Michael go out on to the street. They sit at the kerb, half-a-dozen doors away from number twenty-four. David runs a finger through the deep grooves in the cobbles. "So, is that why your mum isn't called Mrs. Francis anymore?"

He nods. "She wants nothing to do with him."

"And has she said you might have to leave school?"

"No. But I'm sure she's thinking it."

"How do you know?"

Michael pulls his legs to his chest, tugs at his blazer. "How much longer will this last? And we can't even afford a good bit of gammon."

"Does she know about…?" David points at Michael's hands.

He turns his right one over, the marked palm staring up at them both. "She's seen them. But she never asks – you know – why I got them."

It's like the ice has completely thawed; David feels that he can ask him anything now. "But don't you wish the teachers didn't cane you so much?"

"Course, but…" His shoulders drop. He sounds out of breath. "It's happened so many times now, what's it matter if it happens a few more times?"

David refuses to believe him, even though now he's said it twice. "You can't mean that. Surely?"

"Like I said…" he says, firmer. "I don't think I'll be there much longer. So, what does it matter?"

David opens his mouth, very nearly begins his response, but realises, this time, he doesn't have one.

Summer Days

What the summer break will be remembered for most is the rain. At its worst, it shook the windows, thrashed against the walls, and lightning filled the overcast house like blinking streetlamps. All of which meant David spent most of the school holidays indoors. Some days, he would organise games of hide-and-seek or cowboys-and-Indians with Josie and Lily – because if you can't go out exploring the fields and woods, why not go from room to room, exploring them instead? Then on other days – because (when it comes down to it) there really isn't very much to explore in their small cottage – David passed the housebound hours with books borrowed from the library. While the storms slammed hard outside, David learnt more about animals and history and wars.

And not just wars of the past.

Europe – at least, the people in charge there – were clearly brewing another. Just about every day, David would find Hitler's name in the newspaper. There it would be; rigid, immovable, in the headlines and the reports – H I T L E R – like lined-up tin soldiers from Robert's toy shelf.

As with the occupations of Austria and Czechoslovakia, Hitler had given his plan to invade Poland its very own name. *Fall Weiss.* (Translation: Case White.) And it was looking as if he might have some help this time too: a new ally, the leader of the Soviet Union – Joseph Stalin – who, just weeks earlier, had been sat at Britain's side of the negotiating table. And why did he choose to switch sides? Because if the invasion of Poland should be successful, there were a few bits of the country he'd quite like to have himself.

So, over the summer, hardly a day went by without rain – the complete opposite to the previous year – and hardly a day went by, also, without David adding some minutiae of the story to his notebook.

And the more David read about it, the more news bulletins he and his father listened to, the more he heard that word.

The word began with a W. And it wasn't a long word – it only had three letters, in fact – but it carried such huge weight behind it. David would wince, feel his insides convulse, at the simple mention of it.

So, what was it then, that three-letter word beginning with W?

What do you think it was?

The word was war.

Something David always associated with the past, with grandparents and history books. Never something that could possibly intercept and interrupt his own life, now.

But he knew why they were using it, that little W-word – as much as he wished they wouldn't. He knew that, in the end, it might well be the only thing that will halt Germany's bulging borders. If the negotiations fail (and, apparently, there are still some going on) what is there left to try but a bit of war? If you can't work it out inside, at the table, then take it into the muddy garden, roll your sleeves up, and tussle there instead.

Another sodden summer day. Two in the afternoon. David is inside, reading. Out beyond the thin glass, he can hear the steady stream of drizzle sloshing the garden and the path. It reminds him of the wireless being tuned. He sits in his father's armchair, his legs crossed.

"*Ommmm*, naughty." Josie appears from upstairs, wearing her favourite red pinafore and a cheeky, caught-you smile. "Does Dad know you're sat there?"

"Course not." David looks over the horizon of his book. "He's at work."

"I'll tell him when he gets in," she says, hips swaying.

"Fine." David returns to his words. "He won't mind."

"I'll tell him anyway."

"Fine," repeats David. "Just leave me alone."

'mum!" she shouts. 'mum!"

David tries ignoring her, even when she pulls at his legs.

"Get off it!" she says, her voice tinged with laughter as well as desperation. 'mum!"

She's upstairs somewhere, changing sheets. David hears her call down from one of the bedrooms – no doubt telling Josie to be quiet. He puts the book down, unable to focus any longer.

'stop it, Josie!" He swipes at her grabbing hands. 'stop!"

The stairs creak.

"David was being mean," Josie says, weakly, as if about to cry.

"No, I wasn't."

"Never mind all that..." Esther starts coming down, dirty bed linen balled in her arms. "You'll wake Lily. Just leave each other be." She passes them into the kitchen. "In fact – come and help me with tea, Josie."

She slinks off, her tongue stuck out, and when their father gets in, she does just what she promised.

"David was sat in your chair today, Daddy," running up to him before he's even slammed the door shut.

"Was he now?" he says, hanging his coat up.

"Yes." Josie locks eyes with David. "He said you wouldn't mind."

"Oh. Did he now?"

"Yes, he did."

"And what did you say to that?"

"I said I'd tell *you*."

"Right."

Esther comes out from the kitchen. "Hello, darling." Kisses him on the cheek. "Good day?"

"I guess so."

"Good. Come on now, Josie – I need you again."

"But, Mum..."

"None of that – come on."

Josie unfurls herself from Daddy's legs, stomping after her mother into the steaming, hissing kitchen.

"Has she been like this all day?" he asks David.

"Just for a bit."

"And *were* you sat in here?" He pats the chair like an obedient dog.

David nods. "Yes. I was."

"Never." He laughs. "Well, David, that's just…" His mouth hangs open for a few seconds. "Unforgivable. But, I suppose I will – forgive you – just this once."

And then he begins to tell David a new dockyard story. This one is about George Jenkins who, that very day, ended up with a broken arm. Like David's father, George moves the cargo off the ships and trawlers on to the dockside. At best, it's a monotonous job. Each day a city of wooden boxes is built; high, New York-size constructions. (That summer, Robert lent him a picture book all about New York City. The grainy images of skyscrapers and apartment blocks reminded him of how his father had described the dockyard when the boats come in, ready to be emptied. But, back to the story… An arm's been broken – George Jenkins' right arm, in fact.) Like any other morning at the docks, George was trudging back and forth, unloading a tied-up goods ship. "This particular vessel, so as you know…" David's father likes to add extra colour and detail. "Came from over the Atlantic." (So, quite possibly, from New York City itself.) On board, stacked and bagged, was fruit and sugar and timber, much of it soaked by sea spray and cross-ocean rainstorms. While hauling one of the huge, stuffed sugar sacks, George stumbled. Hearing shouts and gruff laughs, David's father found George sprawled out on the dirty dock floor, white over. What he'd been carrying, now settled on top of him like a heavy snowfall. "God knows how much all that's worth," someone said with a chuckle. "Not much now," went another. A few men – David's father included – went to help him up. As one of them yanked at his right arm, George screamed, lashing out with his left. 'sorry. Does it hurt, George?" one of them said. The injured man replying; "Course it bloody hurts."

"Bill!" Esther shouts from the kitchen. "Language!"

"Sorry, love." But he doesn't look particularly repentant, eyebrows raised.

'sounds painful," says David.

"Mmm. I reckon it was, son. But it were funny, too. Not that I'd say that to George's face, of course – not for a few more days anyway. Once the swelling's gone down and he's got all the sugar out his hair – then, maybe, he'll start to see the comical side of it."

Josie skips over to them. "What you laughing about?"

"I were just telling your brother about something that happened at work today."

"Oh, right." And then – because she clearly wasn't all that interested – she skips straight back into the kitchen.

"There you are," David hears his mother say from amongst the fizz of boiling pans. "Boys? Can you get the table set, please?"

After tea, once everything's been washed and cleared away, David's father starts to work on the wireless.

Kfffffff.

Ssssssssss.

Kfffffff.

"Come on – where are you?" He turns the dial.

There should be the sound of somebody talking all the way from London.

Instead…

Ssssssssss.

"Can *I* try, Dad?"

His father looks at him. "Well." Looks back at the device. "I suppose, son. If you want."

He stands back and David takes his place by the cabinet. Slowly, he adjusts the frequency, watches the needle move across the gauge, left to right, back to the left a little, then…

Pip.

"That's it." His father sits down with a satisfied groan.

Pip.
Piiiiip.

"Good evening. You are listening to the British Broadcasting Corporation. The time is six o'clock on Thursday the twenty-fourth of August. This is the evening news bulletin. His Majesty's Parliament has been re-called today by Prime Minister Neville Chamberlain. The decision was made after details of the Molotov-Ribbentrop Pact between Germany and the Soviet Union were made public. Parliament passed a War Powers Act and also ordered the Royal Navy to be placed on a war footing. It cancelled all leave for military personnel and announced that any British citizens still in Germany should return home immediately."

David's father sighs, shaking his head. "There you go," he says.

"What?"

"They've put the Navy on a war footing."

"So?"

But David knows exactly what it means. Later, at bedtime, he tries to fall asleep. But the sheets stick to him, the moon's metallic glow dances in the corner of his eyes, and – worst of all – the words of the news bulletin linger heavily in his mind. He's seen this war-thing looming larger on the horizon for quite a while now – a slowly rising sun, casting its dark light over everything. Tonight, it's the closest it's ever been.

***

The story goes on. But, twists and turns far from over, the next chapter starts strangely.

Hitler goes quiet. In fact, the news bulletin on the twenty-fifth of August – the next day – says that the German Foreign Ministry has cut off *all* communication. At the same time, Chamberlain promises Poland that, should they be attacked, Britain will support them any way they can.

Then, on September the first, the Foreign Ministry in Berlin at last breaks its silence.

And what is it they say?

With what do they break their week-long silence?

What else?

They announce the beginning of the invasion of Poland.

Just like in Austria and Czechoslovakia, little resistance is offered. And as Hitler yet again occupies new territory, David and his friends return to familiar lands.

This school year is an important one. At the end of the third year – the upper fourth – there are exams. Which means lots more homework – as if that was possible. And from the first lesson – English with Mr. Johnson – David can see it stacking up. ("Continue with this in your own time," said the English master. "I want this finished and handed in next lesson," was how Trevithick wrapped up his French lesson. "And *this* is your homework…" announced classics master, Mr. Hennessey, as the bell ripped through the end of last period.)

"For a first day back…" sighs Robert, sitting down in their regular bus seats. "That'll take some beating."

"I remember them saying it'll be tougher in the upper fourth – but I didn't think…"

"Mmm. You're telling me."

The engine wakes up – coughs, splutters, then rumbles gently beneath their feet and through the seats. David leans back. The vibrations run right into him, become a part of his bloodstream.

"Never mind," huffs Robert. "It's not as if I wanted to do anything else when I got home."

David turns to face the window. Watches their morning journey in reverse: houses, pavements, shops, the sign for the dockyard, the factories and worker's yards; the countryside following on, the sun just starting to melt into the horizon. A few more stops, and Robert's home. A few more, and…

Jumping off the bus, David feels the hard ground reverberate up his legs. He puts his arms out, expecting to overbalance.

"David?"

It's his mother's voice. He looks up, looks through the bus as it moves away from the roadside and continues up the lane. Sees her opposite, the shops, like the ones they drove by, still going on behind her.

"What're you doing here? Where're Josie and Lily?" he asks, crossing over.

"I left them with Mrs. Taylor next door."

"Oh."

"There's something I need to tell you." She pauses. Breathes out. "And I thought it'd be best if... if it was just the two of us."

They start walking. Her eyes glint a little; they reflect the fiery, dying sunlight, like David imagines the sea might.

"Look..." she says. "Something happened at the docks today."

He pictures the road-sign again.

"There was an accident. One of the warehouses collapsed."

David just listens; keeps in step with her. Five more paces before she carries on.

"David... your dad was... when it happened, he was... inside."

He wants to ask if he's all right. If... If... If... But he can tell from her voice, the way she reaches down and takes hold of his hand, what the answer to that question would be. And he knows he doesn't want to hear it.

They fetch the girls from number eight. Mrs. Taylor meets them at the door. She tries to smile, but her lips quiver and fail to shape one.

"Come on in," she says, stepping back to let them pass.

"No," says Esther. "Thank you, but..."

"Fine. I'll just get them for you."

She disappears into the cottage. Returns with Josie and Lily. David wonders whether they know, whether they would understand, even if they *were* told.

Back home, Esther makes tea. The girls play by the fire and David watches them: wanting, for the first time in a long time, to join in their daft, little game.

"Do you not have any homework you could be doing?" asks his mother from the kitchen doorway.

He nods. Goes across to the table, sits, and begins to pull out various schoolbooks. He tries to concentrate, cups his head in his hands, holding it in place as he stares blankly at his Latin workbook. But none of it seems to make any sense. He imagines his father arriving back from work, wandering across and peering at what he's doing, stumbling over the words on the page, before giving up completely.

Six o'clock. David switches the wireless on. A habit hard to break. (In the end, he gave up on his schoolwork, thinking, just this once, maybe he should play the part of Robert and ask *him* for a hand. See what he says to that.) He fiddles with the dial, staring at the chair his father would, ordinarily, be sat in.

The crunchy, crackling sound becomes a man's voice. "This is the evening news bulletin," it says.

David continues looking at his father's chair.

"Today, Prime Minister Neville Chamberlain declared Britain to be at war with Germany."

Right. There you go, he thinks. The story goes on – or, is that *it*, over. It's what it's all been leading up to, just what the newspapers have been saying… just what Parfick said would happen… and just what his…

The rest of the bulletin drifts past unheard, the way some people can: people you've had around you as far back as you have memories. They become a part of the background and you forget, really, they're more like the foundation, that without them things just fall away.

His mother comes in from the kitchen. She glances at the empty chair, then at the radio. "Can this go off now, love?"

David nods.

She feels around it. "How…?" Then the voice cuts out. "Oh." She sits, sighs, pushing her pale lips into a stubby smile. "Are the girls all right up there?"

"Josie was reading Lily some fairy tales."

"Right. Good. At least they'll get some happy endings tonight." She sighs again, heavier than before, her eyes wet. "Oh, David."

***

The familiar lands of school don't feel so familiar now. For one thing, everyone knows about Hitler, about the war, about Chamberlain. And the boys' game – now that fills the playground, replicated tens of times.

The news a few days later is that there are more countries joining Britain in declaring war: France, allies throughout the discussions with Germany, as well as places like Canada, Australia, New Zealand – nations knotted to Britain by history.

Soon, though, David isn't only hearing about countries – huge, anonymous groups of people – but individuals.

"My two brothers signed up at the weekend," says one lad in their year.

Then. The story goes on again. Others start talking about their fathers going – the very thing David feared most when the idea of war first poked its way through the news stories. And he starts wondering which he'd have preferred – to see his father sign up, go off and fight, or this… Because, who knows? Though many won't return, many, also, will – and at least that would have left the chance that *he* might too. Instead…

***

More rain, continuing the soggy summer trend; the lane outside the church almost turned to mud. Brown water laps at

David's freshly polished school shoes. His uniform unusually tight, like hands clamping hard, he runs a palm over his damp hair, patting down the bits whipped up in the breeze.

Some more people arrive. He recognises hardly anybody – besides family, of course. David assumes the others must be from the docks and, looking at the quiet, suited crowd huddled under the churchyard trees, he starts thinking of the stories narrated to him over the years.

He stands with his mother and sisters. The older relatives – grandparents and great aunts, great uncles – are inside, keeping dry. Aunt Bessie – that's his father's big sister – holds Lily's hand. She stretches to get away, probably wanting to try out the puddles.

A drop of rain lands on the back of David's neck; begins making its cold way down under his shirt.

Esther nudges him on the shoulder. "He's here," she whispers, her eyes pointing down the lane at the horse and cart moving slowly towards them.

Those gathered under the trees notice it too. Silently, they start to move inside, followed by the rest of David's family who had remained with them outside. His aunt passes him Lily's hand.

Reverend Grainger – having been talking to the men opposite – comes across. "Your husband was clearly well loved, Mrs. Denby."

She smiles and looks at the sodden ground.

The hearse rolls to a stop. The lone horse splutters, its eyes blacked out. Two men jump down, tails and top hats. One of them wanders over; bows his head. "Morning. When you're ready."

Esther looks at the vicar.

"In your own time," he says.

"Right," she sighs. "Children?" She squats to the girls' level, resting a hand on David's arm. "We're going to go inside the church, there, and... we're going to hear all about your dad... and then we're going to say goodbye to him."

"Why?" asks Lily.

Their mother straightens. A cough and a groan. "Just follow behind me, all right?"

They all nod.

"Ready, Reverend."

"Of course," he smiles. "Thank you, Mr. Shimmley."

The men lift the bleached-wood coffin. Two more with hairy faces – who had been stood as part of the waiting crowd – help them, wincing at the weight as it lands on their shoulders. Through the tall, arched doors, David hears organ music gently rumbling, the sound like distant thunderclouds. The vicar walks in first, the men and their precious piece of cargo behind. And following them, David holds both his sisters' hands, one either side, and trails his mother into the church.

Decision, Made

David nudges the front door open, trying to muffle the un-oiled ache the hinges have begun to make. Behind him, autumn winds whirl a-frenzy; dead leaves swirl and fly like starling flocks. Some follow him into the house. He kicks them back out again. The flimsy glass rattles noisily in the window-frames; the wind bumping, reverberating, through the walls, just as if his sisters were running around upstairs.

His mother appears from out of the kitchen. "How's your day been?" she asks, her voice very nearly drowned out by a combination of the weather and the beating clock.

"Fine, thanks." David starts removing his coat, tidies his misshapen hair, then begins taking out his homework.

"Looks like you've a lot to do there."

He nods, eyes peering inside his bag – one last book to find.

"Before you start, there was something I thought we could talk about."

David sits down.

"I've been thinking…" She joins him round the table. "Money's such a struggle."

David wriggles in his seat – these wooden chairs never have been easy to settle in.

"My work at the farm pays a little – but it's only occasional. Now, your…" She pauses, drawing finger-circles on the table. "Your dad never got professional sort of money. But it was always enough – you know?"

David starts to move his books around, making piles, ordering them, as if ordering his thoughts too.

"Of course, you're not really the right age for doing dock-work – and I wouldn't want you down there, anyway. Not now. But we still need the money somehow."

He knows what she's saying. Things need paying for. Even holes in the ground cost something. And they almost couldn't afford one of those.

His mother looks down at the scuffs and blemishes on the exposed tabletop. "I spoke to Mr. Jenkins the other day."

David looks up. Pictures the shop sign, across from the bus stop.

"You know who I mean? The butcher?"

He nods.

"He was very understanding." Each word suddenly seems carefully measured as it slips from her lips. "And at the moment, he doesn't have anyone helping him out. His son's just started down at some university. He's very proud, of course. And I told him all about you, about how intelligent you are – how I've no idea where you get it from."

David takes a paling hardback from one pile, sets it down, opening to an arbitrary page.

"So, when I asked, he said he'd be delighted to take you on. He reckons you'll do wonderfully."

David remains focused on his book.

"So, David?"

"Will I still be able to go to school?" he asks.

She sighs. "No, love. I just don't see how you could do both. But try to think of it this way – education's only good for getting you into a profession, and if you're working for Mr. Jenkins, you'll be doing exactly that anyway. Do you see? And, eh…"

He lifts his stare again, away from the blurry text.

"You'll be earning long before your friends have even finished school."

"But I want to finish school too."

"I know you do. But this is the only way I can see." She pauses again. Leans further over the table. "David, please – look at me…"

He meets her eyes. They seem whiter than normal.

"You're the man of the house now. And I know it seems unfair, and you don't want to do it, but one day – I promise – you'll see the sense in it."

Last Lesson

The next day is Friday. It seems like years have passed in just the space of a few nights.

David stands in the playground. The place looks strangely altered: not as he thinks it should be. A football loops over his head; waving upper fifths shout for it back. The trees, off at the side, swamped with sparrows. The churning undercurrent of motor engines.

The others want to play the game, they want to tell their story, the one that tells of war, the one that is now a reflection of a real war, people out there, playing the parts the real story requires – some will survive, some won't. It feels more like it's their story now: that it's out of these boys' hands. And David's happy to pass it over. Because he has his *own* story to go on with. Perhaps it isn't the one he'd have written, but...

The bell goes.

Walking to final period (his mother's words from the night before replaying... replaying... replaying...), his friends talk about the lesson ahead, about the homework they're going to get handed back to them. One mentions next week. Because, to them, this is simply another lesson, another final period. Next week will just bring along more.

But not for David.

For David, something else is on its way.

Six Days Ago

"Why didn't you say anything?"

Sunday. Six days ago, David started working in the butcher shop. Six days ago, his hands were clean – besides the odd bit of smudged pencil; now, each evening, he struggles to scrub out the dismal shade of pink coating his skin, his fingernails packed red and mucky.

"Why didn't you say anything?" Robert asks again. "You could've at least mentioned it."

David cranes his neck back into the house. Shouts: "Mum! I'm just going out with Robert for a bit." He hears a dim reply from somewhere upstairs. Permission, he assumes.

"So – come on..." He continues with the same question. "Why didn't you tell us?"

"Because... I don't know."

They walk down the lane, right into the low, blaring sun, a faint echo after each of their footsteps.

"Even if I had, it wouldn't have changed it." Then a thought occurs. "How did you find out, anyway?"

"What? Did you think I'd just assume you'd been ill all week?" Like he'd read David's mind. "I overheard Parfick talking with Greening."

David, for a moment, contemplates asking him what, exactly, he overheard, what they could have been saying about him, before realising what a pointless question that would be.

They keep on walking. Everything around them looks white and untouched in the late-autumn light.

"So, what's it like, then – at work?" Robert sounds interested, almost envious.

David shrugs. "I don't know. Maybe it'll get better."

"And it's permanent?"

He nods.

Stopping at a field, they climb the breaking fence. It creaks, unsettlingly, beneath them as they sit. David folds his arms; takes a deep breath. The wind flies in at them, cheeks stinging.

"You would've told me, wouldn't you?"

"I guess."

"What's that supposed to mean?"

"I don't know, Robert." David looks down at the ground. "It's hard to explain."

"Right. It's just, the thing is..." Robert's voice softens. "Now I'll have no one to help me with my homework." He nudges David's arm. "Eh? Which means I'll have to keep coming to see you every weekend."

David jumps down from the fence. "Actually. I better head back now."

"Oh. What?" Robert climbs down too. "We've only just..."

David fronts the march back.

Robert struggles keeping up. "David? Wait."

The silent Sunday countryside endless and empty.

"There's no point me trying, Robert," he says, after a while.

"Trying what?"

"I'm not going back, you know? So, what's the use in bothering with schoolwork – even if it's to help *you*? It'll just be too hard."

"I doubt you'll ever find any of it too hard," replies Robert, close to a laugh.

"No. Forget it. I didn't mean it like that."

A Letter

The letterbox clatters. David wanders over to the front door, toast crumbs scattering his shirt and chin. One of the envelopes – a fading yellow – is addressed to him. He's been working at the butcher's now for two weeks. He turns it over, sees straight away the return address, and tears open the seal. Taking it out, the first thing he notices is the school crest. It reminds him of the letter he got detailing his entrance exam – date, time, so on – not to mention the one that told him he'd passed. (He still has that very letter in the drawer of his bedside table.) David runs a finger over the image. Reads the Latin underneath. *Floreat nostra schola.* The school motto. *May our school flourish.* His stomach gurgles – the first bites of toast working their way down, perhaps. He re-reads the motto (*our school…* But it isn't anymore, is it?), then begins on the rest of the letter.

His mother comes into the kitchen. "What's that, love?"

"A letter," he says, still reading.

"Who from?"

"School."

"Can *I* see?" she says, her hand held out, waiting.

He passes it to her.

"I wonder what this could mean."

The letter is from Mr. Greening. It says he has something to discuss with David, and his mother, and that he would welcome seeing them this week, Thursday, at a quarter-past eleven, in his office.

"Do you think Mr. Jenkins'll mind you taking an hour or so off?" Esther asks, giving him the letter back.

"I don't know." David's struggled every day to work out what Mr. Jenkins will or won't mind. He looks back at the letter, his lips creasing into a hopeful smile.

His mother sees it; mistakes its cause. "Come on, you – it's time you were off."

***

"Please – sit down." Mr. Greening smiles broadly, pointing to two chairs set out specially.

"Thank you." Esther sighs as she sits.

"I was so sorry…"

Esther holds up a hand, looks down at her lap. David notices a frayed hole in the pale-red curtains behind the schoolmaster and his desk. It's his first time in here and it's nothing like as grand as he expected.

"Well, good to see you both. I'm really pleased you came along." He looks at David. "And how are you doing, without us?"

David doesn't quite know what to say.

His mother fills the gap. "Oh, he's doing fine, he is."

She squeezes his shoulder. David squirms. Feels heat in his cheeks.

Mr. Greening looks again at David. "Well, that's nice to hear. Though, in fact, it's also why I invited you both here." Putting on his spectacles, he slides a sheet of headed notepaper across his desk so it's directly in front of him. "Naturally, we were all very shocked by what happened. But, I hope you knew, David, how well you were progressing here – how much all your teachers thought of you. So, to have to lose you – it was a real shame. From what we saw…" The schoolmaster looks at David's mother now. "He really could go on to do absolutely anything. Believe me – there are only a few students like your son at any one time." He picks up the piece of paper. "That's why I took it upon myself to contact an old school friend. He's an architect with offices in the town centre. I explained your situation…" He looks back at David. "Now, to begin with, obviously, with no formal qualifications, you'd simply start out as an office clerk, learning the ropes, so to speak – but he's very willing to try you out and train you up. The pay isn't much, at first, but as you progress – which I'm sure you will – that will too. Here…" He holds out the reply from the architect.

"Mr. Greening…" Esther starts, taking the letter. "Thank you for all you've done – we do appreciate it, both of us, but…"

David repositions himself in the cushioned chair.

"David already has a position, he's already learning a trade, and I don't think it's right that we take him out of that, not now he's settled."

He wonders what could have given his mother such an impression. When has he told her that?

"Of course, Mrs. Denby." Mr. Greening links his hands together like a finger-made pyramid. "I understand. Certain decisions have been taken. But, please, just take a little time to think this over. Talk with each other. This is a considerable offer – I assure you."

David's mother stands, folds the paper and stuffs it into her coat pocket. "Thank you again, sir."

"Not at all," he sighs. "I'll see you out." He opens the panelled door – the one part of the room reminiscent of the rest of the school – and shakes David's hand. "Whatever happens, I wish you the very best." He smiles his wide smile.

Out in the corridor, David hears snippets of lessons. They walk past the classics room, Hennessey's hands banging the chalkboard. He considers walking into the class and just sitting down, like nothing had changed, like the last fortnight hadn't happened.

"Goodbye, then." The schoolmaster stops at the main entrance, holds the heavy door open, sunlight spreading over the stone floor.

"Thank you, Mr. Greening."

"A pleasure."

"Thank you, sir," says David.

"I hope to hear back from you," Mr. Greening finishes. "Whatever you decide." The hem of his school-gown flickers in the breeze.

He nods, replies smile with smile, looking up at the great arched doorway, and then joining his mother to cross the empty playground.

To Do with The Butcher Shop

He was told to come in by the back way: no need to knock, just go straight in. The gate – six, seven feet high – hung limp by one hinge. It scuffed across the concrete as he opened it, scraping over a marked-out path that, presumably, each time someone comes in or goes out, gets etched further into the stone; a mark, a record, of each day passing, to which David was adding, and may well go on to add to for who-knows-how-long.

From out of the half-open doorway, David could hear something. A pounding. Perhaps it was there to welcome him; a marching beat encouraging him forwards into this new, uncertain world. Stepping in, slowly, softly – because, if the right moment appeared, he'd much rather get out of doing this altogether – David found the source of the sound.

Mr. Jenkins was leant over a workbench, a dripping cleaver in his hand, dividing some once-animal into steak-thick segments, completely unaware that – while he did it, while he hacked that thing to bits – there was a boy stood just a few yards behind him, a boy whose chest heaved and ached at each rise and fall of the blade, each time it made that wet, squelching noise.

Eventually, Mr. Jenkins spun round. "Oh," he said, setting the blade down. "David – isn't it?"

He nodded.

The butcher paced a circle round him, working his hands through a bloodied rag. The floor was covered in a layer of sawdust.

"You've missed the delivery."

"Oh. Sorry."

"No. Too late now." He looked down at him. "I got to say, I'd hoped you'd be taller. And…" He jabbed David in the side. "God! There's nothing on you." He laughed – except it seemed closer to a cough; it rattled and growled out of his mouth. "We'll have to sort that out." That laugh again, like a fractious engine.

The butcher began by showing him what everything did – while telling him, also, that he wouldn't be doing any of it himself for a long time. His main job would be a very simple one. Only – said Mr. Jenkins – he'd show him what that was later.

"For the time being, me lad, grab that broom and get the floor through there swept." He pointed into the front of the shop. "I'll come and check it in a minute – and I don't want to see a speck. Right?"

David forced a smile; a nod. Went and got the broom, then made his way into the front.

For a second, he stood still in the doorway. Really, he should have expected it – after all, he'd seen them countless times from the other side of the glass while waiting at the bus stop. But the rack of bodies covering one of the windows, well… It was a shock. He felt them looking at him. Eyeing him up. Even though most of them no longer had heads.

Mr. Jenkins must have noticed. "Come on. Chop, chop," he said, rather appropriately, his cleaver waiting to fall.

David took a deep breath and continued on into the front. He did as he was told. That's what his mother had said to him when she kissed him goodbye. But he worked away from the dead stuff, as best he could, the hard hairs of the brush scraping across the floor as though scratching at the inside of his head. Quickly, he got together a sizeable pile out from under just a few things – bits of dirt and brown paper; crumpled, dead leaves.

In the back, Mr. Jenkins continued with his knife and his meat. (A cow, by the way – that's what it had been, apparently, back when it used to move around. Now it would make about ten, maybe twelve, beef joints at "…and remember this," Jenkins said. "You'll need to learn all the prices as you go along…" one-and-three each. At least David knew he could do that. Remembering information and figures: that was no problem. Ask him again, even if it's in six months' time, without a single reminder between now and then, and he'll repeat it like it's written down in front of him.)

"Let's see, then." Mr. Jenkins came to check what David had done. He wiped his right hand under the counter. Pulled air through his teeth and stood again, over him, dusting his fingers clean. "That'll need another going under, me lad." Turned to the cupboards opposite. "Them, too," he said. Barely time for his hands to reach the floor. "Keep going. I'll check again in a sec." And then he smiled, for the first time since David arrived, then began to whistle, the muddled-together tune almost sweet, unlike anything his appearance or manner had otherwise let on. (But – how long had David been there? Half-an-hour? Who knows? That could easily be a better representation of him, compared to the moody, nit-picky one that had just been on show. Everything has an explanation, every way of behaving, if you follow it back far enough – but then there's not much time for David to dwell on things like that, not when there's meat to be cut and sold, not when there's a floor to be swept...)

"Right. Fair enough." Mr. Jenkins looked either side of him. "I suppose that'll do for a first try. Just go put that broom away. We need to open up."

David went into the back, trying to remember where it had come from. It was obvious that most things had very specific places, so he wanted to at least get that right, without needing to be told. But everything just looked so unfamiliar.

In the front, he could hear the shop bell wobble and chime; the first customer of the day.

Mr. Jenkins greeted them – Mrs. Hebble-something.

A few more things were said.

Paper rustled.

The sound of coins.

"Goodbye."

Then the bell again.

"Come on, me lad," Mr. Jenkins called through. "You've just missed your first customer. A regular, an' all. You know – you'll need to learn everyone by name and what they buy."

He'd already said that, thought David, earlier on when he was showing him round. "Sorry, Mr. Jenkins." He rushed back in, having re-homed the sweeping brush.

"You took your time there, didn't you?"

"Right. I couldn't remember where I'd got it from." He tried to smile again. But the butcher didn't seem amused. "Sorry."

"Your mother said you were a smart lad. Can't say I see it yet."

David looked down at the glass counter, finger smudges marking where Mr. Jenkins had just reached in.

"Just watch what I do, all right?"

He nodded. "Yes, Mr. Jenkins."

"Every time that bell goes, I want you in here, by my side. For one thing, me lad, the customers need to get used to seeing you here."

(He'd said that a lot now... *Me lad... Me lad...* David could feel his skin come alive every time the butcher said it; little shivers running up and down his arms. Maybe it was Mr. Jenkins' way of adopting him as a kind of proxy-son... *Well, the lad needs a father now...*)

David looked again at the white-tiled walls (he'd noticed them earlier while sweeping), the vivid blue letters of the shop name, JENKINS & SON, FAMLY BUTCHER SINCE 1879, spread across the length of one wall. It made David think about the son – the son who wasn't around anymore (except in the name). He wondered if Mr. Jenkins – looking at David, how he wasn't what he'd expected – wished he had him, right now, instead. Was he just like his father – only a younger version? David can't ever remember meeting him. He saw him, once or twice, riding that bike around the village, but that was about it. He was a few years older (wasn't he?), but at the kind of age when just a few years might as well be a few decades.

"Oh." The butcher stepped forward. Someone was about to come in. "Here's Mrs. Butterfield. Right on time."

She looked just like David imagined a Mrs. Butterfield might. Her hair was a light colour – creamy, almost – and she had a soft smile. Her voice was quiet. It sounded like her words came through closed teeth. She spoke with long *ssss*-sounds, like a badly-tuned radio. (*Forgive us our trespasses, as we forgive those who trespass against us…*) With a near-whisper, she asked for half-a-dozen pork sausages and a cut of beef.

Mr. Jenkins leant over the counter. Wrapped up the sausages, once Mrs. Butterfield had agreed with him that they were the six she wanted. Then he took a slab of cow from the side and a clean blade. "This much?" he asked.

"Oh. No. A bit less, please."

"How about now?"

"Lovely. Thank you."

The butcher sawed into the dark-red meat, quick and jagged. He looked like he relished those moments – a chunk of a dead thing in his hands and the chance to hack right into it.

"That'll be two-and-five, my love," said Mr. Jenkins, placing the beef next to the sausages and then wrapping them. He lifted the package on to the counter and Mrs. Butterfield handed him the money. "Thank you." He turned to the cash register. Prodded it a couple of times, until it opened, then placed the coins inside.

David watched as Mrs. Butterfield made her way to the door.

"Cheerio for now," called Mr. Jenkins.

"Yes. Bye-bye," she replied, the door slamming after her.

No sooner had she gone, and someone else was arriving. Mr. Jenkins didn't say who this was – he didn't really have chance before she was opening the door and approaching the counter.

She gave her order.

"Rightio," he said, cheerfully.

"Who's this, then?" she said, looking in David's direction.

"This is David. It's his first day."

"I see," she smiled. "Aren't you Esther's boy?"

He nodded.

"Thought so." Then, her tone altogether different: "Sorry to hear about your father."

David dropped his gaze to the floor. "Thanks," he mumbled. What else do you say?

"That'll be one-and-six, my love." Mr. Jenkins held out his cleanest hand, wiping the other down his apron.

A bunch of rattling, rusting coins passed over.

"Thank you." She bundled the paper-wrapped meat to her chest.

"Get the door, will you?" Mr. Jenkins whispered to David.

He quickly sidled round the counter; beat her to the door handle.

"Oh. Much appreciated, deary." She stepped out; turning around to add: "Pass on my best to your mother."

"I will," he nodded. (Or, I would, if I knew who you were.)

The morning continued in much the same way. And as it went on, David tried to memorise the faces and the names, as well as their orders, Mr. Jenkins' words playing on his mind... "You'll need to learn everyone by name and what they buy."

He repeated a few – the ones he was sure about – to himself, whispering them, carefully, under his breath while Mr. Jenkins made a racket with the chopping boards:

Mrs. Butterfield – half-a-dozen sausages and a joint of beef.

Mrs. Trimmley – three pork chops.

Mrs. Johnson – two pigeons and six bacon-rashers.

Mrs. Davies – four sausages and two rabbits (skinned).

David wondered, too, how often people came into the shop; would it be once a week, two or three times, every day (and, also, whether they really ordered the same things every time. Surely not?). His mother usually came in most days, as far as he knew. And she'd said to expect her around two, just before she goes off to fetch Josie from school. She said she'd want to see how he was getting on. But – what exactly would she see him doing, besides standing around, watching?

Out in the cobbled yard, David ate his lunch. The sun shone, blinking through the wispy, white clouds. He leant against a part-collapsed wall, munching slowly, without really tasting. By a heaped-high bin, he saw something move: a fleshy tail flashing in the corner gloom; a scratching sound, claw on stone.

"What you got there, then, lad?" Mr. Jenkins appeared.

David looked at his sandwich, like he needed to remind himself. "Cheese and pickle." He always has cheese and pickle.

"Ah – good choice." He stood next to him, one hand pressed against the brick. "Though, wouldn't you like some meat in there as well – a bit of ham, maybe?"

David could see the butcher scanning him, up and down. *Want to fatten me up, eh?* "I don't know," he answered, non-committal.

"You'll want to fill yourself up – that's all I'm saying. I could get you something now if you wanted." He gestured inside. "No?"

David shook his head. "No, thanks."

"Fair enough, but…" Mr. Jenkins pointed to himself. "See, it's tough work being a butcher. And you want to look the part too. If customers can see you don't get your fair share of meat, they'll wonder why. They'll wonder why they should keep on buying it from us, if even them that work there don't look to eat what they sell. You see my point?"

"Yes, Mr. Jenkins." (Though – only just.)

"Anyway, thought you might want to read this." He pulled a folded-up newspaper from the pocket of his apron. "I'll give you five more minutes, then I want you in again." And he whistled his way into the shop, the same flimsy melody as before.

When he'd stopped or gone far enough in, so David could no longer hear him, whatever had been by the bin earlier made a dash for it along the back wall. David only really half-saw it, off to one side; a moving, living something, in a place that is otherwise filled with the dead. He wanted to follow it, to see where it was heading, to see if it was making some sort of escape.

But, instead, he looked at the newspaper. They'd stopped getting them delivered at home – partly to save money, but, also, because David had started to lose interest (and just when things had really got going, too…). He read the date first: MONDAY 9TH OCTOBER 1939. Then the main headline: HITLER ANNEXES WESTERN POLAND.

Inside, Mr. Jenkins slammed a cupboard shut.

Five more minutes, David remembered.

And he remembered something else, too – the smile his mother wore when she waved him off.

The sun still shone. He felt it colouring his neck.

Better go back in, he thought, swallowing his last mouthful and closing the paper.

Mr. Jenkins was waiting for him with a pile of six wrapped packages. "This is the main thing I need you for, me lad." He patted the top one. "Did you see that bicycle out the back?"

He had.

"I've a list here – names and addresses. You should know where they all are. So, each of these…" He patted the pile again. "They need delivering."

David carried them out into the yard. The butcher followed behind.

"Just drop them in the basket at the front, there."

He did. Then started manoeuvring the thing from the corner it was crammed into. Bricks on the ground, several rust-rimmed buckets, he lifted the bicycle over them, its rear wheel first.

Mr. Jenkins stood with the gate open, a finger running down the list to check everything was as it should be. "You know where Greens Gate is?"

David nodded.

"And how about New Market Road?"

Another nod.

"Right. The rest of them are in the village, by the Common, so you should be fine round that end, eh?"

David wasn't sure if it was a proper question. He didn't reply, just took the list as Mr. Jenkins held it out to him.

"Take care, lad," he said, flinging the gate shut after David had passed through it.

The first delivery was furthest away. David headed back as if he was going home. But when he got to the fork in the road, instead of taking the right, he took the left turning. Going that way, there was plenty of tree cover; the bursts of bright sunlight bathing the lane thankfully became the anomaly, not the constant. The road curved gently to the right. David started travelling faster – not from pedalling more strongly, but because he'd also started going downhill. He suddenly realised he'd have to ride back. It wasn't the steepest of hills, but, nonetheless…

He propped the bicycle against the garden wall. This was just what he thought Mr. Jenkins would get him doing. He reached in for the first package and checked the pencil marks against what was on the list. It was the right one – half-a-dozen sausages and a cut of mutton. He told David not to worry about money. They settle up at the end of the week. Just knock on the door. Smile. Say who you are. What you've brought them. Then hand it over.

Mr. Fisher answered after the second knock. Scratched at the grey-white hairs covering his chin and cheeks. "Yes?"

David smiled. "Hello, sir. I'm from Jenkins'. Here's your order – six sausages and two pounds of mutton." Smiled again.

"Oh – grand." He held a wrinkled hand out. David passed it to him. "Thank you, son."

"Of course. Bye."

"Cheerio." And the man shut the door. First one done. That simple.

David cycled on, panting his way uphill. He could feel sweat edging its way down his forehead. The next stop was back the way he'd come, except, just before where the butcher shop and the other shops and the bus stop are, he turned off and rode down what, in essence, was a mud path, the bare space between the backs of two sheep pastures. This was New Market Road and it was nothing like the name suggested. For a start, it didn't look new. It was simply a track, a footpath, eight, maybe ten feet wide, walled with hedgerow. Riding along it, David passed a few people. One of them looked like Mrs. Butterfield (could she have only got this far after coming to the shop earlier?). From behind, it appeared to be the same hair: the tight, white curls.

David pushed open the gate. This was another house set out on its own. Something like ivy clung to the walls. A huge conifer – dark leaves and shadows – rooted in one corner of the garden. The door, brushed blue. A circle of frosted glass at a height just above David's head. He knocked. Clutched the packet, the list in his other hand – his evidence, his reason for being there. He could hear voices at the other side of the painted wood – at least two, possibly more. David looked up at the round window, watched the shifting shades of yellow and green, then pink and brown, the voices getting louder. The door handle turned.

"Hello, there."

"Hello, Mr. Clacton."

The man raised his eyebrows.

"Oh, I'm from Jenkins', sir. I'm delivering your order." David looked quickly at the package, needed reminding. "Ham joint, steak, sausages."

"Oh, right." They took it. "You new or something?"

"Yes – just started today." If David didn't know any better, he might almost have sounded pleased, like this, to him, was a day of great pride and accomplishment. But, then – maybe that's exactly what it should be...

"Well – thank you." He looked at the package, as if that too should be thanking David. "Goodbye, then." He made to close the door.

"Bye."

And David started off back down the garden path, the stones crunching under his shoes. Went through the gate he'd left open, shutting it this time. Then, at the wall, at the bicycle, he reached into the basket and pulled out the next one. With a finger, he found the scribbles. His eyes took a second or two to focus, the pencil marks not entirely clear on the paper. It said, LOWCROFT LANE – that was round by the Common. Mr. Jenkins did say all the rest were over that way.

This time there was no one else along New Market Road. The whole length of it – because where David was heading, was where it started – stretched before him, empty. He heard the sheep in their fields, through the hedges, could see flashes of them and their grass-stained wool; but the sounds and signs of people – nothing. It felt like everything had been left to him. David slowed his legs down, eased off the pedals. He could hear birdsong too. He wobbled a little on the bicycle, his progress weaved and wavered, as he started looking round him, into the trees and the hedgerows. David still knew nothing about which sang which song. He hoped to catch the sight of one, its beak moving, the melody clear, unmistakeable. Then he'd know. He'd know what was blackbird and what was robin and why it couldn't be a thrush because their song went more like…

There were young children playing on the Common. David saw their heads turn as he rode past. The road bent to the shape of the green and, to his right, he saw the sign for Lowcroft Lane, the gap in the terraced houses. At a quick guess, he'd say there were ten cottages down there. The packet in the basket was for number seven. David propped the bicycle against the rough-stone wall. Double-checked where Mr. Jenkins had labelled it. Nodded to himself. Opened the gate, closed it behind him this time, then – one step, two step, three step, four – he knocked on the door.

A woman answered. Younger than he'd expected. Probably still just a girl, the more he thought about it. Long, dark hair, which she flung back with her left hand. "Hello?" she smiled, her cheeks plumping.

"Hello," said David, instinctively; then, when he realised she might want to know who he was, what he was doing there, he said: "I'm from Jenkins'. I'm delivering your order." He held it up.

"Oh." She took the package. Noticed the scribbles. Looked to be reading them.

"Does it look all right?"

"Yes. I think so."

"Good."

"Right, well…" She smiled again; rested a hand on the door, her head turned slightly to one side. "Is that… all?"

"Oh. Sorry. Yes," David mumbled. For some reason, he was just staring at her.

"Well. Bye, then."

"Yes. Bye."

And she disappeared behind the door.

David walked back down the short path, the afternoon heat flaring up again. He felt it on his skin, in his cheeks and on his palms.

He took the list out from his pocket. Read it, his finger tracking alongside;

MRS. FISHER, GREENS GATE.

Done.

MRS. CLACTON, NEW MARKET ROAD.

Done.

MRS. KEMP, LOWCROFT LANE.

He looked back at the front door.

Done.

The next one?

MRS. CROSS, WALKER's WAY.

David climbed back on the bicycle. Turned right out of Lowcroft Lane. With the houses to one side, the Common to the other, he followed the road round. Little streets and pathways ran off from it – Lowcroft Lane was one, Walker's Way another. Some had more houses down them, some had none, but led off, instead, into the fields and the woods. (One goes down to the stream where David and Robert sometimes still go to play. The same stream that David and a certain other person will one day use as one of their hiding places, where they play a different sort of game. But that's getting ahead of things…)

David made a right on to Walker's Way. The list said it was for number two. By the gate – which was already open – David leant the wheels. His knuckles grazed against the wall. He winced. "Aaah!" Looked down at his hand. Red lines scratched into the skin – it reminded him of… well… he tried not to think about it. He pressed it into his apron, then grabbed the next parcel.

A man answered this one. "Yes? What can I do for you, son?"

"I'm from Jenkins', sir – I've come with your order."

"Oh." He suddenly grinned. "Hand it over, then."

David thrust it out, like he couldn't wait to get rid of it.

"Thanks very much." He moved off the doorstep; another quick grin. "Well, cheerio, young fella."

The last two deliveries were even closer together, addressed to two of the little terraces that look out across the Common. In fact, their addresses *were* THE COMMON: one was number twenty-six; the other, number forty. David started by going to number forty (because then when he went to twenty-six, he would be heading in the right direction, back towards the shop). Below the four and the zero was a brass doorknocker. It caught the sunlight. David rat-a-tap-tapped, lightly at first, then he did it twice more, stronger. It was like arriving at the butcher's all over again, that sound beating out. Either side of the door were windows, tall, slim. Something flickered in one of them. David stepped back as the door was opened.

A lady looked down at him, a pinny tied to her waist, her hands feeling around inside it. "Yes, love?"

He held up the package, then said, "I've got your delivery, Miss – from Jenkins'."

"Oh. Marvellous. Thank you." She took it from him. "Tell Mr. Jenkins I'll be in on Friday with the money."

David nodded – that was the first customer to mention money – and she nodded in reply.

"Right, well…" She gestured with the package. "Thanks again."

"Yes." David took the hint; stepped back. "Bye."

"Goodbye."

He turned and went. Heard the door close behind him. He glanced down at his grazed hand, then, walking the bicycle a few paces, swung his right leg over.

Just one more to go.

Over on the green, the kids were still playing (though, were there a few less?). It said twenty-six on the gate as well as on the door. No chance of him getting it wrong. Like the last house, there were windows framing the door. David made a fist and knocked gently on the one to the left. It sounded clear – much better than the dull thud had he done it on the door – and very quickly it was answered.

"Yes, son?" The man sounded rushed, interrupted. His head jerked down, and he glanced uncertainly at David's feet. "What is it?"

"I'm from Jenkins', the butcher's – here's your order, sir."

"Oh, blimey – I'd forgotten about that. You caught me on a wrong 'un today, son." He reached out, met David's outstretched arm. "ta." He stood back, tucking the package under his left arm, then started pushing the door shut. "See you next time," he said.

"Yes. Bye."

And that was that.

David returned to the yard. Pushed open the gate. At first, when he heard the awful, splintery creak, he was afraid he'd knocked it full off its hinges. But, turning around, it looked no different. (Must be used to such treatment, poor thing.) He leant the bicycle against a spare bit of wall, the buckets and bricks toppled where he'd left them.

Mr. Jenkins was in the front, serving a customer. "There you are, Mrs. Dale." He handed her some change, sliding the order along the counter so that it was closer to her.

"Thank you," she said, looking up from her bag and noticing David with a smile.

Mr. Jenkins looked down at him. "This is David – the new addition. Just started today, in fact."

"Oh, right." She picked up whatever-it-was wrapped in the paper. "Nice to meet you."

"And you," said David.

She nodded. Then turned.

"Would you like a hand with the door?"

"Oh. Yes, please."

David was already at her side, his hand grabbing for the handle.

"He's good is this one," she said, looking back at Mr. Jenkins as she stepped out over the doorstep.

The bell rang, the door clattered closed, and Mr. Jenkins gave a short whistle, a four, five-second burst. "Good is this one," he repeated, sniffing. "Not sure about that. What happened, lad?" He pointed at the clock. It was nearly four. "What took you so long? You should have been done by three – half-past at the latest."

"Oh." He'd never said, "Sorry."

"Well – I suppose, now you know the routine, you'll do better tomorrow." Coughed. "Saying that, there's different addresses, so... Can't be doing with you dawdling, eh?"

"No, Mr. Jenkins."

"Oh. By the way – your mother popped in while you were out."

"Did she?" He said it like he was surprised.

"She's a lovely lady, your mother."

David smiled. He couldn't think what else to do (or say) in response. Mr. Jenkins matched it with an equally strange one, before going into the back and fetching something from one of the cupboards.

Keys swung and jangled. Mr. Jenkins locked up. Then came through into the back.

"That's more like it, me lad," he said, patting him on the shoulder.

David's skin tingled, tiny spiders crawling up his arms. He looked down at his work – what once would have been a page full of equations and diagrams or a description of some great historical event was now a mound of wood-shavings, flecked red and dirty, in the middle of the butcher shop floor.

"Just take the dustpan, shovel it up, and drop it in the furnace, here..."

He opened the furnace door, the glass of which was smudged with smoke and soot. A charred, white-grey layer left over. David added the sawdust to it: four dustpan lots.

Mr. Jenkins watched him. "Good," he said, as the last load went in. "That's it for the day, then. A fairly average one, as it goes." He smiled awkwardly; his teeth a browny-yellow colour.

"Right," said David, straightening up.

"And don't you worry – we'll have you trained up before you know it."

David remained where he was, dustpan dangling from one hand, sweeping brush held straight at his side by the other.

"Go on, then. Get yourself home. Bet you sleep well tonight – after a proper day's work." He reached out to take the broom and the dustpan. "And... er... pass on my regards to your mother."

"Yes. I will," David said, turning to go. "Thanks."

"You're welcome, lad. See you in morning. And don't be late."

"No. I won't."

And outside, once he'd dragged the gate shut, David looked up to the changing sky and its first few stars, pulled his coat closer to his chest, and ran every bit of the way home.

***

When David arrived the next day, Mr. Jenkins was emptying a new layer of sawdust over the floor. "Ah..." he gasped. No delay in noticing him this time; no chance to get away. "Just start spreading this out, will you? So, there's an even covering."

Outside, a tap-tap-tapping. It had started to rain. David had timed his walk to work well.

The last bits of wood-shavings dropped out of the beige-stitched sack and Mr. Jenkins moved into the front of the shop. David crouched down and began moving the sawdust with his hands. He hadn't been here at this point the previous day, so he didn't know whether this was the best method, whether it would be Mr. Jenkins' preferred method. But, it was early, just gone seven, and he couldn't at that moment think of any other way of getting it spread. He could hear Mr. Jenkins cutting and slicing; a few thuds falling on the chopping board. Then, suddenly, he was in the doorway again, his knife pointing to the corner where the sweeping brush leant. "Same as yesterday, me lad." Meaning the other floor needs sorting. And no comment on the one he was currently working on. "Let's say this is the first thing you do each morning…" said Mr. Jenkins, doing *his* job, getting things ready to be sold. "Without me even needing to ask." He smirked, then started off with another of his aimless, whistled tunes.

So, David got on with it – once he'd finished putting out the wood-shavings, of course. He took the sweeping brush into the front and made a start, under and between, methodically, in a circuitous route, spanning the room – a brand new pattern no doubt to be repeated day after day. Now and then, he stopped to stretch, wriggled himself ache-less so he could keep going a little longer. He'd look around him too. It seemed smaller than yesterday, the front bit of the shop. David felt bunched in much closer, like Mr. Jenkins and the hanging carcasses loomed larger and wider over him.

The noise of the rain increased. Radio static. The spray slapping and falling down the shop windows as though being thrown from a bucket. A band of drummers playing tirelessly on the metal roof. Pausing his sweeping to watch the scene outside, David saw puddles form on the potholed path; ponds, then lakes, little tributaries joining them together, like veins and arteries linking heart with lung. He stared at the drops of rain filling and increasing them, dozens a second, just from the view through this one steamed-up section of glass.

Then, the sound of scales tipping. Bringing him back to the butcher shop. Reality tipping.

"Perfect," said Mr. Jenkins, removing a sliver of pig and placing it under the glass counter. He added another, identically cut, to be weighed. "Good." Repeated the action: twenty-or-so more, trimmed, measured, all neatly arranged and on display.

David looked at the meat, all chopped and sliced, under the counter. He tried to imagine himself holding the cleaver, it shaking in mid-air, the cold flesh in his hands, spots of red on his skin, wiped on his white shirt; then lowering it, the blade digging in…

He thought he heard thunder, a far-off banging, sky-high gunfire. The war came to mind, if only for a second – the idea of it happening within earshot.

"Looks like a rough one today," Mr. Jenkins sighed. "Might be quiet in here. Still…" Laid something else on the scales. "We do get days like that. Suppose you got to learn about them some time."

Lots to learn, thought David – that's what he keeps being told. But it all looks the same.

"Finished?"

David had stopped sweeping. Not quite because he felt sure he'd completed the job. The task had just slipped his mind, other distractions had swept it right out.

Mr. Jenkins came around from behind the counter. Ran his fingers on the floor. Looked under the cupboards and the workbenches. "Good," he muttered to something at the back of where he was checking. "Good," he said again, standing up. "Much better." Then he looked out the rain-smudged window, the one not curtained off with dead pigs. "Ah, blue sky." He squinted; the brim of his hat bowed with his eyes. "It's a ways away, but not to matter – it'll be here soon enough."

And the butcher was right. Years of experience, presumably. At half-ten, the rain stopped, and sunlight started covering the shop floor.

"Now…" said Mr. Jenkins. "I've been getting things ready for the deliveries…" David had been watching him, wondering who it could be for when there was already more than enough set out under the counter. "So, if you like, you can get on with that now."

David didn't realise there was such a choice. "Really?" he said, standing straighter, away from the counter.

"Might as well get it over with, me lad. And, look, it's stopped chucking it down." As if David hadn't noticed. "So…?"

"Yes, Mr. Jenkins."

There were packets strewn over the worktop. Mr. Jenkins gathered them up. "Only four today." He held out a list.

David took it, glanced at it, just long enough to count four names and addresses, then stuffed it into his pocket.

"You all right with them?" asked the butcher, his head slightly turned to one side.

"Yes. I think so."

"Good." He gave David the pile. "Get to it, then."

David opened the gate first, then went back for the bicycle. Somehow it had found itself surrounded by more stuff. Mr. Jenkins must have heaped it all there last night, after David had gone home. He put the packages into the basket and lifted the thing by its frame, left hand on the handlebars, right underneath the seat. When he got it over, it landed with a little bounce and, as he walked it through the gate, the tyres crunched over the chalky stone.

The first two deliveries were just down the road. Lowhouse Cottage and Grangeway Cottage. Before David knew it, the basket was two packets lighter.

He read the list again. The next was near the orchard. He had to ride through it to get there, right through the thick carpet of soggy, brown leaves. The bicycle tyres struggled. David contemplated getting off and walking it, but he knew that wouldn't make it any easier. It'd be like dragging his feet through stagnant, gloopy water.

Beyond the apple trees, there was a group of cottages, arranged in a semi-circle, the fronts staring out across the wooded rows. The second house was the one he wanted. He looked again at the list. It said:

MRS. POTTER
4, THE ORCHARD
BACON (4 rashers) & SHOULDER of MUTTON

David knocked on the door. Gave it a few seconds.

"Coming!" He could hear someone shouting, somewhere inside. When the door opened, David recognised her immediately. "Oh, hello – again," she said. Wasn't it the one from yesterday? Lowcroft Lane? "I work here." David hadn't asked – but he was glad she'd said it. "Is that their order? Mrs. Potter did mention someone should be calling." She held her hand out. "I should've thought it'd be you."

"Yes. Sorry." David thrust it at her – just like yesterday. "What's your job?" he heard himself asking.

"I look after the chickens."

"Right."

She smiled. "What do they call you, anyway?"

"Me? David."

"Nice to meet you, David – I'm Edith." She pointed at her chest. A silver chain glinted and winked at him.

"Well..." he replied. "I better..." He pointed back behind him at the gate. "I better get the last one delivered."

"Course. See you next time."

"Yes," David said, stumbling slightly; the word stuck to his tongue. "Goodbye."

He made the final delivery, emptied the basket, and, as he was riding back, he noticed the clouds gathering again. In the wind, they pulsed and billowed like a bed sheet caught in the breeze and, very soon, it was raining. But – another fine piece of timing – David got back just as the first drops were landing on his neck.

Mr. Jenkins said he could go straight off and eat his lunch, but David went no further than the doorway and sheltered under the overhang of the roof.

By now it was torrential. The rain ran down the grooves in the corrugated iron, like racing waterfalls... *Last one to the ground's a rotten egg...*

He ate quicker than the day before – didn't much want to stand there watching the puddles forming, filling, spreading. There was no offer of the newspaper this time – though David had been the one to pick it up from the doormat and put it on the back counter where Mr. Jenkins tends to stand – and though he didn't really bother reading it yesterday, he did still sense the smallest twinge of excitement when he got it in his hands, how it felt, the ink almost rubbing off on his fingers. It reminded him of the things which, just a few weeks ago, were perfectly normal, but which now... And it wasn't a wholly unpleasant reminder.

Coming into the shop again, Mr. Jenkins was finishing with a customer. They were proving to be a bit of a rarity on this particular day. "There's your change, my dear," said the butcher. "Two-pence."

"Thank you," said the lady.

David couldn't think who she might be – didn't recognise her from yesterday (unless, of course, she came in while he was out on the bike) or from simply having lived round here all his life. In fact, he was starting to find it rather surprising how many people he didn't actually to recognise.

"See you soon, Mrs. Wright."

No – still nothing, thought David.

Mr. Jenkins gestured to the door. Already, David knew very well what that meant. He darted round the counter and met her as she scrambled with her bags and the door handle.

"Bless you, young man." Then she looked back towards the butcher, "Cheerio now," rearranged her headscarf, and plunged into the wet.

Back behind the counter, Mr. Jenkins set off with more chopping and slicing. For what purpose, David had no idea – they'd had hardly any customers and (from the looks of the rain) weren't likely to have many more; and obviously the deliveries had all been sorted too. Perhaps he was doing it just to give himself something to do. Which – if he was honest – didn't bother David at all.

He leant back against the other worktop and glanced to his left at the blackboard. Began reading down it, the meat and the prices. He'd stared at it for most of the morning, so much so that, probably, he'd know it without needing to look. David closed his eyes. Decided to test that theory.

TODAY's CUTS:
LEG of LAMB, 1s 4d
BEEF STEAK, 1s 3d
CHICKEN, 1s 4d
GAMMON JOINT, 1s
BACON (six rashers), 10d or 2d each rasher
PORK CHOPS (2lbs), 8d
PORK SAUSAGES, 1s 2d per half-dozen.

He opened his eyes again. Checked he was right. He was. But he knew he would be. Because if there's one thing he can do, that's remember things.

Outside, the same backing sound playing on, the lane now a near-river. A cyclist struggling past, bike wheels parting the waves. Inside, the clock hit one. A whole hour since David returned from deliveries and just three very wet people had come through those doors. He straightened himself again, pressed his elbows against the workbench, pushed out a long sigh, realising halfway through that Mr. Jenkins was looking right at him.

"There can be a bit of this – waiting around," he said. "That's just what it's like round here. Quiet." He took a few steps nearer to David. "And, what's more, there's lots of folk that don't need us, you know?"

He's always saying 'us', 'we'…

"They have their own pigs or chickens or ducks."

David looked down at his shoes. Spots of oil marked a vague pattern on the black leather. Earlier on, Mr. Jenkins had got him to use some on the wood-shed door ("It's been stiff and creaking for weeks now – been meaning to get around to it," he said as he handed the oil-can over) and, at first, David got most of it all over his right shoe, instead of the hinges.

"Here we go," Mr. Jenkins said, almost in tune with the ringing bell. "Good afternoon, Mrs. Morris – what can we get you?"

"A towel, for a start," she huffed, shaking her umbrella to one side. "Goodness me – what a day."

"Quite, Mrs. Morris – not one for a walk."

"If only I had the luxury, Mr. Jenkins. The only time I get to *go for a walk* is when I come out shopping."

"Yes, I suppose so."

Then she smiled.

(Hennessey used to smile like that. He'd do it after, say, teaching them the basics of Latin grammar, as if he couldn't even understand why he had to explain it, *Surely it speaks for itself.* "Come on, it's very simple, boys," he'd say. "There's just one letter difference. The present active becomes the present passive by changing the *e* at the end for an *i*. So, *amare*, to love, becomes *amari*, to *be* loved. Understand?" Then that smile.)

"But, the shopping won't get done by itself, will it? Even in this weather."

"No. It won't, Mrs. Morris."

"So. Here I am." She stretched out her sopping arms, sighed: "Right…" Then rummaged in her pocket and discovered her shopping list.

"What can I get you?" Mr. Jenkins leaned to one side of the counter, anticipating her answer.

"Well, sausages…" she began, squinting at the slip of damp paper.

"Four?"

"Yes, please."

Mr. Jenkins picked up half-a-dozen. With a quick twist, he removed two, returned them under the glass, and sat the four that were left on some paper.

All the while, Mrs. Morris gazed intently at what else was on offer, one finger picking at her teeth. "And some ham, too," she said, finally.

"Slices or joint?" asked Mr. Jenkins, already turning to grab his slicing knife.

"Oh, slices – you know me."

"That's right, Mrs. Morris – I do."

Carefully, Mr. Jenkins pushed the blade through the meat. "How many is it? Four again?"

"Yes, thank you."

He wrapped them up with the sausages. "So that'll be one-and-four, please." Because he knew that would be the whole of her order.

She dropped the coins into Mr. Jenkins' waiting hand. The cash register sung them in.

"Lovely," she said, tucking the shopping under her arm, then struggling with her umbrella.

"Can you manage? Let David, here, get the door for you."

He'd expected it that time too, was already halfway round the counter.

"Oh, how kind."

As he pulled it open, spray flung in. Mrs. Morris gasped back into the gusty rain, her umbrella having re-sprung, almost of its own accord, by the expression on her face.

"Goodbye, then," she called above the *splitter-splatter*.

"Cheerio," Mr. Jenkins replied.

And David shut the door.

The butcher rubbed his hands together frantically, like he was cleaning something off them. "Gosh! Feels cold out. Put a few more bits on the fire, will you, me lad?"

"Yes, sir."

David went and got some wood from the tin bucket beside the furnace. It had very nearly burnt itself out; now little more than a bed of lumpy ash. He fed the fresh pieces in. Laid them cross-thread, a bridge-way, so the fire could move and conquer. David watched as the frayed, splintered ends turned golden, then black, the flames slowly climbing higher.

"Didn't really notice it till the door were open," Mr. Jenkins said, when David re-joined him. He looked him up and down – something he'd done a lot today and yesterday. "You not cold, either?"

"A little."

"It's just, well – I'm hardly wasting away here…" He punched himself in the stomach – from the look of it, harder than he'd meant to. "But, you, you're… Surely you feel it more than me?" Back to rubbing his hands.

"I don't know."

"So long as you're not over there, freezing from the inside, without telling me," he said, with a smile that quivered quickly to life, before flattening out again, just as fast.

And still it rained. The shop felt like a gloomy cave, the white walls a murky grey – evening set in early. David folded his arms, tight to his chest. Tapped one foot, a frenetic rhythm, hoping, somehow, it might rush time on.

Bah-da-bah-da-bah-da-boom-bah-da-bah-da-boom…

Bah-da-bah-da-bah-da-boom-bah-da-bah-da-boom…

"Stop that, will you?" Mr. Jenkins hissed.

David smiled, weakly. He didn't think he'd be able to hear it.

"It's really irritating – you banging about over there. The rain's bad enough outside."

"Sorry," David mumbled, a little rattled.

"Good. Fine. Doesn't matter." He sighed, his hands feeling the air for something to do. "You might as well take this lot through there – clean it up and put it away." He bundled up the knives and carving tools. "I can't see us needing them anymore today."

David took them in two handfuls. He imagined dropping them. At least one would end up going through a foot. No sooner would he have started, than he'd be going home with a serious injury. (But, then... Perhaps...) He held them under the running tap. The cold water numbed his hands. The bloodstained rag washed redder with each rinse and the white porcelain of the sink swirled pinky down to the plughole.

In the front, David heard Mr. Jenkins start another of his aimless whistles. *Oh. So, it's all right when you... But when I...* David sighed. Tried to ignore it. But as the tune bended its way into the back, that determination very quickly waned. *Ignore it? How can you, when...? Just listen.* He sighed again.

"You all right in there? What you huffing and puffing about?"

"Nothing," David shouted, scrubbing a blotch of blood from the handle of a carving fork, the metal tapping the sink in off-beats.

"Good." And he started back up with his whistling.

David washed the last utensil. Left it draining with the rest. Wrung out the dishcloth.

The clock showed ten-minutes-to-four when David re-entered the front. Mr. Jenkins stood, arms folded, like he'd been kept waiting. David copied his stance at the other side of the counter, at least attempting to look the part in his just-too-long apron and itchy hat. Mr. Jenkins was no longer whistling. Mercifully, his tune ended abruptly seconds after David re-joined him. Instead, he was making odd muttering sounds through his closed mouth – as if there were a group of people inside, debating and arguing. His lips twitched like they wanted out. He caught David's eye, let out an embarrassed sniff, and the voices stopped.

David yawned.

"So, me lad – did you sleep well last night, after a proper day's work?"

"I guess," he replied.

"You'll soon get used to it. Before you know it, it'll be second nature."

And that – in just two words – was exactly what David feared.

***

The previous night, his mother said something. (Of course, she said quite a few things like, "Pass us those dishes…" or, "Just go help the girls settle…" or, "That fire needs some more stoking…" But, before he went off to bed, there was one other thing, one thing in particular, that she said.)

And it was odd, because she never took much of a direct interest in what used to go on every day at school, not really, not since his first few days. It would always be David having to lead those conversations, telling her about the lessons and the tests, and his teachers and his friends. It was just, there was an ease to her smile – the first time there'd been anything close to it in those last couple of weeks – and her eyes reflected the low light like the moon on water. "I can't tell you how important this is, love," she'd said. "What you're doing – it's helping so, so much." David found it hard to believe that the day he'd just had at the butcher shop was, in any way, helping. But he accepted the hug his mother stretched out for and went upstairs to bed.

And once he was up there, he was sure he could hear her downstairs and… though, maybe he got it wrong… but it really did sound like she was crying.

***

At the end of his first week, Mr. Jenkins handed David an envelope. "There you go," he said. "That's your first lot of earnings."

"Oh. Thank you."

"You're welcome, me lad. The first of many more, I'm sure," he said, wide grin.

David folded the envelope, stuffing it into his back pocket, then started to put his coat on. The week had gradually dried out after Tuesday's non-stop downpour.

"I reckon we'll make a good little team, you and me."

That's not what you said the other day...

"Anyway..." Mr. Jenkins stood, arms crossed against his chest, swaying gently on the spot. "You get that nice and safe, back to your mother..." He pointed at the money. "And give her my regards again, of course."

"Yes, Mr. Jenkins," replied David, buttoning himself up.

"See you bright and early – next week."

"Yes. Bye."

And as he was leaving, David looked down at the floor, just by the back door, and spotted a few wood-shavings he'd missed when sweeping up.

***

The rain returned in time for Monday morning: a quick spring of a shower that spanned the length of David's walk to work. His socks felt drenched and clingy and several ice-cold drops found their way down the back of his neck. When he stepped through the door, for a moment, he felt relieved.

Mr. Jenkins was in the front. Chalk scratched on blackboard. David hung up his coat, grabbed the sweeping brush, and wandered into the shop-room.

"Ah..." The butcher looked round at the clock. "Right on time."

That sudden feeling of relief dwindled and disappeared. David started to sweep. The scraping sound of the brush joined in song with Mr. Jenkins' scribbling chalk.

"Ooops! What am I doing?" he muttered, raising a finger to smudge something out. "That's better." Leant back to take in the whole of the board. "Good." And walking away from it, he bent down to check under where David had just swept. "Marvellous." Then he carried on into the back. "Delivery'll be here soon," he shouted over the water tap he'd started running.

David didn't really need reminding of that, the routines of the butcher shop already second nature – like Mr. Jenkins said they would be.

Darkness crowded at the windows, just a hem of light starting to show over the bare fields. David identified vague shapes – the kerb separating paved path from unmade road; the hedgerow – playful, early-rising sparrows flying in, out, then back again; the leaning bus stop sign he always used to wait at. He remembered standing there, the shops waking up, and thought of how, now, he had switched to the other side, to this side, how very soon there'll be another school boy waiting opposite, listening to the shops and the early morning grunts and groans they make, sniffing chopped flesh on the breeze, perhaps after he, himself, has chopped it. David thought of Robert, their walk yesterday, cut short. All the while, he was sweeping. He focused most on the places he knew Mr. Jenkins would check – under the workbenches and cupboards, along the front of the counter, the side the customer stands at and where they might look down. (Throughout the day, throughout most days, David was often ordered to re-sweep that bit of the shop.) The brush whacked the walls, beat against the skirting boards, and tapped and clattered at the under sides of the furniture. Any second, he imagined Mr. Jenkins calling from the back: *Give that a rest, will you? It's blumming annoying.*

But he seemed in a strange mood, actually. No. Scrap that. He seemed in a *good* mood.

Outside, wheels stuttered over damp cobbles.

"Here he is." Mr. Jenkins swung the back door open. "Come on, me lad," he called, already halfway across the yard.

The abattoir man passed Mr. Jenkins a loaded crate. The butcher grimaced as it landed in his arms. "Got it."

David stepped forward.

"Can you manage?" asked the man stood waiting on the cart, seeing his less bulky frame.

"Yes," he replied. They always said that. David held his arms out, rigid like bridges.

"I'll give you the lightest."

The man lowered it slowly. David took hold. Heavier than he expected, the steel of his bridges creaking.

"You got it, son?"

"Yes." He steadied himself; then headed inside. He could feel his apron pulling at his neck and that fresh meat smell shot straight up his nose.

"Just by the other one," instructed Mr. Jenkins when they crossed at the gate.

His arms aching, David carefully put the crate down – cutting into the blanket of wood-shavings Mr. Jenkins had spread first thing.

"Easy does it, lad." Mr. Jenkins was already bringing in his second load. He set it down next to David's. "That's the last of them." (It's always three boxes – except for Fridays.) Mr. Jenkins began removing the wrapped meat and placing it neatly on the side. David followed his lead. This was becoming a well-rehearsed performance; take the crates from the abattoir man who's come on his abattoir cart; unload the crates; then take them back out so the man can take them away again, ready for next time.

Stepping out into the yard, David heard the horses huff, saw their breath cloud the air, and the man telling them to move on, amid a frenzied splutter of sparrow-song. "Get inside, then." The butcher pushed through the gateway. "Can't dawdle all morning."

They spent the rest of their time, before opening up, tidying the mess the delivery had brought. The meat went in its right place – some was put in the cupboards or the cold room; but most of it went into the front, ready for slicing and chopping as and when the customers asked. Monday was always one of the busier days – that and Fridays and Saturday mornings (they shut at lunchtime every Saturday). Mr. Jenkins had stressed this (like he did with everything else he introduced David to in his first few days) as if it must never be forgotten. And he repeated himself as well – three, four times, over and over. *Yes, right, you've said that twice already…* Mr. Jenkins spoke to him slowly and simply, as though he didn't want to stretch him, as though, if he gave him too much too soon, David was likely to snap at the pressure.

But David was feeling a different kind of pressure pressing down. Something that had to do with *why* he was there. Something that had to do with what lay ahead. And that pressure was gradually increasing. The butcher-word still seemed a very distant echo, coming from the far end of a very long corridor, the blue and white apron still alien and uncomfortable (though the colours did match his old school bus). But the more he watched and listened to his new teacher, the more David knew this was it. He could see certain things being realigned, that his future was gradually repainting itself – and this realisation was a heavy weight, far heavier than any crate the abattoir man could give him.

Mr. Jenkins unlocked the front door. Flipped the sign: CLOSED to OPEN. His lips looked ready to whistle, but, fortunately, nothing came out. He took his place behind the counter, at the opposite end to David, both of them soldiers standing guard: silent, facing forwards, ready for the door to open, the bell to ring, and their orders to be given.

The morning passed with a few bursts of regulars. On this particular Monday, they hunted in packs. And as they came, the sun crept out; the thick, seven o'clock clouds dwindling away to leave a blue as blue as David's blue eyes.

"Sausages, please, Mr. Jenkins," pointed Mrs. Davies, her shopping bag held up to her chest.

Mrs. White and another lady David still couldn't name waited behind her, craning round, every now and then, to see what was on offer.

"Certainly. How many?" Mr. Jenkins asked, with a smile that already knew the answer.

"Four, please."

One of the others tutted, then coughed. Mrs. Davies glanced back.

"That's four-and-half-pence." Mr. Jenkins moved the pale, fat fingers of meat, and the paper they rested on, off the scales. "Anything else?"

"Actually, put two more in there, would you?" She glanced behind her again. "My husband deserves a treat once in a while."

"Course, Mrs. Davies." Adding two more, Mr. Jenkins moved them back to weigh. "That's seven-pence now." He laid them on the counter. "Is that all, then?"

"Yes – for today," she replied, rooting through her purse. (She's usually in a few times during the week.)

Mr. Jenkins folded the paper round the sausages, trapping them in. He wiped a hand on his apron, holding the package out in the other.

"Here you go – seven-pence."

They exchanged handfuls.

"Much obliged." Mr. Jenkins turned to the register. Poked at it. It opened, and he dropped in the coins.

The butcher shop sells to a mixture of people. They're those that live nearby because it's where they were born. And where they'll die. Then they're those that have moved to the area because they made plenty elsewhere and want to live out where there's birdsong and sky and less brick, less smoke. So, some of the ladies that come through the door aren't merely the wives of farm-hands and shopkeepers; they're the kitchen maids of city lawyers and retired industrialists whose houses, with their Roman-pillar facades, scatter the city roads.

Mrs. White rested her bag on the counter. "Good morning," Mr. Jenkins said through a sudden grin.

The bell rang, and the door clattered closed. David watched Mrs. Davies' shadow bounce away.

"And what can I get you, Mrs. White?"

She took a while in answering. Ummed. Aahhed. Checked her list. David wondered why she hadn't done all this whilst waiting in the queue. "Do you have pork chops today?" she asked.

"We do, Mrs. White."

They always do. What a silly question.

"Lovely. Two, please."

"Right away." Mr. Jenkins reached under the counter. He slid the pork chops on to another piece of paper. Rested them on the scales, stepping back to read the dial. "That's one-and-four."

"And a bit of steak?"

"Certainly," he said, already wrapping the pork chops.

David could see the steak slices under the glass counter. Mrs. White's eyes lingered on them too. Mr. Jenkins reached in for them, a new piece of paper ready, spread out. He carried them across to be weighed. The gauge wavered – two-and-eight, no, three pounds – then settled.

"So, with the chops, that's two-and-five, Mrs. White."

She paid with a half-a-crown.

"Thank you."

David watched him at the till.

"One penny change." He dropped it into her right palm. "Much obliged."

"Thank you, Mr. Jenkins," she said, finding a place for it in her purse. She moved aside, and the third lady approached.

"And what can I get *you*, Mrs. Donald?"

That was it. Mr. Jenkins had told him about her. She works at Trinity Hall for the Grey family. She looked to have a long list. (Then again, Mr. Jenkins had also said that most of what they eat there – in terms of meat – would be what they farm themselves, not to mention the game they trap and shoot.)

"Three shoulders of mutton, please."

Mr. Jenkins turned to David. "Cold room," he said.

David rushed off into the back.

"What else, my dear…?" He heard Mr. Jenkins continuing the order.

David didn't enjoy going into the cold room. The bodies hung from the ceiling, red raindrops spattering the stone floor. He imagined the door closing behind him and not being able to push it open again. He wedged it ajar with a chair – the only way, also, to keep the light in. At least things were stored in some kind of order. He knew where to look. It had been another part of David's introductory tour round the butcher shop. (*This is where the beef is… and the pork, here… then this is where I keep the fowl – you know, chicken, duck, goose… game birds go here, next to the rabbits… and lamb and mutton over on this shelf…*) Two racks of shelving ran the length of each side wall and held the smaller, chopped-up bits. The lamb and the mutton: they were to the left, second shelf, far corner. Like all the cut-offs, the mutton was wrapped in several layers of paper and tied with string. He took one. Undid the knot, peeling back the paper, just to check he'd got the right animal. Except, looking at it, he knew he wouldn't be able to tell the difference between this or any other meat; it was a sort of reddy-brown colour (and weren't they all?). He folded the paper round it again, re-tied the string, and grabbed two more.

There were four packets already waiting on the counter.

"Ah – thank you, son," said Mr. Jenkins, taking them from him. "Is that everything now, Mrs. Donald?" He placed one on the scales.

"Yes, Mr. Jenkins."

"Right." He looked at his fingers for a moment. "Six-bob, please."

"Thank you," she said, dropping six shilling coins into the butcher's hand. She then proceeded to take one paper-parcel at a time off the counter.

"You all right there?" asked Mr. Jenkins, turning from the cash register.

"Yes – quite fine, thank you." The cotton bag seemingly stronger and roomier than it looked. She slotted the last thing inside.

"All finished?"

"Yes. Thank you – again."

"A pleasure."

"Goodbye, Mr. Jenkins." She smiled David's way too and the bell sang her out.

"Now there's a tidy profit, eh?" Mr. Jenkins grinned, his hands feeling around his apron. "You remember her from last week, don't you? She spent about the same amount. Only the best stuff for their lordships."

"Is that what they are?" asked David.

"Oh. No." He laughed. "Not far off, though – Mr. Grey used to sit in Parliament. So, it might not be long before they make him an actual Lord. Seems to be the way them things go."

Sunlight flooded the shop floor. David could see bits of muck and dust he hadn't swept up. Hoped Mr. Jenkins couldn't.

"I'll make a start on the deliveries, I think," he said. Then, eyeing the front as well: "Just give the floor a bit of a brush, will you?"

David did it to the beat of the blade. There wasn't much to find down there, just a few specks, some blown-in leaves, but he made the job last.

***

Wednesday afternoon. Delivery time. David's schedule ran the same as last week. He'd started by going to the house out at Greystone's Field. Then, he cycled on to Cave Lane. In fact, there were two deliveries down that way. Then the fourth was by the old cemetery, the eerie sound of the crows and jackdaws keeping him company, followed by Greens Cottage – he'd just that minute pedalled back up the hill.

And now...

David's legs were tiring. He struggled into the wind, the lane filling with fallen leaves. Some caught in the wheel-spokes, stuck like wet paper. Just one more package left to do. David crossed the little humpback bridge – which itself crossed the stream, which itself went on to cross the fields – into the Common. Schoolchildren were finishing their day, fresh puddles to explore. Already, some had spotted legs. Others noticed David on the bike, skipped and ran alongside him, faces beaming. A pair of lads weaved between the walking groups – the chaser and the chased. And there were girls who had taken their bonnets off, watching as the ribbon trailed the ground. "Watch it!" shouted one of the mothers, as her daughter nearly swished it through the mucky rainwater.

With daylight fading, David turned on to Lowcroft Lane. Each cottage had its own unique shape and arrangement. Number seven was a squat little place, the garden clotted, knotted, full and unruly. He put the bicycle against the wall, lifting out the packet with the kind of care he used to take over his schoolbooks. The gate gave a squeak{ a prelude to his knock on the door.

A woman answered. Though she was a step above him, David gazed down at her. Her dark, greying hair was bunched tightly in a bun and she wore a tiny, white apron round her waist. Across it, there was a stain. The colour very nearly matched her hazel eyes.

David spoke first. "Oh. Hello, Mrs. Kemp."

"Hello, young man." And, spotting what he held, she flung out a hand. "Is that for us?"

"Yes." David passed it over. (On Wednesdays, they get half-a-dozen sausages and half-a-dozen rashers of bacon. Last Saturday morning, he delivered them a joint of beef.)

"Thank you, my dear – are you new?"

He nodded. This was the first time he'd met Mrs. Kemp herself.

"Thought so," she said. "Take it you live round here?"

He nodded again. "Just up past Nevis Farm."

"Oh. My daughter works near there, at the orchard. In fact, she's there now. Although – I thought she might have finished by now." David saw her glance towards the top of the road, as if saying it, questioning it, would cause her to appear there and then. "Anyway – thank you again, young man." She gestured with the delivery, gave it a little mid-air shake like it was a mystery gift ready to be opened, and stepped back from the threshold.

"Goodbye," David had time to say, before she disappeared behind the shut door.

As he got back on the bicycle, and out on to the main road, he passed the village hall. The doors were barred, the windows black. In the dim light, he could make out the clock above the entrance. It was approaching four. He'd started the deliveries slightly later today. The shop had been busier, first thing in the afternoon, so Mr. Jenkins sent him out about half-two. "Should be back just in time for the rush at closing," he'd said.

The fields passed in a dusky blur, anything a few feet away cast unrecognisable. Some of the potholes took David by surprise and he could hear the tyres slushing through the puddles, feel them splashing his trousers, with no time to avoid them. He knew his mother wouldn't be pleased. *Look at these*, she'd say. *And you need three more days out of them*.

The sound of footsteps up ahead. David had been paying such close attention to the road (at least, the little he could see of it) and to his steering (after, two or three times, jolting over the potholes) that he hadn't realised there was someone coming his way. He looked up. Now they were just a few pedals apart.

"Hello, David." It was Edith.

"Oh. Hello." He slowed down.

"Going home?" she asked.

"Not yet. Just finished delivering."

"Oh, have you just been to ours?"

David nodded. Pointed behind him. "I've just left."

"I've been working too," she said. "Mr. and Mrs. Potter got me helping them in the orchard – after I'd seen to the chickens. We made *seven* huge mounds of leaves." Edith stretched out her arms; grinned. "But it took ages." She glanced up at the sky above them, the rainy-grey clouds still visible against the swelling, bluey darkness.

David heard the clock in the village call the hour.

Evidently, Edith did too. She made to go. "Good to see you," she smiled.

"Yes." David paused. "You too," he managed.

And then she was walking on; and David got pedalling again. He looked behind, every now and then – saw her getting further away, until... there was no one left to see. And then he was turning the corner, the light from the shop windows spilling across the lane in a hazy glow. He was going down the alleyway. Wobbling across the cobbles. Nudging the gate open with the front tyre. Getting off the bicycle. Leaving it to rest. Then stepping inside...

***

A strange thing had started happening. David was beginning to feel restless. Because while he wasn't out delivering, all he seemed to be doing in the shop – besides sweeping and helping customers out the door – was watching. On his first day, that's exactly what he was told to do. "Watch me, lad – then you'll know your way round things."

But, since then, that instruction hadn't changed.

It was Friday. David had delivered early; the afternoon now spread out before him. In came Mrs. Barrat. She wore a rose-red shawl to keep the wind out, which, as she settled herself at the counter, she unravelled to speak.

"Good afternoon," she said – a response to Mr. Jenkins' greeting.

"And what are you after today?"

"Half-a-dozen sausages, please," she began.

Mr. Jenkins set to it. Those that had been prepared before opening had all been sold, and he hadn't got around to doing any more over lunch, so he started on some fresh. There was pig mince ready and waiting. Mr. Jenkins put a couple of handfuls into a metal dish. The device that made the sausages was at one end of the worktop. From one side, it looked like the sort of clamp you'd find in a wood yard: gripping the desk, nuts and bolts, a long, curved handle. And the other end resembled a spout, pointing straight out. Mr. Jenkins went to that side first. He fed the sausage skins – which were made from pig intestine (a fact Mr. Jenkins only revealed after he'd suggested David "See how they feel") – over it. Then he went back to the mince. At the top of the contraption was a square-shaped trough. Into it, Mr. Jenkins tipped the meat out of the dish. With one hand he held the sausage casing still. With his other, he began to turn the handle and the mince was pushed from the trough, through the spout, and into the skins like thick, pinky rope. The last thing to do was tie them in a knot; Mr. Jenkins spun them in front of him, the long coil quickly shortening. Then he slammed them on to the workbench – two bunches of three, half-a-dozen – got some paper, and wrapped them up.

"Anything else, Mrs. Barrat?"

"Just two steak, please."

"Rightio." Mr. Jenkins crossed to David's side of the counter. This time, rather than pounce on it, the butcher's hand wavered. It was perhaps just a few seconds, but David – because he was looking right at the five or six wet, red chunks – felt tempted to point them out. But he didn't. He kept quiet. Because it would have been like interrupting. Last week, he was told to watch. And that *still* hadn't changed.

Besides, after a few seconds, Mr. Jenkins spotted the steak. Carried on with the order.

And that was all David did. He watched. Then and for the rest of the afternoon. Because, what else had he been told to do?

And as he watched, he was trying, too, to find his place amongst the fleshy stench in the air... the dangling blades lined along the walls... and everything in between. Yes, he may have been wearing an apron, the hat may have sat wonky on his head, but what did that mean, really? And he knew it had only been two weeks – but would his responsibilities reach no further than sweeping the floor... washing the knives in the sink... getting sent off on the bike? Not that he could already see himself doing the butcher-thing, the chopping, the slicing, but... He'd lost school for this. For that, he wanted more than a bicycle to sit on and a bit of floor to stand on.

David followed the second-hand round the clock. Four-toc, three-toc, two-toc... Five o'clock. Closing time. Mr. Jenkins swung his bunch of keys by one finger and headed to the door. He locked up. Spun the OPEN-and-CLOSED sign from one to the other. David had already cleaned and dried the cutting utensils – the cleavers, bone-cutters and carving knives; the sawdust was already swept and dumped in the cooled-off furnace, ready to be used up tomorrow morning.

"You might as well get off, me lad," Mr. Jenkins said, looking off to the side.

"Right," David replied, forcing a smile. He went to get his coat. "Mr. Jenkins...?"

"Yes, son." Now he was knelt at one of the cupboards, rooting around inside.

"I just wondered..." He began hesitantly, unsure of his words. "I wondered how long I'll just be watching you."

"Oh, yes."

"I mean, I know there's still lots to see, lots to learn, but..."

"You want to start getting your hands dirty," he smirked.

That's not quite...

"Do you think you're ready?" Mr. Jenkins got up off the floor. David shrugged. He was starting to regret mentioning it.

"You get going, me lad. Have a sleep." Then, with a look David really didn't like: "We'll see what we can get you doing tomorrow, eh?"

Outside, the light breeze drifted through David's slick-straight hair. Normally, he would run home – that's what he did every day last week – but his feet felt heavy, like dead weights. And his head felt just the same. Uncertain. Foggy.

A bus went past. David saw its headlights first, getting brighter behind him, casting all sorts of shadowy shapes ahead; then he heard it, rattling over the unmade, stony road. When he was at school, David had wanted to absorb everything, to learn all that it is possible to learn. Only, that never seemed to include the intricacies of a rural butcher shop. Because, why would he have needed to know about that? But that was then. Now, he does need to know. Now, it seems, that's *all* he needs to know.

Walking home in the failing light, there was still a part of him that wanted out, a part of him that, when it saw that bus, wanted to go back, to jump on board and return. But, at the same time, he knew this re-routing was inevitable – necessary, even, if he and his mother and his sisters were to manage without... David was not a Grammar School boy anymore. He was the butcher's boy. He no longer wore his red and black uniform; he put on a blue and white apron instead. And, tomorrow, he might just get the chance to act the part too.

Fairytales

David walks away from the butcher shop, a third pay packet crumpled in his jacket for his mother to take and use on whatever it is the money pays for. In the quiet, lonely dusk, his footsteps remind him of a ticking clock. They echo and reverberate, timing his journey home.

"And how was your day?" his mother asks him, from the kitchen, once he's in and hung his coat up.

"Fine," he replies – his answers rarely more illuminating.

Josie jumps into the room from four stairs up. The chipped ornaments over the fireplace rattle.

David holds out the envelope Mr. Jenkins gave him.

"Lovely." Big, broad smile.

"What's that?" Josie questions.

Esther steps past David. At the fancy cabinet, she opens a drawer and slides the packet inside. "It's just what we needed, love," she answers Josie. Going back towards the kitchen, she stops, momentarily, to kiss David dryly on the cheek.

"Are you coming upstairs to play?" Josie turns to her brother.

"Not tonight." David sinks into the armchair.

"You always say that."

"Well, sorry – I'm tired."

"There's not time for it now, anyway," their mother calls from the kitchen. "Tea's nearly ready. Josie – go bring Lily down." She comes to the doorway, looks down at her son slumped in the chair. "I can see you've just settled, love, but the table needs setting."

David pushes himself to his feet; a huff and a sigh as reply. He gets the white tablecloth from another of the cabinet's drawers. Whips off the thick-woollen one that stays on the table when they're not eating off it and spreads the white carefully, patting down the creases. From the kitchen, he brings through the cutlery and placemats. Four sets. He lays them out as straight and symmetrical as he can make them. The corkboard placemats first – one for his mother and one for himself, one for Josie and one for Lily – then the knives and the forks, some of which, at the right angle, catch the light from the oil lamps. Each mat has the same image covering them. They depict a harvest. Pale, pastel shades of green and golden-brown. Women in long, plain dresses. The farmer, fingers in his beard, stood on top of the slatted cart as it's loaded full.

The girls come downstairs, Josie helping Lily and her little legs.

Another shout from the kitchen: "Can you lend us a hand, David?"

He wanders in, picking up the dish pointed out to him. Ripped up lettuce leaves.

"That one as well, please." She says it without even looking – must know instinctively that David scooped up just the one dish.

In this second, smaller bowl is sliced tomato. His mother carries cucumber and chopped carrot. She'd already taken through a plate of buttered bread.

The girls sit in their usual places. Lily sways in her high-cushioned chair. It's the only one with arms and it's tucked in tight under the table, so she's no escape. Josie will have lifted her into it – she normally does, she enjoys doing that, even when Lily's all arms flailing, resistant, tantrum tears, because she'd rather stay upstairs playing.

They mostly eat in silence. Next-door-but-one's dog barks so clear it could be in the room. Maybe it knows they're eating.

"There's not a window open, is there?"

David looks round, leans over his plate to see into the kitchen. "Doesn't look like it." But he suddenly feels a chill lick his neck; starts thinking there is one open after all.

"Will you read to us, David?" Josie asks, once everything's been washed and put away.

He checks the time. "I suppose." He half-smiles and gestures to the stairs. "Come on."

"Straight to bed after that, you two."

"Yes, Mum," replies Josie.

In the bedroom, she flings David a scuffed hardback.

"Which one tonight?"

Looking over his shoulder, the contents page open, Josie nibbles a finger, deciding. "That one."

"Rose-Bud?"

She nods. Wide smile. "Yes, please."

"Lily?"

She's nodding too, already was before he turned to her. "Ose-Bub," she tries.

They shuffle next to David on the bed, one either side. He wants to help Lily, holds out a hand, but she won't let him. Still, she happily uses his arm as a pillow; he feels her head pressing into his elbow, burrowing in snugly.

"Ready?"

"Ready," says Josie, contented sigh as she settles her chin on his knee.

David starts to read: "Once upon a time there lived a king and queen…"

Downstairs, he can hear his mother switching tablecloths and straightening chairs. The dog gave up a while back, thankfully.

"The queen had a little girl that was so very beautiful that the king could not cease looking on it for joy, and determined to hold a great feast…"

This is one he's read them several times now. They got his father to read it to them too, over and over. He remembers being read to from this book as well, when he was their age. He always thinks of that when he's up here with his sisters. He would stare out from beneath his bed-sheets at the fading green of the cover, half his father's head obscured. And his voice, normally so serious and level, would charge with energy in the same way it did when he used to tell David about his day at the docks. It was something he often said – "I may not know much, but at least I can read to you. At least I can give you that." So maybe, in doing this, in copying his father like this, he was *giving* something to his sisters. Giving back a little of what he'd been given and what they are now missing.

"Are they asleep, then?"

"Just about." David sits back in the armchair, facing his mother. She's patching a sock, a slightly paler black filling in the worn-through gap.

"I don't know how you put holes in these so fast."

"Mum?"

"Yes."

In the window, David catches a glimpse of the moon, one bite missing. He gets up to draw the curtains.

"Oh, thanks, love – forgot about them."

"It's fine. Mum – you know when we saw Mr. Greening yesterday and he said talk about it? Well, we still haven't talked about it."

"What's there to talk about?" She looks back at the sock and the needle and thread.

"But, I thought…"

"You've already got a position, full-time, so what do you need something else for?"

"He said this one'll be well paid."

"Not to start with, it won't. And, what's it matter? We're doing all right as things are. And the way you're going, you're likely to start earning more in the future. Aren't you?"

"I guess." (Mr. Jenkins had said that… "You'll be on full pay before you know it, me lad…" when they were talking the other day.)

His mother moves on to another sock.

David yawns – just the thought of the butcher shop makes him tired. "I'm going to bed," he says, standing, stretching.

"Good idea, love."

He bends down, kisses her forehead, her hair parted perfectly, then he heads upstairs. The first step groans like a falling tree.

"David?"

He stops.

"You do understand that this is the best thing; for me, for the girls, *and* for you, too? I honestly can't see any other way." She sniffs. "As good as Mr. Greening's offer is, we've got to stick with what we've got. What if this architect office job falls through? How can we stop a thing like that happening? You see? It's better this way."

David nods. She might be right. When she puts it like that.

His mother holds the half-mended sock up to the light, checking the stitching. "Anyway – night-night."

"Night, Mum." Going up, each step after the first groans too, a whole forest floored by the time David's reached the landing.

In the Snow and By the Stream

Another Sunday. David watches the clock. At around ten, the garden gate clatters into the hedge.

"Robert's here, Mum." David opens the door, leaps across the doorstep, shouting behind him: "Bye!"

Heavy snow fell this winter. Everything wiped white. The empty fields and the bare, black trees, the rough-tiled rooftops and chimneystacks – all covered over. Piles of the stuff at the side of the lane. Long, white corridors.

Still. It looks set for a clear day: the sky a pale orange; slim, wispy clouds drifting here, then there. This has become their new habit. Every Sunday. This.

"William and Michael keep saying they want to come," says Robert. "But their Mum's won't let them."

"Right."

It is a long way from here into the town.

They walk slowly. David scoops up chunks of snow with his shoe, tipping each load to one side, like his feet are spades and he's got something to uncover.

"So, what've you done this week?"

"Nothing. The usual."

"What's the usual, then?"

David sighs. "You want to know what an average day's like?"

Robert smiles. Nods.

"Well. I get there first thing, about half-seven, and I take my coat off, hang it up…" David opts to go into the greatest possible detail. Maybe then Robert will see just how dull it really is. "I pick up the sweeping brush, then I go into the front, where the counter is and where the customers come in, and I sweep the floor in there. Mr. Jenkins comes to check it and normally tells me I need to re-sweep some of it, like under one of the cupboards or something. Then, on Mondays, Wednesdays and Fridays, the delivery man comes from the abattoir and we put all the stuff away – some of it goes in the front or stays in the back and the rest of it goes into the cold room. After that we get things ready for opening up. Get stuff weighed. Write the prices on the chalkboard. Mr. Jenkins slices bits of ham and pork, cuts the steak, does the sausages, that sort of thing..."

"Don't you get to do any of that?" Robert interrupts.

"You what?" David looks up, takes his eyes away from the snow passing under his feet.

"Do you get to chop things up?"

"Well, yes – I did this week. But that was the first time, so..."

"What was it like?"

David scratches his left ear. "It was..." The truth? Can he come completely clean? "It was strange."

"What do you mean?"

"I mean..." He hadn't even been this honest with his mother. Gradually, even that is getting more difficult. "I'm not sure I liked it, really." His skin tingles. Perhaps it's the cold. Or perhaps it's something else.

"Why not?"

"Because... I don't know." David gives up explaining. He can't really explain it to himself, so putting this vague feeling into words so that someone else can understand...

Footsteps fill the gap.

Then Robert continues: "What's Mr. Jenkins like?"

"Well – he's strange, too."

Robert laughs. "Why's that?"

David sniggers too – can't help it once Robert's started. "He just is. You never know what mood he's going to be in."

"Sounds like you." Robert's still giggling.

They get as far as the stream. David expected it to have frozen over, but the water gushes frantically across and down the dip in the rocks. Robert finds a stone in the snow. Turns it over. Brushes off the slush to see the simple, grey markings. Nothing too striking, not one for the collection; he slings it into the stream. David watches it bounce against a raised bit of the bank, then get taken and carried a few yards downstream.

"Thompson's calmed down a bit, you know?" says Robert.

"Has he?"

"He's still like he always was – itching to finish things first and get the best marks, that kind of thing, but – I don't know – he doesn't go on about it like he used to."

David nods, staring down at his feet. He can hardly remember what Thompson looked like – no, what Thompson *looks* like.

"No, it sounds good at the butcher's…"

David turns to face him.

"It does." Robert reads David's less-than-convinced expression. "I wish I was earning money instead of sat in lessons all day."

David sighs, almost wants to laugh again. "And I wish I was sat in lessons all day, rather than earning money." He shakes his head at the white-over ground. "Want to swap?"

"But, think about it – you get a head start on all of us. And you never really needed school anyway – you were always far too clever for it."

"But I miss it."

Robert nods. "I wish you were still there as well. But I bet before you know it you'll be running your own shop and then I'll come in and ask you for a job and you'll give me one just so you can boss me around."

"That does sound quite fun," David admits.

At the other side of the water, a shelf of snow shunts forward, dropping into the stream.

"Are you going to try and chop something up next week, then?"

"I think I'll probably have to," says David.

"Good. Then you can tell me what it feels like." They swap smirks. Robert draws a circle with his right foot: then suddenly straightens up, flash of inspiration; "Oh. How big are the knives you use?"

"Erm…" David gives his best guess, using his hands to show the width, then height, of one of the meat cleavers.

Robert looks impressed. "I still haven't asked my mum whether she'll start using your shop. The other one's just a bit nearer to us. But she goes on Saturdays sometimes – so if she says yes, I could come with her and see you."

"Yes. Suppose." David feels a little embarrassed at the idea.

"But, then, I could just come down anyway – couldn't I?"

"Well. Except, Mr. Jenkins might not like you coming in just to see me and then not buying anything." David tugs at his scarf, glances behind him at the holes their footsteps left.

If Mr. Jenkins is in one of his moods, well – it wouldn't take much to make it worse. And that's the last thing David wants...

Rations

David steadies the cleaver. Not quite as heavy as it used to be. Tight grip round the handle. He wonders, briefly, how sharp it actually is. The sort of question Robert would have. If he followed the curve of the blade with his fingers – barely touching it, just the slightest contact – how badly would it break the skin?

"Go on, then," Mr. Jenkins prompts him. A nudge on the opposite elbow.

David drops his wrist.

"That's the way, me lad."

Mr. Jenkins grabs one of David's shoulders, squeezing it. David pulls away and sets the knife down. Three steak cuts pile limply like a half-built staircase. Pink splodges spatter the workbench, his apron.

"Now – didn't that feel better?"

David nods (out of habit, if anything) glancing at the resting blade, then at the sawdust beneath his feet, the stone floor peeping out.

"You're getting the hang of it now." The butcher smiles. He sounded satisfied, genuine.

"Shall I finish in there?"

"Yes. Good lad."

David goes into the shop and picks up the sweeping brush he'd left propped up by the front door. He squints through the window, past the OPEN-CLOSED sign and condensation. Most of the snow has melted, about four weeks after it first came down. (And the snow showers continued, intermittently, for the following fortnight.) He watches some children passing, on route to little school, their scarves waving in the breeze. Mr. Jenkins starts slicing again and David remembers the job in hand, the sweeping brush in both his hands...

"Are we done yet?" Mr. Jenkins wanders in, pieces of steak concertinaed on the wooden board. He starts setting up the display. Brings stuff out from the cold room. Chops some more in the back. The letterbox clatters and the newspaper lands open on the doormat. Mr. Jenkins goes to collect it. "Don't worry," he says, bending down. "I won't look at it for too long – I know you'll want your turn as well." He chucks it on the sideboard. "Right. Let's check this floor…" The butcher crouches, knees flexed, his left-hand skimming under one of the cupboards. He brings it back out. Holds the palm flat. Takes a long look. Feels with his other hand. "Good." Moving to the next place he wants to check. "Then we can get the blackboard sorted and open up," he says, commentary mapping out their day. "Just go back under that one, will you? Right into the corner." Mr. Jenkins points at the workbench he normally stands at. "Then that's it for this morning."

David does it. Sweeps a few more bits out.

"Fine. Good job." Mr. Jenkins nods at them collected on the floor.

David knocks it all on to the dustpan, carrying it carefully to the bin in the back room.

"While you're through there, lad…" Mr. Jenkins waves a worn-down lump of chalk. "Grab that chair and we'll get these prices done."

The first flurry of customers ends. Mrs. Butterfield ambles off and David stares at what's left: the empty pavement, the quiet lane.

With a sigh, Mr. Jenkins picks up the newspaper. He holds the front page at eye-level, his pupils zigzagging it. "Never good news," he mutters. Sighs again, his breath catching the top left corner of the paper. "Oh…" He suddenly, briefly, puts it down; starts prodding the air with an index finger. "Just check the floor round by the counter's still nice and clean, eh?"

"Yes, Mr. Jenkins."

Not much needs doing, but David takes his time anyway – that way he looks extra thorough.

"Marvellous, son," says Mr. Jenkins, after David's put the broom in the back and come out again. "Here…" He holds the newspaper in front of him. "There you are."

David takes it. "Thanks." Leans on the workbench, reading his way slowly down the first page. Mr. Jenkins was right; most of it isn't good news. Another trawler's gone missing out in Arctic seas. A local man has been found guilty of fraud, forgery and theft – one other, forty-three, found dead as a result. Several obituaries; funeral notices.

Then there's the war.

Like every other day, it makes up most of the print. Though, it seems very little has actually happened so far. Today, the main report is about the Belgian army preparing themselves for invasion. Sounds familiar. First, Austria. Then, The Sudetenland. Czechoslovakia. Poland. Now, Belgium.

For the last few weeks, David's been adding to his notebook again. Mr. Jenkins lets him take the newspaper home – though he hides it from his mother, smuggling it upstairs, and looks at it there, on his bed whenever the girls aren't around.

The door handle turns. The hinges creak. David looks up; the shop bell shaking, chiming. He folds the paper in half. Puts it neatly, softly, on the worktop.

"Good morning, Mrs. Davies – how can we help you?"

He'd started saying "we" and "us" much more in front of the customers.

"I'll have half-a-dozen rashers of bacon, please."

"Certainly." Mr. Jenkins reaches under the glass counter; finds the pink, ear-shaped bits of meat, dropping them with his right hand on to the piece of paper balanced in his left. He lays them on the scales. Checks he's got six – not more, not less. Then looks at the numbers. "That's fine, my love – anything else?"

"And a tin of corned beef, Mr. Jenkins." She points to the line of yellow and red cans at David's side of the counter. He passes one across.

"Altogether, that'll be two-bob, please. David? Would you deal with the book?"

Mrs. Davies pays Mr. Jenkins. Then she puts some stapled-together sheets of paper on the counter-top. On the front, in black capitals: RATION BOOK. David finds a pencil. Marks down the amounts.

"There you are, Mrs. Davies," he says, sliding it back and smiling, his eyes focused on the book and her hands, rather than her face.

"Thank you, love." Putting it away.

Mr. Jenkins slams the register shut. "And that's your bacon, Mrs. Davies."

"Lovely." She puts that in her bag too, then the corned beef can. "Cheerio." Turns to leave, opening the door and slipping, momentarily, on the slush outside.

The ration books are new. The government issued them a few weeks ago, one for every household. The idea being that, because it's harder now to get things into the country, and because so much of what's made and grown is needed by those that have signed up to fight, there has to be a limit on how much people can have, so that nothing runs out. At the moment, the restrictions only include bacon, butter, sugar, and people are allowed a certain amount – four ounces of ham or bacon each week – and it gets recorded in their books. (Which, very quickly, became David's job.) Mr. Jenkins looked one over. Scratched his forehead. Ruffled his hair. Then shoved it across to David, saying: "You deal with that, lad." Now, the customers instinctively pass it to him and he pencils in what they've just bought, so they don't get any more than they're entitled to.

The shop bell rings again. Mrs. Green comes in.

"Good morning," says Mr. Jenkins. "What'll it be this time?"

She asks for ham joints, passing David her book. He scribbles in the numbers – that's her done for the week.

"Anything else?"

"No, thank you." She puts the ham in her bag. "That's me for now." Turns towards the door. "Ta-ta."

"Yes. Bye for now."

She'll be back later in the week, no doubt, for her regular cut of beef. David reaches for the newspaper, looking up at the clock: nearly lunchtime.

"You getting the knack of that, lad?" Mr. Jenkins asks.

"Sorry?" He puts the paper back down.

"The ration books – you following them?"

"Oh. I suppose."

"You suppose?"

"Well – it's simple enough, really."

"Oh. Good." Mr. Jenkins turns his hands to the resting knife laid next to him on the side. He picks it up, runs it through his apron, then lifts it, tilting it in the light, before placing it again on the workbench.

David returns from doing the deliveries. He kicks the packed-in snow from the soles of his shoes, then steps inside, hanging up his coat.

"All right out there?" Mr. Jenkins shouts through from the front.

"Fine, thanks." (Though there had been a few hairy moments going down the hill to Greens Gate when it was that skiddy he thought he might end up over the handlebars.) David straightens his apron, his hat, and goes into the shop. "Been busy?" he asks.

"Not too bad," says the butcher. "And – eh – I did a few ration books myself, you know?"

"Right. Good." David *had* wondered how he managed when he was out on the bicycle.

The clock chimes the quarter-hour. Fifteen minutes to four. The display under the glass counter largely empty, some of the plates already heaped up on the side.

"Shall I make a start on these?"

"Oh. Yes, please, lad."

David takes them into the back. Runs the kettle under the tap, then puts it on the stove.

"Is there not any left?" Mr. Jenkins stands in the doorway. "I didn't think I used it all." He holds up his mug of tea.

"Doesn't matter," says David. "I don't mind boiling some more."

"Fair enough."

David strikes a match. Watches the water start to bubble, warming his hands over the blue flames. Someone comes into the shop: a man. Probably not a customer then, he thinks. Mr. Jenkins says, "Thank you," and then the door goes again. David hears what sounds like rustling paper. Then a fist lands on the worktop. The butcher moves round the counter. "Closing early," he says, turning the sign.

"Oh."

He's in the back now. "So, don't bother with that."

"Really?"

"No. You get home. I'll sort it out."

David walks over to the coat stand. Removes his apron. "Are you sure, Mr. Jenkins?"

He nods. "You heard what I said – clear off."

Blood, Toil, Tears, Sweat

Summer looks to have arrived early. April was unusually dry (its customary showers flooded March instead) and now May has begun drenched in sun.

In the shop, the smell of sweat mingles with the whiff of wood-dust and cut flesh. One on top of the other, they layer the still, stagnant air.

"Of course, Mrs. Hebblethwaite. Did you hear that, David?"

David nods, holding the cleaver at shoulder height, then plunging it *thwack* through the pig-meat. He turns, presenting his effort. "Are they all right, Mrs. Hebblethwaite?"

"Oh, they'll do nicely, young man," she says, with a grin.

"We'll just check they're the right weight, dear." Mr. Jenkins takes over: picks the two slices up, plopping them on the scales. "They'll be fine. David – three-and-a-quarter ounces in the book, please." Then, facing the customer: "Would you like a couple of rashers to make up the full amount?"

"Oh…" Takes a moment. "Go on, then. Yes."

"Right away." He gets her some bacon. "Call that a full four ounces, then, me lad."

David crosses out the three-and-a-quarter, replacing it with 4OZ. Gives Mrs. Hebblethwaite her ration book back.

"Thank you."

"There you are." Mr. Jenkins passes her two bundles of paper.

"Thank you," she says again.

"That's one-and-two, please." He pats David on the arm. "Go on, lad – you're nearer the register."

"Oh…" David holds out his hand, takes the coins, the exact amount, and shifts to the till. Slowly, he presses the buttons (*is this right?*) and the register jolts open. The money rattles in.

"Thank you very much, Mrs. Hebblethwaite," says Mr. Jenkins, finishing off.

"Rightio."

"See you next week."

The bell rings and the door shunts shut.

"Good work, me lad." The butcher turns again to David, face set blank, before dodging past him, into the back.

David breathes out. "Thanks," he says, too late for the butcher to hear.

Fingering the frayed ends of his apron, David glances down at it: at the straight, top-to-bottom stripes of blue and white. Pink spots mark it – some which were put there today, just now; others that were done earlier in the week. (David's mother waits until Saturday afternoon to put his work clothes through the wash – alongside everything else the week produces: the dirty dresses the girls come in with after messing about in the garden; the tops that have had food dropped on them when they – especially Lily – eat messily.) Running two fingers over the dry blotches, he gets a sense of things done. A few months previously, he could never have thought that. He used to proudly compare his apron with Mr. Jenkins'. His unmarked, an unblemished record; the butcher's covered with days-old stains, each one the mark of something killed, cut up, and sold. Now, there's very little difference between the two.

"Did you hear the bulletin last night?" Mr. Jenkins shouts over the tap.

"No," replies David. Their wireless still hasn't been used since…

"Well…" The sound of rushing water stops, and he comes back through. "Looks as if the Gerry's are getting closer."

"Really?"

"They reckon they'll be halfway into northern France by tomorrow. Which reminds me – just pop into the paper shop and see where ours has got to."

"Right." David unfastens his apron – he *had* noticed the newspaper missing – folds it and leaves it on the side, laying his hat on top.

Outside, the lightest breeze passes through David's hair, lasting a few seconds, then coming to nothing. The newspaper shop is three doors down. Next to Jenkins' there's the greengrocers, then the bakery, *then* the newsagents. In the windless air, like it is in the shop, the smells mix and mingle. The heavy dead cattle stench (which David is now well used to – another thing he could never have said months ago) fades into the crisp smell of a ripe, ready apple orchard, an earthy vegetable patch, before a whiff of pastry just pulled from the oven overwhelms them all.

There's a bell above the newsagent's door as well. Heads turn as he steps inside.

"Good morning, young man." The shopkeeper stops rearranging the confectionary.

"Good morning, sir."

"How can I help you?"

"Mr. Jenkins sent me over, wondering where our newspaper was."

"Did it not get delivered?"

David shakes his head.

"Oh, that boy – I am sorry. Here." He holds one out. "Pass on my apologies."

David nods and leaves. He tucks the paper under his arm, wants to start reading – but decides it's best to wait until lunchtime.

For a few weeks now, the storm on the mainland has been growing, the sky darkening. Hitler's men lined the borders of their western neighbours – France, the Netherlands, Belgium, Luxembourg – before (on the tenth of May) crossing over and beginning to invade.

Meanwhile, in London: Parliament, unhappy with Prime Minister Chamberlain's actions up to and into this war, called for a vote of 'no confidence'. The vote took place and (also on the tenth – something about *that* date, perhaps) Chamberlain resigned.

Which brings us to today, the fourteenth of May: there's news in the paper about who's taken over. His name is Winston

Churchill (a name dotted throughout David's notebook – he often spoke out against Hitler and how he should be dealt with before war was declared). It quotes a speech he made the previous day in the House of Commons. He said: "I have nothing to offer you but blood, toil, tears and sweat..."

Could this be the turning point? Or is this German advance irreversible, now that it's got going? Like the tide battering the beach, irresistible? You can run away, spread your spine against the cliffs, but the water will still reach you and pull you under.

"Leave the door open, will you?" shouts Mr. Jenkins, louder than necessary. He holds the cleaver high, slams it down, then leaves it to lie on the side. "That's the last of them, son. Just three today. Give it an hour or so before you get started." Mr. Jenkins lifts his left hand to his shirt collar, smudging it with blood. "Blimey! It's hot in here." He undoes a button, fanning his neck.

David puts the newspaper down. Blindly re-ties his apron.

"Enjoy lunch?"

He nods, now squaring his hat.

"What was it? Same as usual?"

"Yes," says David, still not tired of cheese and pickle.

"You know you only need say and I'll give you a slice of something to go with it?"

"It's fine. Honestly."

"Just so you know," says Mr. Jenkins, holding his hands up, surrendering his offer. He moves some pots to the sink, piling them staccato for David to sort out later. "How's your mother, me lad?"

"She's..." David's never quite sure how to word these things, how to sum up the little he knows about another person's state of mind. "She's well, thank you... considering... everything."

The butcher nods calmly, to show he's listening, taking in, understanding.

"She's always busy, you know? There's always something that needs doing." David smiles, as if accepting some of the blame for that heavy load.

"Well, if there's anything *I* can do..." But he doesn't go into any more detail (under what circumstances would he...?).

The sound of the bell, the door opening – Mr. Jenkins darts into the front, "Hello, there," and David follows him, the afternoon session suddenly under way.

When David returns from his delivery round, he finds Mrs. Cresswell waiting at the counter, tapping her foot impatiently.

"Hello?" he says.

"At last, young man – where've you been?" David opens his mouth to answer, but she carries on: "Two pork chops."

"Right." Fortunately, there are several remaining on display. He reaches in for them. Moves them over to the scales and checks the numbers. "That's one-and-three, please."

She has the money ready; thrusts it in his direction.

"Thank you, Mrs. Cresswell." He gets her change, passes it to her, then wraps up the pork chops and hands her those too, thankful he has no need to ask for her ration book on this occasion. "There you are."

She reluctantly thanks him and leaves, the door slamming hard after her.

Checking no one else is there, ready to come in, David ducks into the back. "Mr. Jenkins?" Not quite a shout, but close enough. "Mr. Jenkins?"

No reply. Just the tick of the clock. David roots around the tops of the workbenches. He might have left a note; a reason; an explanation. He goes into the front again. Starts checking those counters, but Mrs. Bradley bustles in.

"Oh. Hello. How can I help you?"

"Hello, there – how are *you* today?"

"Yes. Fine, thank you."

"Good. You on your own?"

Looks like it. "Yes," he says. "Mr. Jenkins just had to pop out." Though where... "I hope *I'll* do instead."

"Course, dear. Now..." She passes him her ration book. He remembers making a mistake on this one last time. He spots the smudged pencil marks; the attempt to rub it out. "Four rashers of bacon, please."

"Right away." David peels four apart, places them slimy on the scales. "That looks like seven-pence, Mrs. Bradley."

"Lovely. Here." She passes him the exact amount.

"Thanks. I'll just..."

Some clatter in the back.

"Oh, Mr. Jenkins," smiles Mrs. Bradley.

David tries carrying on regardless. Like he'd expected it. He rings in the order. Places the bacon on the counter-top. Mr. Jenkins now stands next to him.

"Must be nice, eh? Knowing you've someone you can rely on if you're needed elsewhere?"

"Sorry?"

Mrs. Bradley tries again. "I said it must be nice..." she says. "To have someone you can leave here to look after things while you pop out."

"Oh. Yes. He'll be running the place in no time." There's an odd tone to his voice. David knows he's never been Mr. Jenkins' first choice, but it's hardly *his* fault.

She goes on to talk about the weather – this heat, like being in an African desert. "Anyway – best make a move before everywhere else closes. Cheerio."

"All right."

"Bye, Mrs. Bradley."

The questions have been slowly forming since he came back from the deliveries.

Mr. Jenkins opens the cash register. Flicks through the pound and shilling notes. *What? Don't you trust me?*

David looks up at the clock. Four-thirty. He wonders how long he could have been gone. Mrs. Cresswell really didn't look happy.

"Mr. Jenkins?"

"Mmm." He turns around. Slams the till drawer shut.

"Where were you?"

"Me?"

David nods. "I got back, and you weren't here. Mrs. Cresswell was just stood there."

He pulls air through his teeth. "Was she all right?" Though he doesn't look especially bothered.

"She did look a little put out."

"What? She have a go?"

"No."

"That's all right, then. Looks like you managed."

"Yes, but…"

"I just had to sort something out, all right? I got a letter and… It needed dealing with."

"Right."

"Maybe I should've locked up, turned the sign round." His eyes dart side to side. "Still. No lasting damage. Deliveries all right?"

"Yes. Fine."

"Good. Now – let's make a start on clearing away."

***

Red spots dot the porcelain. David holds his head over the sink, pinching his nose between two fingers.

"Right. That should stop it, lad."

Mr. Jenkins leans in towards him. David pulls away.

"Right. Course." He steps back. "I'll just sort things out in here."

With his left hand, David turns on the cold tap. Rests his arm on the metal basin. He can hear him in the other room making the sausages. The back door is ajar.

Mr. Jenkins comes in again. "Get some fresh air, if you want." Picks up something from one of the sides. "Sorry… I don't know what…"

David takes his advice: goes outside. He leans by the wall, one shoe pressed against the brick.

This isn't the first time. He did it the other day too. Gave the same excuse then. His hand slipped. He didn't mean to. It'll never happen again.

But perhaps David should have known. Perhaps he should have known this is where it was heading. A thump on the nose for... What? Just being there, the butcher's boy? *Come on, it's what you're here for, son.* Yes. He should have known. Stood in that sopping churchyard – wasn't it obvious?

***

The letter arrived with the last post. Mr. Jenkins looked like he'd been expecting it. "Right," he sighed. "That's that, then."

"Sorry?" said David, innocently.

"Don't..." He turned away. David just watched his shoulders rise and fall. "It's probably best if you went home, lad." Still turned around.

"Oh."

"What? Don't you think I can manage on my own?"

"No. I didn't..."

"I coped, didn't I, before *you* came along?"

"Course."

"Go on. Get out of here."

David went and got his coat. Slipped out of the back, not another word, wondering (part of him hoping) if he meant he wanted him to go altogether.

It rained, just as it did when David and his mother were last in that place. The torrent drowned out the sound of the person speaking from the lectern, the weak light shaping strange shadows across his face. Mr. Jenkins was in the front pew. Beside him: Mrs. Jenkins (shorter, older, than David had pictured; Mr. Jenkins quickly introduced them to each other before things got started).

The shop was shut for the day. Which reminded him. The name above the door, and on the walls, and on the delivery bike... JENKINS &...

Given what happened – and where – there was nothing to bury. So, it didn't quite feel like it should, there being no wooden box to stare at, no box to imagine what was inside. As instructed, they stood; sang; sat. It all seemed over very fast and, after, David waited in the grounds with his mother and one of their neighbours who – it turned out – knew Mrs. Jenkins (and therefore the whole family) rather well.

"It's such a shame," muttered Mrs. Falmouth.

"Yes," sighed Esther.

David held the umbrella.

"Margaret..." (That's Mrs. Jenkins.) "Margaret did say she didn't like the idea of him going out there."

"Mmm."

"But he'd made up his mind. There was no stopping him."

David could feel his mother looking at him. He knew what she was thinking.

"It's just such a waste, isn't it?"

Mr. Jenkins was sheltering, arms folded, in the church doorway, under the rain-lashed seventeenth-century brickwork. Someone was talking to him, but, besides a few nods, he didn't seem to be listening. David caught his eye. The butcher looked away.

Mrs. Falmouth went over to speak with Mrs. Jenkins.

"We'll get going shortly," said David's mother. "When Irene's finished..."

David smiled. "Fine." He swapped the brolly from his right hand to his left.

"Do you not want to go and speak to Mr. Jenkins?"

"Oh. No. That's all right. He'll..." He'll what? "I'll see him tomorrow."

***

He comes out into the yard. "Look, lad: I'm sorry. Right? I shouldn't have done it. It was wrong of me." His hand is shaking, he stuffs it in his apron, but his voice is perfectly clear, steady. "But – come on – you can't stay out here all day." He gestures to the open door. "I could get the deliveries ready if you like. You could do them early today."

David nods blankly.

"Right," he says. "Give us a few minutes."

He's acting like it's all fine, like it's all sorted. But maybe it is – as far as he's concerned.

David perches himself against the bicycle frame. Feels, gently, around his bruised and bloodied nose. A bit of red comes off on his fingers. He wipes it down his apron. It hardly looks out of place. At least his mother won't notice. And he certainly isn't going to tell her – so long as they're no obvious marks elsewhere. Besides, she'll probably blame him anyway. *What did you do to deserve that, then?* He thinks of Michael, stood in front of the whole class.

The butcher emerges with a stack of packages. "Here you go." He puts them in the basket. Stands back.

"Thanks," mumbles David, starting to turn the bike round.

"Maybe you should just clean yourself up a bit first."

"Oh."

"People'll be wondering what happened to you." He tries to smile. It doesn't quite work, though. Turns into more of a pained scowl.

David washes his face in the outhouse, peering into the dusty mirror hanging wonky by a piece of brown-dyed wool. As much as Jenkins doesn't want anybody seeing him like this, David would rather nobody found out too.

When he comes out into the yard again, he can hear the butcher back inside. David carefully, quietly, wheels the bicycle into the alleyway and sets off.

The cool breeze stings his throbbing face. Perhaps Mr. Jenkins really meant his apology. Perhaps he won't do it again. This time. After all, his son has just… you know…

He rides into the common. A couple of men (though they can't be more than a year or two older than David – in fact, probably the same age young Jenkins was when…) stand in uniform outside the village hall, smoking. Who knows if they'll make it back. Maybe one will and the other won't.

He passes a news-stand, the headline clear and simple: GERMANY OCCUPIES THE NETHERLANDS.

The story goes on. The tide rushes in. Listen carefully and you might even be able to hear it breaking, crossly, on the rocks. Belgium and Luxembourg have gone too, swallowed up by the German advance. This pattern – one invasion following another – must surely come to an end at some point. But will that be because they try for one too many or because there's none left to take? If recent newspaper articles are right (and they generally prove to be), France could be teetering too. Their war is as good as over – so Churchill discovered in a visit to Paris. It may soon just be Britain left standing, the cliffs scratching at their backs, at David's back.

***

The news on the twenty-ninth of May: Parliamentarians question whether any good can come from this continued resistance. Would surrendering, now, be Britain's best option?

Churchill doesn't believe so. He makes his case. He asks for courage.

The news on the thirtieth: Parliament votes to continue.

A Pair of Willow Trees

"William and Michael heard them too," says Robert. "Obviously."

He and David wander down the centre of the empty lane. Another Sunday morning.

"William wanted to go down there to see, but his mum wouldn't let him – she was scared it wouldn't be safe."

The Germans have arrived. Unable, so far, to come by land and sea, they've come, instead, by air. David's listened for the last few nights; heard the distant sirens, the explosions. Even the village has begun to fill with sandbags and military vehicles, while Robert's journey to school has – he says – become a daily game of spot-the-difference. Each morning revealing another street flattened. Half the houses between William and Michael turned to heaps of rubble. How long before it's their turn? And the docks too – the German planes seem especially interested in them.

Up ahead, past the slight rise in the road – an anomaly in this very flat region – the lane angles round, watched over by three terraced houses. Opposite them, on the inside of the curve, is the duck pond. David and Robert sit down on one of the iron benches, white paint peeling in huge strips. Two weeping willows dangle long fingers into the water. Most of the mallards rest on the far bank. A few dredge the bottom, their oily-green or patchy-brown (depending whether they're male or female) tail-feathers pointing to the sky.

"Oh," smirks Robert. "My mum wanted me to say you looked very smart yesterday when we came into the shop."

"Right."

He's still smirking. David can't help joining in.

"Did you like my hat?"

Robert nods. 'suited you."

The sun flickers across the rippling surface.

"Did you hear about the bomb that didn't explode?"

"Down by the sewage drain?"

"At least no one got hurt. Not that time, anyway."

But that's just it, thinks David. Plenty of people have been hurt. This is no game. It hasn't been for some time. Those that were near this bomb that didn't go off – they were just lucky. Which doesn't mean they will be next time. And this is the lesson David's beginning to learn (yes, he can still learn things – he doesn't just need school for that): that the long arms of war – he looks back at the willows shadowing the water – don't just reach out to grab the soldiers and the men in charge of them, they reach out for everyone else too, one way or another.

"Thompson asked about you the other day."

"Did he?"

Robert nods, teeth gripping bottom lip.

"In a nice way?"

"I guess – he just asked how you were." Robert sits up, lines his back against the curve of the bench. "He did look like he was actually interested."

"What did you say?"

"I told him you were fine, that you're doing well, why wouldn't you be…"

He still hadn't told anyone about Jenkins' temper.

"Oh – and another thing – William had to go see Mr. Greening. You'll never guess why."

"William? Mr. Greening?" He's in no mood to play. "I don't…"

"You give up?" Robert leans forward. Doesn't wait for David's response. "He's been entered for a special exam – a few people have. And guess what else?" He breaks into another grin. "Thompson hasn't."

"What sort of exam?" David feels heat in his cheeks.

"Advanced mathematics." Robert jumps to his feet; starts muttering about cramp in his legs.

"I didn't realise…"

"No," he winces. 'me neither. But he's really good."

"You all right?"

"Fine. What time is it?"

David looks up – the sun straight, central, in the sky. "About midday," he answers.

"We should go, then." Robert starts to limp back. "I said I wouldn't be late back this time."

***

Another Sunday. David and Robert are by the pond again. They start by feeding the ducks, a quacking crowd gathered at their feet. David tries to aim for the ones at the back, the less pushy ones, but very soon the crusty end of the loaf Robert's mother gave them has run out.

Robert brushes his hands clean. "All gone," he says, moving to the bench and sitting down.

David does the same, holds his hands up, his evidence… *See? Nothing left…* then sits next to Robert.

The sun peers through from behind the clouds, barely a spot of blue in the sky.

"Did you read how many were killed the other day?"

David turns to his friend, nodding. Robert's been showing more specific interest in the numbers and the names. "And there'll probably be more tonight," replies David, rubbing his chin with his right hand.

For over twenty consecutive nights, the Germans have bombed London. And this isn't something just confined to the capital. At some point since war broke out, every city in the country has faced attack from the *Luftwaffe* (that's the name for the German air force). Strategic bombing, it's called. They target ports and factories. Or they fall on gas works and military bases – anything that might give them an advantage.

At least, they did. That *used* to be the plan. Because now, in London, whenever they strike, reports in the newspaper the next day say how they're not just going for those obvious targets – for the docks and the water works – but they're hitting houses, sometimes whole roads. (Something David and Robert – not to mention William and Michael – know all too well.) They say that the Germans are bombing to break spirits, they're bombing for surrender. You could call it a different kind of strategic attack.

***

November. Robert is up to the lower fifth and David's now done more than a full year at the butcher shop.

"So, he wants to keep you on?" asks Robert.

"That's what he said."

"Good. It is good, isn't it?"

"Mum reckons so."

"But *you* don't? I thought you liked it now."

David doesn't know what to say. That's what he tells everybody. *Yes. It's fine, thanks.* But the truth is the beatings – and that's what they are – are becoming more frequent. Mr. Jenkins doesn't even apologise anymore. And he knows his mother will side with the butcher. Because they need the money. *He's doing us a favour, you know – taking you on, training you up.*

"David?"

He looks up.

"Is something wrong?"

"No." He notices a crane fly on the bench between them. "I was just looking at this."

"Oh." Robert takes the bait. "Let's see if it'll crawl on to me." He holds his left arm out and it starts inching up his shirt sleeve. Robert grins. "Eh? You know what I found out about Thompson the other day?"

"No," says David, perplexed that the sight of a daddy-long-legs creeping up his arm made Robert think of Charlie Thompson.

"Well, his dad joined up right away – you know, when war broke out."

"Right."

"But – and this wasn't Thompson telling us, so…" He lets the crane fly down. "He's been killed."

"Gosh! But – how do you know it's true, if Thompson hasn't…?"

"He's been off for weeks now."

"Are you sure?"

"Positive. I think I'd have noticed him around…"

"No, I mean…" David shakes his head. He feels a single raindrop on his neck, flinching, and on the water, he suddenly notices here-and-there ripples.

"William said he might not come back – you know, because…" Robert slows down. "Because you didn't."

"Maybe he won't." David stares at the water and the banks, the ripples spreading, the wind picking up, the willows bowing lower, creaking louder. "If he's… If that's really what's happened… I don't blame him."

"Anyway…" smiles Robert. "What were you saying about the butcher shop?"

David thrusts a palm out. "Look…" he says, standing. "Best get a move on."

"Oh. Right."

Robert gets up too. David's already back on the lane.

"Wait up, then."

***

"So, William was right," says Robert.

"What about?"

"About Thompson."

David nods, his eyes following the stone he's just kicked forward. "Doesn't surprise me," he manages to say.

They reach the pond. A cold, late-November day; their breath leaves ghostly marks in the air.

"So, Thompson didn't come back at all?" asks David.

"No."

They sit down. Some of the ducks venture towards them: hopeful, vocal. "We don't have anything," smiles David, locking eyes with one particularly brave male pecking at his shoelace.

"Can I ask you something, David? Something I've wondered for a while?"

"Sure."

"Do you...?" Robert hesitates.

David notices the yellow in the willow leaves. Reflected in the water, they look like flowers in a bluey field.

"Do you miss your dad?"

"Well..." David's surprised he's not already been asked this. He'd be as curious, if it were the other way around.

"If you don't want to..."

"No, it's fine."

"I just..."

"I know."

"Wondered."

David lifts one leg on to the bench, tucking it under the other. "I suppose I don't really think about it. I mean – I try not to, anyway. Mum never talks about it, so... And it can't be changed, you know...." Though he does wish, sometimes, when Jenkins has finished with him and he's bent double in the yard...

"Right. Sorry, if... you know..."

"No," sighs David. "It's the way it is. Can't change it."

"But do you really...?" Robert breathes in. "Do you really believe that?"

"Why? What else can I believe?"

"But I mean... Can you really just get on with it?"

"I have to. What other choice do I have?"

"I don't know," Robert admits.

"I used to just want to go back to school." David uncrosses his legs, plants both of them back on the grass. "Pretend like nothing had happened, like nothing had changed. Part of me still wants to, but..."

The soft clatter of feathers; two mallards flying in. Their feet skitter on the pond and, when they settle, they close wings and join the others. The wind playing in the willow branches sounds like a whispered welcome.

"And you're not the only one," reasons Robert.

"You mean Thompson?"

"Not just him – lots of people have left since first year."

"How many's lots?"

"Well, a few." Robert cracks a grin; it seems out of place. "Four or five."

And what about Michael, thinks David. If money was the problem there, like it was... is... for his own family, then he's surprised Michael isn't one of those boys. After all this time, how have they managed?

"How's...?"

But David waits. How much does Robert know? Anything? He can't imagine Michael having told them. Even after all this time. Especially after all this time. And Robert would've said, wouldn't he? *You'll never guess what Michael told us the other day...*

"So, how're William and Michael?"

"They're fine," he answers, illuminating as ever. He jumps to his feet, rubbing his shoulders. "Fancy walking on? We could do a circuit, go around at Cotterill Farm."

"Mmm." David stands too. "Sounds good."

Cotterill Farm is half a mile on from the duck pond and nearly two miles, roughly, from both David and Robert's houses. To get there, you pass fields, endless fields, which, if they don't contain crowds of cows or sheep, six or seven horses, then they contain crops – wheat, barley, rapeseed, sugar beet – all bunched in, growing to be made into something else. The fields are then, sporadically, interrupted by houses. They come in threes and fours; where there's one, there's bound to be two or three more.

Further on, a man enters one such house. David and Robert watch him.

"Isn't that...?"

"Mr. Jenkins?"

"Is this where he lives?"

"No. He lives near the Common. I think."

"But this is nowhere near…"

"I know."

"I wonder what…"

David shrugs. Short of running after him, knocking on the door he's just closed… "Maybe I'll ask him tomorrow," says David, knowing full well that's the last thing he'll dare do.

"Want to turn back?" asks Robert. "In case he sees us?"

David nods; then points at a break in the fence. "Shall we just cut through here? We can get around that way, down the footpath."

Robert starts off and David follows him, looking back, briefly, back at the squat little house and the holly bush peeping, red-eyes, too many to count, over the garden wall.

The Story Goes On

June, 1940. France – after several weeks wobbling, teetering – finally surrenders. The Germans – aided by Italy – marched through, taking town after town. Amiens followed by Boulogne-sur-Mer followed by Calais followed by Paris. By the end of the month, the Channel Islands are taken too – the first bits of British soil to feel the press and stamp of enemy boots. Putting them just the shortest stretch of sea away. Look, there, to the right. Lift a hand to your forehead. Squint. Can you see them?

Hitler draws up his next invasion plan. He calls it *Operation Sea Lion*. It relies on victory by air *and* by water. Which is relying on a lot. Even the men in charge of his air force and navy have reservations. And they show no fear in sharing them with him. Hermann Goring, commander of the *Luftwaffe*, says it should be rejected, that Britain is in no way weak enough – not yet, at least; and the man from the German navy (the *Kriegsmarine*), Erich Raeder, responds in a similar way. But – and why would he be anything else – Hitler remains firm, convinced. He states: "As England, in spite of her hopeless military situation, still shows no signs of willingness to come to terms…" (that is, to give in and do as we say…) "I have decided to prepare, and if necessary to carry out…" (even though I've been advised not to…) "a landing operation against her."

So, by July, the *Luftwaffe* start their daytime raids. They begin over the Channel Sea, before the attacks shift to the shipyards, the military airfields and aircraft factories – anything that might destabilise Britain's ability to fight back. Then the campaign changes, in a way even Hitler had not planned for. No civilian victims – that had been his intention; military, industrial, commercial targets only. But, whether by accident or by aim, the bombs start to fall, not on the airfields, but on the cities. They fall on Bristol and Portsmouth. They fall on London. And, in retaliation, they fall on Berlin too. Something else Hitler failed to foresee. And this Berlin bombing leads to those fifty-seven consecutive nights. Now, no longer is it a weapons factory or an R.A.F. barracks. Instead, it's Bob and Joan's house down the road; it's the street your granddad grew up in.

The pendulum that had been swinging Germany's way at the start of this bombing campaign is beginning to turn in the opposite direction. Hitler postpones his invasion. Then postpones it again. Meanwhile, the British air forces begin to claim victory. And by the middle of September, *Operation Sea Lion* is delayed indefinitely.

Still. This initial threat may have eased. But it doesn't stop the planes. They keep on coming and the bombs keep falling. Remember? Those fifty-seven consecutive nights? Which is without mentioning the raids on other cities. The centre of Coventry is all but flattened. Liverpool, Southampton: they suffer extensive damage too. Hitler's resolve to batter and pound the British Isles is unaffected even by the apparent failure and abandoning of his great invasion plans.

Still. As these planes continue to come, and as the bombs they carry drop, the R.A.F. continues, too, to gain the upper hand; the effect Hitler hoped for – to force some kind of surrender or deal – an increasingly unlikely outcome.

Though there is no decisive date, by the time October ends, so too does the full weight of Germany's aerial campaign. The threat of invasion nothing more than a mention in some lad's notebook.

The story goes on. And for Britain, there is another battlefield. Hitler's friends, the Italians, are making trouble in North Africa. In Egypt, in the Sudan, British troops (with *their* friends, the Indians) are positioned as Italy advances from neighbouring Libya. Their job is to defend and preserve these far-off, dusty desert regions of the Empire from what may well become the successful invasion Hitler couldn't force more directly from across the Channel: the other way into Britain, if you like, through its back door, its overseas territories.

In the beginning, it's all attacks and counterattacks, spread across the summer and autumn while the German planes continue to empty themselves over Britain. But into December and what could (perhaps) have been termed skirmishes are now (most certainly) sieges. The Allies – that's the British and the Indians – capture Sallum. For the Italians, this is the extent of their first campaign into Egypt. The Allies hold position (and this group of men now also includes Australians). Then, they start to advance. Bardia and Tobruk are taken; Derna and Beda Fomm follow. Which means they have crossed the border into Libya. Making *them* the invaders. In February "41, Benghazi – the Italian stronghold – is captured. What's left of the retreating army, only the next day, surrenders.

But.

Wait there.

It's never quite that simple, is it?

At this point, the story changes. Churchill orders the victorious men away. Help is needed in Greece. They must prevent another German onslaught. And that provides the Italians – and it provides Hitler, more importantly – with an opportunity: some time to regroup, reassess. He agrees, finally, to place German troops in North Africa, sending them under the leadership of a man called Erwin Rommel, and as the fighting rekindles, their effect – *his* effect – is almost immediate. Into March, and the British advance is starting to reverse.

June, 1941. The news on the twenty-second: Germany begins its invasion of the Soviet Union (codenamed *Operation Barbarossa*).

Over the long course of events, the German-Russian relationship has ummed and aahhed. Though the Soviets have been – for the most part – on the Allied side, Hitler and Stalin have, nonetheless, maintained close contact. At times, the Soviet

Union has even been willing to join with the Germans – if there's something, territorially speaking, to be gained from it.

But, that's just it. All along – surprise, surprise – the vast lands of Russia have been high on Hitler's own invasion list too. And, with the British operation crossed off that list, this, evidently, is the next one down.

They strike from three sides. The main attack pushes through from occupied Poland; while the Romanians – who are another of Hitler's friends – cross the southern Soviet border; and, aided by Finland, a further influx of German troops floods the cold, cold country from the north.

For centuries, invaders have led their men into Russia. Remember Napoleon's Grand Army? It's like Mr. Parfick said. Another history lesson ignored. And as the press and stamp of German boots are felt on Russian land, Stalin orders a scorched-earth policy. The same treatment dished out to Bonaparte. Burnt land. Which drew him deeper, desperately, into the country.

Still. All looks well for Hitler. Perhaps, this time, the lessons have been learnt. They take Riga, Vitebsk, before finally reaching and capturing Smolensk – crucial, if Moscow is to be taken too. At the same time, the armies in the north close in on the other major Soviet city, Leningrad. By September – ten weeks into the campaign – it is completely surrounded.

Meanwhile, out in the Pacific, there's another of Hitler's friends and another of Britain's. On one side, America – yet to actually declare war – and, on the other, Japan – who, alongside Germany and Italy, are the third part of what are known as the Axis Powers.

The Americans have been giving assistance to the Allies, something the Japanese – and no doubt the man in Berlin – do not like. And so, they have begun sending their planes and their pilots (*Kamikazes*, these men are called: because they plunge themselves and their aircrafts at their targets, rather than leave the job to the bombs which – let's face it – always have a chance of missing). And what is it they're flying into, nose first? U.S. air and naval bases, of which the Pacific Ocean has a fair number, and in which (this collection of military communities) there is one in particular – a naval base, to be precise, called Pearl Harbour.

On the seventh of December 1941, it is attacked. By this, the Japanese intend to put a stop to any American plans to aid the British in the south-east Asian region.

Of course, the result is quite the opposite.

Now, let's jump ahead a little, just for a moment, to May, 1943. The news on the thirteenth is that, back in North Africa, the Germans and Italians have surrendered. Their great advance under Field Marshal Rommel became a retreat as the British forces pushed them all the way from the Egypt-Libya border to the Tunisian capital on the Mediterranean coast.

At one point though, the situation had looked grave for Britain. You remember? After early progress, their campaign suffered when, in the early months of '41, Germany sent its troops to bolster the struggling Italian forces. At the same time, the familiar prospect of a German invasion was brewing again in Europe – this time in Greece – and certain divisions deployed in Africa were called upon to pitch in across the Mediterranean. Leaving a weakened, more inexperienced bunch to protect what had just been won.

The effect of Germany's introduction into this North Africa campaign was quite instant. El Agheila was re-captured and Allied generals taken prisoner, then Fort Capuzzo, Bardia and Sallum were secured, before the tactically advantageous Halfaya Pass. Really, the only remaining British stronghold was the port of Tobruk and thankfully – because the Royal Navy managed to maintain its supplies – Rommel and the German-Italian forces were unable to break it. This created, for a short time, a sort of stalemate. Because Tobruk was vital – even to the Axis supply-line – and the repeated effort Rommel put into trying to take the port meant certain resources were drained from their other forces elsewhere in the region.

In May 1941, Britain broke the standoff. Their intention was to push the Germans and Italians back beyond the Egyptian border, freeing up Tobruk from the Axis siege. However, the offensive failed. Fortunately, though, all this did was reinstate the stalemate. And in the meantime, the Allied forces regrouped and reorganised – which, of course, is just what Rommel and his men did too.

There were tactical triumphs for both sides in the months that followed. Britain and its allies pushed the Axis defence-line back again, recapturing much of the territory it had lost and re-drawing the front-line at El Agheila. But, in the summer of "42, the Germans and Italians finally captured Tobruk. Which put them in a position to try for Cairo. Only, as they advanced, the Allies managed to hold them back. Another of those stalemates – but this one came at just the right time for the British. Again, they rebuilt and re-equipped. Then, after halting the Axis advance, they pressed on, defeating them in a second battle at El Alamein, pushing them west before, in January 1943, the Libyan capital, Tripoli, fell into British hands.

The pendulum finally swung decisively one way – this marked the start of what was to end the North Africa campaign.

Returning to the Soviet Union: the Germans are nearing Leningrad. Hitler orders that no prisoners be taken, and the German forces push to within seven miles of the city. But this is as far as they get. German casualties stack up. Hitler becomes impatient and decides, instead, that the only way Leningrad can be taken is by starving it. All the while, on the road to Moscow, things are stalling there too, and the Russians start mounting counterattacks. The Germans decide, eventually, to pull forces from the siege of Leningrad and send them to support the more-crucial march on Moscow.

On the second of October 1941, the battle for Moscow begins. The German forces close in on the capital by taking Oryol, then Bryansk and Vyazma, catching the Soviets completely off-guard; Moscow's first line of defence breached. But then the weather starts to play its part – didn't Mr. Parfick mention that in his history lessons too? First, the rain falls. The roads to Moscow turn muddy, delaying German progress. Supplies begin dwindling. On the thirty-first of October, Germany's High Command call a halt to proceedings. Which provides a welcome reprieve for the Soviet army. Though their supply situation looks far better than the German's, it gives them pause, more importantly, to re-organise and firm up their positions.

On November the fifteenth, Germany re-starts its advance. But the ground is hardening, the temperatures falling. Sound familiar? Slowly, they creep closer to Moscow. The weather worsens. The *Luftwaffe* can't even get off the ground. And, with the Soviet army using the earlier interim to boost its numbers by several hundred thousand, the Russians launch a huge counter-offensive and push the Germans back some two hundred miles, permanently denting any hopes of a successful invasion.

The story goes on. And just a short crossing from North Africa, the Allies land on the island of Sicily, beginning a new campaign in Italy. Within weeks, before they've even hit the mainland, the Italian leader, Mussolini, is removed from government and an armistice is signed with the Allies. Of course, this smooth passing does not last long. On the tenth of September 1943, the Germans move in and occupy Rome. Finally hitting the mainland at Salerno, the Allies (that's largely, in this case, the British and Americans, who finally joined the war officially after the attack on Pearl Harbour) are bombarded by counterattacks. It takes many weeks before the area is fully in their hands.

Meanwhile, the instability in Italy's government is matched on its streets and in its cities. As there has been in France and other occupied territories, there is a growing movement of anti-Nazi, anti-German resistance. In Milan, explosions are reported; while in Naples – spurred on by the Allied advance – the opposition is such that they manage to free the city from German rule.

Another month passes. Much of southern Italy secured, the British and American forces reach what's called the Volturno line – the first of many defensive barriers from which the Germans plan to delay and obstruct the path to Rome.

Then, the news on the thirteenth of October: Italy declares itself at *war* with Germany. The Axis powers are turning in on themselves.

But – like time dancing around us, the many threads of this knotty war tangling at our feet – the story must go on…

A Girl Called Edith

"What can I get you, Mrs. Harris?"

She scanned the little on offer, turning back to the paper in her hand. "I'll take the sausages this time."

"Certainly. It's three, isn't it?" She nodded, and he reached under the glass counter. No need to check the weight. "That's three-and-half, then, please," he said, wrapping them up and swapping them for the coins and the Harris" ration book. He sorted that out first. Handed it back. Then strode to the cash register. "Right. Thank you very much, Mrs. Harris." Turned back. Smiled. "See you next time."

"Yes. Thank you." She went for the door handle. Set the bell off.

"Oh..." It was Mr. Jenkins. Breadcrumbs round his lips. "Cheerio, Mrs. Harris." She raised a hand, the vaguest of smiles, before stepping out and shutting the door. "How's it been? Not missed much, I suppose?"

David wrinkled his nose. "No – just her and Mrs. Carroll." He looked at his apron, smudged blood across the up-and-down stripes. "Shall I start on the deliveries?"

"Yes, lad."

This was *his* job now. Though most of the stuff was already cut and sliced – in one form or another – it was up to David to put it all together according to however many orders there were. It was a Tuesday. Which meant there were five orders. And David knew exactly who those five belonged to. Mrs. Jones wanted her ration of sausages; Mrs. Trimmley always got ham on Tuesdays; Mrs. Baker had lamb; as did Mrs. Bosworth; and Mrs. Turner would be expecting pork chops.

Outside, it was raining. The sky the colour of night. David didn't fancy being out in it, the wet running down his neck like cold fingers. Mr. Jenkins dealt with the next customer. Got David to grab a few things from the cold room while he was through there. With the door opening and closing a few times, and the back one ajar, he could hear the pace of the rain fading and noticed sunlight starting to paint itself across the shop floor.

When he'd got everything ready, David jotted down his list. Asked Mr. Jenkins to check it. "Should be done by four," he said, passing it back with a nod. The doorbell ordered him into the front again. "Good afternoon, Mrs. Wright, what can I...?"

David stuffed the list in his back pocket and gathered the packages in his arms, just managing to pull the back door to on his way out.

There was a December bite to the wind. David's breath went before him. But at least the rain had ceased; the clouds, mostly clear, the sun now blinded his way.

Mrs. Jones lived near the Lacey Farm. He went the longer route, the one that passed the apple orchard – though he had heard clearly what Jenkins said, knew what that might mean should he be late back. But it was easier on the bike tyres that way.

Though that wasn't the only reason David did it.

Two-thirty. She finished about now. That's what she'd said, wasn't it?

Looking up, away from the golden glare, a sparrow hawk glided silently in search.

Then, there she was, waiting for him; her left hand raised and waving. "Hello," she said. "Where're we going today?"

"You mean you can't remember?"

"No." She shook her head, unashamed grin.

"This way first."

David got off the bicycle. Walking alongside it, alongside her, his right arm brushed Edith's left every few strides.

Between the orchard and Lacey Farm, she told him about her day with the chickens and the Potters. Then they turned off the lane. David propped the bike by the fence, took out the top order, and pushed open the wrought-iron gate, holding it back, creaky, for Edith. She stepped through, did her best in avoiding where it was muddiest, the horseshoe prints and thick (compared with those of the butcher's bicycle) tyre tracks.

Edith pulled a face. David couldn't help laughing.

"What?"

"Nothing."

"Mum'd get angry if I got these shoes all dirty."

You work in a chicken coop, he thought.

Nearer the house, Edith held out her arm. "Can I knock for this one?"

David pulled the package away, closer to his chest.

"Come on."

She snatched for it, got hold of his hand. For a second or two, David let her grip tighter, the warmth of her skin merging with the warmth of his. Then he fought her off.

"Next one," he said.

Mrs. Jones was happy to see them. Well – to see her order. "Bless you, treasures." She took it and held it like a returning friend. "You manage anything extra today?"

"Sorry. Not today. But I'll try to next time."

"Bless you," she said again, stepping back from the doorstep. "See you Thursday, then."

"Yes, Mrs. Jones. Bye."

They raced back through the field. If Edith's shoes weren't muddied before, they were now. It had even reached the hem of her skirt.

"Your mum won't be pleased."

"Sorry?" she panted.

David nodded; gestured to her legs.

"Oh, no!" But she was smiling. "It'll be all right. She can bark, but she can't bite."

David imagined her, blunt teeth bared.

"So, where's next?"

He peered into the basket, double-checking. "Springhead," he answered.

They followed the road back round. David spotted Lacey in one of the sheep fields. The haywain packed full, he was forking huge clumps into the feeding trough.

"Did you see your friend yesterday?"

"Yes," David nodded. Of course, he had – every Sunday, that's what they *always* do.

"Have you told him about me yet?"

"Not really."

"So – no?"

He shook his head, lifting the bike over a sudden rise in the asphalt.

"Are you embarrassed?"

"What?"

"You must be."

"No. No, I'm not. It's just…" He sniffed at the cold air. "It's private."

"Like a secret?"

"Suppose."

The lane ahead split in two.

"Is it this way?"

She pointed to the right and David gently grabbed her arm, moving it to the left.

"Oh."

Mrs. Trimmley lived in a hunched, one-floor cottage, one of the few that still had straw for a roof and, as they got there, smoke drifted from it into the clear sky.

"Here you go." David passed Edith the delivery.

"Thanks." She took it, held her pale hand over his for a little longer than necessary, then went to ring the doorbell. With the shrill tone echoing in David's ears, she stepped back from the door, glancing at him, momentarily, teeth on show.

A person's shadow danced in the frosted glass. "Oh, hello," said Mrs. Trimmley. "Is that for me, my dear?" Edith gave it over. "Thank you." She glanced at David too. Polite nod. "Well – pass on my best to Mr. Jenkins, won't you?"

"Yes."

"Goodbye."

"Bye."

Mrs. Baker lived near the duck pond. On the way, Edith took hold of David's hand and, for about the length of five fields, she didn't let go. It was what he'd been waiting for, though he hadn't quite known how to start it off himself. He looked across at her, just to see what her face was saying – since her mouth was saying nothing – but there was just this simple, set smile, and her eyes seemed bright from the sunlight, and her skin felt so warm, and the whole thing just felt like… Like what they'd been out there for all along. Forget the bicycle walking beside them, the packages wrapped in paper, the houses they were going to, and where he was going *back* to – especially where he was going back to…

Then, in front of them, David saw someone approaching. Plainly, Edith did too. She pulled her hand away, an awkward grinned glance.

"What?"

Quick shake of the head. *Not now*, it said.

"Hello, love." The lady recognised Edith. "How are you? How's your mother?"

"Well, thank you."

"Good to hear it." She caught David's eye from below her flowery bonnet. "Well, I mustn't stop. Lots to do. Send her my best."

"Of course. Bye, Mrs. Mallory."

David waited until she was out of earshot. "You know her?"

Edith smiled again. "No. I just guessed she were called Mrs. Mallory."

"Right. You sure *you're* not the one who's embarrassed?"

"No," she shot back, adamant; then, not so: "But…"

"But?"

She sighed. "I mean, I've still not told my mum about this."

David hurled a stone forward with the end of his works shoe. It caught the front bike tyre on its way. "What is *this*, anyway?"

Edith started to laugh, taking hold of David's hand again. "I'm not sure. But I like it."

"Me too." With his hand in hers, how could he say otherwise?

"You think we'll have enough time later on to… you know?"

"If we get a move on."

So that was just what they did. David did the business at Mrs. Bosworth's and the last one – Mrs. Turner's pork chops – was on the way to the Common.

As they got closer, they turned off into one of the fields. David left the bicycle – like earlier – propped up by a tall hedge, half-swallowed by the bare branches. In one corner of the field there was an old cattle shed, empty besides a few mice and spiders. The floor was hard concrete, littered with leftover hay. Three of the five windows were without glass: one boarded by a very dark wood; the others completely vacant, like the structure itself.

For a moment, they stood a foot apart. David stared at her. Right into her grey eyes. Offered her a weak, runny smile; then a laugh, started by the gurgling in his belly. Then he closed his eyes. And all he could feel next was the dry touch of her lips. But it was warm too. It was warm like her hand wrapped round his, her lips wrapped round his. Then she unhooked her hand from his sweaty left one and started moving it up and down his arm, elbow to shoulder, down to wrist, and up to shoulder again. The year that was between them seemed suddenly larger. Next, she was grabbing at his clothes, the cotton clinging to his neck, his chest. Her lips came away from his and David opened his eyes.

"Do you know what we're supposed to do?" she asked.

"What?"

"Don't worry." She smiled and shook her head. "I'll show you."

"Will it take…?" David tried to say, but Edith had already got going, and the rest of what he was wanting to say seemed suddenly irrelevant.

They took the final package on to Mrs. Turner's. When she asked why they were so late, David managed to mumble something about being held up at the last place. Which was half true. Only, the last place wasn't quite to do with deliveries. In fact, it had nothing at all to do with deliveries. And – anyway – wasn't it only three-thirty or thereabouts?

"Thereabouts, maybe, son – it's gone four."

"Oh." David just about hid his panic.

Mrs. Turner thanked them and shut her door.

"I really better go. Mr. Jenkins'll be livid." He clambered on to the bike, clamped hard the handlebars.

"You all right?" Edith was stood in his way.

David nodded. "It's just…"

"Course. Tomorrow?"

"Yes. Same time."

"Good. Can't wait."

"Sorry. Have to…" David worked the bicycle backwards, away from her toes. "But, that was…" He didn't know what word to use; how, even, to describe it. "You know?"

Edith smiled, staring right at him.

"See you tomorrow," he said.

"Definitely."

***

Another Sunday. When Robert called, he was a little late and David wasn't quite ready. He dashed to the door. It had been a while since he last sat by the front window, watching the second-hand catch up with the hour-hand, anticipating his friends' arrival. This particular Sunday, he was helping his mum in the kitchen. She'd decided, on some whim, that the cupboards needed a sort out and when they were moving things, from one pile into another, David noticed the strain showing in her arms. Sometimes she used the work surface for support, or her knees, if they were sitting, working through the floor cupboards.

So, when Robert called, she took it as an excuse to stop. "Go on, love," she said, standing. "You get off. I'll leave it till you're back."

David looked at the mess around them.

"I promise," she added. "I won't touch it till you're home."

"I could just say…"

"You can just say nothing," she smiled. "Go."

"Sure?"

"Go," she sighed. "Have fun."

David rushed to the front door. Opened it, his left arm simultaneously unhooking his coat from the coat stand.

"Hello," said Robert.

"Hello. You all right?"

"I'm fine."

Then a sound. Other voices. Excited. Laughing. William and Michael leapt out from behind the hedge.

"Oh. Woah!"

They exchanged grown-up handshakes. Told David it was good to see him. He couldn't count how many times Robert had said, "They'd like to come, but their mums won't let them." But there they were. And now that they were, David felt stuck for what to say, out of practice almost. He nodded along as they – mostly William – told him about school. Robert looked at him awkwardly. It was a subject he hardly brought up anymore. Must have noticed what it did to David when they talked about it. The blank eyes and drawn-out sighs. But William went on. He talked about the new subjects they get to do now they're older. The tests and the homework – worse than it ever used to be, he insisted. The new schoolmaster.

"Sorry?"

"What?"

"Where's Mr. Greening gone?"

"Has Robert not said?"

Robert smiled; short shrug of the shoulders. "I thought..."

David knew exactly what he thought. But – of all things – he might have mentioned...

"He's left. There's been someone else since we started the lower fifth."

"Mr. Fitchley," added Michael.

"What happened?"

"The war," William replied, simply. "He went off to fight. So did Hennessey. So did Finch."

"And so did Moore," said Robert, making up lost ground, perhaps.

"But David won't know him. He came after. Remember?"

"Oh, right. Forgot."

The trees were full again, a budding white and pink, dressed for a wedding. Sparrows raided the hedgerows.

"Sounds like a lot's changed. What's he like – this Fitchley?"

Robert rolled his eyes; creased his lips. "Don't know." He looked at William.

"Could be worse – I guess."

"He is strict, though," Michael interrupted.

"True."

"Even you've been whacked." Michael meant William. The roles have well and truly changed. Surely, if things had been different, Michael would be saying that about David.

"Running down the hallway," William explained. "Right past his office, just as he was coming out."

"Bit daft, really," grinned Robert.

William held out his right hand, shook it limp like it's only just been hit.

"Hurts, don't it?" said Michael.

Some things hadn't changed, then.

The sun, for a moment or two, went dim behind the shifting clouds, the boys' shadows disappearing.

They walked down the middle of the lane, peeling off to the sides when motorcars or farmer's carts needed to pass. They decided to wander down along the stream and follow its course up to the Common. The banks were soggy after the overnight rain, the current gushier, much fuller, than it would be ordinarily. William lobbed a splintered plank into the water after testing it – unsuccessfully – for an improvised bridge. David leapt from tree-root to tree-root, avoiding the mud so that his shoes – which are also his work shoes – remained relatively clean.

Robert and Michael stretched on ahead. David decided – because he may get no other opportunity – to ask William something. He lowered his voice, just in case. "How *is* Michael now?"

"What? You mean?" William showed him his right hand again, flipped it over, knuckles to palm.

David nodded. "Is he still being caned a lot?"

"No, actually – it's really not that bad. I know he said, about Fitchley – but everyone's been done by him, just about. He's *really* strict."

"Oh."

"Even Robert – did he not tell you?"

"No. He didn't."

"He got caught talking, to Patterson, while Fitchley took Latin. He went mad. Gave him ten slippers on *both* hands. Right there and then."

For once, David felt relieved not to be there at school with them anymore.

"But..." Getting back to the original subject. "You're sure Michael's..." Which word to use, without giving it away?

"What?"

"Well, when I left, he still wasn't, really, himself. It seemed like something had changed..." Which it had. And David realised how close he was getting. "Anyway – he seems better now," he added, in a rush, convincing William, it seemed, but far from settling the question in his own mind.

Late-morning church bells sounded out from the Common. A crow suddenly landed, big, cawing, into the tree above them. David looked up, half-blinded by the fiery daylight. William was talking about planes and bombs. Where had been hit and what remained to be hit. David remembered Robert telling him about the Picture House near school. How he went home, passed it, same as usual, on the bus, and by the next morning the bricks that were walls were just dusty piles scattered across the pavement and into the road.

David and William caught up with the other two.

"All right?" said Robert, as if they were only just meeting up.

William nodded, speaking for both of them.

"My dad told me something interesting the other day..." Robert nudged David on the arm. He wondered whether Robert was aiming this just at him or all three of them. "How they're lots of places in Germany being bombed too."

"Oh – by us, you mean?"

Robert nodded.

He was right.

Essen and Lubeck. Hamburg and Rostock.

"Hitler..." and David started to smile, just couldn't help it. "Well – he isn't very happy about it."

"I'll bet," said William.

"But..." David dropped the grin. "It'll probably mean more attacks on us, you know?"

"Course," added William, his smile disappearing glumly too.

They started to see houses, squat brick things with chimney smoke and garden gates. The noise of the stream became a distant static; the path followed the buildings, not the water. Soon, the single houses were rows of houses. And then they were looking at the Common, the sun glinting off the grass.

The four of them walked on to the green – ten, eleven, twelve paces – and sat cross-legged in a circle. Instinctively, almost, they each began picking at the short blades of grass, pulling at them between finger and thumb.

"You deliver round here, don't you?" asked Robert, glancing round and behind him at the houses.

"Oh. Yes." David's eyes darted down to the ground.

"So, come on..." William picked things up. "What's it like working in a butcher shop?"

The one question David still wasn't sure he had an answer for.

"It's..." Began to attempt. "It's fine, it's..." His friend's faces looked to be asking for more. But he wasn't going to tell them some of the things that really went on. "It's pretty dull. Same old routines – you know?"

"Like what?" Because – actually – how were they to know the butcher shop routine?

"Well. You get the same old customers…"

"Like my mum," Robert jumped in, cheeky grin.

"Yes, and like Robert said…" He pointed to the houses on sentry duty around the Common. "I do deliveries too, to the same places every week."

"Which ones?" William shifted position so that he was half-in-half-out of their circle.

"Oh…" David stared for a few moments at the terraces and cottages. He found number twenty-six. "That one – with the blue door and green curtains."

"I see it," said William, oddly excited, like they'd started a new game. "Where else?"

"Well…" David searched for number forty or fifty-four. "Oh, there, that one, number forty, with the fancy white gate."

"Yes. Got it." William swivelled back with a smile.

Crows landed noisily on the grass, calling like frosty mornings, jabbing necks and beaks at each other.

David looked up, towards the houses again. Someone was coming over to them. Someone female.

Now, is that…? The hair looks…

Then she smiled. No mistaking.

Then she was right next to them, her shadow covering bits of their trouser legs and faces and the circle of green between them.

And then she was saying: "Hello."

And David wasn't. He just about managed a smile.

"Hello," repeated Edith.

"Yes. Sorry." Broader smile, verging on the embarrassed – but which reason to pick. "Hello," he said finally. Then to the boys, "This is Edith," clearer than he thought it might come out.

They gave her low, shy nods. Mumbled hellos.

"I deliver to her family," David clarified.

"Yes," says Edith, adding: "That's how we met." Which, to the boys, looked to warrant some explanation.

"And she sometimes helps me – with the deliveries."

"Oh. Do you work at the butcher's too?" croaked William.

"No – at the orchard."

"What? Picking apples?"

"No. I look after the chickens – they belong to the Potters…" As if the others would be well acquainted with the Potter family.

More mumbling. Then nothing. These chatty boys rendered silent by a girl one year older than them.

Edith pulled fingers through her hair. Switched legs, turning to look at the pavement and the road, a bit busier than the average Sunday. "I better…" She started to make her excuses. "I better be going." Then her eyes connected more certainly with David's. "See you… *later?*"

Which he knew meant tomorrow, same time and place. "Yes. All right," he replied, as nonchalantly as he could, given the tingling in his arms – which he thought he'd long since got over.

Robert, William and Michael managed stronger goodbyes and Edith held up an embarrassed hand, turned, and went. David kept an eye on her, while the boys returned to talking about bombs and school and (their idea of) butcher things.

"So, what would you say is the best way to…?" William stopped. "David?" Noticed his attention focused elsewhere. "You hear me?"

"Yes." Slight untruth. If he was being honest. "Go on."

"No. Just wondered, how do you slice the perfect ham joint?"

"With a really sharp knife," answered Robert.

William retorted to that by slapping him on the knee.

"Hey!"

"Seriously."

"I *was* being serious," grinned Robert. "It'd come out rubbish with a pair of scissors. Or a spoon."

Edith disappeared over the little humpback bridge. David looked at William with a smile.

"Are *you*…?" he began.

"What?" said David.

"No. Nothing." Then, returning to his first question: "You never said about the ham joint."

"Oh. You don't want to hear about that. It's boring. Now…" David got to his feet. "Shall we start heading back?"

"What? Already?"

Later, David spoke to Michael on his own. Robert and William lingered behind them, playing about on the bank of the stream and in the snaking tree-roots. He started aimlessly at first. "Been good this morning, eh?"

"Mmm," he responded; nothing more. His hands typically thrust in his pockets.

"Glad you could *all* come out," David continued. "Like being back at school." Which it really hadn't been – he just wanted to gently tilt the conversation towards it. "What's it like now, anyway?"

"You heard what the others said."

"Yes, but... *you* didn't say what..."

Michael rolled his shoulders, mouth shut, stubborn – same old Francis.

"I suppose I wondered how you were."

"Fine."

"You're still there, then."

"Well..." His face lightened. "Clearly."

"You know what I mean."

Michael sighed. "Just don't worry about it, David."

"Can't help it. You're my friend."

"Do *you* want to talk about what happened to *your* dad?"

No, if he was honest. But, then, how did this become about him? "Michael, that's..."

"What? Different? It's not – not really. Mine's gone. Yours has too."

The other two caught up with them.

"What you talking about?" asked Robert.

"Nothing much," lied David.

"Oh, has Michael not told you yet, then?"

"No. It doesn't..." Michael began to protest.

"What?"

"Just leave it."

"Nonsense," said William. "I'll tell him if you want."

And he did. Apparently, Mr. Francis signed himself up. Conscription having been re-defined again – you could now be as young as eighteen or as old as fifty-one – his father, so said Michael, was first in line to fill out the papers.

"Where is it he is now?" William asked.

Michael took a second to answer; glanced in David's direction first. "Africa."

"Fighting Rommel, eh?" Robert nudged David on the arm.

"Right," said David, a thought quickly occurring to him and refusing to leave. How long will it be before Michael reports the terrible news that his father'll never be coming home?

***

It didn't take long for Edith to notice the marks on his skin.

"What's this?" she said, pointing to a bruise on David's chest.

Mr. Jenkins put it there the other day. But he didn't tell her that.

"It's nothing. I just caught it with the bike," he said. "I was trying to put it away and hit myself on the handlebars."

"Right."

Edith rested her lips on it. To start with, it tickled. David squirmed slightly, but the more he did the more she held position.

"What's wrong?" she sniggered, looking up at him.

"Doesn't matter," he smiled. "Carry on."

And she did, her kisses moving further down his body until she was undoing his belt and hitching up her dress.

***

They met in the usual place. "We'll have to be quick today," David told Edith. "Jenkins wants me back by three."

"Oh, right."

She checked her watch. That only gave them an hour. One hour for deliveries and – more importantly – that other little thing.

They got to that first. Just in case there wouldn't be time later.

In one of the wheat fields, stalks half their height, David dumped the bicycle and followed Edith as she crawled ahead of him into the crops. They crouched down and began undressing, stopping every now and then to let their lips meet.

"Sorry about yesterday," said Edith, as David helped her out of her blouse.

"Oh."

"Did your friends say anything after I left?"

"No. I thought maybe…" He eased her into the right position. "I just thought William might have noticed something."

"Really?"

"But he never said anything."

Afterwards, David stood up. Checked that they were alone, that no one would be able to see them, then began dusting bits of the field from his trouser legs while Edith sorted out her clothes.

"Best get a move on," he smiled, then glancing again: ahead, behind, left, right. "Come on. It's safe."

"You've got some orders for the Common, haven't you?" she said, putting her perfect white arms back through her top and getting to her feet. "Take them first, then I'll go on home and you can finish the rest without me."

"Oh. Fine," nodded David.

"Then that should get you back by three. Right?"

And why not? Why shouldn't she do that? Because the real reason for them meeting up – their fumble in the farmland – has been and gone, for today at least – leaving behind nothing but the grass stain on her skirt (though how long will her mother keep believing them to be careless accidents?) and the aching sense that, one day, these secret moments may cease their secrecy.

The sun was huge and glorious above them. If only they could have felt it a little longer on their skin, with the gentle breeze shunting through the wheat-shoots.

"I've talked to my mum about you, you know?"

"What?"

"Not properly – don't worry. She doesn't know about... this." She put her hand over his as it clutched the handlebars. "No, I mean – we talked about..." Edith shrugged her shoulders. David felt a slight tremble run down her fingers. "About feelings, you know?"

"Oh, right."

"David? You do *love* me, don't you?"

He'd assumed that's what she was talking about, when she mentioned feelings, even hoped she'd use that very word – but to turn it round on him...

She asked him again. "You do love me, don't you?"

"I..."

He didn't know what to say. He knew the word: thought he knew what it meant, what it felt like, but now...

And suddenly she was apologetic: saw the unease in his face, perhaps; the year there is between them, maybe...

"Sorry. I shouldn't have brought it up, not now..."

Then, when? How much further will they have to go before it becomes something they *can* talk about without one – or both of them, for all David knew – feeling flushed and queasy?

"Forget about it," she said, carrying on along the lane. "Come on. Don't want Jenkins getting mad, eh?"

He knew what that felt like, at least.

For a little while, they walked a few paces apart. Edith took the lead. (So, no change there, then. She led him that first time into the field, into the run-down cattle shed. She took his hand, showed him where to touch, what to do once she'd unzipped his trousers. But. It wasn't really like that now, was it? Take earlier on. It was *him* pushing *her* to the ground. It was *him* telling *her* how to move, what worked best. So, that year difference – it didn't really count for much anymore.)

"Edith?"

She stopped; looked back at him.

He caught up to her. "So – what did your mum say about it?"

"You mean…?"

They carried on walking. He signalled for her to hold the handlebars again.

"You mean about…?"

Now *she* couldn't even say it.

David nodded. "What did she say it felt like?"

"She said it felt like this."

He smiled. "Good. That's good. Because – I think I do."

"What? You can't stop thinking about me?"

"No." Shaking his head.

"And your heart leaps when you see me?"

"Yes."

"And when you're with me, it's like there's nothing else going on in the world?"

"Yes."

"Oh," she smiled, her fingers feeling in the grooves and bumps of his hand. "Sounds like we've got a problem, then."

"Good."

***

A minute after leaving the house, David realised he was whistling. It was three years since that first October day in the butcher shop, and that tune – which he quickly halted – was a sudden reminder.

The sky was clear above him, daylight beginning to spread broad brushstrokes.

So, three years. Longer than the time he spent at school. And what did that count for now? But, best laid plans… Perhaps it was always supposed to be altered. For one thing, he probably wouldn't have seen the inside of that cattle shed from down on the floor, felt the warm touch of Edith's body against his own, if he'd still been at school.

Seven in the morning. He turned the corner. Shop lights spilt across the concrete. Opposite – he always checked – the bus stop remained in shadow beneath the great, wide oaks. David could hear the rooks. Looked up and saw their stick-and-twig colony; two-, three-dozen nests, occupying the highest reaches of the trees.

Inside, David found Mr. Jenkins in the cold room. "Morning," he said, so the butcher wouldn't be spooked (or worse) when he came out and found he was no longer the only one in the shop.

"Morning, lad," he heard him say as he wandered over to the coat hook. He emerged with a full tray. "Now – most of this is for the deliveries." Mr. Jenkins set it down noisily on the counter. "I want you to get them done before lunch today."

"What? You mean – do the deliveries before lunch?"

"Yes." Mr. Jenkins looked down at him. "That's what I said, isn't it?"

"Right." But what about Edith, he thought. She'll be expecting him at the normal time.

"We're getting something special from the abattoir and it can only come in the afternoon – so I need us both here for when it arrives."

David nodded. Picked up the sweeping brush.

"It's for them at Trinity Hall, you see."

"Right." He wasn't all that interested. He was just wondering what Edith would think when he didn't show up.

"They put in a special order last week. Some big do they're having." He disappeared back into the cold room. "Though why they need so much just for a few posh bits in dinner suits, I've no idea." He came back out. Another tray-full. "Still. They're paying for it. So, who am I to question them?"

***

"Turned up today, eh?"

"Sorry. It was Jenkins. There was some delivery we were getting, so I took the orders round in the morning."

"It's fine. Don't worry. I assumed it'd be something like that."

She took hold of the left handlebar and started walking alongside him. Another bright, mild October day – the second in succession.

"You weren't waiting long were you?"

"No," she smiled. "I gave you half-an-hour. Then I left."

"Sorry."

"You've said that already." Then, a little later: "But I've been thinking. You're sixteen in a few weeks…"

"Six," added David.

"Right. Whatever. But, after your birthday, I'd quite like to tell my mum about you. And…" (There's more, is there?) "Maybe you could tell *your* mum too."

For a while, David didn't know what to say in response.

Edith continued: "It'd just be nice, you know? I know there'll be all these questions. Like, how long have you known each other? How serious is it? And my dad – he might not be happy about it…" (That doesn't sound good.) "But I want them all to meet you. And I want to be able to go around to yours too and play with your sisters, you know, and bake stuff with your mum, and…"

She made it sound so simple.

But maybe it was.

"What will you say?" David finally responded.

"How do you mean?"

"Well. How are you going to tell them? What words will you use?" (Typical David – thinking about the minute details.)

"I don't know. I haven't thought about that yet." (Typical Edith – getting ahead of herself.)

"What if they don't approve?" he asked, when they'd done the first delivery.

"Why wouldn't they?"

"You said it yourself – your dad might not like the idea."

"Yes, but – he doesn't like the idea of food from tins and Mum still gives him corned beef in his sandwiches."

"So?"

"So, he'll get to liking it – he'll get to like *you*. Why wouldn't he?"

"Right. So, what will you say, then?"

She leant across and kissed his cheek. "I'll think of something."

***

His birthday was a Sunday. Rather than meet up with Robert, William and Michael – because now, most weekends, it's all three of them – he'd arranged, instead, to see Edith.

David peered into the kitchen. "I'll see you later, then, Mum." He made to go.

"Eh! Come here first."

She stood in the doorway, holding her arms out. David walked towards her. Put his arms out too.

"I'm *so* proud of you," she sighed into his shoulder.

"I know," he replied, muffled by her cardigan, which he could feel unpleasantly on his lips and tongue.

She released him. Stepped back. "Have a good afternoon."

"Thanks. I will."

"What time do you think you'll be back?"

"About three."

"Right. And you're sure the boys don't want to come back for some tea?" (Because, of course, that was who he told her he was seeing.) "I'm sure I can manage to get something sorted."

"No. It's fine. They've got to be back home so they're ready for school and everything."

"Course they have. Another time maybe."

Edith waited for him by the stream in the copse. "All right?"

"Yes," he replied.

It felt strange not to have a bicycle tagging along.

"You?"

"Mmm." She kissed him. "Great."

They perched next to each other on one of the felled trees. David remembered first noticing this one had fallen a few days after a particularly rough thunderstorm.

"Good day so far?"

"Yeah, you know – fine."

"Good." She smiled, inching closer, resting her head on David's right shoulder. "I don't really have anything planned. I just wanted some time with you – you know – where you don't have to rush back to the shop."

David turned his head, so it nestled on hers, the right side of his face tickled slightly by her hair – odd that he didn't mind that quite as much as his mother's itchy cardigan.

"Oh." She straightened. "I did make you something though." Edith rooted around in her bag. "It's nothing, really." She passed it to him. "My mum's been showing me how to crochet. So, I thought I'd do you a scarf – for when you're out doing deliveries."

"You mean when *we're* out doing deliveries."

"Right. I told her it was for me. That's why it's that colour." She looked down at it in David's hands. "Hope you don't mind."

"No. I like purple." He unfolded it. Began winding it round his neck.

"Here…" She was stood in front of him now. "Let me."

David watched her mouth as she put it on him.

"There."

"Thanks."

"You fancy…?"

David nodded. "Where do you think…?"

"Here?"

"Really?" David looked around. Though he'd never known anyone, other than him and his friends, come this way for a Sunday lunchtime walk. "It's a bit nippy."

Edith smiled. "Doesn't matter." And she rested a hand, right where his heart throbbed fullest, and leant in for another, longer kiss.

David got up and fastened his belt. Brushed the dead leaves from his knees. Edith remained on the ground, her legs hunched up against her chest, her back pressed square against the horizontal tree trunk. Her top was unbuttoned, and her underwear lay at David's feet. He picked it up, cleaned some soil off the clasp and the padding, then dangled it by her head.

"Here you go," he smiled.

She took it off him. "Thanks." But didn't put it on. "Come on." She patted the space beside her. "Come and sit with me."

He did.

"We've got some more time, haven't we?"

David took hold of Edith's left wrist – the one that wore her watch; brought it slowly towards him. Quarter-to-two. "Plenty," he said.

"Good." She sighed and settled her head against the sharp bark.

David couldn't help looking at her bare, white chest – there was a beauty there he still didn't quite understand. He caught Edith watching him. She smiled; kissed him on the neck, the skin she'd exposed resting perfectly on his arm.

"Sorry," he said.

"What for?"

Sometimes he thought perhaps he shouldn't just stare at her, but he really couldn't resist. "Doesn't matter."

With one of her cold fingers, Edith started drawing circles round one of David's new scars. "Does it hurt?" she asked him.

"What? That?" He looked down at the bruise.

"Mmm." She seemed to be studying it.

"No." Though it did a bit – less so now, but when it first happened…

She rarely asked him now about the marks. Perhaps she knew. Perhaps she'd always known.

"Did you say your mum had invited the boys to tea?"

David nodded slowly.

And then she was standing and dressing herself properly, checking her skirt was on the right way around.

David stood up too. "What? Are you going?"

"Sort of."

He put on his coat. "What do you mean?"

"Don't you think it'd be easier to tell your mum first?"

"Wait. Edith? Tell her what?"

"About this. About us."

"You mean everything? You mean *this*?" David pointed down at the ground, at the tree against which they finished.

"No, not everything – that would be silly. Just us. How we feel."

"I don't know."

"Come on. It'll be nice. You say you've a brought a friend after all. Introduce me."

"Introduce you? Like, what? Hello, Mum. So, I know I've never mentioned her, but this is my girlfriend, Edith. I wasn't really meeting my other friends and I thought I'd bring her back with me to see you. Look – she made me this scarf."

"Something like that," she smiled.

David sniffed. 'something like that," he repeated.

"What's wrong?"

"I don't know," he sighed. "I don't know what you're expecting."

"Look. I just want to…" She reached out for one of his hands, either of them, just the feel of his skin. "This is great. But I want to get to know you better. And your mum, your sisters, they're all a part of that."

"You're really sure?"

She nodded.

"Cause this could really change things."

"I know."

The front door was ajar, and the girls were in the garden. They looked puzzled as David walked up the path with someone they'd never seen before. They dropped their dolls on the grass – which was long overdue to be mown; another of David's jobs now – and followed them in.

"Mum!" called David, stepping inside. "I'm back."

Esther came out from the kitchen, tea towel in one hand, dinner plate in the other. "Good. I was just… Oh." She'd spotted Edith. "Hello. David?"

"This is Edith, Mum."

"Hello, Edith – nice to meet you." She looked again at David, the same question etched into her face.

He had thought of a few ways of starting, on their walk over; Edith had made a suggestion too; but, right at that moment, he couldn't recall any of them. "She's a new friend. I mean, we've known each other quite a while, but…" He looked over at Edith, then behind at his sisters. "I thought maybe she could stay for tea, since…"

"Oh. Of course. More the better." She ducked back into the kitchen, then returned empty-handed. "Maybe, girls, you could take Edith upstairs and show her your dolls. I'm sure she'd like that." She shot a stare at Edith. "Yes?"

"Yes, Mrs. Denby."

"Some of them are in the garden, Mum."

"Well go and get them, then." Then she disappeared into the kitchen again.

David edged closer to Edith. Whispered: "We'll tell her properly later – I promise."

"It's fine."

Then his mother was back in the room. "I hope you like ham, Edith."

"Oh, yes – very much, thank you."

"Good," she said with a very deliberate smile. "David – come and give me a hand while the girls all go upstairs."

"Oh…" He looked quickly at Edith.

"I hope your parents know you're here."

David hadn't even thought of that.

"Yes. We have Sunday dinner quite early – at lunchtime – and I told them I'd be back quite late."

"Right. And they don't mind? You do that a lot, do you?"

"Oh, no – not really – but they know they can trust me."

Josie and Lily came back in; started going up the stairs.

"Don't forget Edith, girls."

She took the hint and followed them up. David headed to the kitchen.

"So…." His mother leant over the stove, wooden spoon in her right hand. "When was it you met her, then?"

"I was delivering to her house and she answered the door."

"She not at school, then."

"No. She works for the Potters at the Orchard."

"Right. Picks apples, does she?"

"No, actually – they have chickens and she looks after them."

"Oh – similar line of business to you, then, if you think about it."

David had *never* thought about it. He wanted to say that surely it was more like what you did at the farm. But instead: "I suppose so," he said.

"And did you just bump into her on your way back?"

"Yes," lied David.

"Good job I have a bit extra, then – isn't it?"

The pans started to steam and hiss wildly. David rolled up his shirt sleeves.

"What do you boys get up to, anyway?"

"Sorry?"

She pointed to his trousers. "You're covered in muck."

"Oh…" David hadn't realised it was so bad. He'd assumed he'd cleaned it all off.

"You still play that blumming shooting-war-game-whats-it?"

David nodded – though it'd been a thing of the past since the real one began.

"Pass us the salt, please."

"Here."

She added a bit to the biggest pot.

Unless he was mistaken, David could hear giggling coming from above.

"You can set the table if you like – that'd be a big help."

David went over to the cutlery drawer and got what he needed – five sets, not four. Just like a few years previously when there were always five at the dining table.

"Girls!" shouted Esther from the kitchen doorway.

They came down fairly swiftly. Edith followed behind, broad smile.

"All right?" he said, quietly, when she stood close by, watching him put down the last of the placemats.

"Fine."

"Right…" Esther looked at the table. "How about you sit there, David?" She pointed to the seat his father used to sit at.

"Sure?" he checked.

"Yes. And Edith…" She stood by David's chair, clamped both hands firmly on the backrest. "You can go here."

She sat down.

"That's where *I* usually sit," said David, pulling his father's chair out.

"Oh, well – if you want…"

"No – just saying."

"Josie – *you* can help me serve up."

"Yes, Mum."

And Lily joined them at the table. "Edith liked *my* doll best."

"Oh, did she?"

"Yes."

"Well, I didn't quite say that…"

But Josie was back in the room, a plate in each hand. "That's yours." She put it in front of her sister, then edged along to Edith. "And that's yours."

"Thank you."

"But you said you liked her hair," spluttered Lily through half a potato.

"Well, yes – that's true."

Josie returned with her plate and Esther had David and her own. Once they were all sat, once the knives and forks had begun their work, little more was said.

"I hope this is all right for you, Edith," said Esther, part way through.

"Yes, Mrs. Denby." She quickly swallowed what was in her mouth, flinging a hand up to hide the fact. "It's lovely."

"Good. David doesn't bring many friends round, do you?"

"Well, Robert's been quite a bit – and the others too, a few times."

"You must be a very good friend, my dear." She did that quick, deliberate smile again – as if it was all some elaborate joke designed solely for her – and then took in a mouthful of peas. Then again, later, when their plates were all but cleared: "So – you look after chickens, I hear?"

"Oh…" Brief glance at David. "That's right."

"Nothing to be ashamed of, love – I've done a bit of that in my time." (His mother, occasionally, took work at one or a few of the local farms when they were busy and in need of extra help. Most of the time it would involve the cows or the sheep, but sometimes it had to do with the chickens.) "Interesting little things, aren't they?"

"I suppose so."

"Got characters of their own, they have."

That was something Edith had said to David a few times.

"Yes. Actually – there's a few I've given names to."

"Oh, yes – like what?"

"Well, there's one called Poppy, and another called Gran – because she's the oldest and got white and grey feathers. And then there's one always falling over so I call her Tripping." She looked across at Lily who was putting all her effort into stabbing what remained of her peas with her fork, chinking the plate in the process. "Anyway – silly, really."

"Well – I guess you spend so much time with them, it's only natural you notice these things." She stood up. "Finished?"

Thanks." Edith held out her plate. "Would you like a hand with the dishes?"

"Yes – that'd be wonderful."

Edith let her take her plate, but then began gathering the rest up. "You sure you're finished," she said to Lily.

"Yes, thank you."

David stayed at the table with his sisters. They started arguing about who Edith liked best out of the two of them.

Then Josie leant in, glancing at David. "No, actually, I think she likes David best."

"Oh," he said.

Lily stuck out her tongue. Why on earth would she like a *boy* best?

"Really? Why do you think that?"

"Because, when we were in our bedroom, all she wanted to know was what was yours, and where did *you* sleep, and which book did you look at the most, and she said how you'd told her loads of things and that you were really clever, so – *that's* why."

When they were done in the kitchen, his mother came out, still holding the tea towel. "How about you show Edith what you got for your birthday."

"Yes." He stood up. The squeak of the chair as it shifted over the boards. "All right."

She followed him up silently just as she had done earlier with the girls. David reached under his bed and pulled out a white box. Inside were some shoes.

"They're for work," he told her.

"Oh. Smart."

"But Mum says I'm to wait until my other's have fallen apart." He put the lid back on. "And then there's this…" He stretched across the bed sheets and lifted a book from off the bedside table. "It's about the ocean," he explained, opening it randomly.

"Right. Do you fancy just sailing off somewhere, then?"

"Not exactly – no. It's just interesting."

"Do you not ever think that, though – about getting away to somewhere you've never been before?"

David shook his head. That had never occurred to him. "Why – do you?"

"I have done. Not much, but… sometimes."

He put the book down beside him on the bed. The light outside draining into dusk.

"I think I should probably get going now."

"Right," nodded David.

"This has been good, though – being here. I'll go down, say goodbye to everyone – but don't worry about walking back with me. I'll be fine."

Esther had other ideas however. "David?" Noticing him without his coat or shoes. "You not going to see her home safe?"

"I'll be fine, Mrs. Denby."

"Nonsense. Go on, David."

They stuck to the main lanes, their shadows indistinguishable in the creeping blackness.

"Sorry. I know it wasn't quite how you'd planned."

"Probably for the best."

"You think?"

"It'd been silly turning up and announcing it like that."

"Suppose."

"This way we all get to know each other gradually."

David sniffed – another cold coming on.

"I am invited again, aren't I?"

"Course."

"And, soon, I'll sort something out with *my* parents. My birthday's not that far away, either."

She inched closer, so that they were touching without having to hold hands. David heard what sounded like an owl; the sudden rustling of something in the field. He huddled even tighter.

"The Caribbean," Edith suddenly announced.

"You what?"

"That's where I'd go – if I had the nerve."

"Why there?"

"I saw a picture once. It looked beautiful. And whenever I think of going somewhere else – you know, somewhere completely different – that's what I see."

"Do you think you'd ever be able to do it? Just leave?"

"Yes." Then for a moment she rested a hand on the small of his back. "If someone took me with them."

When he got in, the girls were sat by the fire and Esther was watching them from her armchair.

"Happy birthday, son," she said, once he was settled opposite her. Then she sighed and went on: "I guess I never realised how grown up you were getting."

"How do you mean?"

"Courting already. But I suppose me and your father were around your age when we met."

"Wait. I never said…"

"You didn't have to *say* anything. A mother sees these things. But, don't worry, she seems like a nice lass." She sat there, nodding to herself, not even looking at him, like she was about to drop to sleep.

David decided to head up himself, and he took the girls with him, just as his mother shut her eyes.

***

The ground was damp after another short, April rainstorm. They waited it out under the trees.

"So, would you do it?" asked Robert, once they'd got moving again.

"Join up, you mean?"

"Course," William answered for him.

"We wouldn't have much choice," added David.

"Suppose."

They walked the perimeter of one of the unused fields. There was a man and his dog with the same idea, half a lap ahead. Michael stooped down to grab a fallen branch. Began prodding it into the hedgerow.

"How do you reckon Edith would be about it?"

"What? Signing up?"

Robert nodded, his hands rooted in his coat pockets.

"I think she'd support it. We've talked about it a bit."

"What about Helen?"

"The same, I think," replied Michael.

Just before his sixteenth birthday, Michael left school. Just as David had expected. (Though it had taken much longer than he expected too.) He started working in a haberdashery as a trainee sales clerk. At first, he would tell them about business things: how much – and what – he'd managed to sell that week. But soon he was talking about the others that worked there: the girls, and this one girl in particular called Helen. And when he finally told them they'd started seeing each other, a few evenings at the pictures and a bit of holding hands, it only took David a few more weeks to find the courage to tell them about Edith.

"So – do you just get made to go and sign up?" asked William.

"I don't think it's quite like that."

"Oh."

"I don't really know."

"I think they send a letter," Robert chipped in. "Someone my mum knows, their son has just turned eighteen."

"Right."

"Mmm. That's what *I* heard too," added Michael.

Suddenly they all knew how it worked. But all David knew was that as soon as he reached his eighteenth birthday, he was going down to the nearest civic hall and filling in every bit of paperwork they gave him. Anything to get away from the butcher shop.

***

The bell chimed.

"Good morning, Mrs. Beedall. How are you today?"

"Can't grumble, thank you. Yourself?"

"Oh, you know…" He watched Mrs. Beedall feeling around inside her handbag, emerging with her purse and her ration book. "What're you after, then?"

"*You* tell *me*," she said. "What is there that's good today?"

"We've plenty of beef."

"Right." She peered through the glass at the stuff all plated and priced.

"It's a good cut, this one."

"Yes?"

"The best."

"Go on, then. You've convinced me." She placed her ration book on the counter. "I could do to get some sausages too."

Mr. Jenkins looked over the pencil marks. "Right. We can do, say, three. But that'll just about fill you up for the week."

David turned from sorting out the beef, double-checking it on the scales, then wrapping it up.

Her lips screwed, Mrs. Beedall took a moment to decide. "Fair enough," she said finally. "Three sausages, please."

"That's not a problem." Mr. Jenkins leant in under the counter and grabbed them. "What'll that be, David?"

He went over to the cash register. Rang it in. "One-and-three."

"One-and-three, please," repeated the butcher. He passed the coins – exact, no need for change – to David. "Thank you very much, Mrs. Beedall."

"Not at all." She stuffed them into her bag.

"See you next time."

"Cheerio."

And the bell chimed her out.

"Now – go get us some more sausage meat, lad."

David went straight to the cold room.

"You see it?" called the butcher.

"Yes, Mr. Jenkins." David closed the heavy door, but, turning to go through into the front, he caught the leg of one of the counters with the heel of his left foot. The pig mince spilled on to the floor, the metal dish spinning off towards the furnace.

"What are you doing in there?" Mr. Jenkins appeared in the doorway.

"Sorry."

Seeing what had happened, he charged over to David. Knocked him down to the ground, stamping hard on his right hand. David tried not to make too much noise – that only ever seemed to encourage him.

"Sorry," he tried again.

"That'll come out of your wages," he said, lifting his foot and pushing past him into the cold room. "Good job we've plenty more." He emerged with a second container, stepping on his other hand too. "Woops! Now clean all that up."

***

David had filled four notebooks and, looking through them, he could see his handwriting grew more fractured, more intense, his daily entries longer. There were some good signs for the Allies – the invasion of Italy had begun, there had been German submarines sunk in the Atlantic; but the picture across the rest of mainland Europe looked rather more shaky.

It was October, now four years since he left school; late Saturday afternoon, the last dregs of daylight.

Edith was over again. She found the books in his bedside table drawer. "What're these?" she asked, one journal already spread open on her lap.

"Oh..." David jumped up beside her, having been rummaging for something else under his bed. "They're nothing." He held his hand out, hoping she would pass them back to him.

"What's it about?"

David watched her eyes scanning the page.

"Are they all like this?"

"Mmm."

"They're about the war, aren't they?"

"Yes," he nodded. "I just like to, you know…"

"Write it down," she offered.

"Right."

She flicked on a few pages. "How long does it take you?"

"Not long. I do a bit each day, so…"

"Mmm. I thought it might've been your diary."

"Oh – what? And you were just going to open it and see what I'd put, eh?"

"I guess so," she smiled. "I need to know what you're saying about me."

"And who says I'd be saying anything about you."

"Oh. *I* see," she laughed, closing the notebook.

Listening carefully to what was going on downstairs, David leant across and kissed her left cheek. It was still red from the cold walk over.

"Do *you* have one?" he asked. "A diary?"

She nodded cautiously.

"I know what I'll be looking for then, next time I'm round."

"Oh, really – I'll have to start thinking of somewhere to hide it."

And she kissed him back, soft and square on the mouth. David couldn't help focusing on the noises below them. But they carried on, and he felt Edith's hand rest – perhaps accidentally – round about his upper thigh. She pulled away from the kiss; smirked.

"Not here," whispered David, his lips and Edith's lips still barely apart.

She left her hand there.

"What if…?"

She pressed harder. Said: "What?"

He couldn't think – what? why? – not with her so close, not with her hand…

Edith gently loosened his belt and felt her way inside, her cold fingers tightening further. David winced, and she caught it with a quick, strong kiss, her hand still holding him hard.

"Is that...?"

"No. Edith, stop."

Her grip loosened. "What?"

"We can't – not now."

"But I was only going to..."

"I know, but..."

"Suppose." She sat back. Helped him out with his trousers. "What do you reckon your Mum would've done if she'd caught us?"

"Don't know."

"Mine'd go mad, I reckon." Then, after a brief pause, she asked him: "Do you think Michael and Helen have done this yet?"

"No idea. But you know Michael – it's not the sort of thing he'd tell us about."

"So, you don't talk to your friends about this?"

"No. Why would I?"

"Don't know. Just wondered."

"Why? Do *you* talk to *your* friends about this?"

"Might do."

He could see her smiling without even needing to look.

"Really?"

"Well – I can't talk to my mum about it, can I?"

"No, but..." Why do you need to *talk* about it? What is there to talk about? "I just thought... It's private, isn't it?"

"I don't tell them every little thing."

"So?"

"We just talk. You've nothing to worry about. Promise."

David still hadn't met Edith's friends and, right at that moment, he was rather glad he hadn't.

A Few More...

October, again. In a month, David will be eighteen. He's counting down the days. Has been, really, for years.

Speaking of which, it was William's birthday the other week. He did what all these boys are going to do: went straight into the town and put his name down; signed it off on the dotted line.

"And was that it?" David asks him.

"Pretty much – they just said come back on the twenty-first with the rest filled in."

"Can't wait till it's my turn," he sighs.

"Won't you miss selling sausages?" grins Robert.

"I'll get over it."

"Won't you miss Edith, more like?"

David looks at William. "I..."

That hadn't really occurred to him. But he's right. There'll be a distance between them that they haven't felt before. It's not as if he'll be able to break away – like he can at the shop – and meet her for... whatever... in some field.

"I'll write," he offers.

But it sounds so slight. It's just not the same. It's not the same as...

Still, he thinks, anything has to be better than going into that shop every day, not knowing what kind of mood Jenkins'll be in. He can't quite believe that he's managed to keep it all hidden from everyone – especially Edith, who must know every inch of his skin by now. And every time it happens, he just thinks about Michael, all those times he watched him at school...

The tree branches creak and wave, fallen leaves swirling at their feet. The wind batters David's back, pushing him along like a firm, parental hand. *That's it. Keep going. Not far now.*

And there isn't far to go, is there?

A few more delivery rounds...

A few more circuits of the shop floor with the sweeping brush...

And a few more blasts of the butcher's temper...

PART TWO

Now & Then

Now

David switches the radio on, tilting the aerial forty-five degrees or so towards the bread-bin, then grabbing the kettle. At the sink, he fills it two-thirds, puts it on the hob, and lights the gas with a blue flash. He sets the cups and saucers out on the worktop, then goes and pulls back the curtains. Condensation covering the bottom half of the window, he can see the blurry shape of the young lad next-door mowing the lawn. He glances at the clock. Half-past eight. A loose thread dangles from the right arm of his pyjama top. He starts winding it tight round one finger. Only then does he realise what the newsreader is saying.

Argentine naval ships have entered...

He turns the sound up a few notches – the hiss of the boiling water starting to drown it out.

The House of Commons will today debate its response...

Edith walks in. She starts to speak, but he quickly shushes her.

The news report continues. It mentions something about a military task force, a statement from Number Ten. Then it ends, and the next story begins – a huge earthquake in Central America.

"What is it?" she whispers, eventually.

"This is how it started last time," says David, reaching for the teabags and checking on the water.

"How what did?"

"Won't be long before there's others getting involved. Then what'll happen?"

Edith doesn't answer. But she isn't meant to.

He finishes making the drinks. They sit quietly at the kitchen table. Radio voices discuss the new book by some up-and-comer (what did they say his name was? Somebody Swift?) – one of the reviewers calls it ambitious, more accomplished than his previous offering; the others seem less convinced. Then a politician is on to introduce what he calls an "overdue, much-needed" agricultural initiative, to do with the growing of crops.

Sadly, for him, the interviewer sounds unimpressed; far more interested in talking about Argentina and the South Atlantic.

Edith sips softly at her tea. She's been dressed a few hours now; dusted and polished most of downstairs – apart from the kitchen – the bathroom and bedrooms next on her list.

Outside, the clouds break. The forecast – sunny spells and high temperatures for the time of year – may just prove correct.

David gets up to make some toast. "Want some?" he asks, firing up the grill.

Edith shakes her head.

"You already...?"

Edith nods her head.

"Right." He hadn't heard. Normally he does. Normally he listens, tries to pick out what she's doing from the sounds, like smells, wafting through the house.

Like with the tea, David lays out the plate and the butter and the butter knife ready, before crouching down to check on the bread. He doesn't like it too well-done. He pulls the grill tray out, turns both slices over, and puts them back under.

"Don't know why you bother," says Edith. "More like warmed-up bread the way *you* have it."

He peers under the grill again. Almost there, just another couple of seconds. It has to be *that* precise. He watches the bread begin to brown off.

"Anyway..." Edith gets to her feet. "I'll get on."

He nods, "All right," at the same time as removing the tray and turning off the grill. He covers both slices with plenty of butter and sits down to eat, the radio still talking away on the worktop.

It seems they finally have someone on who's there to speak specifically about what's brewing off the South American coast. Some typical, Tory-sounding chap; all he's got to say is maybes and we'll-sees and it's-not-really-clear-at-this-stage. Hardly worth bothering with.

David takes his time with the washing up. Notices him next-door again: now he's hauling things out of the shed – making a right noise of it too.

Does he have to? Really?

Then something little and bright lands on the fence, followed by another (a juvenile, its plumage less developed). They sing – two, three notes – and then they're gone. As far as he can recall, that's the first goldfinches he's seen this spring.

Edith reappears. "Just go careful in there, will you?" She's talking about the downstairs bathroom. "I don't want to have to re-do it, now."

"No," he says, rinsing the last of the crockery and standing it to drain.

"No, what?" Edith waits in the doorway.

"No. I'll be careful."

"Good. I'm upstairs now."

"No, you're not," he says.

She doesn't seem to appreciate the joke. Turns and starts up the stairs.

He dries his hands. The lad next-door's still clattering on. For a few moments, David stops and watches. He's up to this kind of thing every weekend. Then, worrying he might be spotted, he returns the hand-towel to its hook and heads for the door.

Sunlight fills the hallway. Vases catch and re-direct it.

He wonders where the dog's hiding himself. Thought he might have come in while he was making breakfast.

"Billy?" he says, his pitch peaking.

The dog emerges from the sitting room.

"There you are. Where've *you* been hiding?"

He comes and rests his body against David's right leg. He stretches down and strokes his side.

"You been out yet?" he says.

The dog stares up at him.

"Yes? No?" He straightens up. "Come on, eh?"

David goes to the back door. Billy follows him.

"There you go."

The dog trots happily out and David closes it after him.

"Just let Billy out," he calls up to Edith.

"Right."

"Going for a shave."

"Right."

In the downstairs bathroom, he unbuttons his pyjama top and folds it, leaving it on the side of the bath. Fills the hand basin lukewarm, looking for a while at the shadowy reflection, then gets a good dollop of shaving foam in both hands and spreads it even across his face, like butter over toast. Reaching for the razor, he dips it into the water, then, in steady strokes, starts clearing the white stuff off again. It always reminds him of painting a wall. Only, in reverse.

Then

It felt like a steak knife poking around inside his leg. The metal frame of the camp-bed creaked. David lifted a hand to his eyes. Rubbed a bit of the long sleep out of them.

"Finally, with us, then," said a female voice.

"Sorry?" Everything looked a blur. David closed his eyes again.

Then it was a man speaking, saying hello and asking if he could take a look at him.

"What...?" He coughed through the rest of the question.

"Don't worry," the man said. "You're on the mend." He put David's leg back down, gently. "You just need plenty of rest." And then he left.

Daylight. David could hear birdsong and – at intervals – jet engines. He tried to sit up. The bed creaked again. He expected someone to come and stop him. He tried looking round, but his vision was still unfocused, cloudy. *I've not...* A horrible thought suddenly occurred to him.

"Well, hello there."

Was that the same girl as last time? He rubbed his eyes. When *was* the last time? He didn't know whether he'd slept for hours or for days.

"How do you feel?"

"Not sure," he answered.

"How's your leg?" she asked, more specifically.

"Sore."

"Yes." She leant over him, helping him sit more comfortably. "It will be for a while. But you're in very good hands here."

"Right."

"Can I get you some water?"

"Please."

She returned with a jug and a tumbler. "I'll put it just here, shall I?" She set them down on the cabinet to the left of his bed.

"Thank you."

"You're very welcome. I'll be back to check on you shortly."

What for? he thought. But he smiled and nodded.

***

When the news reached them, those in the hospital that could shouted and cheered.

HITLER IS DEAD, declared the newspapers.

In the days that followed, the German leadership, which was already fragmenting, was left to crumble completely. From all directions, the British, the Americans, the Russians, marched into Germany, and on the seventh of May 1945, Karl Donitz (appointed Reich President by Hitler the day he died) officially signed Germany's surrender to the Allies. (Though the Japanese held out a few months longer, the war was all but finished.)

But that was never how David imagined it would be. When the idea of war was simply that – a fantasy in a young lad's head, a game enacted on the playground – he and Robert, and William and Michael, would talk endlessly about the parts each of them would play. How it would be a great adventure. How they'd all be there, together of course, when Germany finally fell. How they'd witness, with their own eyes, the capture of Hitler and the other German officers, perhaps even be the ones to haul him out of his bunker – which he'd taken to, when things had started turning conclusively in the Allies" favour.

Instead, David was in a bed in a military hospital on the south coast of England. That was where he watched it all from, the end of the war, the end of Hitler. That was the end of his great adventure. And Robert... or William... or Michael...? He had no idea where they were, whether they were even...

After about a week, the pain in his leg began to ease. He was able to get out of bed, to walk himself to the toilet, rather than rely on the nurses, and he was able, also, to go outside.

The hospital had some grounds; nothing particularly special, just a lawn, a bird feeder, some benches and pot plants. But, as often as he could manage it, David would take himself out there to sit.

In fact, it's the place he first saw goldfinches.

But that's beside the point...

Out of all the boys in there, he seemed to be the only one showing any obvious signs of improvement. Which he should have been thankful for. Except, he would look at them – the ones with reddened bandages on their heads and the ones that never seemed to wake up – and then he would look back at his leg. He could hardly see the mark. The doctor said there was shrapnel in the wound, but that had long since been taken out.

So, was that it, then? All that waiting; is that what it had amounted to? A cut on the leg?

He'd have got worse staying on at the butcher shop.

In fact, he *did* get worse.

The days went on, and, to David, it all felt once-removed. He didn't feel like an injured soldier (could he even call himself a soldier? What had he done to warrant such a name?). Yes, the medical people kept saying they needed to keep him in longer, that there was still a danger of infection, but he would see, every morning, in the paper, the mopping-up, the return to the negotiating table, and it was like he'd played no part at all. The whole thing was at such a distance.

But maybe that was just as it should have been?

After all, when he was younger, all he ever saw or knew of the war was either ink on newspaper or voices from the wireless. Lines in his notebook.

Nothing had changed, then.

But yet – and this is what David sat and thought about most in those hospital grounds – *everything* had changed. Because David had wanted to be a part of it; he'd even encouraged his friends to want that too. He'd seen it as an honour, a duty, something to be proud of. He'd entered it, much like he had entered school, with an unflinching anticipation, which never actually took on any definite form, was more like the idea of something than the reality, and he'd left it feeling as if he'd barely touched it, just grasped at it, blindly, in the mist.

***

It was a while before he heard about the others. He was back home by then and, one evening, the telephone rang.

Edith answered. "Hello."

David watched her face. Moved closer, because he sensed it might be for him.

"Course," she said. "Here he is." She held the receiver for him to take. "It's Robert."

"What? Robert Fitzgerald?"

She nodded.

"Hello," he said.

They met up the following day – which, just for old times" sake, happened to be a Sunday.

"Glad to see more than one of us got out of it alive," said Robert, shaking David's hand and patting him firmly on the opposite shoulder.

What? Does that mean...? "So, do you know what happened – to the others?"

Robert nodded and gestured that they should sit down.

"Both of them?" said David.

"Apparently William was somewhere in Italy – Ancona, I think – and Michael ended up fighting the Japs."

David sighed. "How do you know all this?"

"I was invited to both their funerals – well, their memorial services. You were too, of course – but you were still in hospital."

"So – did Edith know about this, then?"

"Yes. But, she thought it'd be better if *I* told you."

"Right."

"When you came home, she let me know, so…"

"Here we are," David smiled. "Can I get you a drink?"

"No, let me."

They went inside. It was mid-afternoon, but the sunlight was failing to make any significant mark on the pub's interior. At the bar, they ordered their drinks, then went and sat down in one of the less gloomy corners. Talk about the war was avoided – not implicitly, just instinctively. The fact they were both there, that they at least had made it out, was as much as the other needed to know. The only mention came when Robert asked David if he'd recovered from his injury.

"What was it, exactly?"

"My leg." David patted the relevant limb.

"And it's not too bad now?"

He shook his head. "No. Hardly notice it."

"Good."

He didn't even ask what had happened, how he'd been injured, how he'd come to spend so long in hospital.

"So, what're you doing at the moment, then – for work?" asked David.

"I'm an apprentice draughtsman."

"Oh." Robert always was good at drawing; a skill David could never quite master himself. "Do you like it?"

"Mmm. Can't complain."

"And what sort of stuff do you draught?"

"It's really not very exciting," shrugged Robert. "We design systems for things like water storage and drainage."

"Right. Sounds a bit rubbish to me," grinned David.

"You could say that. What about you? You back at the butcher's?"

David drew in a deep breath. "No, I'm… I'm looking for something else."

"You better hurry up," said Robert, smiling.

"What do you mean?"

"Well – a man in your position needs a job."

***

Nine days after he woke up, David received a letter. He recognised Edith's handwriting on the envelope immediately and quickly opened it. She'd begun to get a little frantic, it said, because her last few letters hadn't been answered. (He hadn't received any, as far as he knew.) All sorts of thoughts came to mind, naturally, until a reply finally came from someone in the army telling her about his injury, but not to worry, it was nothing too serious, and that he'd been transferred here (they enclosed the hospital address and apologised for any undue stress the delay might have caused). *And don't you worry*, she added at the end, *everything seems to be going fine with me, so Mum reckons – only I don't want you missing it, so hurry up getting better and get yourself back here.*

He'd been meaning to write to her for a few days. Let her know he was all right. But he was putting it off. He didn't want to have to tell her what had happened to him. Not because he wanted to spare her the gruesome details: more because – odd as it sounded – there were no such details, not really, not in comparison to… And Edith had told him, repeatedly, before he left and in every letter since he left (those that he'd received, read, and replied to, at least), how brave she thought he was – she'd said the same thing again in this new letter – and, if anything, that word was the last he'd use to describe himself. Those others in the hospital – yes, *they* were brave. But, him? No.

David thought about that morning on platform three when he and Edith said goodbye. They'd sat, hardly talking, with cups of tea. They could hear the trains rumbling in and out. David kept checking the station clock.

"When's it due?" Edith asked, eventually.

"Twenty-three minutes past."

"We can go and wait, on the platform, if you'd rather."

"No, not just yet. In a few minutes."

Edith nodded and took another sip.

The station was filling up around them – young men, there for the same reason. There to make the same journey. But a journey to – where exactly? Surely, they wouldn't take you straight to the front-line – of which, at that point in the conflict, David knew all too well, there were several. (In fact, it turned out they took you to a training camp on the North Yorkshire moors, where for a few weeks you're covered in mud, rain and bruises.)

Watching them arrive, David even thought he recognised some of them. Were they in one of his old classes? Was that…? And he remembered Robert and William, who – only weeks earlier – were waved off from here. He thought about Michael, his turn yet to come. All four of them: the adventure just beginning; their schoolboy game grown very real.

Twenty-past. Edith tapped his hand. "Think it's here," she said, just as David, himself, noticed the approaching sound.

They stood up. He hauled his pack on to his right shoulder.

There was still no sign of the train. Perhaps the bodies on the platform were hiding it from view.

David turned to Edith. Smiled. It was all he could think to say.

"I love you," she told him.

He nodded. "I love you too."

Steam started swirling around them. The noise was deafening. He glanced round. The train – still pulling in – suddenly towered over everyone.

"I'll see you soon," he heard her say, just.

David edged closer, partly knocked by someone in the crowd. He rested his lips on her left cheek. Then stepped back and looked at her.

Edith smiled. "You sure you've everything you need?"

"Yes. Bit late now, anyway."

"I could get it sent on."

It felt like they were shouting at each other.

He kissed her again, on the lips.

"I love you," she repeated. "Look after yourself." Which seemed a little inadequate, given where he was going.

But David nodded. Reassured her; rubbing her arm. He could hear the train start to board. The conductor blew the first whistle.

"You know what I mean," said Edith, resting a hand on her stomach. "It's not just me who needs you safe back now, is it?"

Three weeks before David was due to leave, he found Edith in the bathroom at her house. "Oh," he said. "Sorry. Didn't realise you were..."

"No," she said, reaching out for the door handle. "Come in. There's something I need to..." She closed the door. She sounded flustered. "I think something's up."

"Like what?"

"I think maybe... I think I'm pregnant."

"What? Edith – are you sure?" Of all the times, just when he was about to disappear for God-knows-how-long. "Have you seen a doctor?"

"Not yet."

"Well, maybe you should, first, before..."

"What if Mum finds out?"

"But if you are, she's going to anyway."

"Oh, God!" She sat down on the toilet; her pale, bare legs suddenly very porcelain-like. "What do we do?"

David knelt down next to her. "Don't know," he muttered.

"Some use you are."

"Thanks."

"Oh," she sighed again. "Sorry." Ran a hand through his hair. "I just never expected..."

"Mmm. But you just couldn't resist me, could you?"

"Oh, don't!" She gave a sort of half-laugh. "Not now."

The next day, Edith met David, as usual, to help him with the deliveries. But there was no visit to the old cowshed or no detour into one of the fields. The first thing he said to her: "Have you decided what to do?"

She just looked at him.

"Right. Well. Let's think..."

But he couldn't. This wasn't something that could be easily fixed, like the bicycle chain going, and for a few more turns in the road, neither of them said another word.

Then: "There is one... possible... solution."

"Right?" David turned to look at her.

"We get married." Three words, said with utter simplicity.

"You serious?"

"What?" She sounded upset, offended. "You don't...?"

"No, not that – I just..."

"Think about it."

David *was* thinking about it.

"The problem is how do we tell our parents, about the..." She gestured to her belly. "But you're going away, right? So, we say we want to do it, get married I mean, before you go, and then... well... then it solves everything."

"Does it?"

"You got a better idea?"

"No. But it's a pretty big solution."

They'd reached the garden gate of one of the delivery stops. David picked up the package and walked up the path to the front door. Edith waited with the bike.

"It's not that I don't want to marry you," said David, once the delivery was done and they were moving again and no one else – that he could see – was around. "But there's already plenty going on right now. How will we find the time?"

Edith didn't answer.

David directed them, with a drop of the shoulder, down the next lane.

"Sorry," he said. "I didn't mean to..."

"No. I'm just thinking."

"Oh."

"See, I know what you're saying – but how else can we...?"

She left her question unfinished. David had to sort out the next order, leaving her at the garden gate, still trying to find the end to her sentence.

"What do we do, then?" she said, soon as he returned and clanked the gate shut, as if he knew full well what the solution was but was insisting she work it out herself.

"I don't know," he said.

They carried on up the lane. A gent with wire-rimmed glasses passed them going the other way, wishing them a good afternoon.

"Right," she said, once the man was far enough away. "Put it this way then; forget about the baby."

"It's not really that easy."

"Just do it – forget about it."

David nodded.

"Would you want to marry me?"

"Well..."

"You're not going away, either – everything's just... normal."

"And this is *you* asking me, not the other way around?"

"Come on, David. If I hadn't have told you I liked you in the first place, we'd never have got going."

"Suppose," he said.

"Right. So – come on, then. What do you say?"

"Yes." One word, said with utter simplicity.

"Yes, what?"

David laughed. "You can't have forgotten already. Yes. I'll marry you."

"What? You *would* marry me? Or you will?"

"I will."

"You sure?"

"It was *your* idea, Edith."

"No, I know. I'm just..."

"What? You don't want to now?"

"It's a big thing, David – don't joke about it."

"I'm not."

"How're we going to tell our parents?"

"Wasn't that the original problem?"

Finally, Edith smiled. "Suppose."

"What would you prefer – tell them we're getting married or tell them you're pregnant?"

"Well, when you put it that way."

They started, that evening, by speaking to David's mother.

"You're *what*?" she said.

"And we want to do it in the next two weeks," added David.

"Gosh!" gasped Esther. "You two don't do things by halves, do you?"

They looked at each other.

"Why so soon?"

"Well…" David thought that part would have been obvious. "I'm going away, aren't I?" She can't have forgotten that little thing, surely. "So, there's no other time, before…"

"You could've thought about this sooner, though."

Edith joined in. "It's only just started feeling real, Mrs. Denby."

"Esther, please."

"Right, sorry…"

"Especially now you're going to be…"

"Yes, I suppose, but – you know – since he might not…" She avoided David's gaze. "Since he might not…"

"Yes, well – let's not dwell on that, love."

"It's just this seemed like the right time."

"Mmm. Perhaps you're right," she smiled. "But it'll hardly be the best start to married life – separated for… well, goodness knows."

"I know," said Edith. "But I'd rather that than not at all."

It was a much trickier conversation to have with Edith's parents.

"But are you sure this is the best time?" Edith's mother looked particularly at David. "You've a lot going on at the minute."

Edith answered for him. "That's why we don't want to wait, Mum."

"Yes. I understand that, but... What does your mother say about this, David?"

"She wasn't sure at first, for the same sort of reasons, but she said she'll support us."

"Mmm. I just don't know..." muttered Mrs. Kemp.

Her husband had barely said a word yet, so Edith tried to draw him in. He'd usually side with her. "Come on, Dad."

"Don't need to talk to *me* about it," he said, his voice low and dry. "Sounds like you've both made up your minds anyway." He got up to leave the room. "If you've just come for my blessing, I suppose I can give you it – but that doesn't mean I'm happy about it."

"Dad?" Edith followed him out.

Mrs. Kemp called after her, "Leave him, love," and David just sat there, staring uncomfortably at the front room door. It was like the first time he visited, after Edith had introduced him and told them they were seeing each other.

"Sorry about that, David, love."

"Oh. No. It's fine."

"He doesn't... usually..."

"I know."

David glanced round the room, trying to avoid Mrs. Kemp's eye. He could hear Edith shouting for her father, the back door closing.

"You two seem..."

David was worried about what she might say.

"Well, you always seem very happy together, far as *I* can see."

He nodded. Smiled. Relieved.

"But marriage is… It's a big decision."

"I know, Mrs. Kemp."

"Right. You have to be really sure."

"I am," he said. "I love Edith." Which he realised he'd probably never said out loud to anyone other than Edith herself, not even his own mother.

"Yes. I can see you do. And I know Edith loves you. But it isn't just about loving each other – because feelings can change, you know?" (Was she still talking about them? Or something else?) Mrs. Kemp snapped to her feet. "Anyway. Can I get you another drink, just while they're…?"

"Err – yes, please."

But Mrs. Kemp had already whisked his cup away. "Back in a tick."

She left the door open. David peeked round after her. He considered getting up, going to help, just to stretch his legs more than anything – which ached after another day's pedalling – but David felt like a stranger all over again, intruding on something very private. He wondered whether him being there was just making it worse. Would it have been better for Edith to have told them on her own?

"Too late now, anyway," sighed David, quietly, to himself and the watching ornaments lining the mantelpiece.

He caught his reflection in the mirror. The high-backed armchair looked to tower above him. The thought of marriage and children suddenly seemed absurd. Perhaps that was what Edith's mother was trying to get through to him.

Mrs. Kemp returned to the room. She set his tea down by his feet.

"Thank you."

"You're welcome, dear."

"Are they…?"

"Just on their way through, I think."

"Right."

Then there they were. Silently, they sat back in their seats.

Mr. Kemp was the first to speak. "Edith and I have had a chat."

David wondered whether it was more like Edith had chatted and he had listened.

"Now I can't say I'm delighted about the idea."

"Dad?"

"But – you do, both, have my blessing."

He reached out and shook David's hand. It was – unsurprisingly – the firmest handshake Mr. Kemp had ever given him.

"So, what did you say to him?" asked David, when they were leaving for an early-evening walk.

"To Dad? Just that I love you and you love me and, with you going away, we wanted to do it before you went."

"Right. So, you didn't say anything about...?"

"Oh, God, no! Don't you think he would've come in, all guns blazing?"

"Suppose." David tried not to think about it. A few of his fingers still hurt – though it was the handshake combined with some earlier Jenkins-related treatment.

"And what would be the point in that, anyway?"

"I know."

They turned a corner in the lane. They weren't far from the duck pond and the bench David and Robert always used to walk to. The weeping willows: their long, leafy fingers.

"We *are* doing the right thing, aren't we?" asked David.

"Course," replied Edith.

"You're sure?"

"Look. I know it feels like we're hiding something from them."

"Which we are."

"But – we do love each other, right?"

David nodded.

"So, we're not lying about that, are we?"

"Suppose."

"And that's the important thing."

"So, you don't think they know something's up?"

"Why, do you?"

"Don't know. It's just... They might think it's all a bit sudden."

"But we said, didn't we – you going away, us getting ready for it, made us realise..."

"Right. I know."

"David?" She grabbed his hand, gently, but, also, there was no way of him resisting – she'd certainly got that from her father. "Stop worrying."

***

Two weeks in the military hospital, and David still hadn't been told whether he could leave. There were others, seemingly in a worse state than he was, being discharged; so, what was the hold-up? He could walk, just about, and it wasn't like he'd had a serious head injury either. He could understand their reluctance in letting him go if that had been the case. But he was getting better, wasn't he? At least, that's what they kept telling him. But then when the question of going home was mentioned: "Oh, well, no – we best keep you here a little longer. The wound isn't completely healed. There's still the danger of infection."

And as things began to be cleared up on the mainland, the hospital, naturally, became busier and messier. Lots of youngsters – boys David's own age – started arriving, in need of being fixed. He ended up with a kid next to him whose right arm had been blown off on the way to Berlin. (Though how they were going to fix that, David had no idea.) And then there was someone else, in one of the beds opposite, whose left leg looked like the Gerry's had used it for target practice. But instead of saying, "Right. We need this bed now. Come on," and kicking him out, they packed them in closer, like tinned fish, until David was in danger of finding himself in the bed next-door if he rolled over too far.

What was more: because of this lively stream of patients arriving and departing, David was being asked again and again about his own injury, about his side of the war. And he was finding that with each re-telling, the details grew foggier. He began to lose grip on them. They were becoming lost to the mist.

We were in the Netherlands, right? He would run through it, to himself. Marching towards the German border. Then what? We were getting close to the river, the Ij-something. Was that when we were attacked? It must have been. He could remember little bits of that, how could he forget – seeing guys, friends of his, just drop to the floor and not get up? It was horrible; not worth remembering. But then, how did he get from there to here? There was a part, a rather important part, of the story missing. But, looking at his leg, thinking about the condition it was in when he first woke up, he knew it can't have been very pleasant, whatever it was that happened. Maybe that was about as much as he needed to know.

As often as he could – and when his leg allowed him, because, if he was honest, it was still more painful than he dare let on to the doctors or nurses – David took himself out, alone, into the small, walled garden at the back of the hospital grounds. That was the place in which he read and replied to Edith's letters. After the long, unfortunate delay, they had very quickly fallen again into the rhythm of writing to each other. As soon as he'd received something, and read it thoroughly, he would begin composing a response.

On the fourteenth of July, David got another letter. It was from Edith. And only the day before, he had just sent her a reply to her last letter. It can't have got there so fast, usually it took a couple of days, so David quickly ripped the envelope open. He didn't even wait to go outside. The letter was short, its contents clear.

Dearest David,
I have just given birth. She is a beautiful, healthy little girl. Come
home quick.
All my love,
Edith

He read it again. Perhaps he didn't quite believe the simplicity and the enormity of what was written on the little square of notepaper. He smiled as he looked over that first line for a third time. *I have just given birth.* He imagined Edith, worn out, her throat sore and her skin sticky, a crying child in her arms, frantically scribbling those words. She can't have meant it quite so literally, he thought. Surely, she doesn't mean just that *minute* given birth. He went to check the date in the top-right corner, but she'd forgotten – unsurprisingly – to include one.

Now he really did need to get home. The next time one of the nurses came to see him, he showed her the letter.

"Oh, goodness!" she said, smiling. "You never said." Then, knowing exactly why he'd shown it to her, she added: "But we can't rush things, you know?"

"But…"

"We've got to make *you* better first, all right? Then we can get you home to see your daughter."

But I *am* better, he thought. Though even at that point, there was an uncomfortable twinge spreading its way down his leg.

Later that day, the doctor came and examined him. He prodded and poked at the wound. David stifled pained winces. He asked him how it felt, whether it hurt.

David lied. "No. Nothing," he said.

But the doctor still didn't look sure. "I'll check you again in the morning," he said. "First thing. Then – maybe – we might be able to sort something out."

"What? You mean…?"

"I mean maybe you're ready to be discharged."

"Thank you, doctor."

He started walking away. "Don't thank me yet."

That night, David had a dream. He was alone, in the middle of what appeared to be a huge wheat field. The stalks of grain were so tall he could barely see the blue of the sky. It might even have been where Edith and he used to spend some of the delivery time together. But there was no sign of anybody else.

He began to walk. There was nothing with which he could orientate himself, nothing to tell him in which direction he should go, so he simply went straight forwards.

Every so often, David stopped and looked around. Then he carried on. There seemed to be an urgency. He *had* to get out of there. Though he wasn't really certain why.

Then he started hearing strange sounds. Like something scuttling. This must have happened a dozen times. Something scuttling. Like it was following him.

He thought about calling out. Maybe it was just Edith playing a trick. She'd been waiting for him and seen him coming, so she wanted to frighten him.

The light was starting to fade. He could hardly see two steps ahead. David looked down at his feet (he had the distinct thought that he should check they were still there, doing their job) and sure enough he was wearing his old butcher shop shoes. The very first pair, which his mother bought him, and which he wore until they fell apart. They were even splattered with bits from the shop – blood and sawdust. So that must be it, he thought. He must be on his way to meet Edith.

He heard the sound again. It didn't really seem like a person. Could it just be the wind? He could see no movement in the wheat stalks, but... What else could it be?

He kept on walking. The darkness had practically blindfolded him. He thought again about calling out. "Hello?

Anyone there? Edith?" In a minute, he kept on saying to himself, in a minute I'll try it; just a few more paces, once I've got past...

The rustling repeated itself. It sounded so close this time.

"Who's there?" he stuttered. His voice felt shaky, like someone else's.

David waited a few moments, glancing carefully to either side, squinting at the blackness. His breathing had become even more frantic.

He managed to ask again: "Who's there?"

***

On a cloudy, Thursday morning, David and Edith got married. (Now, if you'd said to him a month ago... Or even two weeks ago...)

They had just a few days, a little over a week, to get it all together. Mrs. Denby and Mrs. Kemp took the reins. For which Edith – and David – were very thankful. It had to be a registry office – not enough time to organise a church ceremony, which was a sore point for Edith's mother – and they invited just a few friends and close family. David asked Michael to be his best man – Robert and William had already been seen off – and Edith, appropriately, chose Helen to be her maid of honour. Apart from them and a few of Edith's other friends, the rest of the gathering was made up of Edith's parents, David's mother and sisters (both of them – quite reluctantly, in Josie's case – on bridesmaid duties), and a couple of aunts, uncles and grandparents from both families.

David wore his father's old suit. The last time it had been worn – according to Esther – was at his grandfather's funeral, David's father's father, who he was much too young to remember meeting. Similarly, Edith wore the dress her mother had been married in. Mrs. Kemp painstakingly spent her evenings in the run-up adjusting it, insisting David didn't visit the house whilst she did so. Because that would be bad luck, she'd said. And there wasn't much about this wedding that was traditional, was there, so they should at least stick to some element of ritual.

Stood beside Michael, David waited on the steps of the registry office.

"Hope it doesn't rain," he said.

Michael's eyes glanced up at the clouds. "It'll be fine."

"Better be," he sighed.

"You all right?"

"Just nervous."

"Bound to be. I was shaking."

Michael and Helen were married about three months earlier in Helen's parish church. It was one of the last times the four of them – he, Michael, Robert and William – were all together. William was best man that day – only a fortnight or so before he set off for Europe – and David couldn't help wishing the others were stood there with them.

His mother and Edith's mother arrived. The rest of them – Edith, her father, Helen, Josie and Lily – would be arriving, squashed up, in Mr. Kemp's car.

Esther hugged David, kissing him on the cheek. "You look lovely."

"Thanks, Mum," he said, his cheeks starting to redden. He was very aware of Michael next to him. Funny how easy it was to feel like a schoolboy again trying his uniform on for the first time.

"Can we go in yet?" asked Mrs. Kemp.

David looked over his shoulder at the main entrance. "I don't know."

"I'm sure we can," she said. "Come on. You can't be stood out here when Edith arrives."

Someone pointed them in the right direction. The minister was waiting in the room. He showed David and Michael where they needed to stand, showed Esther and Mrs. Kemp where they were best sitting.

"Are you expecting many friends and family?"

"No," smiled David, glancing round the room. It seemed a little large for them.

"Well, we have ten minutes or so. Maybe..." He looked in Mrs. Kemp's direction. "Maybe you wouldn't mind waiting outside and directing people in."

"Oh," she said, getting to her feet. "Of course."

"And then you can let me know when..." He checked his notes. "When Edith is here, as well."

The car pulled up around five minutes later. Mrs. Kemp returned to the room and gestured to the minister, as if David wouldn't know what she was referring to.

The other guests began to take their seats. The minister came back in the room. "Ready when you are," he said.

"Oh." David straightened himself, checked his tie, his collar.

"Just stand more..." He pointed to a spot on the floor a few steps to David's left. "There. That's it. Right." The minister looked to the back of the room. Nodded. Music began. "Please stand."

David had never seen Edith in such a fancy dress before. She looked so different. He was used to her in cotton skirts and floral blouses, overalls covered in chicken feathers.

The whole ceremony didn't last much more than a quarter of an hour. They left the room arm in arm, and David wondered how on earth, in a week's time, he'd be able to say goodbye to her, the realisation that he might not return suddenly hitting him harder than it ever had.

***

But he *was* returning. David finally boarded a train home. It had been three days since Edith's letter telling him about their new little daughter and he hadn't had time to write back, to let her know he was on his way, so as the train arrived at the Paragon station, there was nobody there waiting for him.

He limped off the platform (it suddenly felt worse again), out of the main entrance, and then, leaning against the rough-stone wall, David lit a cigarette. He watched as people passed into and out of the station. Nobody really looked at him, apart from the odd glance, and David wondered why. Couldn't they tell? Couldn't they tell where he'd come from?

David stubbed his fag out on the brick and then began to make his way down the main road. The pain in his leg had eased and there were still spots of rain on the pavement that hadn't quite dried up from an earlier shower. Several taxicabs drove past, but he only had enough change for a bus. At the stopping point, there were a few people already waiting and David stood, to one side, against a silver-birch tree.

The traffic started to build a little. David didn't know what time it was – forgot to check in the station – but he assumed it was about four or five in the afternoon.

"Excuse me," he said, to the man nearest him.

He turned around. "Yes?"

"Do you have the time?"

"Yes. Quarter-to-five," he answered, straight away, without checking his wrist or pocket.

"Right." Close enough, he thought. "Thank you."

Something small darted noisily out of the tree. David looked up, hoping to catch sight of it, mid-flight, only to see a pair of pigeons land, clumsily, and begin pecking at the cracks in the pavement. He watched as they edged towards him. Perhaps he was so still they hadn't even noticed he was there. They got to about six inches from his right foot, before turning back and retreating to a safer distance.

The sound from the passing cars was almost deafening. Yet the longer David leant against the tree, the closer he felt to falling asleep. Once or twice, he let his eyes close. Just for a few seconds. Nothing more. It was less a voluntary thing, more an unavoidable inevitability. Then, when he'd shut his eyes for maybe the third time, he noticed a change in the motorised lullaby. And it reminded him, unexpectedly, of cold mornings and freshly baked bread.

As the bus slowed to a stop, David stretched and yawned. He let the other people on first, since they were there to start with. One of them – the one who'd told him the time – nodded a thank you. Then he paid the conductor, took his ticket, and sat down in the last spare seat. He tried getting his leg into a comfortable position, but it was tricky in the cramped space.

This was one of the few bus journeys he'd made since leaving school. Robert should have been there next to him, quizzing him about the previous day's history or mathematics homework. But though the familiar motion of the bus made it seem that way, they weren't children anymore. Far from it. Whilst in the hospital, David had considered trying to find out about Robert – as well as William and Michael – perhaps by writing to Robert's parents. But, whenever he did, all kinds of horrible scenarios played through his head and, rather than press pen to paper, he would simply convince himself they were fine, that there was nothing he need worry about.

The bus left the main road, continuing its route through some of the newer, residential areas: the tall terraced housing replaced by squatter, boxy things with flat roofs and front porches; the streets no longer arranged straight like grids, but instead in a more uneven pattern of little avenues and cul-de-sacs lined attractively with grass verges. The landscape of the city had changed dramatically in the last few years – thanks mostly to the *Luftwaffe* and their bombing raids – and the bus route also took them past great areas flattened by the bombs, where temporary, pre-fabricated houses had been put up to deal quickly with the huge numbers of people made suddenly homeless. Whole streets had gone. Some still remained piles of brick and concrete, while others had been cleared, ready for when re-building could begin.

Crossing the city boundary, trees and green began making up more of the landscape. David started to feel like he was finally home; the farms, the fields, the winding lanes, all smiled back at him like friendly faces. This part of the region had been unaffected during the German air raids – at least on the surface.

David could remember hearing the sirens, the sound of dropping bombs, explosions – even, sometimes, see the fires climbing high into the night sky – from his bedroom window. But there was still that distance. He'd find out about it, properly, in the paper the next day, like it was something happening over in Belgium or the Soviet Union.

It was more than a year before he ventured into town to take a look at the damage for himself. The street two blocks up from William's had just been hit, a few days previously, and all four of them went to see it, climbing on the rubble like the other children, as if it was merely something new to play on, a tree felled in strong winds.

They reached the Common. David got off the bus and went down Lowcroft Lane.

"Oh!" gasped Edith, opening the front door. "What you doing knocking? You should've just walked straight in." She stood back, let him get in and over the doorstep, before grabbing him and hugging him and kissing him. "I was still waiting for you to write back and tell me when you were coming."

"I know," he said. "But I only got told last night. There wasn't really time to write."

"Never mind," she said, gently shutting the front door.

"I just wanted to get back – soon as possible, you know."

"Well. The main thing's that you're here now. And you get to meet…" She motioned to the living room; dropped her voice to a whisper. "You get to meet your little girl."

She led him in. The electric light was off, and the only sound was the clock on the mantelpiece.

"She's sleeping." Edith gestured to the basket on the armchair.

David nodded. "Where're your mum and dad?"

"Out."

"Right." Then, looking again at the little child: "Shall we just leave her to…?"

"No. Don't be daft."

Edith let him past. He tried crouching down, but his leg hurt. "Sorry," he winced. "I can't."

"What?"

"My leg."

"Oh. Right. Hold on a minute." She returned with a chair from the kitchen. "Can you sit on here?"

"Thanks," said David. "That's better. It's just, bending it, like that..."

"Course."

"The doctor said it'll take a while for it to get back to normal."

He set the chair facing the basket and peered in at her, sleeping.

"What do you reckon?" Edith asked him.

David didn't reply straight away. The whole thing felt like it had happened without him – though, for obvious reasons, that wasn't possible. But suddenly there was this little person, lips creasing and crumpling into a contented, slumbering smile, and it was *his* job – and Edith's – to look after her.

"What do you reckon?" she repeated her question.

"She looks lovely," he said, simply.

"You know we still need a name."

"You mean, you haven't...?"

"I couldn't. Not without *you* here."

David looked at her again. "Do you have any ideas?"

"A few," she said. "What about you?"

"I've not given it much thought – to be honest."

"No. Course."

"So..."

"Well, we don't have to think of one right away. You've only just met her, anyway."

David nodded; smiled.

"Maybe we should sleep on it."

Of course, once they were in bed, Edith seemed less inclined to sleep. As soon as David was settled, his leg causing him more pain than he was happy to let on, she leant over him and began kissing him: first on his cheeks, then his lips. "I'm so glad you're home safe," she whispered, sitting up a little and taking off her nightdress. "It's been such a worry, all these months, not hearing from you for so long."

"Edith?" he said.

"Right. Sorry." She kissed him again, on the neck. "I'll be quiet."

"No," he said. "It's not that... I can't really..." He almost mentioned his leg. Then he remembered her mum and dad, across the landing. "It's just... It's been a tiring day."

"Don't worry about that," she said. "You just stay where you are."

Afterwards, Edith laid back down next to him. He could feel her breath on his bare shoulder, her warm body against his.

"I've missed this," she said.

He turned, carefully, to face her. "Me too."

She reached for his hands. Held them tight. "I wish we could just lie like this all night."

"Mmm."

"But I've already lost too many night's sleep as it is."

"She not been sleeping too well?"

"Just... very broken, you know. It's normal."

"How many times have you been getting up for her?"

"Depends. Usually a couple of times."

David listened for a moment. She was only at the other side of the room.

"We best get some rest while we can, then."

"Mmm," sighed Edith. "Suppose so." But she didn't let go of his hands right away.

At about half-two, David's eyes shot open.

"Here we go," he heard Edith say, pulling back the covers. "Thought we might get away with it this time."

"What?" said David, following her out of bed, tripping over his pyjama legs as he tried getting them back on.

"Why don't *you* try?" she said. "You've still not held her yet."

"But I don't..." He looked over to the bedroom door, expected Edith's parents to come rushing in. "Shouldn't you put something on?"

"Why?"

"Your mum and dad," he said, nodding in the direction of their room. "What if we wake them? Do you want them seeing you...?" He'd forgotten how beautiful she was: her milky skin and roughed-up hair, her lips, her breasts.

"No. They'll just leave us to it. Anyway..." Edith held her out towards him. "Come on. There's nothing to it."

"I don't..."

"You've got to learn some day. Just put your arms out."

Which he did, trying to copy the position Edith had them in. She passed her over.

"That's it," she smiled. "Just watch the head."

He looked down at her: into her big, brown eyes. She was still crying. I can't be doing this very well, he thought.

"Are you sure we won't disturb them?" he said.

"Promise."

He tried rocking her, gently – he'd seen Edith do it earlier, before they came to bed. But that seemed to have no effect either.

"She's not..." He looked over at Edith, who was busy rearranging the covers in the basket. "Maybe she's hungry."

"Mmm. I think she must be. Here."

He handed her back.

"See? Good job I didn't bother putting my nightie back on, eh?"

Edith sat on the edge of the bed and David perched next to her, just watching the two of them: one gazing up, the other gazing down; connected in every possible way – perhaps in a way greater than he could ever hope for.

"What about Jessica?" he said.

"Sorry?"

"There was someone in our division. He kept talking about his girl back home. Her name was Jessica. And I remember thinking how I quite liked the sound of it."

"Mmm. What do *you* think?" she said, looking at the child in her arms. "*Jessica.*" She was still feeding. There appeared to be little or no reaction. "Do you like that?"

"It was just a suggestion."

"No. I like it," she said. Then, to the child again: "Oh. Are you done?" She moved her, so she was sat on her left knee. "Are you full up now? That was quick."

"Do you want a tissue?" he asked, noticing they both still had bits of milk on them; the child round its lips, Edith round her left nipple.

"Yes, please."

David grabbed one from the dresser.

"Thanks." Edith wiped the little one's mouth, then cleaned herself up too. "This is a bit of a pain, to be honest," she said.

"Oh."

"Leaks out all the time. See?" She dabbed at her other breast as well, the one she hadn't been using.

"Right."

She smiled. "But you didn't need to know that, eh?"

"No. I meant… I think it made you look…"

"What? Like a mess?"

"No. You looked… beautiful… both of you."

"You think?" she said, bouncing the baby on her leg. "You hear that, Jessica? Daddy thinks we're beautiful."

Gradually, as the weeks passed, David's leg began to improve. It began to feel stronger, more like it used to, and the pain was increasingly less noticeable.

The army was still paying him. But that was due to run out in under a month. So – right there – was a rather big reason for him to get better.

One morning, when he'd been home just over two weeks, he went out to get a few things from the grocer's – the one in the Common, *not* the one near Jenkins'. Parked outside one of the houses, only around the corner from Edith's, was a van belonging to a painting and decorating company. David read the side...

ARNOTT & son
PAINTERS and DECORATORS
Est. 1912

...and imagined himself in white overalls, his face and the palms of his hands covered in paint stains. Well, he said to himself, that has to be better than pig's blood – or my own blood, for that matter.

Now

"Jessica and the boys'll be round soon."

"There's plenty of time before that," he tells her, glancing at the clock. "It's not even ten yet."

He reaches past her for the dog-lead.

"Come on, fella."

It races in from one of the other rooms.

"Just don't go too far, then. I don't want you tiring yourself out too early."

"How old do you think I am?"

"You know what I mean."

"Yes. Thank you." David bends down to clip the lead on, narrowly avoiding a face-full of tongue. "And thank *you*," he laughs. "Come on."

They turn left out of the garden gate. The dog immediately lifts its leg at the nearest fencepost, seemingly unaware that most of what comes out is bouncing off the pavement and spattering his legs and feet. It feels milder than it was earlier when David popped out to leave toast crumbs on the bird-table. He may yet regret putting on his jacket. Though – looking up while the dog finishes peeing – the sky is settling into a murky grey, so perhaps he'll end up feeling relieved after all that he wore his coat when it starts chucking it down.

The grass verge is covered in blossom, like confetti in a churchyard, and that pile of stuff near number six's garage seems to have grown even more since yesterday. How they can bear to let it get like that – let alone add to it – is beyond David. One of the black bin-liners is split too. No doubt clawed (perhaps, pecked) open by something. It just looks a mess. He pulls on the lead, so the dog's nose isn't drawn in that very tempting direction.

"Keep moving," he urges him on, away.

The dog raises its leg again by the base of the streetlight just a few yards further up, holding it still for a few seconds, then putting it back down.

"Is that all this time, fella?"

The metal and the concrete seem hardly damp.

His name (that is, the dog's name) is Billy. They've had him for nine years now, ever since he was born. Their old dog, Kim, had a litter of seven and Billy was the one they kept. It was David's decision. Edith said they should sell them all – that had always been the original plan – but he just couldn't bear to see this one go. He always seemed much more attached to David than any of the others. So, it would have felt cruel to let him go elsewhere. He's very like his mother too – in character and in appearance. Even Edith would admit she likes having him around – especially since Kim had to be put to sleep five summers back.

He finds himself whistling. Quickly, David turns it into a *hum-hum-hum*.

Billy appears to have found something interesting in the bark of an oak tree. The amount of times they've passed it, he can't imagine what there is there that he can't have smelt before. He can guess, of course. And he's probably right. He gives Billy a few more lick-and-sniff seconds, then gets him going again.

Rounding on to the main road, he spots Mr. Jones from number thirteen walking their fluffy little thing. It always yaps at Billy whenever they cross ways and Billy tends to just stare at it – which is precisely what he'd do if the daft dog tried the same on him. (Though maybe he'd be tempted to bare his teeth a bit too.)

"What're they like?" Mr. Jones always says.

What's yours like, you mean? he always thinks.

They exchange friendly nods and good-mornings. As anticipated, the yapping starts and Mr. Jones laughs it off with the usual words.

"Bye," David manages, above the noise, and they carry on in opposite directions.

Nearby, there used to be a school. It closed about six years ago. The buildings were half-knocked down and the kids that went to it – in fact, it was the senior school Jessica attended for

her last two years after they first moved into the area – were all
given places in other local schools. Behind it ran some train-
lines. You went that way if you were heading north or north-
west – to York or Scarborough or Newcastle. But now that's
closed too – the tracks buried beneath brambles and nettles. So,
what you're left with is a site the size of, roughly, three football
grounds: empty, abandoned and overgrown.

Billy loves it. So, David makes sure they come this way once
or twice a week, certainly every weekend. And while Billy's off
doing God-knows-what (or, more accurately, dog-knows-what),
he takes the chance to wander aimlessly for thirty minutes, as if
he were really in some greener, quieter place and not
surrounded, actually, by buildings and engines and people.

Because, haven't you noticed? The dawn chorus is motorised
now. Think about it. What is it you first hear when you wake
up? It's not birdsong anymore, that's for sure – at least, not
round where David lives. No. Listen. What can you hear? That
low, droning tone? It's carsong.

This place has the appearance of a kind of accidental nature
reserve. He's seen birds here that would never venture into his
or next-door's garden – and if they did, it would only be because
this place has attracted them to the area. You even get kestrels.
David reckons they nest in what's left of the schoolhouse,
feeding on the voles and shrews he's sometimes spotted
scurrying about in the undergrowth. What at one time would
have been the playing fields has grown, rather naturally, into an
inner-city heath. And since the school shut, nothing has been
done to reclaim it as anything else. He's heard about no council
plans for a new housing estate here, no business proposals that
it should be turned into a brand-spanking branch of whatever.
But, really, that's its charm to him: that, to all intents and
purposes, it's been forgotten about, left just to get on with itself.
You get people like that as well. And – in a way – they're the
most interesting people of all.

Though he's yet to bump into anyone out here – which he still
can't quite believe – David's sure others must come here too.

There are trodden-down pathways, criss-crossing like train-track – many more than he and Billy could have made alone. Not to mention discarded drinks cans and crisp packets – though they could have easily drifted this way on the breeze.

Today, he does a full circuit of the site, as if it were cross-country day and the games teacher wants a lap of the field. Billy goes off grubbing in the thick bracken. Though David isn't entirely sure where he is, besides the odd movement in the tangled branches, Billy no doubt has one eye fixed on him the whole time.

Once David has ambled all the way round, he heads in the direction of the old buildings. With none of the windows boarded up, almost all of the glass has been smashed over the years by kids hurling bricks and stones. Which means if it isn't dog walkers that come here regularly, then it's teenagers with nothing better to do. The wildness of the undergrowth is halted close to where the main entrance to the school would have been. The concrete yard remains intact, besides a few cracks and fissures through which thistles and dandelions have begun to push, and the doors swing ajar in the gentle breeze.

Creak.

David turns around – though he's not really certain from which direction the sound came.

Billy stops. Like he's been caught up to something.

"All right, boy – you carry on."

He looks back at the old school, at the main doors. Must have just been the hinges on those things, he thinks. Surely, they've rusted almost to nothing by now, anyway.

"Come on then, fella," he says again to the dog, turning to leave.

A few moments later, when David shakes the lead, Billy trots happily up to him and allows it to be reattached.

"Right," he sighs. "Let's head back."

The clouds start to break, and he notices a familiar shape in the sky, high over the field. One of the kestrels (could it have been watching him, waiting for him to leave? Could that have had something to do with the noise?) hovers, hangs, as if another, larger creature, invisible, has hold of it. Then it drops down and out of sight. David smiles to himself – seeing the kestrel, it makes the visit worthwhile somehow.

Billy pads alongside: his pace slower, but no less eager. This, then that, grabbing his attention. The weekend cars whip past – day trips and family visits. But Billy remains oblivious to all that. He squats on the grass verge. Watching him – though it always seems like he shouldn't be – David gets the plastic bag ready: turns it inside-out so it covers his hand completely. Billy steps away, a sideways glance at what he's left behind. It feels warm through the bag – not wholly unpleasant. He turns it back the right way. Ties a knot. All the while, Billy stands, waiting, until David gives the lead a little tug, a simple word or two, "Keep going," letting him know they're off again.

Between here and home, there's just one public bin to swing it in. He tells himself not to forget about it. The last time he trailed a full bag through the hallway and out to the back garden, Edith went ballistic. (Maybe the lesson, though, is simply not to let her see you doing it.)

They return to the main road, retracing their steps. Billy pauses to smell things he's already sniffed at the first time round (just in case – what? Something's changed, been added?). David humours him, a few times, then starts growing a little irritated by it.

"That's enough, boy."

Pulls on the lead.

"Let's keep going."

He checks his watch. Quarter-past eleven. Plenty of time before Jessica and the boys arrive. What was Edith worrying about?

David lets Billy linger at the next tree, his tongue working its way through the grooves and valleys in the rough bark. Then, reaching the top of their street, David drops the little, black bag into the bin with a hollow *thud*. Like a blade hitting a chopping board.

The lad from next door creeps past in his car. Their eyes meet. Polite nod and awkward smile. He must be off out to some hardware shop, so he can carry on whatever it is he's started. It's what he does most Saturdays. It winds David up sometimes. In fact, they're lots of things doing that at the moment.

Then

They told him to go around the back way. The gate'll be open, the main bloke said.

But it wasn't.

David tried again. Perhaps he just hadn't pushed hard enough the first three times. He threw his left shoulder into it too.

Nothing.

"Hello!" he shouted, yanking at the handle.

"Hold on!" he heard, from somewhere inside the house.

David stepped back.

Rushed footsteps over the cobbles. The gate shook, and the bolt was unfastened.

"Sorry about that – completely forgot."

"Oh, no – no problem."

The man stood aside and let him through. A strange smile creased his lips, not looking too sure whether it should stay there or not. He clearly hadn't shaved yet. Two fingers scratted about in his dirty-grey bristles. "Come in," he said, pointing to the open door. "Just about ready."

"Thanks."

They'd only met yesterday. It was Edith's idea really. David told her how he'd seen their van, around the corner, at number sixty-three, after going to the shop, and she'd said: "Well? Why don't you ask them? Can't hurt, can it?" David shook his head, all the while thinking about his leg. And so, he went out again, later that day, popped his head round and asked if they were looking for anyone extra, another set of... David held out his hands. "Can't go wrong with a pair more," said the older man, and before David knew it, he was writing down his address on a scrap of paper, telling him to come around, first thing, and we'll take you on for a few days, see how it goes.

He gestured to a wooden chair. "Take a seat."

"Thanks," David said again.

"Want something to drink?"

"No, thank you."

"Fair enough." He picked up a mug, some of the boiling contents swilling out as he did so, then left the room, adding: "Just be a minute."

"Right."

David looked around. There was a little mongrel thing curled up in one corner, seemingly uninterested in him – the only movement David noticed was when a fly buzzed about by its ear. He moved uneasy in his seat. There was an apparent wobble to the chair – one leg shorter than the others, or one longer. He tried to remain steady. The wallpaper (which would once have been, what, a yellow colour?) stained from years of cooking. Shelves stacked untidily.

He heard the man in the hallway, calling up the stairs.

"He'll be down soon – then we can get off," he said, when he came back into the room.

He was talking about his son, Harry – the one in ARNOTT & SON. They were introduced, briefly, yesterday.

"You sure you don't want a cuppa?"

"No, thanks."

Arnott put his now-emptied cup into the full sink, after rinsing it a few seconds under the cold tap.

David heard footsteps above him; spotted Arnott's eye looking up, to the ceiling.

"That's him ready, I reckon," he said.

And, sure enough, the next set of footsteps came down the stairs, through the hallway, and into the kitchen.

He and David nodded to each other.

"Ready?" His father suddenly sounded impatient.

"Yes. I'll just..." He reached for something on the sideboard. Slipped it in a trouser pocket. 'ready."

"Good." Then Arnott was shouting again, "We're off now, love," no doubt to his wife, somewhere else in the house. David thought he heard a faint reply, but Arnott and son were already halfway through the back door.

They climbed into the van, the company name painted on the side. Just like the butcher's bike. It was all *very* familiar.

Mr. Arnott started the engine. "We're working in the town," he said, once they were settled on the road.

"Oh, right." David wondered if they often did, whether it was another result of the bombs.

"We're at one of the hotels," he continued. "Should take us a while, this one." (He didn't specify exactly how much time "a while" amounted to.)

They passed the row of shops: JENKINS' at the end. It didn't look open, which it should have been by that time. David glanced down at his watch. Ten-to-eight. And suddenly realised that Arnott might actually know Jenkins. After all, they hardly live a million miles from each other. His wife probably shops there, he thought – though he couldn't ever recall serving a Mrs. Arnott or Mr. Jenkins ever mentioning one (and he did reel off a huge list of regular customers that first day) and he certainly never delivered to their place.

"We've been wondering about getting someone else for a while – haven't we, son?"

The younger Arnott nodded.

"The odd one's helped us out from time to time, but then they go off again, you know – find something else. It didn't help when the war were on, of course."

"No," muttered David. He remembered his friends.

"How long did *you* serve?"

David hesitated. Tried recalling whether he'd even mentioned it. "Just a few months," he shrugged. Then, because he thought it only seemed polite: "Did you…?"

"No. Failed the medical. Which were a blessing, really."

"Oh." David wanted to ask what was wrong, why he failed it.

The day's job began by unloading the van. David helped Harry with the ladders, then the scaffolding, while Arnott senior managed a few containers (one in each hand) and some dustsheets balled under his left arm. For a first shift, it looked like a rather challenging one. The hotel foyer had a large, domed ceiling. David remembered the entrance hall at school. He wondered how on earth anybody ever got up there to clean it.

"Hope you've a head for heights," said Arnott.

David smiled, then started helping to put up the scaffold. The metal frame, followed by the wooden boards and dustsheets, spanned the length of one wall, directly opposite the reception desk, leaving enough room for the hotel guests to come and go beneath through the main doors.

By half-ten, they were finally ready to paint. Arnott worked on the lower level, while David and Harry settled themselves at the top. There were bare patches of plaster in the ornate coving – another feature reminiscent of school – and they began by carefully chipping off the rest of the old, peeling paint. David could hear the hotel traffic behind and below them: the service bell yet another reminder – this time of the butcher shop. He moved carefully along the scaffolding. He didn't quite trust the structure – in large part because he had helped to construct it – but he was also beginning to feel a few sharp twinges in his leg.

At first, David and Harry spoke simply to apologise for getting in the other's way or to ask for something – a scrap of sandpaper; a dustpan and brush – to be passed over. Eventually, though, Harry brought up the subject of the war.

"What rank were you?" he asked.

"Private."

"Oh." He looked him square in the face. Smiled. "Sorry."

"What?"

"Nothing." He shook his head. "Where did you serve?"

"The Netherlands."

"Right. So, when the Gerry's were pushed back?"

"Yes, except – I got injured, before that, so…"

"What?"

"Well, I was in hospital, recovering, when all that happened."

"You missed out?"

"Yes." Like he needed someone else telling him.

"Still – it's more than *I* did."

David chipped the remaining flecks of original paint, then looked across to see the next bit that needed doing. They were almost finished – at least, this first, preparatory task was nearly finished.

"Were you not old enough?" David had been trying to work the boy's age out all morning.

"No. I only turned eighteen a few months ago."

David nodded. "Would you have wanted to, then?"

"Too right," he answered. "It's better than this."

"Maybe," muttered David, diplomatically.

"You prefer this to what you did out there?"

"I don't know. I didn't really *do* anything out there."

"More than me," he shrugged. "Anyway – what was your injury?"

"My leg." He tapped the affected area.

"What happened?"

"We were ambushed. They started shooting at us."

"The Gerry's?"

"Mmm. Firing grenades, you know. A few of us dived behind our supplies truck, but – one of the grenades landed right near where we were and, before any of us could move, it…"

"Did anyone…?"

He nodded. Pieces of the puzzle had been slowly falling back into place; he was starting to remember more about that day in Holland. "There were three of us," said David, his eyes fixed to the wall rather than the boy asking the questions. "I were the only that made it."

Mr. Arnott came up to check on them. He'd been working on the level below, adding a thick stripe of royal blue that would eventually run the length of the whole room. "How're we doing?"

"Fine," answered his son.

Arnott wandered along, nodding as he went. "Good," he said, a few times. "Be about ready to paint, I reckon." Then he checked his watch. "We'll have some lunch first. Then we'll crack open the paint and get going."

It was half-twelve – so said the clock above the reception desk. They descended and went to stand outside, just around the corner from the main doors of the hotel. Edith had made him cheese and pickle. She'd looked rather bleary-eyed that morning – so had he, probably – and the baby sat bawling and beautiful in the high-chair. Her crying was the sound they said goodbye to; the last thing he heard when he closed the front door. Perhaps, he thought, it'll be what he opens it to as well.

"You married, then?" Arnott pointed to his ring.

David looked at it as if it shouldn't be there. "Oh," he said. Swallowed what he'd just taken in. "Yes."

"How long?"

He thought for a second. "Nearly eighteen months."

Arnott nodded and had another bite. "Harry, here..." he spluttered, showing off far too much of his food. "He'll be getting around to that soon."

"What?"

A playful smile broke across the man's lips. "Come on, son. You've been courting her long enough."

Harry looked like he didn't want to talk about it.

When he'd finished his sandwich, Arnott pulled a pre-rolled cigarette from his pocket and lit it with a match. David took that as permission and began to smoke too. He offered Harry one, held the packet out for him to help himself, but he smiled and shook his head.

"We should finish the job by the end of the week, I reckon."

"Right. Then, where next?"

"Nothing's lined up at the minute. That's the thing with this trade. But there'll be something soon. There always is."

And David wanted to ask Arnott whether they'll be taking him on, whenever that next job materialises.

"Anyway..." he said, dropping what remained of his cigarette on to the pavement and stubbing it with his right boot. "Won't finish it stood out here, eh?"

"No," smiled David, quickly finishing his own ciggy and following them both in.

The next day, they set themselves up behind reception, trying – as much as possible – not to disturb the booking girls. It was about eight in the morning and, even then, they looked to be busy with a steady flow of arriving and departing guests. David repeatedly apologised as he edged his way around the congested space. There were three girls on duty, then the three of them, besides all the scaffolding and ladders, so it was actually a relief to get up and work above them.

He and Harry, like the previous day, started by chipping the old paint back to the plaster. David was surprised about how comfortable he felt up on the scaffold.

But his leg continued to prove a bit of a problem.

Which, of course, he did his best to disguise.

It had felt tight in the night, stiff like cramp. Edith had noticed, asked him what was wrong halfway through undressing him.

"Nothing," he'd mumbled.

But though she carried on, began unbuttoning his pyjama bottoms, she knew he was in pain, that they better not continue, and she laid down next to him, shuffling herself so they were at least touching, shoulder to shoulder.

"Is it your leg?" she asked him.

"What?" He had hoped he'd hidden them well, all the little bursts of pain – which usually seemed to happen when Edith was climbing over him… arching her back… easing him in… her lips pressing against his flesh…

"Does it still hurt?" she asked again.

"Now and then," he admitted.

In the darkness, he heard her sigh, felt her move next to him, then felt her kiss him on the arm.

"You need to tell me these things," she said. "Don't keep it all to yourself. Like you did with all that Jenkins' stuff."

***

To begin with, David had been quite good at hiding the marks and bruises from Edith. Even when she had him undressed – but perhaps there were other things on her mind – she didn't seem to notice. Or maybe she just thought it best not to ask. When she did start to notice – and when she started asking questions – David shrugged them off as accidents. When Jenkins gave him his first black eye (how could she miss that, it was staring right at her?) he told her, his bottom lip trembling, that it was the back gate. It had been a silly mistake, he'd said, *his* silly mistake, and she giggled and called him clumsy. Then she kissed it better. (Her cure for everything.)

Of course, there was only so long he could laugh them off like that. They were becoming more obvious – the lumps, the cuts. And she was asking more and more questions. "How did you manage that one? What, on a cupboard door? You must have slammed into it pretty hard."

So, he had to tell her. He made her promise not to tell anyone else. Not even his mother. Not even Robert.

"But…" she said.

"No," he said. "Promise?"

"All right – I promise."

He told her when it started, how every time he said he'd knocked his head on the worktop or fallen off the bike, it had really been Jenkins.

"What are you going to do about it?"

"What do you mean?" It was a question he'd never asked himself.

"Well – you can't just go on like this." She reached out and took hold of his bruised hand, running a finger softly over the blackened skin. "What if he really hurts you next time?"

David tried to smile. "No. It's fine."

"It's not fine. I can't believe you're only just telling me this."

She seemed genuinely hurt. But wasn't *he* the one with the cuts and bumps?

The next time it happened (what was it that time – a jab of the butcher's elbow square on the nose?), Edith asked him why he didn't just go somewhere else.

"It's really not that simple. I can't just leave. Mum needs the money. If I leave the shop, what'll she do then?"

"But…"

She reached out and he pulled away.

"He's hurting you," she said.

"Look…" David took her hand in his. "I turn eighteen in three months. Then – that's it. I can sign up and we won't have to worry about it again."

David's last day at the butcher shop started just like any other. Pushing the gate open, it carved an even deeper groove into the concrete. Mr. Jenkins had his back to the door and David managed to hang his coat up and put on his apron without him realising he'd arrived. He turned to put something in one of the cupboards, finally spotting him.

"Blimey, lad," he said. "When did *you* sneak in?"

"Just now."

"Right."

David headed through into the front, picking up the sweeping brush as he went.

"You going to miss this, eh?"

David didn't answer, didn't think he was supposed to, and the butcher carried on in the back.

About four weeks earlier, on a Saturday afternoon after they had shut up for the day, David had gone into the village, into the parish hall. In his hand, he held a government-stamped letter and he joined a short queue, about seven or eight others roughly his age all with similar-looking pieces of paper, at the end of which were two older men, in uniforms, sat at two tables. They each had a tall stack of papers, and when the boys stepped forward, they asked for their name and age, writing both down, then handed them some sheets from the top of the pile in return for the one they brought with them, explaining that they were to return with the forms completed as soon as possible.

"Next, please," said the man on the left.

David was now first in the queue. He was being beckoned over.

"Name, please." He didn't look up, just held his pencil ready.

"David Denby, sir."

"How are spelling Denby?"

"D-E-N-B-Y."

"And your age?"

"Seventeen."

Finally, he lifted his head to look at David. "And when are you eighteen?"

"In a fortnight."

"What date exactly?"

"The eighteenth of November."

"Right."

He peeled some pieces of paper from the pile, his other hand hovering for David to place the initial letter into. "Fill these in," he said.

David took the new paperwork.

"Return here with them in two weeks."

The following Monday, David had to tell Jenkins. He was worried – not surprisingly – about how he might react. (Last week, he'd got a whack round the ear just for dropping a steak chop – when they were in the back, of course; never in front of the customers.) So, he arrived that morning feeling very queasy. He'd been getting that way, anyway – fearing, in general, what was in store, what kind of punishment he could expect – but this was a different kind of queasy. At the first sniff of fresh flesh, when he walked through the door, he could feel his stomach churning.

"I'm just going…" He ran out to the toilet.

For a few minutes, he knelt down over the cold basin, trying not to catch his reflection in the water.

Jenkins came to find him. David listened as his footsteps got nearer, looked at the crack under the door as his shadow approached.

"You in here, lad?"

"Uh-huh." His voice echoed.

"You all right?"

David took a deep breath before answering. "Yes."

"Well…" said Jenkins. "Don't be too much longer, eh?"

"No. I won't."

David made sure he'd gone back inside before emerging from the outhouse. It was tempting to just leave. The gate was so close. Closer than the back door. He could slip out and peg it home or round to Edith's in ten minutes (provided he didn't feel like throwing up again). But yet he knew he'd never dare do that – not even after all the things the butcher had done to him.

"Oh." Jenkins sounded surprised to see him.

David did his best to smile and walked past him to sweep out the front of the shop.

"Feeling better?"

David lied. "Yes," he said.

The regulars came and went at their regular times. You could set a clock by them. In fact, David barely needed to check the time anymore – he knew the routine better than Jenkins now; he knew that if Mrs. Banks had arrived it must be half-past nine and that Mrs. Merrilees would be along in a few minutes (two-and-a-half, to be precise).

It was a murky morning: low cloud and drizzle. The customers would arrive, damp and grumpy, and stand for a few moments by the door, adjusting to the change in conditions, before approaching the counter and giving either David –

because it was a long time since he had been seen simply as the butcher's boy – or Mr. Jenkins their order.

"I'll be wanting sausages, please, love."

Mrs. Michaels passed David her ration book. He looked it over.

"We can do you two," he said. "Then that leaves you some more for later in the week."

"Fair enough."

David reached under the counter for the sausages. Laid them side-to-side on the paper and wrapped them up tight. "Is that everything?"

Mrs. Michaels had her money ready. She nodded and dropped it into his hand.

"Thanks."

Mr. Jenkins emerged from the back, just as she was leaving. "Cheerio, Mrs. Michaels," he said.

She smiled and let the door slam shut.

"I might just pop in and see Keystone." (That was the man at the newsagents.) "You'll be fine for a few minutes, won't you, lad?" He asked the same question every time he needed to go somewhere – which was lately becoming more frequent.

"Course."

"I'll only be a few doors down if you want me." He unfastened his apron and left it scrunched on the worktop, then went out through the front door.

David was relieved. He was whenever Jenkins popped out. It was like he could breathe properly. And it gave him some more thinking time too. He wanted to tell him sooner, rather than later, but most of the morning had gone – it'd soon be lunch, and then he'd be going out on deliveries. Which, actually, might be better, he suddenly thought; perhaps Edith'll be able to help – she always said the right thing.

When Mr. Jenkins returned, he went straight into the back and began getting the delivery orders ready.

There were a few more customers in the run-up to midday, though it did seem quieter than the average Monday.

Jenkins said he could eat fifteen minutes early, if he wanted. "You might as well, lad. Think I can manage on my own."

So, David stood in the yard, a nasty wind swirling around, trying to stomach his sandwich. In the end, all he could manage was a few bites. He binned the rest and just waited there, for his time to run out, watching the tops of the trees over the wall as they waved tauntingly at him in the breeze.

He met Edith by the stream, just outside the village.

"You all right?" she said.

"No, not really."

"Oh." A grin worked its way across her face. "I know what'll cheer you up."

She came up alongside him. Reached a hand into his pocket. He tensed, couldn't help it, felt himself start to harden, and she grabbed for it with her fingers. For a second, he considered undoing his belt, letting her have a proper hold, but then he pulled away.

"What?"

"I just... I don't think I'm in the mood."

"You're always in the mood."

"Well..." he said. "Not today."

He perched against a fallen tree. Edith settled there next to him.

"Has something happened again? Has he...?"

"No. Nothing like that."

"Then, what?"

"I need to tell him, that I've signed up, but..."

"You're worried he won't like it?"

David nodded. "And I don't even know what to say, you know? How do I tell him?"

"You just... tell him, dopey. That bit's simple."

"And what if he doesn't like it?"

"He can hardly do much to you that he hasn't already, can he?"

"Suppose."

"And, anyway – you've not really got a choice in the matter, have you?"

"No."

"So – there's not much he can do about it."

That's the thing about conscription – once you're the right age, the decision's made for you.

David went over to the bicycle.

"Oh. Guess we're going, then."

"Mmm. Better had."

"You sure you don't want to… really quickly…?"

David looked at her there in her rose-print dress. He imagined it hitched up, her legs exposed. He imagined it heaped on the floor while he… while they… But…

"No," he said. "Tomorrow. There's an extra order today, so…" He turned the bike around, began walking it over the mud.

Edith left him halfway through the route. "Tell him," she said. "Make sure you do it before you leave."

She held out her right hand. David took it in his. Then they kissed.

"Just think…" she said, a few seconds later. "In a few months, you won't have to worry about this anymore."

David smiled.

"So, don't back out, eh?"

"I won't."

"Good. And I'll see you tomorrow? Same place?"

He nodded. As if they'd go a day without seeing each other anyway.

"Cause you promised, remember?"

"I know."

And it was always a promise worth keeping.

David made it back to the shop just after three.

"Any problems?" asked Mr. Jenkins.

"No."

"That's what I like to hear, lad. It's been fairly quiet here, as it goes. Feel like shutting up early."

David asked if there was anything that needed doing.

"There's a sink-full in there."

"Right."

He rolled his cuffs up and turned on the tap, almost forgetting to put in the stopper.

"You get that new one delivered all right?"

"Mmm."

"You find the place?"

"Yes. It was just around the corner from the Swinson's cottage."

"Ah! Well there you go, then." Jenkins *had* said, before he left, that he wasn't quite sure where it was.

David took the kettle from the stove and added some of the water to the sink. Dipped a hand in to test the temperature. Poured in a little more.

Jenkins appeared in the doorway. "Soon as its five, you get off, lad. So long as you remember to sweep the floor."

Now would be a good time, he thought. But then the shop bell chimed. He looked at the clock. Three-ten. Which meant it was Mrs. Green.

"Good afternoon. What can I get you?"

She'd come for her Monday usual: half-a-dozen rashers of bacon and a couple of tins of corned beef.

David took his time washing-up. He liked how the warm water softened his skin. It was especially pleasant at this time of the year. And having just returned from the delivery round.

Two other customers arrived. David listened to their orders and to Jenkins' responses, that familiar rhythm: one he knew better than anything he'd learnt about, say, iambic pentameter at school.

He left the pots and trays to drain on the side. Re-filled the kettle, placing it carefully above the fire. Really, he was just finding jobs to do, rather than go back into the front. And, all the time, there was a conversation going on in his head – a conversation that needed to be spoken out-loud.

"Mr. Jenkins…?" he said, finally out of unnecessary tasks and finally in the front again.

"Yes, lad?"

"I've signed myself up." No point skirting round the issue.

"Signed up for what, lad?"

He must know, thought David. He must know what I mean.

"For the army."

"Oh. Is that right?"

David nodded.

"You really want to…?"

"Yes. I do. But – it's not really up to me, anyway."

"I know, lad. How long, before…?"

"Well, I'm eighteen in a few weeks, so I've got to wait until then, before it's all official."

"Right."

"Sorry."

"What? You think I can't manage here without you?"

"No. I didn't…"

"I was a butcher long before you were *born*, lad."

"I know."

"Don't you worry about me."

"No."

"Besides – I knew this were coming. So, I've already started asking round for someone new."

"Oh." He was that easy to replace, was he?

"Might get them in, before you go, now that I think about it. You could take them on deliveries with you."

"Good idea," smiled David. He thought about how much he should tell them, whether he should warn them. He wished someone had warned him – or his mother. Maybe it would have changed her mind. Maybe he wouldn't have had to leave school. Of course, some good had come of it; he may never have met Edith if it wasn't for the butcher shop.

She didn't like the sound of someone else joining David on the delivery round. "That's not fair," said Edith. "I'm the one who helps you do the deliveries."

"But Jenkins doesn't know that, does he?"

"Come on – he must do."

"What do you mean?"

"The amount of times people have seen us together – someone must have mentioned it to him."

"Well, he's never said."

"Doesn't mean he doesn't know."

David had never even considered it before. The idea suddenly worried him. He thought it was a secret of theirs, didn't like that Jenkins might have known about it all along and – worse, for some reason – not said anything.

They turned off in one of the fields. In one of their usual spots, obscured by thick hedgerow and tall, untended grass, David kept the promise he'd made the day before.

He let Edith undress him; watched silently as she removed her own clothes. Then before they went any further, David took hold of Edith's left hand, ran his fingers slowly up her arm, then resting it gently on her cheek, stepping closer, he pressed his lips firmly into hers.

It was an oddly mild November afternoon, thankfully, and afterwards they lay next to each other, their bare arms linked.

"We should be getting on," he said.

"In a minute," she replied.

David sat up. Reached for his shirt, the first thing he could find in the heap of their discarded clothes.

"I wish we didn't have to…"

"Have to, what?"

"Go."

David smiled; observed, for a few moments, the rise and fall of her chest. He bent down and kissed her.

"Don't *you*?"

"Yes," he said. "But…" He picked up her skirt. Flung it at her, covering part of her face and her left breast. "Afraid we have to."

"At least you managed to tell him," said Edith, once they were back on the delivery route.

"Suppose."

"I'm proud of you," she added, quite unexpectedly; it was normally his mother who said that sort of thing.

Mr. Jenkins kept mentioning it: the fact that it was his last day. He told every customer that visited the shop. David would start to serve them, lean under the counter for their slices of beef or their sausages, then Jenkins would say: "It's his last day, you know."

"Oh. Is it?" they'd reply.

"Uh-huh. He's signed up. Leaves in... When is it, lad?"

"Three-and-a-half weeks."

Then they'd wish him all the best, or say what a good job he'd done, what a quick learner he was, or that it was nice to get to know him – not that he felt like he really got to know any of them, beyond what bits of meat they purchased – and David would smile and thank them, as if it wasn't the tenth or the twentieth time the same conversation had been repeated.

And then Jenkins would make a point of saying, to everything – like when he was getting the delivery bike ready – that it was the very last time he'd be doing it. "How's that feel, lad – doing that for the final time?" (Not that David had ever said he'd never be returning to the shop, once he'd served his time in the army. Although he had, definitely, decided exactly that. Perhaps Mr. Jenkins just didn't expect him to return. After all, that's what happened to his son.) And David would – much as he did when all the customers said their piece – just smile and nod and say, "Don't know," adding, 'strange," which was a lie, because it actually felt really good, it felt like a relief, like something being removed, something David had, yes, got used to, but had also grown to resent even more than he thought possible.

So, when he left there that day, the sun setting, the sky a canvas of swirling pinks and fiery orange, the walk home seemed to take on an entirely different character: reminding him of the times when he used to make his way to and from the bus stop, a time when all the world seemed alive with possibility.

***

They were at the end of their week in the hotel foyer. Arnott directed them as they removed the scaffolding.

"If you start by putting these in."

He set to unbolting the wooden boards and David and Harry began taking them outside. To David, it seemed like they had spent their whole time at the hotel either building or dismantling the scaffold. Fitting it all in the van was a puzzle he now knew very well. They laid the boards flat. Went back for some more. Like stocking up the cold room or sweeping the shop floor: a routine he would have to get used to.

Three days into the job, Arnott had said – once they'd packed away and begun to drive back home – that they could do with his help on a more permanent basis, if he was interested.

"Yes," David had replied. "Course I'd be interested. Thank you."

"Well, you're an hard worker – I can see that. It'd make a big difference to things. Believe me."

"No. Thank you," said David again.

Edith was delighted when he told her. "What did I say? You never know unless you ask."

David had been the one to see the van, parked around the corner, but it was Edith that talked him into asking if they had any work going. She looked very pleased with herself – as well as with him.

David sighed and sat down.

"Your leg all right?" she asked, resting a hand on his shoulder.

"Bit stiff – that's all."

"Well, you stay there." She moved over to the stove. "I told Mum I'd make us all tea, so… What do you fancy? Your choice."

Arnott slammed the van door shut. "Job done," he smiled, planting a firm hand on his son's back. "Now. Want a quick drink, before we get back?" He and Harry both looked at David – their minds clearly already made up.

"Go on, then."

They left the pub just after nine. So, it was getting on for ten when David got back to Edith's.

"What's all the noise for?" she hissed at him as he tripped over the doorstep.

"Nothing," he said.

"Sshh! You'll wake Jessica."

"Oh. Right. Sorry."

He started taking his jacket off. For some reason, his left arm was stuck.

"Here," sighed Edith.

She grabbed him, spun him round, then yanked his arm out of the sleeve.

"Thank you."

He leant in for a kiss, but Edith pulled away and hung up his coat.

"I'm shattered," she said.

"Oh. Me too." He forced a yawn.

"Right. Looks like it." She made for the stairs. "By the way, your tea's through there."

"Oh. Thanks."

"Don't get too excited. It's been sat there two hours."

A little while later, David tiptoed into their bedroom. He peeled off his socks, only staying on his feet because he managed to fling a hand out and catch the side of the bed.

"You'll wake the whole street up at this rate," said Edith, sitting up and switching a light on.

"Oh," smiled David. "You still up?"

"Can't sleep with *you* making all this racket."

"In that case..." He pulled back the covers and climbed in. "Why don't we...?"

"No, David – not now."

"Why not?"

"Because... Look at you."

"What? Not handsome enough for you?"

"You just need to get some sleep – all right?" She turned the light off. "Night-night."

"Do I at least get a kiss goodnight?"

"Fine," she said, her lips finding him in the darkness. "Happy?"

"Very happy."

"Good."

"But I'd be even happier if..."

"What did I say?"

"I know, but... Come on."

He felt around for her, felt her body melting to his touch.

"But I'm tired, David."

"Just stay where you are, then."

She sighed, let him move aside her nightie, and when he kissed her, her lips pressed back into his, holding them in place.

"See?"

"Just get on with it, eh?"

Edith helped him slip off his pyjama bottoms; directed him inside her.

"That all right?" he said, as they started moving together. "Will I do for you now?"

"Mmm." She kissed him again. "You'll do."

"So, what happened to you last night, anyway?" asked Edith, the following morning.

"I went for a few drinks with the Arnott's."

"Seemed like a bit more than a few."

"Mmm." He raised a hand to his forehead. "I think it might've been. Can't really remember."

"Right. And what do you remember about when you got in?"

David thought for a moment. Took another bite of toast. "Why? What happened?"

"Well you made a right racket for a start. I'm surprised Jessica slept through it all."

"Did I? Sorry."

"Do you not remember it at all?"

"I'm not sure. Maybe." Something came to mind suddenly: the taste of Edith's skin. "Oh. Did we…?"

She nodded. Looked through into the hallway, in case her parents were around. (Even though they were married, had been for months – and even though they had a child – they were both still cagey about certain things around their parents.)

"I think I remember *that* – well, some of it."

"I should hope so too," she whispered.

"What do you mean?"

"Because you were the one going on about it, pestering me until I gave in."

"Oh. Sorry. What else happened?"

"That was about it – thank goodness."

David finished his breakfast. Started on the washing-up.

"It got me thinking, though," said Edith, leaning next to him against the worktop. "It'd be so much better if we had our own place, wouldn't it? Then we wouldn't have to worry about waking up Mum or Dad and we could… you know…"

"Mmm."

(At least, he thought he knew.)

"What do you reckon?"

"Well, now that I'm earning again, I guess there's no reason why we can't start looking into it."

"Right. And – I've been thinking about *this* too."

"What?"

"Well, if we have our own place – a bit more room, you know – then we could have another baby too."

"Oh."

"No, don't worry." Her voice dropped again. "I'm not saying I'm pregnant again."

"Good."

"Well…" She grinned. "I don't think I am."

***

In the north of the city – as in many other parts of the city – the council were building new houses. Thousands were needed to replace the ones the Germans had bombed. But they weren't just offering them to the families made homeless in the raids. There was also a surplus number of properties, ones that didn't already have intended tenants, and the council were making them available to any other interested families.

"What do you think?"

David showed Edith the advertisement. It had been in that morning's newspaper.

"You reckon we've a chance of getting one?"

"Course."

She looked at the image.

"It does look nice."

"I know. So, I put our names down. All right?"

Just a few weeks later, a confirmation letter arrived, and a few more weeks after that, David, Edith and Jessica were moving into their new home.

"Look at this."

Edith inquisitively opened doors and peered in to rooms.

"Right. In a minute."

David set down the box he was carrying. Trailed back to the car for the next. Mr. Kemp passed him on the garden path.

"Where shall I put this one?"

"Just anywhere for now."

They hadn't much to unload. Most of it was Jessica's or Edith's. By the time David returned with his second box-load, Edith was already unpacking the others and filling up kitchen cupboards. Mrs. Kemp came down the stairs holding Jessica.

"The bedrooms are a good size."

"Mmm."

"Is your mum coming at any point?"

"Not today, but she said she'd give me a hand, later, with the wallpapering – give me a break, you know…"

"Right." Mr. Kemp emerged from the front room, after dropping off another box. "Busman's holiday, eh?"

"Exactly," smiled David. "Anyway – how much more is there?"

"Almost done."

By the middle of the morning, everything was out of the car and in the house and they were all sat round the kitchen table with a cup of tea. Jessica was bouncing on Edith's knee.

"She seems settled today," said Mrs. Kemp.

"Yes." Edith smiled. "She must like it here."

"Mmm. I still wonder whether the town's the best place for a youngster to grow up."

"Not this again, Mum."

"I know this looks like a pleasant enough area. But those streets we drove down to get here – they were filthy."

"You're worrying about nothing."

"And what if war breaks out again? I couldn't bear to think of you living here with all that going on."

"War's not going to break out again. Tell her, Dad."

"Edith's right, love. They'll be fine here."

"I still…"

"Mum, just drop it. Please."

David glanced at his watch. It was almost eleven.

"Thanks again," he said, looking at Mr. Kemp. "I'm not sure we could've managed on the bus after all."

"No, don't be daft. What's the point in having a ration of petrol if we don't use it now and then?"

"Suppose."

"In fact, I can't remember the last time that car was used. I'm surprised it got started, to be honest."

"Well – we really appreciate it, Dad."

"We should probably be getting back actually." Mr. Kemp stood up. "Come on, love."

"Really?"

"Yes. Come on." He stretched. "We'll leave you three to it. Let you get settled in. Properly."

On the doorstep, David and Edith waved goodbye – Edith manufacturing some movement of the arm from Jessica. They watched as the car disappeared down the road, then stepped inside and shut the door.

"Well..." David raised his eyebrows. "Welcome to your new home, Mrs. Denby."

"Why, thank you. It's rather nice, isn't it?"

"It certainly is."

With Jessica in her arms, stretching to break free, they wandered from room to room, talking about what could go where and what colour they'd like on the walls and what the view was like from the windows.

"It's just right," smiled Edith, in the main bedroom.

"Mmm. It'll do."

"Woah! Don't get too excited."

"Come on," he said, letting his right hand linger softly on her shoulder. "Let's go do some more unpacking."

***

David brought in both sets of stepladders, one in each hand, leaving them, to one side, in the doorway with the paint tins. He went back out to the van, where Arnott and son were sorting the rest of the things.

"Is that everything?" asked Harry, bucket swinging from his right hand.

"Yes, son." Mr. Arnott slammed the door shut.

They were working in a solicitor's office. STEEPLE, GREEN, FRANKS & ASSOCIATES. While they got to laying the dustsheets, the typists carried on around them, copying up whatever handwritten notes the men in smart suits brought them. The job was simply a new coat of paint: one in every room; a nondescript, cream shade in this big, busy space, then more of a plush blue for the private offices.

It was almost lunchtime before David looked much further than the wall he was painting. But he heard one of the clerical girls. She sounded familiar. He turned around. She was chatting – softly, but he could still make her out, quite clearly – to the person opposite her. It looked like the right colour hair, from behind. And when they did finally get out for something to eat – a little later than usual – she was there, by herself, stood on the pavement with a cigarette.

David made his excuses, "Just a minute – I'll catch you up," and went over. "Helen?" he said.

Just as she was raising her head, David thought there was still a chance he could be wrong. "Sorry?" she shrugged, now looking right at him. "Do I...?"

"David Denby – I'm a... I *was*... a friend of Michael's."

She sighed. "Oh, of course. I remember." Then she held out her fag packet.

"Don't worry." David reached into his coat pocket. "I've got my own."

"Fair enough." And she took another puff. Exhaled. "So..." She pointed to his spattered overalls. "This is what you're up to now. I thought you worked in a shop somewhere."

"Yes. I did."

"How come...?"

"Just wanted to..." He lifted his ciggy to his lips. Took a drag. "You know..." Breathed out. "Do something else."

"Where was it you worked?"

"Jenkins' butcher shop."

"Right. Don't blame you, then – all that blood." She inhaled deeply, then added; "I should probably get myself some lunch."

"Right." David stepped aside. Watched as she started down the street.

"You coming?"

"Oh." He thought, if anything, from the looks of her, that he was being a bit of a bother. "Yes."

She took him to a café around the corner. He spotted Arnott and Harry on the way. They ordered sandwiches and a pot of tea and sat down.

"I'd normally have another..." She gestured to her packet of Benson. "You know, if I was on my own."

"No. Have one. In fact..." He held out his. "Take one of mine."

"Why?"

"I need to cut back."

"Right." She accepted his offer; slowly slid one out and lit it.

"Well, really, it's Edith telling me to cut back."

"Oh, yes, of course – how is she?"

"Not so bad – it's just, with Jessica, she doesn't think it's such a good idea."

"Who's Jessica?"

That's right. She wouldn't know, would she? "Our little girl," he smiled.

"Oh, goodness – I didn't realise you two had... When did this happen?"

"Well Jessica's about ten months now."

"Right," she smiled.

"So... Anyway, that's why Edith doesn't think it's such a good idea me smoking."

"No. Guess not."

"So, you're helping me out really."

The lady that served them brought over their things.

David tucked straight in. They were only delayed in getting out for lunch by about half-an-hour, but, when you haven't eaten since first thing... "Do you always come here?" he asked, between mouthfuls.

Helen nodded. "Most days – I need to get out of the office, have some time, to myself."

"Well, I'm sorry if…"

"No, I didn't mean that. It's nice to see you again."

"Mmm. You too."

Helen topped up his tea, then added some more to hers.

"So how long have you worked at the solicitor's?" asked David, remembering where her and Michael had met.

"Seven or eight months, something like that – just after I found out about…"

He finished the sentence in his head.

"Like you, I guess – I needed a change."

David thought about that morning at the registry office, about how Michael had reassured him, based on how he had felt, just months earlier, at his own wedding. He and Helen had looked so happy together. They always did. Never, for one second, did David think that…

They returned to the office for half-past one. Arnott senior and Harry were already back to work. They waited for Helen to settle at her desk before commenting.

"What's the story there, then?" asked Arnott.

"Just an old friend," replied David, reaching round him for the tin of emulsion.

"Is that right, eh?"

David nodded; hoped Helen couldn't hear them.

"Just an old friend," repeated Arnott, before turning his attention back again to the wall and his paintbrush.

As the job progressed, David gradually saw less of Helen. She and the other clerical girls ventured rarely into the lawyer's offices – they had their own secretaries for that. But there were a few times the two of them crossed paths. The day they were in Steeple's office, David had just been out to lunch and Helen was heading out that way. They very nearly clattered into each other.

"Sorry," said David, before he knew whose arm he had hold of.

He looked up.

"So, did she?"

"Oh. David."

"Helen. How are you?"

"Fine. You?"

He nodded. "Yes – fine, thanks."

The green of her eyes suddenly reminded him of the green all the classroom doors were painted in. He could see Michael outside the head's office. The idea that they might, one day, be contracted to re-paint the place occurring to him too.

"Going for lunch?"

"Yes."

"Same place?"

"Yes."

"Right. I've just been. Not to… there. Somewhere else, but…"

(He'd gone to the fish and chip shop with the Arnott's, then stopped off on the way back at the tobacco stand.)

"I should…" She readjusted her handbag on her shoulder.

"Course."

She stepped away.

"You know…" David called after her. "I'm sure Edith would like to see you too, if you…"

"Right." She gazed down at the pavement. "Maybe." And then she went.

That weekend, David telephoned Robert. Besides that, first time, they'd met on just a couple of occasions since their returns from the continent.

"Look…" he said. "I know we haven't really…"

"No."

"But I just thought…"

Robert had moved into the town too, into one of the badly bombed areas where rent was cheap. He was studying at the university, with plans to maybe become a teacher.

"What'll you teach?"

"Don't know," he smiled. "Literature, I think."

David offered him a fag.

"Yes, please."

Struck a match.

"Thanks." Robert ran a hand through his mucky-blonde hair. "You still painting and decorating, then?"

"That's right."

"You like it?"

David nodded. "Hmm. You know."

"You never said why you didn't go back to the butcher's."

"Well…" That question again. "Just… had enough of it." Which was true, in part.

"And how's Edith?"

"Good, thanks. She said hello."

"And the little one?"

"Good too – can still cry the house down, mind."

"Really?"

"Oh, yes." He stubbed his ciggy out in the ashtray. "And are you… seeing anyone?"

"Yes, as it happens." A smile crept across Robert's lips.

"Oh, right – who?"

"We met at a dance one evening. Her name's Martha. We've not really known each other long, been on a few little dates, that's all."

"But you like her?"

"Mmm. I do."

"Well, that's great. I'm pleased for you."

It was like they were still fourteen and sat on that bench by the duck pond.

"You know who I've seen this week?"

"Who?"

"Helen."

"What? Michael's…?"

David nodded. "She works in the offices we've been decorating."

"Where's that?"

"In town – one of the solicitor's offices?"

"Have you spoken to her?"

"Yes. A few times."

"How does she seem?"

"Don't know. Quiet. But she always was."

"Was she still wearing her ring?"

"Yes," said David. It was the first thing he'd noticed, when she was outside, lifting the ciggy to her mouth. The sunlight caught it like broken glass.

After a few more moments, Robert stood up. "Same again?"

"Please."

David waited outside. They were directly beneath the creaking pub sign. THE WHITE BUTTERFLY. It was late, getting dark, but there were plenty of cars and people still around. The streetlamps gave off a dull-yellow glow and David noticed a mark on his left shoe. Blue paint. Must have missed it, earlier on, when he had the polish out.

"So…" started David, when Robert had returned with their drinks. "When are you next seeing this Martha?"

"Tomorrow, actually. We're going to the pictures."

"Sounds nice."

Robert smiled. "Should be." He took a quick swig. "Bet yours and Edith's evenings are a bit different nowadays."

"You could say that."

"What's it like – being a father?"

"Oh, you know…"

"Well – no, not really."

"Right," David smiled. "It's sort of hard to describe."

"But you like it, don't you?"

"I guess. It just feels kind of…" But he couldn't quite think of the right words. "I don't know."

"What?"

"Well, Edith just looks so... at home with it all, you know – whereas I'm still trying to get used to it."

"You know she probably doesn't feel as comfortable with it as you think she does."

"You reckon?"

"Ask her."

The idea sounded ridiculous to David. What would she think of him if he asked her that?

"I don't know. It's like she's a different person – not, in every way, but..."

"We shouldn't have gone away, should we?"

"What?" The question seemed to come from nowhere.

"We should never have signed up."

"But we didn't really have a choice there."

"I know, but... All it's done is mess things up."

David nodded in agreement – though, he also wanted to ask why Robert would say such a thing. What exactly had the war messed up for him? They still didn't really speak about it – barely brushed the subject; and, whenever they did, it was always side-stepped and avoided. David didn't even know where Robert ended up serving.

They parted with a handshake, a firm pat on each other's shoulder, and the promise that they would meet again, soon.

David took a slow walk home, keeping to the main streets. Every corner revealed fresh evidence of the mess of war. Just like Robert had been talking about. Certain areas of the city had begun to be rebuilt, some were even finished, like theirs, but still others remained rubble. And many of those that hadn't given in to the bombs looked like empty shells; whole terraces, down at least one or two streets, completely abandoned. David hadn't been to this part of town before. It seemed like an entirely different country compared to the semi-detached houses and front gardens of the estate where he and Edith lived.

It was a mild evening, summer just kicking in, and David was surprised to see plenty of children still out, playing games. Several times, he found himself, when stepping out to cross the road or passing the end of a ten-foot, in the middle of a football match. He passed the ball back, once or twice, to shouts of "Here, Mister!" – wondering at what point had he crossed the line from boy to mister. He hadn't ever really noticed. Though perhaps that was another consequence of war.

When he arrived home, Edith was cradling and shushing a crying Jessica.

"That's it," she said, softly. "Sshh, now."

The little thing carried on regardless.

David took off his coat and hung it on the peg.

"She had been sleeping quite well," said Edith, once Jessica had finally given up the fight.

Edith laid her carefully in her cot. David followed her into their bedroom, switching off the landing light.

"I mean, she managed a few hours."

"Well, let's hope she can manage a few more, then."

David began getting undressed. Edith was already in her nightie and just slipped back under the covers.

"Did you have a nice evening?" she asked.

"Yes, thanks." He rested his clothes neatly on the back of the chair which was also, at that time, when any spare money was spent on baby things, playing the role of bedside table.

"How's Robert?"

"He seems all right, I think." Though David knew that wasn't quite true – Robert saying they should never have signed up still playing on his mind.

"And *is* he…?" (Because, really, it was Edith that had put the question in his head.)

"Yes. Her name's Martha."

"Oh, right. He say any more…?"

"Just that they've only been out on a few dates."

"Well, you never know. Everything has to start somewhere."

David smiled and got into bed.

Jessica stayed still and sleepy for almost three hours. Then she woke again. David waited a few moments, not long, expecting to hear and feel Edith leave the bed. But when she didn't – and when Jessica didn't stop but continued on ferociously – he peeled the sheets back and staggered blearily over to the cot. He reached in and picked her up, a little uncertainly.

"Come on, Jessica," he said, like her crying was something that could be reasoned out of her.

David glanced towards Edith. She still hadn't woken, still hadn't shifted – the only movement being the slow rise and fall of her breathing. He considered going over to her, nudging her on the shoulder. But if Jessica's crying hadn't roused her – *still* hadn't roused her – then what difference would a nudge make?

David shushed her again. "That's it," he said, rocking her gently. "Go to sleep now." But apart from a slight adjustment in volume – thankfully, in the right direction – it seemed to have little effect. "Come on," he tried again. "Come on, Jessica." He looked over at the bed, not so much at Edith (who he couldn't face waking now; she just looked so peaceful, somehow – unlike Jessica).

He was starting to wish he hadn't got up either. But he had, hadn't he? He had got up. Leaving him with a screaming child to pacify.

David sniffed the air, he sniffed near her bum, checking that wasn't the cause of her distress. No. All seemed normal. Normal baby smells. He wondered whether she was hungry, but she was a few hours early for her usual feeding time.

"What's wrong?" he said. She might have, after all, suddenly (and extraordinarily) developed the ability to speak and explain herself. That would certainly help with a few things. Edith would probably appreciate that.

He looked again at the bed. David thought about saying something too. Considered, again, the nudge. Just a gentle tap. Nothing more. Barely there. But enough. Enough to wake her.

"Edith?" he whispered, placing his right hand on whatever arm she had emerging from the bedsheets. "Edith?"

David noticed something in her face twitch.

He repeated her name. "Edith?"

Then her eyes shot open. "Oh. What?" She sat up. "Is everything…?"

"I can't get her to sleep again."

Edith stood up. Offered to take her. "How long have you been…? How long have I…?"

"Just a few minutes." Though it felt much longer.

"Come here, my love." She held Jessica close to her. Kissed the top of her head. "Calm yourself down."

David stood there watching. Edith rocked her up and down – there was both a gentleness and a firmness to it. But it had the required effect. Within a few minutes, Jessica's cries reduced to hardly any sound at all.

"There we go," sighed Edith, kissing her again. "That's better now, isn't it?"

"Much better," said David.

"I wasn't talking to you," she smiled. Edith perched on the side of the bed, still cradling Jessica. "What time is it?" she said, looking up at the clock.

David looked too. "Quarter-to-three."

"Soon be up for a feed, won't I?"

He sat down beside them. "I didn't want to wake you," he said. "Not at first, anyway. But then I couldn't get her to settle, so…"

"Don't worry. I can't believe I didn't wake up."

"No. Me neither. I didn't think anybody'd be able to sleep through all that. At least it means she might sleep through feeding time."

"I doubt that very much."

And Edith was right. She woke up again. Half-four. On the dot. Only, David wasn't awake to see it this time.

"Did you sleep all right in the end?" asked Edith, as soon as he was downstairs and in the kitchen.

David assumed he must have done. "Yes, thanks," he said.

"Good."

"Did she not...?"

"What? Jessica?"

"Mmm. Did she not wake up again?" Because he couldn't remember having heard her again.

"No, course she did. But you were sound asleep, so I just left you."

He sat down. "Sorry."

"What for? I got another hour or so afterwards."

Was that meant to make him feel better or worse?

David slid the newspaper towards him. Scanned the front page.

"Cup of tea?"

"Please," he nodded.

Edith filled the kettle, lit the hob, and then joined him at the table. "So..." she said. "What's the plan today?"

"Don't know. Don't have one." He opened to the first page. "Might go out for a walk later."

"Oh. You could take Jessica with you."

"Mmm. I could," he said.

"You'd like that, wouldn't you?" she said to Jessica, grinning in her high-chair.

When later arrived, Edith helped make sure David had all he would need. "Right. She's only just eaten, so..." She stood back. "I think you're sorted."

David opened the front door. Began to manoeuvre Jessica and her pram over the doorstep.

"Don't you both look lovely together," smiled Edith.

"We won't be long," he said, the memory of last night fresh in his mind. What if that happens again and he can't get her to shut up?

He wheeled Jessica to the top of the street, then turned right down the main road. It all looked very quiet: just a few Sunday dog-walkers; a couple hand-in-hand. David tried to keep the pram as steady as possible, avoiding any bumps in the path, so that Jessica stayed settled and – crucially – silent. He wondered whether she could sense his nervousness, whether that alone would set her off. They say animals can smell fear, so does that translate to children too? And if so, rather than attack, do they just react by bawling their eyes out? He hoped not. It would hardly be the relaxing walk he'd originally envisioned.

Of course – as Edith probably well knew it would – the reverse started to happen; the motion of the pram seemed to be sending Jessica calmly off to sleep. She yawned up at him. David smiled in reply.

He rather liked her this way, he thought. If she could just be like this all the time… If she could've just done this last night…

The clouds suddenly broke. The sunlight blinded David and he lifted a hand to block it.

As he walked and pushed the pram, the houses along the main road grew from small, squat semi-detached places – like theirs – into great, three- or four-floored terraced houses, dating back to the Edwardian or Victorian period. Despite the apparent grandeur of those buildings – an impression mostly felt because of their size, something he always remembers sensing when at school – many of them also looked sadly run-down, the result – again – of bomb damage. He imagined himself in one, in one of the big front rooms, re-painting the walls.

After fifteen minutes going in one direction, David crossed the road and began to return home. Jessica was fast asleep by this time. David hadn't expected this little adventure to work out so well. Edith would be pleased with him, bringing her home like this.

"How did you get on?" she asked.

David raised a finger to his lips.

"Oh. Sorry." She repeated her question in a whisper, peering into the pram. "How did you get on?"

"Fine," he said. It was like she'd sent him out for some kind of lesson – how to walk your child without tipping them out of the pram or losing them completely.

"Did she take much settling?"

"No. She just… nodded off." He didn't know how else to explain it. "She was no problem." And he never expected he'd be saying that.

Edith pushed her into the kitchen. "No point taking her out of here just yet."

David followed her through. Sat down again with the paper, most of which he'd read twice.

"Where is it you said you are next week?"

"The bank on Corton Road."

"Course."

"Should only take a few days."

"Right."

***

In the bank on Corton Road there was a girl. She worked as one of the cashiers. She had light-coloured hair, down to just below her shoulders, and she had pale, freckled skin and a mouth that always seemed to be in use. Her name was Martha. At first, David thought it was funny, how he'd only just seen Robert, who'd mentioned this girl he'd just met, a girl called Martha; but then he began to wonder whether this girl wasn't just another girl with the name Martha – which wasn't so remarkable a possibility in itself – but that she was in fact the same Martha that Robert had been talking about.

"Pass me that brush on your way up?"

David handed it to Harry.

"Thanks."

And clambered up alongside.

They were filling in the detail on the coving – a leafy pattern of green and gold. It was fiddly, time-consuming, and David had already made a number of mistakes, which he'd washed off sloppily with a spattered rag, and done his best to go back over.

It was their third day and they were behind the counter. He could hear Martha chatting to the girl next to her. She'd mentioned a boy before – though no name – and they were talking about him again.

"Where's he taking you tonight?"

"Not sure yet," she answered.

"Oooh! Mysterious."

"No, not really."

"Is he not that sort, then?"

"Don't think so."

"Not so far?"

"No."

"So how many times you been out with him now?"

"This'll be the fourth."

"He'll be popping the question soon."

"Oh, don't be daft!"

"No." Then the friend lowered her voice, but David could still hear every word. "I don't mean *that* question."

The bank closed at five. David thought all the bank girls had gone, but while he and the Arnott's were packing away, he found himself alone with Martha.

She smiled. David smiled back. Reached down for the last of the paint pots.

"Do you want me to…?" She grabbed the door for him.

"Thanks."

David had to shuffle past her, felt a part of his body brush hers. She dropped her gaze.

"Sorry," he said.

Outside, he said goodbye to the Arnott's and began to make his way home. A few minutes in, he realised there was somebody else behind him. He spun round, just out of interest, to see. It was the girl from the bank.

"Oh!" she said.

David couldn't tell whether it was genuine surprise or not – surely, she would have watched him leave, known who it was she was following. He waited for her to catch him up. Said: "Hello again."

"Hello."

"Are you heading this way?" He pointed up the road.

"Mmm."

"I could… walk you home, if…"

"I think I can manage, thank you."

"No, I didn't mean…"

"But, yes – I'd like that."

"Oh."

"I'm Martha, by the way."

"Martha," he repeated, as if he didn't already know. "I'm David. Nice to meet you."

They went, roughly, in the right direction for David to get home too. She told him about herself, hardly broke off at all to ask *him* any questions. She told him about her parents, how her mother wasn't well, and her father went to fight and never came back. She told him about the bank, who she got on with and who she avoided. But what she didn't tell him was anything about Robert – or about any boy, for that matter.

When they got to her house, they stopped, under the spotlight of a streetlamp.

"Well, this is where I live."

"Right."

"Thank you for walking me."

"No. It's fine."

"Are you finishing up tomorrow?"

"Yes," he nodded. "It should all be done tomorrow."

"Oh." She didn't sound so certain. "Good."

"I better let you…" David gestured to the front door.

"Yes, of course. Thank you again."

"Not a problem. Bye."

"Bye."

And he watched her turn – the shape of it, the flow of her movement, reminding him of Edith – open the door and go inside.

The next day, David thought she might be ignoring him. She barely looked at him, barely smiled, as if they'd never spoken, but when they were finished packing away – the job finally done too – there she was waiting for him.

"I thought… perhaps you could walk me home again."

"Right. Suppose so," he said.

And, again, she told him about herself – some of it the same, some of it different. But as he listened to her, as he watched her there next to him, David began to see something he hadn't really noticed the previous evening. Under the glow of the lamplight, she looked beautiful. Maybe it was the green in her eyes. Or the way her hair rested on her left shoulder. Maybe it was the way she didn't seem interested in him at all.

At her front door, David waited for her to speak.

"Do you want to come in for a cup of tea?"

He hesitated. Then nodded.

Once they were in, the only light coming from the back of the house, David took hold of her hand.

"Wait," he said.

Then, without another word, he kissed her. And, rather than pull away, she kissed him back. After a few moments, more to catch their breath, they stopped. Martha put a finger over her lips, then raised it, pointing upstairs. He followed behind her and she took him into her bedroom, softly shutting the door. David began to undress her. Martha just stood there, let him remove everything, item by item, then watched as he took his own clothes off. He placed her on the bed, kissing her neck, her breasts.

When everything was over, they laid side by side on the single bed.

"This can't happen again, you know?"

"You mean...?" Martha lifted his right hand, ran a finger over his wedding ring. "Why did you even...?"

"I don't know." Which really was the truth. He hadn't meant to. Had no idea this was what was going to happen. "I'm sorry, if..."

"What for?"

"I hope *you* don't regret it."

"No." She pressed her lips into his shoulder.

"But don't you...?" He stopped himself.

"Don't I what?"

"Don't you have someone you're seeing?" Meaning Robert.

"Oh. How do *you* know?"

"I heard you, the other day."

"Right. Well, that's nothing much, really."

"Oh. What's his name?"

"Why's that matter?"

"It doesn't," lied David.

"Frank," she said.

"Sorry?"

"His name – it's Frank."

"Oh." He tried to hide his relief.

"Anyway..." She nudged him with her elbow. "You better get dressed. I need to get you out of here without my mother seeing you."

They carefully crept down the stairs. Martha held his hand, guiding him down behind her. She opened the door, whispered something in his ear which he couldn't quite hear, then clicked the door shut, leaving him alone on the street.

All the way home, David tried working out why he'd just done what he did. Maybe it was simply because he liked the way she looked. Maybe it was because he couldn't remember the last time he and Edith had. Or maybe it was because *he* was the one taking charge, not Martha; he was the one doing the undressing, getting her in the right position. And maybe it was because she let him, because she gave into him.

By the time he was back, David had resolved to forget about it – along with all the other things he was trying to forget: his forays on the mainland, his time in the butcher shop, even those couple of years he spent at school. None of it mattered now – not the war, not Jenkins, that playground, not even this girl he'd just… It all belonged the other side of his front door, the other side of this point in time, which – he told himself – would have no bearing, no relation, to that which was to come.

And all that was fine. Most of the time. Things would tick along as they always had. Most of the time. But then, every so often, he would remember her, remember how she looked, laid next to him on the bed. And he wouldn't always try to push that image away. Sometimes, he would let it stay, let it take shape, add detail, words, things he should've said, things she might've said in return.

Then about a year later, he was still working with the Arnott's and they had a job, a domestic one, two streets from Martha's house. When they were done for the day, he waved the van away and then began to head towards the house. Checking his watch, he knew it was about the time she would be arriving home – that is if she still worked at the bank. He found the right place straight away. He considered knocking, had almost formed a fist, lifted his arm, when…

"David?"

He dropped his arm back down to his side. "Oh. Martha."

"What're you doing here?"

He was flattered she'd recognised him. But he didn't have much of an answer for her. "I'm not sure, really. We've got a job, just up the road. I started thinking about you. I'm sorry…" He stepped back. "It was a bad idea. I'll go."

"No," she said. 'don't. Please."

They didn't give in at first. To start with, they talked, perched on the side of the bed. She was living there alone now. Her mother had finally passed away and she was only managing to stay in the house because her aunt was helping to pay for it.

After a while, she asked him again. "So why did you come here? Really?"

"I guess I wanted to see you."

"But what about your...?"

"You mean Edith?"

"Right. What about *her*?"

"Look, I don't want to be here. I just... I couldn't help it."

"Do you love her?"

"Yes. Course I do."

"Then what about me? Why are you here with me instead of at home with her?"

David said nothing; he had nothing he could say. It felt like a very long time sat there on the bed.

"I should go," he said, finally. But he didn't stand up, didn't even try.

"You're still here," she said, after a few more moments.

"If I love her, then why... why do I still think about *you*? Why do I still think about what we did?"

This time it was Martha's turn to respond in silence.

"And why...?" He turned to look at her. (Was she even more beautiful than he remembered?) He didn't want to say it. But he did. "Why do I want to do it again?"

They gave in. One moment, Martha was sat there looking at him, her hands placed neatly on her lap, the next she was underneath him, her blouse pulled open and her skirt bunched at the waist. One moment, David was asking the question, "Why do I want to do it again?", the next he was kissing her, holding her chin steady with one hand and fumbling at his belt with the other.

After, their breathing heavy, their skin charged and sticky, they laid next to each other on the bed. Her dress heaped on top of his shirt and trousers heaped on the floor. That why-word fizzed even more so around David's head.

"Is this it, then?" sighed Martha. "I'm not going to see you for ages again – until you remember me and decide you want to see me?"

"Don't."

"Don't?" She propped herself up by her right elbow. "Why should I just let you turn up here, when you feel like it? Why should I just wait around for you?" Now *she* was doing it, using the why-word. "It's not fair. It's not fair, when..." Martha stopped, dropped her arm and laid down again.

"What?"

"Doesn't matter," she said. "Go on. You better go, I suppose."

He didn't feel like he had much choice. David gathered his clothes together. Began getting back into them. He looked across at her on the bed, felt like he might be about to stiffen again, then turned away.

"We hardly know each other. We've spent more time... in bed, than we have talking."

David wanted to dispute that, knew she was probably wrong, but instead continued buttoning up his shirt.

"It's just... Oh, I don't know what I thought might happen." She was sat up again, shrugging her shoulders. "But this is as far as it can go. Right?"

He nodded.

"You need to forget about me. And *I*... I need to forget about you."

David waited while Martha dressed herself. She didn't seem to mind him watching her. Why would she, given that she'd let him remove it all, let him in where – he assumed – she'd let no one else?

They trudged down the stairs. Before opening the front door, they paused, let their lips meet one last time.

"I'm sorry," he said.

"Me too. Now. Go."

She turned the latch. The dull-yellow of the streetlight crept in and David stepped out, into it, and though his neck strained to turn, he stopped and instead just listened for the click of the door, then began to walk home.

***

David was in that field again. But this time, looking down at his feet, his work shoes were spattered with emulsion. In fact, wasn't that the same colour they used to paint the bank?

Inching on to the ends of his toes, he tried to see over and beyond the wheat-stalks. The field seemed endless. He glanced behind. There was nothing to signify its beginning or end.

So, David did all he could do. All he could think to do. He began to walk. He brushed aside the grain with both arms, very soon starting to wonder, starting to worry, that he might not be managing to go in a straight line.

Then, he heard the sound. At first, it was just the once. But it made him stop. He listened.

"Hello?"

Listened again. Thought he could hear some far-off birdsong.

David carried on. It suddenly occurred to him that maybe the *swish-swishing* might simply have been from the movement of the crops as he pushed through them.

But then it started again. David could hear it on top of the noise he was making. So, it had to be something else, didn't it? There had to be something else there.

"Hello?" he said, louder, rooted to the spot.

It was carrying on. Like something scurrying through the field. Scurrying *towards* him. David looked for movement. The noise was growing.

"Who's there?"

(He daren't say, "What's there?" Though that was more what it sounded like. And what could it say back anyway?)

The scurrying was becoming a running.

"Who's there?"

The running a thundering.
"Who's…?"

***

"I've got some news," said Edith. "Good news."
"Right?"
"I'm pregnant."
"Oh."
Before he could say anything else, she had her arms around him, her face pressed into his chest.
"Isn't that great?"
"Fantastic."
"I mean, I know it'll be a bit of a struggle. But you're earning enough now, aren't you?"
David nodded.
"And I know we hadn't talked about it for a while, but Jessica's nearly two now – it'd be nice for her to have a little brother or sister. Don't you think?"
"Mmm," he smiled.
But there wasn't a lot of time for David to get used to the idea. He returned home from work one evening, a few months later, to find Edith crumpled on the kitchen floor, her back against the cupboards, a pool of blood by her feet and staining her skirt.
"What's happened?" He rushed over to her, dropped his things in the hallway.
"I don't know," she said, tears in her eyes.
David rang for the doctor. He came, examined her, sat them both down, and told them the news – the good news turned bad, turned bloody.
Edith kept apologising. Whilst, inside, David blamed himself. Saw it as punishment. Which, yes, *he* deserved. But, Edith? All she'd done was love him, trust him.
He tried to reassure her. "No," he said. "It's not *your* fault. Like the doctor said: this is just what happens sometimes."
But that seemed to make no difference.

For several weeks, before they each drifted off to sleep, they would lay utterly silent, their backs facing one another. Night after night after night. David couldn't help wondering whether it would ever return to the way it was, whether it had changed how she felt about him. And, worse, he couldn't help wondering, too, about that girl. If he wasn't careful, there she was, on the bed, her body moving under him: that image always lingering, waiting, in his subconscious.

She said it again, almost from nothing: "Sorry."

"Edith, please. There's no need. I've told you." He sighed. "We'll try again."

He hadn't said that before. And as soon as he had, he thought perhaps he shouldn't have done. Edith excused herself. Bundled a load of laundry into her arms and disappeared upstairs.

As usual, that night, they got into bed. David rolled over on to his side and settled into a comfortable position. When Edith joined him, he felt her brush his back. Assumed it must have been unintentional. David closed his eyes. But she did it again. He felt her warm breath on his neck.

"Edith?" He turned.

"I'm not promising anything," she said.

"What do you mean?"

Then she kissed him.

"Are you sure?"

"Think so."

At first, she did seem uncertain: hesitant, even, about how it all worked. She let David do most of the manoeuvring and, when he entered her, she winced sharply.

"Sorry." He withdrew. "Are you all right?"

"It's fine," she smiled. "Just... not used to it, I guess."

He tried again, slower. "Better?"

She nodded. Arched up and met his lips. Their bodies linked, working together, they each made noises, involuntary, like delighted sobs, until... The moment arrived: the seed sown in the soil. Edith pulled him closer; kissed him. She told him she loved him, said it a second time, and he responded – a little breathless – in the same way.

"I love you too."

Weeks became months. And still – after plenty of trying – Edith wasn't pregnant.

David continued his reassuring. "Don't worry. It takes time. We just have to be patient." But he was running out of things to say, platitudes to placate her with, and beginning to wonder whether it would ever happen. It was typical: when they hadn't meant to – both times, in fact – it happened; and now when they were really wanting it to...

David put it down as something else to blame himself for. Though – of course – he never said that aloud, tried his best not to show it. Instead, he began to offer his painting and decorating services to neighbours and friends at weekends and on evenings. He told Edith it was to save up some extra money. "For when the new baby comes." But that was only a little bit true. Because David was starting to see what this desperate yearning for something just beyond reach was doing to Edith, and he didn't like the way it looked, didn't like what it was making her into. And he could see, also, that it was something, in large part, that he was responsible for. The same thoughts played on in his head, over and over. If only he hadn't... If he'd just stayed away... If... If... If...

But he had, hadn't he? He'd done it. And this was the result. Giving Edith another baby wasn't going to sort it. Not entirely, anyway. It certainly wasn't going to stop the voices in his head, the accusations. Then again, why should he be free of them? He'd earned them. They weren't empty or false. Every word was true.

Once, he nearly told her. Blurted it out. The guilt was overwhelming him, and he could see no other way of controlling it. But then he couldn't. He couldn't say it. Couldn't say the words. "Edith, I..." Because he knew it would change everything – even though, in many ways, in the most significant way, it already had.

Gradually, their attempts to conceive became less frequent. Edith's desire to try – and to only, later, experience the numbing disappointment – was spent. Which David understood. He gave up trying to talk her round. Got used again to the silent, back-to-back night after night after nights.

It was in the spring, the following year, that David returned home with their first puppy. His thinking was that it may go some way to alleviating Edith's baby pangs. She'd commented before, once or twice, when out and about, seeing other people with little dogs on leads, how nice it might be to have one of their own, how she'd always wanted one growing up, but never had.

When it came to it, though, the gesture was met with very little enthusiasm. "What did you get that for?" she said, practically scowling at the poor thing.

"Well, I thought, you know… You've always said how much you'd like one."

"When've I said that?"

Selective memory, he thought. You definitely have. "Well, I must've… misunderstood."

"Mmm. You'll have to take it back."

"I can't take it back."

(He really couldn't. He'd just bought it from some bloke in the pub. David didn't even know the man's name. Couldn't recall ever seeing him in there before. The whole thing seemed daft now.)

"Well, I don't want it living here."

"Edith?"

"No. Get rid of it."

After a few hours, she backed down slightly. Her position became one of indifference; David had bought it, so it would be his responsibility. Everything. The walking. The feeding. The shitting. All of it.

"Fine," he said.

And the dog conveniently became just another excuse to leave the house. If ever he saw Edith, that look aching across her face, he'd say: "Come on, Benny – time for a walk." He knew it probably wasn't the best way of dealing with it (it wasn't any way of dealing with it, was it?), but anything he did or said only served to make things worse. He couldn't give her the thing she wanted most, so whatever else he offered was never going to match up.

One place to which David liked to take the dog was by the river. There was space there for Benny to run as he pleased. There were other dogs too, other pets *and* their owners – an aspect to dog ownership David could have happily done without, the small talk and doggy phrases lost on him – but because there was so much space, it wouldn't take long for he and Benny to find themselves utterly, peacefully, alone again.

David would have to drive there – it was a few miles from home and if they walked there, which they could, Benny would've been shattered before they even arrived. To an extent, David wondered whether that defeated the object, but after a few times, he soon forgot about those misgivings.

As soon as he hopped into the car, Benny would know, just by the direction David turned on to the main road, where they were going. The whole journey there – which was never much more than five minutes – he would be crying and pining to get out and get there. Even that didn't bother David. In fact, it made him smile. It made him like the silly thing even more. Which came as a surprise to him. He had expected to grow irritated by it, by its dependence on him. But the opposite seemed to be happening.

One day in the summer, when Benny was – by David's best guess – about four years old, Edith suggested her and Jessica come along with them for their walk by the river.

Jessica was nearly six, settled into infant school, and though Edith did nothing to encourage it, her and Benny were very close too. He'd let her do anything to him. Prod him in the mouth. Pull at his tongue. Mess with his ears. His only reaction was to lick her and offer her something else, another part of his body, to play with.

David didn't answer Edith's suggestion right away.

"Come on," said Edith. "Why not?"

"No." He hadn't said they couldn't. "Course."

The short drive was spent in almost-silence – the only chatter came from Jessica, at first trying to get her mother's, then her father's, attention, before finally deciding to converse with the dog, who responded typically with a wet tongue across the face.

They arrived. Parked up and got out. Benny raced off ahead. David looked out at the water, made half-golden by the midday sun.

"I want to walk next to *you*, Daddy," said Jessica.

"Oh." He was a few paces in front. "Come on, then."

Edith continued, a few strides behind. David kept glancing back, catching her eye, smiling.

"This is nice," she said, eventually.

"Mmm," nodded David. "I like it here."

"Yes. I can see why."

Jessica had wandered a bit further in front. Benny was off God-knows-where – though, no doubt, he knew exactly where they were. When the path curved round, taking them nearer the riverbank, they came to a bench. Edith gestured to it. David nodded. They told Jessica not to go out of sight, then sat down.

For a few minutes, they said nothing to each other. Simply stared out at the water. Some days, David had been here when the cloud was so low you could hardly see any of the river, let alone across to the opposite bank. On this occasion, though, there were no such difficulties. He began wondering what Edith might be looking at, whether she was looking in that direction too, when she finally spoke.

"I'm sorry, you know?"

"What for?"

"I've not always been… myself, lately."

"You've nothing to be sorry for," he said – which only made him think of the things *he* had to be sorry for, which only ever reminded him of one thing in particular.

"But I know I've been difficult, just because… you know…"

Of course, he knew. And, suddenly, the thought occurred to him that he wanted her to know – wanted her to know everything. He glanced round, to see where Jessica was. Was this the place, the time – really?

"Edith?" he said.

She turned. "Yes?"

He was looking her right in the eyes.

"What is it?"

He opened his mouth to answer.

Now

David checks the time again. It's two minutes later than when he last looked. Chucks down the newspaper. It lands, untidy, on the kitchen table. "Edith?" he shouts.

He hears her start down the stairs. "Yes?"

"What time did we say?"

She looks at the clock too. 'twelve-thirty."

It was gone one.

"This lot'll be ruined," he points at the pans he's been keeping an eye on. "You tried phoning?"

Edith shakes her head. "No. Don't fuss about it. They'll be here soon."

"Could've done all sorts in this time."

"Oh, nonsense," she sighs and leaves the room.

"When you say you'll be somewhere, at a certain time…"

"They'll have just got held up."

"They know we eat at one."

"Yes, love."

"But it's always what suits *them*, isn't it?"

Edith returns from the hallway. "Why don't you see if there's anything you can be doing in the garden?"

"What?"

"Just a suggestion."

"No – we made an arrangement…" He swipes his right hand through the air.

"I know, but…"

"I'm not going to start changing my plans for them."

"Fine." She turns to leave again. "But I've got stuff to get on with upstairs, so…"

"Right. *You* do that." He picks up the paper. "I'll stay down here."

Then

His boots – and the feet swelling and tingling inside them – felt like lead weights, like the ones they stuffed their packs with during training. They'd been going over three hours now. They started out some time around six, ate early at five, with the aim of reaching the next checkpoint by eleven. His water ran out miles back. He looked up, to the left, but the mists had hardly lifted and the wall of poplars lining the road meant there was little else visible. The supply wagon crawled at their backs, and he tried to remember whether they'd already crossed the border, or whether that was where they were still heading. The road seemed to be getting worse. He did his best not to get caught out by the potholes. Mud sloshed at his legs, spotting the trousers of those in front.

Five days. Five days since they landed on that beach – parts of it still burning, bodies still... If he'd known when he was younger, when Robert was telling him all about his holidays in Scarborough, if he'd known that would be the beach he first set foot on, he might never have wished that he could go there with him, or that his parents would take him, just for the day, him and his sisters, so they could play in the sea and the rock pools, catching crabs and getting seaweed tangled in their toes. Because if that's what a beach looked like, if that's what you saw...

The march went on. Just like the story – which he, now, boot-marks left behind him in the pot-marked road, was in some way a part of. Playing *his* part. Doing his duty. Leaving his mark. Same as when he helped carve that line in the concrete, every day he arrived and left the butcher shop.

They reached a crossroads.

"Company, forwards!" came the order.

Stretching to see over the men in front, there was still no sign of that checkpoint through the heavy mist. But he noticed again the ache in his ankles. Strange how he'd forgotten about it. He nudged his rifle up a little, so that it rested more comfortably on his shoulder, and took another deep breath.

Then, the story changed.

It started with a shot.

The people around him, the officers, began to shout.

Then, there were lots more shots.

He got pushed back. It happened really fast. He fell to the ground, banged his head, but managed to stumble to his feet again. Then he felt someone pulling at his shirt. "This way!" they yelled. But it was hard keeping up. He nearly fell again. There were too many people in the way, too many of them just lying there, on the ground.

They made it to the supply truck. There was him, the one who grabbed him, and two others. "Check you're loaded," hissed the first guy. He started messing with his rifle. Caught his finger on the catch. He couldn't think straight. It was like he'd never held one before. What's *this* for?

Then David saw it land and roll towards them. The others were still getting their rifles ready. And before he could say anything…

Now

Through the kitchen window, if David leans over the sink at the right angle, he can see the cars as they pull into the street. He counts twelve false alarms. Three of them frustratingly similar to the silver Ford he helped pay for.

Then they arrive. He checks the clock. Ten-past two. He turned the gas off the pans half an hour ago.

"They're here!" he shouts into the hallway.

Edith comes out from the dining room. "There. See," she says, like it's all gone to plan.

He lets her open the door. She waits there, in the porch, with her arms folded to shield herself from the chill, and glances back in his direction.

"Hello, Grandma," he hears one of the boys say.

"Sorry, Mum – we just... you know..."

"It's lovely to see you," says Edith. "Hello, Samuel. You've grown, haven't you? Soon be taller than me."

"How's Dad?"

"He's inside." Then she whispers, but he can still hear her: "A bit upset."

"Oh."

"Yes," he says, going to meet them at the door.

"Hello, boss," waves Mark, Jessica's husband, the youngest grandson, James, clinging to his other hand.

"What time did we agree?"

Jessica hesitates. "I..."

He turns to Edith. "What time was it?"

"Twelve-thirty," she answers.

"Right. Sorry. You know how it is, though."

"No. I don't, actually."

"Oh."

"When you make arrangements to be somewhere, at a certain time, you arrive at that time – maybe a bit early – and if you can't, then you call, to let them know."

"Yes, Dad." She sounded like a little girl again.

"Dinner's ruined."

"No," Edith chips in. "It isn't. The chicken'll be fine. We'll just have to warm it up again."

"You know when we eat."

"Yes. We just…"

David shrugs. "Just, what?"

"Well, Mark's parents wanted to…"

"Thought so."

"What's that supposed to mean?"

"You make it perfectly clear that you'd rather stay there than with us…"

"They've got more room – that's all. And you don't want the boys waking you up at all hours. James still isn't sleeping right through…"

"Oh, dear," says Edith. "I thought he was…"

"Anyway," smiles Mark. "We coming in or what?"

Edith laughs. Steps back.

"No."

"Jessica?"

"No. I can see we're not welcome."

He glares at her. "Might be for the best."

"Come on, kids."

"Jessica? Don't be daft." Edith shoves him on the shoulder. Hisses at him. "What are you…?"

"You heard her."

David watches them head back towards the car. James asks what's going on, why aren't they staying. Edith follows them to the kerb. Jessica just shakes her head, leans in to kiss her on the cheek.

Mark starts the engine and Edith waits by the side of the road while they pull away and out of the street.

"I…"

"No. Don't," she says, heading back inside.

"I might take the dog for a walk."

"I don't care what you do, David," she answers, pushing past him and disappearing upstairs.

PART THREE

Afterwards

Afterwards

David adjusts the seat, inches it closer to the steering wheel, and starts the engine. The car radio turns itself on automatically. To begin with, it growls and spits static; then a voice breaks in, saying...

The skies over Baghdad were last night filled with...

He changes gear: second to third. Turns on to the main road.

At this stage, it is unclear how many civilian casualties...

David reaches for the dial, finds one of Beethoven's symphonies in full bloom, appropriately; the sun breaking through the clouds, blinding, for a second, his view of the road.

He couldn't have picked a worse time to set out: three-thirty, kids and pushchairs swarming across the zebra crossings. Then again – he didn't have much of a say in the matter. The girl on the phone didn't really explain. She just said that he should get there, as soon as possible.

Eventually, David finds a parking space. He pulls past and reverses in, slow, steady, then gets out, locking the door. David lifts a hand to his forehead and looks for the ticket machine.

The girl on the phone didn't really have to say very much. All explanation came when she said *where* she was calling from. Anyone ringing you from a hospital is hardly going to be ringing you with good news, are they?

David can't decide how much money to put in. Because – how long will he be here? He glances behind him, spots the growing queue, and settles on five hours. It only costs fifty pence more than three. He goes back to the car, sticks the ticket on the windshield, double-checks he has everything he needs – wallet, keys – and starts off for the main entrance.

The girl on reception sounds like the girl on the phone. "Right, Mr. Denby – take a seat and I'll call for a nurse to take you through."

"No," he says. "It's fine. I'll stand, thanks."

"OK," she smiles, then picks up the telephone. David looks at his feet while she speaks to someone somewhere else in the building. "They'll only be a minute," she says, when she's put the receiver down.

"Thanks. Can you tell me what...?"

"The nurse will explain everything, Mr. Denby."

"Right. Course."

He stands back and a woman with blonde, bobbed hair approaches the desk. Her right hand trembles as she speaks and, with her left, she holds on to a young girl who, herself, clings tightly to a stuffed bear with one eye missing. Doctor won't be able to do anything for that, thinks David.

"Mr. Denby?"

He turns around.

"My name's Amy – I've been looking after your wife. Would you like to follow me through?"

He nods.

She holds the double-doors open. "Just this way," she says.

David follows her between rows of cubicles – most with their curtains pulled back. He tries not to look at the people inside. The nurse directs them through another set of doors. Then he sees her, in one of the beds, a man leaning over her.

"Dr. Philips..." says the nurse.

He straightens.

"This is Mr. Denby."

"Right. Thank you." He comes around the bed and stands beside him. "Mr. Denby – it seems your wife was found unconscious."

"What? Unconscious?"

"The paramedics did what they could and managed to stabilise her and bring her in – but she really is very poorly."

"How could this...? What's wrong with her, exactly?"

"There's severe bruising to her head and chest – probably a result of the fall. The main thing we're concerned about right now is internal bleeding. She's stabilised at the minute, but..."

"Can I speak to her?" asks David – though he doesn't really know why, now that he's said it. It just seemed like the right thing to say.

"Well, she hasn't been responding. Mr. Denby – does your wife have a history of this kind of thing? Has this ever happened before?"

"No," he says, moving nearer to her. "Please. I'd like to speak to her."

"Well. OK. Perhaps a familiar voice will help." The doctor steps away. "I'll just be over here," he says, pointing to a corner of the room.

David looks down at her. But he doesn't know what to say. It's hard to recognise her under all the tubes and wires. "I... Edith..." He reaches for her hand. It rests limp in his. "What do I do?" he whispers, impulsively – the first thing that comes to mind. "I don't know what to do."

"Mr. Denby?" The nurse rests a warm hand on his shoulder. "Would you like to sit?"

David takes the plastic chair from her. "Yes. Thanks."

"Take as long as you need."

He watches her at the other side of the room. There are other patients, other families, and, actually, he'd rather look at them than look at Edith. After half-a-minute or so, he takes hold of her hand. There's a thick, purple bruise, which wasn't there when she left the house. He lifts it towards his lips, but...

The sound coming from the machines changes from a *beep-beep-beep* into a continuous tone. The line passing along the screen turns flat.

He drops her hand. "What?"

The nurse rushes back across.

"I didn't..."

Followed by the doctor: "Just stand back, please, Mr. Denby." He checks her eyelids with a little light. "Get on to theatre," he says to the nurse. "We can't wait any longer." She disappears from the room. The doctor turns to David. "We're going to have to take her up to the operating theatre."

Two guys with shaved heads and facial hair come in and start to wheel her out the room.

"Can I...?"

"You'll have to stay here." The doctor follows behind the trolley.

"Would you like to come this way?" The nurse, Amy, is suddenly by his side again. "I'll show you to the relative's room."

She rests a hand on David's back and steers him in the right direction. "Just in here." She opens the door. It's like a dentist's waiting room. Out-of-date magazines. Kids toys, untidy in one corner. "Would you like a tea, a coffee?"

"No."

"OK. When I know something, I'll come and see you."

A few minutes later, the door opens again. David looks up, expecting to see Amy, but the woman and the girl with the teddy from earlier are brought in by another nurse, a young fella with thick-rimmed glasses. They sit down opposite.

"Can I get you anything?" he asks.

"No, thank you."

"Right. Let me know if you change your mind." And he leaves them to it.

David watches the girl climb on the woman's lap. "Look..." She points to the play things, but the girl shakes her head and hugs her soft-toy closer. The woman reaches down for her handbag. Takes out a blue asthma inhaler. Ingests two squirts and puts it back in her bag, sighing and shutting her eyes.

David notices a loose thread in the carpet. He stares at it for... He's not really sure how long, exactly, but he suddenly realises the woman across the room is talking to him.

"Excuse me," she's saying. "Are you OK?"

He looks up. It takes a few seconds for his eyes to re-focus.

She repeats her question. "Are you OK?"

"Not especially," he says, honestly.

"No. Silly question, I know. You just looked a little... lost."

"I suppose I am," he says, not sure how to explain it further, should she ask, and not sure, either, whether it's even the best way to describe what's going through his mind. Because he has no idea what any of the things he's thinking and feeling add up to.

The little girl climbs down from her mother's knee and goes over to the toy corner. She finds paper and felt-tips.

"Want to do some colouring?"

The girl nods.

"Come here, then." The woman points to the table between where they're sitting and where David's sitting.

"How old is she?" he asks, once she's settled and started filling her page with blue sky.

"Three. Do *you* have kids?"

David nods. "A daughter."

"Right," she smiles.

"She's grown up, of course – got children of her own." He turns away, looks expectantly at the door, only to see a pair of paramedics passing with someone new on a trolley.

"Do you mind me asking why you're in here?"

"Well..."

"Sorry. I should mind my own business."

"No. I..." David glances back at the girl, who, now, is concentrating on making her grass sufficiently green. "It's my wife," he tells her. "She collapsed."

The woman does a sort of sympathetic gasp, then asks: "Will she be OK?"

"I don't know," shrugs David.

"Right. I'm sure they'll make her better, you know... I'm sure she'll be fine."

David wonders what medical knowledge she possesses that makes her so certain.

"Is your daughter on her way?"

"Er..."

"Sorry. I'm being really nosey, aren't I?"

"No." Well, yes, he thinks. "It's just a bit... What's the word? It's a bit complicated."

"Oh," she smiles. "Fair enough. I'll shut up now."

The woman stands up, moves over to the low-set window with its office-block blinds. David considers asking her why *she's* here, since she asked him. He's about to, when the door opens.

It's the male nurse that brought them in. "Miss Dobson? Would you like to come this way, please?"

"Yes." She picks up her handbag. "Come on, Jess."

The name startles David. Though he doesn't know why it should matter, it still does. His heart, which he could already feel pounding, lurches like the aging motor it is.

"Time to go now."

The girl scrambles to her feet, leaving her picture half-done.

"Don't forget..." David points to the teddy and the girl, looking nervous suddenly, sweeps it up.

"Thank you," smiles the woman. "I hope everything with your wife..."

David nods; doesn't need her to finish the sentence. He manages to say, "Thank you," and then they go, and he's left alone again.

The next time the door gets opened, the young nurse, Amy, walks in, followed by Dr. Philips.

David stands up. "How is...?"

"Mr Denby – please, sit." The doctor perches on the chair next to him. "Your wife suffered severe internal trauma..."

He notices they're already talking about her in the past tense. Does that mean...?

"It seems there was some kind of build-up of tissue, on the brain – that's what caused her to lose consciousness. I'm sorry. We were unable to resuscitate her."

David stares blankly at the name badge pinned to the doctor's shirt pocket.

"Is there anyone you'd like us to call, Mr. Denby?" asks Amy.

David shakes his head.

"Right. You sure?"

He nods his head.

"Well, in a few minutes – if you'd like to – you can come through and see her."

"I think I'd like to go outside," he says.

"That's fine. Sounds like a good idea – some fresh air. Would you like me to…?"

"No." David returns to his feet, stiffly this time. "I'll be all right."

Amy points him in the right direction and he finds his way back to the main entrance.

Apart from one bench occupied by gowned-up smokers, the others are free. Missing one, going for the third along, David sits at the end not already spattered with bird crap. The cigarette cravings he used to feel when he first quit suddenly return and there's a booth with flowers and magazines and chocolate bars for sale. David wanders across.

"Ten *Benson & Hedges*, please."

The shop assistant takes them from the shelf and rests them on the counter – which is essentially a pile of yet-to-be sold newspapers. "Three-nineteen, please."

He hands her a crumpled fiver. "Oh." He suddenly remembers. "And a lighter as well."

She passes him the ciggies and a blue, clear-plastic lighter. He looks momentarily at the fluid moving inside.

"There's your change."

"Thanks."

Back at the bench, David lights up. He pushes the smoke out slowly through his teeth. Watches it linger in front of him, then drift and fade away. To begin with, it does the trick. But after a few more drags, David's mind creeps back inside the hospital. He goes over what the doctor said. *We were unable to resuscitate her*. He wants to ask them why, how hard they tried. He wants to know how this happened. How does someone just fall over and die like that?

David hears footsteps behind him.

"Mr Denby?"

He turns; looks up.

"You can come and see her now?"

"What?"

"Your wife."

"Oh. No. I don't think I can."

Amy sits down next to him. "I understand," she says. "But it can help."

"How?"

She smiles, softly. "I don't know – to be honest. But I've seen it help lots of other people in the same situation. You can just sit there, or you can talk to her. It's up to you."

"I don't know. What would I say?"

"You can say what you want – tell her how you're feeling."

David stares straight ahead, at the main road; cars and the number two bus clog the tarmac, the tail-end of rush hour.

"Or you don't have to say a thing."

"Where is she?"

"I'll show you."

The people in the room stop what they're doing, their eyes darting to the door.

"Mr Denby's just going to have some time alone with his wife," says Amy, grabbing him a chair and putting it right next to the bed. "We'll just be outside."

David sits, slowly. To begin with, he simply looks down at his hands resting on his lap. He daren't face her there on the trolley. The room is unbearably quiet, impossibly still. His chest throbs and he can't think what to say. Or whether he *should* say anything. Is that how this works?

Finally, he looks at her right hand. He remembers lifting it, earlier – the kiss that he never quite…

"I don't understand," he says. "I mean – I don't understand why, how. I don't know how I could've let this happen to you."

Because it had to be down to him, surely – that was what she always said. *You're the reason no one comes see us anymore. You're the reason our grandchildren don't want to visit.*

He stays there barely five minutes. When he leaves the room, Amy, the nurse, is waiting for him.

"I've a few forms, Mr. Denby, for you to sign – if you don't…"

"No," he says. "Pass them here."

She hands him the papers and scrapes around for a biro. "Just there." She points with the ballpoint. "And then again there. It's just for the hospital records."

"Fine." David rests the form on the counter, catching the eye of another nurse on one of the computers. He tries the pen. Nothing. It merely scratches a faint line on the paper. "Doesn't work," he says, giving it a second go.

"Here." Amy offers him a different one.

"Thanks. Wish everything was so easily replaced." He signs his name, twice, and slides the forms back her way. "That it?"

David closes the front door quietly, checking the latch has dropped. He finds the dog in the kitchen, waiting to go out. He lets him into the garden and, instinctively, turns on the radio. They're still debating the intervention in the Middle East. David fills the kettle at the cold tap, flicks the switch, and pops through to the sitting room to draw the curtains. He realises, on the way back into the kitchen, that there are two mugs on the side, left out from earlier; his favourite (garden birds of Britain) and Edith's (a beach scene in Scarborough – he finally did get someone to go with him).

The clock strikes the quarter-hour.

During the drive home, David got to thinking about calling someone. He'd refused the offer at the hospital, but he knew people should be told.

He looks again at the time. It's gone nine.

There's only one person he can bring himself to call.

"Oh." He always sounds surprised when someone at the other end answers. "Hello, Josie." Then, for a moment, he stops, wondering how to begin. "Something's happened..." he says.

The doorbell rings. David sees a version of his sister through the frosted glass.

"You made good time," he says, stepping back. "When did you set off?"

"First thing – just after eight."

"You'll want a drink, then?"

"Please."

Josie follows him down the hallway and into the kitchen. The dog gets up from his basket to sniff round her feet.

"I had hoped you were calling for a different reason."

"Oh. What's that?"

"No, I meant... anything."

"Right. Sorry to disappoint you."

She smiles. "Was she...? Will she have been in any pain?"

"I didn't ask. There was a lot of bruising."

"It's horrible. I'm so sorry."

David squeezes as much he can out of the teabag, then leaves it on the side, balanced on a teaspoon.

"Thanks." Josie pulls out a chair; sits. "Are you not...?"

"Just had one." He joins her at the table. The dog transfers his interest to him.

"Alf sends you his best."

David nods. "How is he these days?"

"Fine. He just gets worn out so easily. He couldn't have managed the long car ride."

"Right. I didn't realise it was so bad."

"He went for some tests the other day." Josie takes her first sip. "We should hear back about them after the weekend."

"But he's... well, besides that?"

"Oh, yes."

"Good."

She takes another mouthful of tea, then asks: "How was Jessica when you spoke to her?"

"Well…"

"You did call her?"

He looks down at the varnished oak of the table-top.

"How else do you expect her to find out? The next time she rings to speak to her? You need to tell her, David."

"I know."

"So…?"

"No. I was going to."

Josie gestures in the direction of the hall, the phone by the bottom of the stairs.

"Well, actually…" says David. "I was hoping, maybe, you might."

She simply shakes her head.

"You heard how I was last night."

"And I don't blame you, but – she'd want to hear it from *you*."

David isn't so sure of that, but he doesn't say so. He stands up and goes into the hallway. Josie watches him from the kitchen, turning in her seat.

"What do I say?"

"Exactly what you said to me."

"Which was…?" he asks, genuinely.

"You just told me what had happened."

"But the doctors don't even know, exactly, what happened."

"David – you need to tell her."

He sighs and picks up the receiver. The notepad which serves as a phonebook already lays open at her number. He taps in the digits. It rings a few times, enough time to…

"Oh. Hello. No, it's not, it's your father." David pauses, briefly, glances at Josie, before carrying on. "I've got something to tell you."

"All right?" asks Josie, once he's hung up.

"She's coming straight here."

"Course."

"She's got Friday's off now evidently."

"How did she sound?"

David shrugs his shoulders. "Upset."

"Not surprised. Do you want me to wait with you until she gets here?"

"It's up to you. It'll be a while."

"If I'm getting in your way, I can always..."

"You drove a long way, Josie – I'm hardly going to chuck you out after half an hour."

"Right. But I could pop out for a bit. Give you some peace. There are a few people I could call in on."

"No. Honestly. It's fine." He straightens up.

"Well, in that case – why don't we pop out for a drive?"

"Where to?"

"I passed the bridge on the way here. It's been years since I've had a walk by the river. We could take the dog with us, fill a flask."

"Maybe." It had been a while since he'd gone down there.

"It might be good for you – a change of scenery."

"So long as we're back before Jessica arrives."

"Course." Josie finishes her tea. "That gives us plenty of time."

They park up along the foreshore. Josie pulls in beside an optimistic ice-cream van. David gets out, goes to open the boot, and the dog belts off to the water's edge, running uneasily over the stones. They follow, carefully, behind him, heading towards the bridge.

"I still remember all the stuff on the telly about this being built," says Josie.

"Sorry?" Concentrating more on not tripping.

"The bridge," she points. "When they were building it."

"Oh. Yes. Me too."

"It was nice because – even though Alf and I had moved away well before all that – it was like we were still around here, in a way, watching it grow."

It was certainly an event, seeing the towers go up, then the road between them. David looks up at the huge, stone pillars, his neck aching – imagine trying to paint one of them, that's what he thought back then – then he turns and faces the water and the bank opposite.

"So – did they not even have an idea about what could have caused Edith to... collapse like that."

"They said it was something on her brain."

"What, like a tumour?"

"I suppose. It was – you know – just a matter of time before..."

"Mmm."

David lifts a hand to his forehead. "You know what?" he says. "I've still never gone across it."

"The bridge? You're kidding," says Josie.

"No."

"Well..." Josie rolls back her sleeve. "Why don't we?"

Bundling the dog back into the boot, wet feet and, well, wet everything else, they set off.

"My purse should just be in my handbag, there." Josie points blindly to the space where David's feet are. He feels around. Finds it. "We'll call it my treat, eh?"

"Do you have to pay both ways?" he asks.

"Yes. That *is* how it works."

"Seems a bit silly."

Josie shrugs.

"I mean, for a silly little drive – not really worth it if you'd rather..."

"No. Nonsense. We're here now, anyway," and she stops at the tollbooth, winding down the car window and reaching for her bag.

"Two-forty, please," says the attendant.

"There you go," smiles Josie.

The barrier stutters up and they drive through. David looks out of the passenger-side window. It takes a while before they're not just going over road or trees or train-track, but over water. And, with the sun reflecting brightly across its surface, you'd be forgiven for not noticing how much mud and silt there is lurking in that river.

"What do you think?" Josie asks him.

"It's all right," he says, informatively.

On the south side of the water, David notices the docks; several tankers arriving and departing. It reminds him of the trawlers – though, as far as he knows, they've never done that kind of thing round here. But it reminds him, also, of St. Andrew's – now a place recognised, mostly, for its big-name shops and American-brand restaurants. At one time, not all that long ago, you'd have taken a trip down there to buy the latest catch – a bit of tuna or skate or cod – not the latest camera or sofa or top.

Once they're off the bridge and driving back over land again, Josie pulls into the first lay-by and stops the engine.

"What're we…?" starts David.

"We're getting out," she says.

He unfastens his seatbelt, the dog moving expectantly in the back, and follows her out. She's already halfway down the concrete steps, heading towards the public footpath.

"Wait up," he says after her.

The two riverbanks are as distinct from each other as David is from Josie. The north shore, where they've driven across from, has that awkward, stony beach, whereas this other side has mudflats, which shift impulsively with the tide. David spots some little wading birds scurrying about on the wet sand. Every time the water washes close to them, they move, like they're one entire body, out of its way… only to return again when the water pulls back.

"What're you looking at?" asks Josie.

"Just the birds, down there," he points.

Josie squints. It takes her a little while. "Oh," she says. "I think I... Don't know how on earth you clocked them."

They walk on, Josie setting the pace.

"There's bound to be all sorts of stuff round here," he says. "You just have to look."

"Suppose," she says – though the natural world never did interest her like it did David.

"Anyway. How far are we going?" asks David, knowing the path laps most of the estuary.

"Not much further."

David follows behind her. His eyes dart from side to side. Because there could well be something about to swoop down from the sky or appear from the reeds growing in the space between the footpath and the sandbanks. And David wouldn't want to miss that.

"Look..." says Josie, suddenly, but calmly.

David comes up alongside her. "Where? What?" He looks first at the water's edge, then scans the tops of the bulrushes.

"There," Josie nods in the direction of the river.

But, apart from the murky water and the bridge, David doesn't understand what there is to see. "What am I looking at exactly?" he asks.

"It's strange, isn't it? Seeing it all the way over here."

David realises what she means. "I suppose so," he says – though, really, it all seems rather nondescript, from such a distance. Those buildings across the river could belong to anywhere. "Do you think we should be getting back now?"

Josie checks her wrist.

"The dog'll be wondering what's happened to us," he adds.

"Mmm. Come on, then."

"I won't stay much longer," says Josie, back at the house. She empties the flask into a mug and sits at the kitchen table.

"Do you not want to see Jessica?" asks David.

"I just think it's best if I go – leave you two to it."

"Right." David shrugs. "If you want."

The clock in the hallway strikes twice for the hour.

"I can't see her being too much longer."

"No." Josie gets up again, puts her mug in the bowl and starts to wash it.

"Here." David joins her at the sink. "Let me."

"I don't mind."

"I know, but..."

Josie steps back; sits down again. David hears the dog behind him moving around.

"You still not tired out, eh?"

"He looks it," smiles Josie.

David turns. "Suppose he is getting on a bit."

"Like us."

"Mmm." He wrings out the cloth, leaving it draped over the taps.

"Sorry. That was..."

"Don't worry."

David sits opposite her at the table. His weezy breathing, the beat of the clock in the hall, fills the silence for a few minutes.

"Shall I go?" says Josie. "Give you a bit of time to yourself, before Jessica arrives?"

"No. I..."

"It's all right. I don't mind. Alf'll be expecting me back soon anyway – there's only so long he can survive on his own."

David shifts in his seat.

"Oh. No. David – I didn't mean..."

"It's fine, Josie. Go – if you want to. I've Finn here to keep me company..." He points at the dog now half-asleep in his bed – though what company he'll be in that state... "You've got nothing to worry about."

"But I do. I *do* worry about you. Have done for a long time."

"I'm fine." He gets up. Takes the dishcloth and starts wiping the worktop. "Besides – Jessica's on her way, so..."

"Right." Josie stands. Lifts her cardigan from the back of the chair. "But I'll call you. Tomorrow."

David nods.

At the door, he lets her hug him and she says: "I just wish I could've visited for a different reason."

They step back. Exchange smiles.

"Give Jessica my love."

"Yes." David opens the door. "You got everything?"

"Think so." She starts along the path. "Speak to you soon."

"Bye," he says, watching as she gets into her car, starts the engine, and pulls away from the kerb and down the street.

Jessica arrives around half-three. She has a few bags with her, dumped on the backseat.

"Do you mind giving me a hand with these?" she asks, shyly.

David follows her to the car and takes the bigger of the two holdalls.

"All right?" she checks.

He nods and they head in.

"I hope you don't mind – I thought I might stay a few days."

"Oh, right."

"At least until..." (She means the funeral.) "I thought you might need some..."

David shoos the dog away from the bags.

"Well. Anyway. I didn't want to leave you on your own."

"You didn't have to," he says, walking, leading them, into the kitchen.

"I know. If it bothers you, I can always find somewhere else."

"No, I didn't mean..."

"I don't want to cause you any more problems."

"You're not. You won't," he adds. "It's fine."

"I just wanted..." Jessica sits at the table. "I just wanted to be here."

David stands a while at the worktop, half an eye staring out the window. The sound of next-door's kids coming home from school and tearing into the back-garden creeps in past the thin glass.

"Which way did you come?"

"Up the A6, then off at junction four."

David nods. "Was it busy?"

"No, not really."

"Good. I thought there were road-works on the A6 at the moment."

"No. Not that *I* saw."

"Right."

"Dad?"

"Yes."

"How *are* you?"

"Oh." He rolls his shoulders. "You know."

"Honestly, Dad."

"I don't know. I..."

"Do you want to talk about it?"

David shakes his head. Because, where would he start? Right now, it just looks like a mess, like a knotted bundle of... string... that can't be untangled and, even if he were to try and untangle it, he knows it'll probably just go on unravelling until... until...

"Shall I put the kettle on?"

"Help yourself."

Jessica takes it over to the tap, fills it and sets it boiling, then says: "I better phone Mark actually. Can I just...?"

He nods, sitting down and pulling the newspaper – which has waited, unread, all day on the kitchen table – towards him. David glances, unfocused, across its front page.

The sound of the water in the kettle increases in volume.

Jessica returns. "Mark sends you his best," she says.

"Right. Thanks."

The kettle clicks off.

"You having one?"

"No."

"OK."

He watches her search the cupboards.

"Where're the cups?" she asks, after two attempts.

"Here," he points, getting up from the table. "This one."

"Thanks," she smiles, choosing the Scarborough beach scene.

"No. You can't... That one's..."

Jessica puts it back. "OK. Sorry." She picks another – plain blue. "This one all right?"

He nods.

"Look..." she says, dropping a teabag into the mug and reaching for the kettle. "Are you sure you wouldn't rather I stayed somewhere else?"

"No. It's fine. I'm just..." But that's as far as he gets.

"I know this is difficult – and I don't want to make it any harder for you."

"I might have a drink, actually," he says, getting up again.

"Oh, well – let me."

"No. I can take care of myself, thanks." That comes out sharper than he intended.

Jessica steps back. "I know."

"Sorry."

They sit down together.

After maybe half-a-minute, Jessica says: "Please, just, let me help. I don't mean, you know..." She points at his mug. "I don't mean with making cups of tea – I know you can do all that. But, look – there's lots to arrange. And I want to take some of that stress away from you. If you'll let me."

David stares at the chaffinch on the side of his cup, trying to remember what there is directly opposite, facing Jessica – it's either the blue tits or the robin.

"Please, Dad," she says. "You don't have to do this all by yourself."

He looks up. "What're you suggesting?"

"Well, we need to ring the church, organise that – and then let people know about it – so, maybe, I could do that for you."

David nods. "If you don't mind."

"Course I don't."

He turns the mug slowly round. The chaffinch disappears, replaced by a pair of nesting blackbirds, their beaks touching.

The sound of number forty's car alarm wakes David. He looks at the clock. Seven-ten. He tries closing his eyes again, tries pushing the sound somewhere else, but then he hears movement, too, downstairs. It isn't straight away that he realises who it is. For the briefest of moments, he questions who is in the house, how they got in, before…

He remembers.

David gets dressed. Quickly combs his hair.

"Morning," says Jessica, her back to him. "Tea?"

"Please."

"You hungry?"

"No." David sits at the table. "Not just yet."

"Well I might…" She gestures to the bread-bin. "I might have a bit of toast, if that's all right."

"It's fine," he says. "Has the paper arrived?"

"No." She helps herself to two slices. "How did you sleep?"

David shrugs.

"Me neither. Lots going through my head, I think."

"Mmm."

"Speaking of which – I thought I'd call St. Eustace's today, since it's just down the road. Do you think she'd…? Do you think Mum'd like that?"

"Don't see why not."

"Did she ever really tell what she would've liked?"

"No. We never really discussed that kind of thing."

"Not at all? I know it's…" The bread pops up, suddenly. She pushes it back down, feeling around in the cupboard below for a plate. "Well, I'll get on to it later."

Jessica waits until David is out with the dog. When they return, she has a piece of scrap paper in her hand.

"There're a couple of dates they can help us out with."

"What's that?" he says – not that he'd forgotten exactly (how could he?), just that, with the dog's water dish to fill and his coat to take off...

"The church."

"Oh, right."

"They can do next Wednesday, Thursday or Friday."

David hangs his coat up; re-enters the kitchen.

"So?"

"I don't mind." He can't see what difference it makes.

"Friday?" suggests Jessica. "Gives us more time to let people know."

"Fine." He opens the door to stop Finn whimpering.

"What time?"

"Don't know."

"Eleven? Then there's time to have some lunch with everyone after."

"No. I don't want any of that."

"Oh, I just thought..."

"No. Eleven, in the church, then..." David moves a hand flat across his chest. "That's it."

"Right. I said I'd talk to you, then call them back, so..." She goes into the hallway. "I'll just be a minute."

David moves over to the back door; watches the dog do zigzag laps of the lawn.

Jessica comes in again. "That's that sorted, then."

"Good."

"He's just going to pop round on Monday, about half-two."

"Who is?"

"The vicar – to talk about... to talk about Mum."

"Does he have to?"

"Yes. That's how it works. He needs to know a bit about her, so he can do the service."

"Right. But... Do *you* mind...? I'm not sure I could."

"Well – we'll see him together though? I'll do the talking, if you want, but I'd rather not do it by myself."

"Fine."

"Now..." Jessica reaches for the kettle. "Tea?"

"No, thanks. I might just sit outside for a bit."

"OK. Good idea." She returns the kettle to its cradle. "Actually, there's something else I better just deal with while it's on my mind."

David sits on one of the garden chairs: the one not decorated white and brown by the birds. Finn eyes him suspiciously, then gets back to pawing at clumps of grass. David glances round, noticing all the little jobs he still hasn't done. What if he forgets again? That trellis needs straightening. And the shed door wants new hinges. Who'll remind him to get all that done?

The back door opens.

"Dad?" Jessica stands next to him. "I just spoke to the funeral people. To give them the details – of the service and the church. They said they know Reverend Butterfield quite well, so..." She sighs. Then adds: "They said we can go see her – if we want. I know you probably..."

"I'd rather not," says David. "If *you* want to, that's up to you, but I don't think I could see her... like that."

"No, I know. But I said we'd get back to them about it, so just... please... just think about it."

She goes back inside. And David *does* think about it. How can he not? It's *all* he can think about. Maybe to other people, it would make perfect sense. A way of saying goodbye. But, right now, the last place David wants to be is one of those rooms, even if Edith is there with him. Because, she won't really be there, will she? It'll be just like it was in the hospital – everything still, everything halted; and the silence, the absolute silence.

"I spoke to the funeral directors again," says Jessica, later. "I think I'm going to go see her. Monday morning. So... if you wanted, we could go... together."

"Right. I don't think so, but..." David gets up from the settee.

"Course. It's up to you."

He looks at the carriage-clock on the mantelpiece. Time for Finn's afternoon walk. "I'm just going out with the dog."

"OK. I'll make a start on tea, then."

Monday morning arrives. And so does the inevitable question.

"Are you coming?" Jessica says it like it's a drive to the shops.

"No. Thanks, but… I can't."

"That's fine. I'm still in two minds about it myself, but… It feels like the right thing to do."

What? So…?

"I just can't see what good it'll do."

"It might help," smiles Jessica. "That's what the funeral director said."

"The nurse said that too – when I saw her in the hospital."

"Right."

"But…"

"I guess I just need to say goodbye."

David nods.

"How about you come with me?"

"No. Jessica – I said…"

"Just in the car, OK? There's a park opposite. I'll go in – and then we can go for a little walk afterwards. What do you say?"

"I'm sorry," says David, somewhere between the park entrance and the duck pond.

"What for?"

"Because I'm still here – and your mum isn't."

"Look, Dad…"

Jessica stops. David takes a few steps before he realises.

"I know we've had our issues, but – you must know – I'd never think like that."

"No. It's just… earlier…" He could tell, when she returned to the car, that she'd been crying. "You looked really upset."

"I was," she smiles.

They find a bench and sit down. The sky is overcast. David hears laughter coming from the playground. It sounds like a foreign language.

"Thanks for coming with me," says Jessica, resting a hand on David's left arm.

"Well. I didn't quite…"

"You know what I mean. I might never have gone in if you hadn't come along too."

"Really?"

"Mmm. But I'm glad I did." She sighs. "You know, it's going to be a really tough week."

"I know."

"So, I don't want to hear you talking rubbish like that again."

"What?"

"Stop apologising. It's all in the past."

"OK," nods David. But that's just where… That's just where Edith… He can still barely acknowledge it in his head, let alone out loud. The words feel… what? … like there must be some kind of mistake, some sort of mix-up.

Dead. Edith. Is.

Dead. Is. Edith.

Is. Edith. Dead.

Yes.

Edith. *Is*. Dead.

"We should probably start calling people, you know – let them know about Friday."

"Mmm."

"I'll do it. I'm not suggesting you…"

"No. Maybe I should."

"It's fine, Dad. Just write me a list so I don't miss anyone out."

Shortly after quarter-past two, the doorbell rings.

"Hello," says Reverend Butterfield. "I know I'm a little early. Is it…?"

"That's all right," says David, standing back. "Come in."

"Thank you."

"Can I take your coat?"

"Oh." He starts taking if off. "Very kind."

David hangs it up. Turns again to face him.

"My condolences, Mr. Denby." He clasps David's right hand in both his – larger, rougher, than he'd have thought they would be; more like builder's hands than vicar's hands. "Was it your daughter I spoke to on the phone?"

"That's right. She'll be down any moment."

Upstairs, the toilet flushes.

"Would you like a drink?"

"Oh, yes, please – tea, milk, no sugar."

"Right." David starts for the kitchen.

"Where do you want us to sit?" asks the reverend.

"Oh. In there." He points to the sitting room.

"Rightio. Do you mind if I…?"

"No. Make yourself comfortable."

"Thank you," he smiles, pacing slowly in.

Jessica comes down and into the kitchen. "All right?"

"Just doing him a tea."

"OK."

"Do you want one?"

"Yes – I will, thanks." She gestures to the front of the house, to the sitting room. "I better just say hello."

David nods, then reaches into the fridge for the milk. "I'll be through in a minute."

Jessica opens the front door. "Thank you, Reverend."

"Not at all." He smiles in David's direction. "It was nice to meet you both. I hope… well… I hope it all goes as well as it possibly can on Friday."

He steps out.

"Goodbye. See you on Friday," says Jessica.

David merely smiles, watches as the door is closed and Reverend Butterfield's head shrinks and shrivels to nothing in the frosted glass.

"Right..." sighs Jessica. "What do you fancy for tea?"

David follows her into the kitchen. "You all right?" Normally the question would be aimed the other way around: her asking him.

"Fine. Just... you know..."

He nods. Tries to look understanding, but she nudges past him to the sink and starts filling the kettle.

"Something to drink first," she mumbles. "You want one?"

"Yes. Please." David watches as she sets it boiling, gathers the mugs and a teaspoon, removes the milk from the fridge. He tries again. "You all right?"

Jessica turns around. Rolls her shoulders uncertainly. "It's just hard, isn't it? Talking about her when she's... not..."

"Sorry."

"No. It's fine. We need to talk about her."

"But – I could have said a bit more in there."

"You said enough. Anyway – we made a deal, didn't we? I'd do all the talking."

"Mmm."

"Now..." She straightens up. "Don't know about you, but I'm starting to feel pretty hungry."

Friday morning. Josie arrives at half-eight. Her and Jessica put their arms round each other with barely a hello-how-are-you.

"She had a good, long life," David hears Josie whisper in Jessica's ear. She said the same thing to him one night when they spoke on the phone.

"Alf not with you?" he asks, when they separate.

"No. He's not had a good week, really."

"Oh."

"He's fine," she adds quickly. "Just not up to the journey."

Jessica offers her a cup of tea and they all wander through to the kitchen.

"How many are you expecting?" asks Josie, once they're all sat down, mugs in front of them.

"Not many. We only invited – how many was it, Dad? Thirty?"

"Something like that."

"Close family on yours and Dad's side, obviously quite a few from Mum's family, and then a few friends, so..."

The dog cries at the back door. He can probably hear Josie's voice. David gets up to let him in.

"And will I be seeing your boys?"

"Yes," smiles Jessica. "They're on their way. Mark reckoned he'd be here by about nine and James is coming with his new girlfriend."

"Oh. I won't have met her, then."

"No. I've only met her twice, I think. She's called Karen – seems lovely. And then Sam's bringing the girls. Actually – did Dad tell you?"

"Tell me what?"

"No." David shakes his head. "I forgot."

"Well..." A smile extends its way across Jessica's lips. "Sophie's expecting again."

"Oh, that's wonderful. Isn't it, David?"

He nods. "Mmm. Wonderful."

"She's only four months gone, but..."

"I see."

"Because – you know – they were trying again for a while, but... they had a few problems."

"Yes. I did know about that."

"Right. But it seems to be going a lot smoother this time round."

"Well – that's something to look forward to, eh?"

"Yes. Touch wood." Jessica taps the stained oak table-top.

"And how old is Rebecca now?"

"Four."

"Goodness."

"I know. She's starting school in September."

"It doesn't seem that long since she was born."

"Mmm."

The bell goes again. On the doorstep, James gives David a stiff hug, his right hand patting him on the back a little too hard.

"Sorry, Granddad."

"Thanks."

They step back. James introduces Karen.

"Nice to meet you," nods David. "Just…" He gestures to the back of the house. "Just go straight through."

In the kitchen, James does the introductions again and Jessica starts making them each a drink.

"What time does it all start?"

"Eleven."

"Is Dad on his way?"

"Hope so," smiles Jessica. "When we spoke last night, he thought he'd be here around nine."

"What about Sam?"

"Don't know when to expect them."

"But they're all coming?"

"As far as I know."

"How's work going, then, James?" asks Josie.

"Good, thanks."

James qualified as a vet three years ago and began working in a rural surgery about eighteen months later.

"It's just so different to working in the town."

The phone rings.

"Oh," says David, looking at Jessica. "Would you…?"

"Course."

"So…" starts Josie, again. "How did you two meet?"

"Through a friend – his girlfriend is good friends with Karen and a group of us met up, we were introduced, and just sort of spent the rest of the evening chatting. It was really…" He shrugs. Looks a little flushed in his black suit.

"That was Sam," says Jessica, returning from the hallway. "They'll be here on time for the service, but they're going to be a bit delayed. Apparently, Rebecca spent most of last night in their bed."

"Oh, dear."

"Upset tummy. She'll be fine. I think she can be a bit fussy, you know. I love her, but... if I were Sophie, I'd be a bit firmer with her."

"Yeah, right, Mum," grins James. "You fuss her worst of all."

"Well. She is my only granddaughter."

James rolls his eyes. Looks redder, again, in the face.

"What is it *you* do, anyway, Karen?" Josie returns to her quiet interrogation.

"I work at a small surveyors, in the accounts office."

"Oh, yes."

"Mmm. It's really not that interesting," she adds.

"No, I'm sure it is," says Josie, diplomatically.

"I worked in a fruit-packing factory for eleven years," says Jessica. "Apples and oranges mostly. Doesn't get more exciting than that."

"Tell Karen what *you* used to do, Granddad."

"Oh. Not much. Painting and decorating, then joinery – for the council, at first, but then I was laid off and started working for a private firm that specialised in gardens – you know, fencing and sheds and that."

"And you were a butcher, before all that," says Josie.

"Were you?" says Jessica. "I didn't..."

"Not for very long," he says, dismissive.

"Well, a few years. Did your mother never tell you? That's how they first met."

David nods.

"It was after our dad died," Josie explains. "Your dad left school and started working for the local butcher."

"And how did you and Mum meet exactly?"

"Just out and about," he says; adding: "I used to deliver to people's houses. Hers was one of the first I went to."

"I never… Why did you never tell us?"

David shrugs. "It was a long time ago."

"But even when the vicar was round the other day, you never said any of this."

"How come you stopped doing that, then?" asks James.

"Well, the war was on," Josie continues for him. "So, when he was old enough, David left to fight."

The doorbell goes again. David gets up to answer it, his chair scuffing across the lino.

"Mark – come in."

"Thanks." He shakes David firmly by the hand. "I'm really sorry about…"

Everyone keeps apologising. Like they were personally involved.

David leads him into the kitchen. "Mark's here," he says, unnecessarily.

"Actually, can I just use the bathroom?"

"Course," nods David.

"Want a drink, love?" shouts Jessica, as he disappears up the stairs.

"Yes, please."

The final, expected *tring-tring* of the doorbell comes just before half-past nine.

"This'll be Sam and Sophie," says Jessica.

David returns to the kitchen with them. Rebecca, who is resting in Sam's arms, is immediately the focus of everybody's attention.

"How is she?" asks Josie.

"Fine," answers Sophie. "A bit under the weather – but nothing too bad."

"And, how are you?" Jessica points at Sophie's stomach.

"Good, thanks. Everything's going well so far."

"What time are we going to the church?" asks Mark, to no one in particular.

"The car's coming at quarter-past ten," says Jessica, casting a glance at the clock.

"Are we all getting in?" asks Sam.

"Well, I think there are two – so Dad and us two..." She waves a finger at herself and Mark. "And maybe Josie too – we'll go in the first car. Then the rest of you should all fit in the other."

There are a few people waiting outside the church. David doesn't really recognise anybody in particular. The others stop to speak to them, but he heads inside. The vicar is lurking at the back, thumbing through a thick little blue book. The heavy door shuts behind him with a boomy *thud*.

"Mr. Denby," says Reverend Butterfield, walking over.

"Hello."

"You're not alone, are you?"

"No. Everyone else is outside."

"Right. Good." He checks his watch. "So, you're sure you'd rather not follow in behind the coffin?"

David nods.

"Not a problem. I'll show you where you'll be sitting."

He leads him to the front, then points to the pews on the left-hand side.

"Just in here, OK? But – you know – you can wait a while before you take your seat."

"Thanks. Is there a loo?"

Reverend Butterfield takes him through a side-door, to the right of the building. The floor of the room it leads into is bare, unpolished boards and there are cupboards running the length of one wall. He takes him through another door.

"There's only the one, I'm afraid. Just in here."

"Thanks."

David shuts the door, struggles for a few seconds with the rusting lock. He undoes his belt and lowers his trousers. This visit is more out of nerves than necessity. It takes a while before anything arrives. When it does, it barely colours the water. He waits a moment, tries forcing a few more drops, then zips himself back up.

The main body of the church remains empty. Even Reverend Butterfield, it seems, has gone outside. David sits in the front-left pew he showed him to. It's quiet in a way he can't enjoy, in a way he can't appreciate. Because he's inside, not out, so he can't hear the birds or the wind. Instead, all David *can* hear is the blood rushing past his ears, like speeding traffic, and the occasional architectural groan. The way the tall, slim windows let the light in reminds him of the old school hall. Even after all this time, that place will come to mind. David will remember the thread of a lesson or, once when he was building a bureau, the scent of the piece of mahogany he was using made him picture, immediately, the panelled corridor near the schoolmaster's office.

The door opens. David turns around. People begin to come in and take their seats.

Back at the house, Jessica and Josie make sandwiches for everyone.

"So..." says Mark. "How did you and Edith meet?"

"Oh," says Jessica. "We had all this before you arrived."

"Sorry. Didn't realise."

"We met when I was about fifteen, working in the local butcher's."

"You were a butcher?"

"For a bit. I did deliveries and hers was one of the houses on my route."

"What? So, she answered the door?"

"Yes."

"Then, what?"

"We just kept seeing each other around until... you know..."

"Bit like us, eh?" says Jessica, glancing at Mark.

"So how did you two meet?" asks James.

"Come on – you know all that."

"But Karen doesn't – and Dad might've forgotten."

"I can remember it perfectly well, thank you."

"How could you forget?" smiles Jessica. "Best day of your life, wasn't it?"

"Well…"

"Eh! Careful."

"I know."

"It really isn't that exciting, Karen," says Jessica. "We met at the bus station. We were both on our way to work. He started talking to me – and then we just kept on seeing each other, most mornings. How long did it take you to ask me out?"

"Oh, a good month, I think. I was convinced you'd say no."

"I nearly did."

"What?"

"Just kidding."

"How long did it take *you* to ask Edith out?"

"Actually, it was the other way around."

"Really?" splurts Jessica, through a mouthful of ham sandwich. "That was… unconventional."

David nods. "Your mother was – and she was a year older too, which at that age, back then, meant a lot."

"I never knew any of that."

"Did your Mum never tell you?"

Jessica shakes her head. "But I don't I think ever really asked."

Sam and Sophie are the first to leave. Rebecca fell asleep shortly after they got back from the church, so Sam carries her out to the car and fastens her in. The rest of them linger on the doorstep, watching.

Sophie kisses David gently on the left cheek. "Take care of yourself," she says.

"Thanks. I'll try."

Sam tracks back up the garden path. He comes to David first, while Sophie makes her way round the rest of the group.

"Look after yourself, won't you?" smiles Sam – as if David hasn't already heard that a thousand times, as if he might decide not to. "We'll try and pop up again soon, if…"

David nods. "I'd like that," he says – and he thinks he actually means it.

"We should probably make a move too," says James.

"Well…" says Karen, quietly. "It was nice to meet you all."

"Come here." Jessica reaches out for a hug.

"Oh." Karen accepts it awkwardly.

"Hopefully, next time it'll be under better circumstances."

"Mmm." Karen steps back; smiles.

"Have a safe journey back." Jessica hugs and kisses James.

"You have everything?" asks David.

"Yes, thanks." James turns from his mother to David. "It was good to see you," he says, smiling awkwardly. "We'll be in touch."

"Thanks."

James shakes his hand, pats his right arm.

They watch them drive away, then head inside again and into the kitchen.

"Fancy another cuppa, Josie, or are you…?"

Josie hesitates, looks at David before answering: "Yes. Go on. I'll have one more and then get off."

Mark crouches beside Finn's basket. He lifts his head in anticipation. "Hello, little fella. How you doing?"

"He knows something's up," says David.

"Right."

"Well, they do notice…" says Josie. "When people…"

Mark gives him a final, firm pat on the back, then sits back at the table.

"Which way will you be going back?" asks David.

"Who?" Mark points at himself. "Me?"

David nods.

"Motorway. Just quicker."

"Right. And are you all packed, Jessica?" he says, realising he hadn't seen any bags in the hall.

"What?" She doesn't turn around, the kettle just coming to the boil.

"I said are you all packed?"

"Oh. No. I'm not going back. Mark – I thought I'd said."

"Yes," he says. "You did. I never… It was your dad asking, not…"

"Dad – I thought you would've… I'm not going to just leave you, straight after…"

"Right. I didn't…"

"Unless – do you want me to go?"

"I just thought…" What? The first chance you got, you'd be out of here? Because that's what he would've done.

"There's still lots to sort out," she says.

David wants to ask, Like what? But he doesn't. He just nods, slowly, fires a quick smile at Josie and says, "Yes," when she offers him a drink.

Jessica makes tea.

"What a day, eh?" she says, setting the plates down and taking her seat opposite David.

"I know," he nods.

"How're you feeling?"

"Not sure, really."

"Mmm. It was nice seeing everybody, though, wasn't it?"

"Suppose."

"I know it would've been nicer if… well… you know…" She lifts her fork to her mouth. "It's a shame Auntie Lily couldn't come. Was it just that she couldn't get flights sorted?"

"No. Her doctor's advised her not to fly."

"Right."

David thought Josie had mentioned that earlier, shortly before her and Mark left.

"I'll only stay a few more days," says Jessica. "Promise."

"Fine."

"I just... Well, I worry about you, Dad. You seem – I suppose you always have seemed – closed off. I mean, I'm your daughter and feel like I hardly know you. I found stuff out about you and Mum today that I should've known years ago." She pauses. Moves food around her plate. "Most people can remember their dad taking them places, reading them bedtime stories, but I... I try to picture you when I was growing up. But I can't. It's like you're not there."

"I did work a lot," offers David.

"Mmm. I guess I just wish... I don't know... Maybe it's because of what's just happened..." But that's where the conversation ends, and a few mouthfuls later Jessica says: "Anyway, I was thinking..."

David looks up.

"While I'm still around, I could help you sort some of Mum's things out."

"Well..."

"We'll just make a start."

"I don't know."

"It'll have to be done eventually."

So, let's wait until then, thinks David.

"Anyway. It's just a suggestion. We don't have to."

In the morning, David finds Jessica already in the kitchen. She makes him some toast; places the jams and butter in front of him on the table.

"Any plans for today?"

"Me?"

"No. Finn." She turns to look at the dog. "You up to much today, Finn?" He lifts his head, briefly, before resting it again. "Course I mean you."

"Right. Sorry."

"So...?"

"No. Nothing special."

"Well – how about a drive out somewhere?"

"Like where?"

"I don't know. But it's got to be better than sitting around here all day. We could take Finn with us."

David rolls his shoulders; drinks some tea.

"How about the bridge park? You always used to take... What was his name?"

"Benny."

"That's it. Benny. You always used to take him out there. Before there was a bridge, of course."

"Mmm."

"So – come on. What do you say?"

"Josie drove us out here," says David, getting out of the car.

"Oh, right. When?"

"The other day, before *you* came over. We parked up on the front, had a walk by the river."

"Well, if you'd prefer...?"

"No. Here's fine."

Jessica locks the car. They're in the visitor's car park, which is surrounded by woodland and footpaths. Finn disappears into the undergrowth.

"Guess we're going that way," smiles David, and they follow after him.

Slim shafts of sunlight light the path: a dry, clear morning.

"You know when you were a soldier and you'd gone off to fight?"

"Yes."

"Did you manage to keep in touch with Mum?"

"To start with – but after a few weeks the letters stopped coming through."

"That must have been horrible – not knowing if she was all right."

"Oh. No. I knew she'd be fine. It would've been harder for her, wondering if... well... wondering if something terrible had happened to me."

"Which it did."

"Mmm."

"You don't talk about it much – what it was like out there."

"That's because I wasn't out there for very long."

"Well, what did Mum think about you going?"

"She understood. I think. She knew it was something I wanted to do, so…"

They come to a gateway, beyond which is the river. David steps aside and lets Jessica through. Finn begins to look a little worn out – his stride and bounce more plod and trudge. He staggers down on to the pebbles of the foreshore. David and Jessica sit, instead, on the embankment and watch as he stumbles and trips his way to the water.

"You ever thought about living somewhere else?" asks Jessica.

"Like, where?"

"Anywhere."

He glances momentarily at the bridge. "No," he says. "Edith always wanted to."

"Really?"

"Well, when we were younger, before we got married, she used to talk about it sometimes. But… It's too late for that now."

"Oh, I don't know."

David shakes his head. "Besides. It's the same round here as it is anywhere else."

"I just thought… you know… a new start…"

"I'm too old for new starts, Jessica."

"No. Don't be silly," she says, placing a warm hand on his knee.

"Mmm," he smiles, placing his hand on top of hers and looking out, past Finn, at the sun scattered and reflected in the dirty, silty water.